D0056390

Katharine Kerr's
Novels of Deverry,
The Silver Wyrm Cycle

Now available from DAW Books:

THE GOLD FALCON (#1)
THE SPIRIT STONE (#2)
THE SHADOW ISLE (#3)

Forthcoming from DAW:

THE SILVER MAGE (#4)

The Shadow Isle

Book Three of *The Silver Wyrm*

Katharine Kerr

DAW BOOKS, INC.

DONALD A. WOLLHEIM, FOUNDER

375 Hudson Street, New York, NY 10014

ELIZABETH R. WOLLHEIM

SHEILA E. GILBERT

PUBLISHERS

www.dawbooks.com

Jacket art by Jody A. Lee.

DAW Books Collectors No. 1439

DAW Books are distributed by Penguin Group (USA) Inc.

Book designed by Elizabeth Glover

First Printing, May 2008
1 2 3 4 5 6 7 8 9

For Elizabeth Pomada

AUTHOR'S NOTE

Despite what you may have heard or read elsewhere, THE SHADOW ISLE is not the last book in the Deverry sequence. It is, however, the beginning of the end, Part I of the last Deverry book, as it were. The true end will be published soon as THE SILVER MAGE, also from DAW Books.

PROLOGUE
IN A FAR COUNTRY

You say that the three Mothers of All Roads run tangled beyond your power to map them. Why then would you ask to travel the seven Rivers of Time? Their braiding lies beyond even the understanding of the Great Ones, so be ye warned and stay safely upon their banks.

—*The Secret Book of Cadwallon the Druid*

LAZ WOKE TO DARKNESS and noise. Gongs clanged, men shouted. Not one word made sense to him, and no more did the sound of water lapping and splashing. He could smell nothing but water. Pain—his hands burned, but the rest of him felt cold, soaked through, he realized suddenly, sopping wet. How his hands could burn when he was sopping wet lay beyond him. The gongs came closer, louder. Waves lifted him and splashed him back down. *Floating*, he thought. *I'm floating on water*.

The shouting came from right over his head. Hands suddenly grabbed him, hauled, lifted him into the air while the shouting and the gongs clamored all around. Hands laid him down again on something hard that rocked from side to side. The shouting stopped, but the gongs clanged on and on. Through the sound of gongs he heard a dark voice speaking. *Not one word of it!*

The voice tried yet another incomprehensible language, then a third. "Here, lad, speak you this tongue?"

Lijik Ganda, he thought. *Just my luck*. "I do," Laz said aloud. "A bit, anyway."

"Splendid! Who are you?"

"I don't know." Laz put panic into his voice. "I don't remember. Where are we? Why is it so dark?"

"It's not dark, lad. There's a lantern shining right into your face."

"I'm blind? I don't remember being blind."

Voices murmured in one of the languages he couldn't understand. Someone patted his shoulder as if trying to comfort him. The rocking continued, the splashing, and the gongs.

"Here!" Laz said. "Are we on a boat?"

"We are, and heading for the island. Just rest, lad. The ladies of the isle know a fair bit about healing. It may be that they can do somewhat about your eyes, I don't know. I'd wager high that they can heal your hands at the very least."

"They do pain me."

"No doubt! Black as pitch, they are. You just rest. We're coming up to the pier."

"My thanks. Did you save my life?"

"Most likely." The voice broke into a wry laugh. "The beasts of the lake nearly got a meal out of you."

Beasts. Lake. Blind. None of it made sense. He fainted.

When Laz woke next it was to light, only a faint, fuzzy reddish glow, but light nonetheless. Most of him felt dry and warm, but his burning hands lay in water, and water dripped over his face. The smell of mixed herbs overwhelmed him; he could smell nothing beyond plant matter and spices. He could hear, however, women talking. Two women, he realized, though he understood not one word of what they were saying. The pain in his left hand suddenly eased. A woman laughed and spoke a few triumphant words, then lifted the hand out of the water and laid it down on something dry and soft.

"I think me he wakes," the other woman said in Deverrian.

"I do," Laz said.

"Good," Woman the First said, "but there be a need on you to stay quiet till we get the burnt skin free from your right hand."

"Is it that you see light?" Woman the Second said.

"Some, truly."

"Try opening your eyes."

With some effort—his lids seemed stuck together with pitch—he did. What he saw danced and swam. Slowly the motion stopped. The view looked strangely blurred and smeared, but he could distinguish shapes at a distance and objects nearby. In a pool of lantern light two women leaned over him, one with gray-streaked yellow hair and a tired face, and one young with hair as dark as a raven's wing and cornflower-blue eyes.

"My name be Marnmara." The young woman pointed at her elder. "This be Angmar, my mam. The boatmen tell me you remember not your own name."

Laz considered what to say. He'd not wanted to tell the boatmen his name until he knew more about them, but these women were doing their best to heal him. He owed them the courtesy of a better lie. "I didn't, not right then, but it's Tirn. I think I have a second name, too, but I can't seem to remember it."

"There be no surprise on me for that," Marnmara said. "Whatever you did endure, it were a great bad thing."

He started to lift his left hand to look at it, but Angmar grabbed his elbow and pinned it to the bed. "Not yet," she said. "It be not a pleasant sight, with you so burned and all."

"Burned." He formed the words carefully. "How badly?"

Angmar looked at her daughter and quirked an eyebrow.

"I doubt me if you'll have the use of all your fingers," Marnmara said. "But mayhap we can free the thumb and one other. The right hand's a bit better, I think me. Mayhap we can free two and the thumb."

"Free them? From what?"

"Scars. They might grow together."

Panic struck him. *Will I be able to fly again?* The one question he didn't dare ask was the only question in the world that mattered.

"Why is the pain gone?" he asked instead.

"The herbs," Marnmara said. "But the healing, it'll not be easy."

"It's very kind of you to help me."

"I will heal any hurt that I ken how to heal," Marnmara said. "Such was my vow."

"We have your black gem." Angmar held up something shiny. "Fret not about it."

"My thanks." Dimly he remembered that he once had owned a pair. "Not the white one? I carried a gem in each hand."

"The boatmen did find this one clutched in your left hand. Your right hand trailed open in the water. I think me the other be at the bottom of the lake by now."

"So be it, then."

He realized that he could now see Angmar more clearly. Whether because of the herbs or time passing, his eyes were clearing. What had blinded him? *The flash of light.* He remembered the pure white flash and the sensation of falling a long, long way down. *Why didn't I listen to Sisi?* For that, he had no answer.

Angmar glanced at her hands, flecked with black. Marnmara picked up a rag from the bed on which he lay and offered it to her mother, who began to wipe her fingers clean.

"Those cinders are bits of me," Laz said.

"I fear me they are." Angmar cocked her head to one side and studied his face. "Need you to vomit? I've a basin right here."

Instead he fainted again.

"I hear that the island witches have a new demon," Diarmuid the Brewer said. "Maybe he's that snake-eyed lass' sweetheart, eh?"

"They're not witches," Dougie said. "Avain's not a demon, just a mooncalf. And how many times now have I told you all that?"

"Talk all you want, lad. You're blind to the truth because of the young one. A pretty thing, Berwynna, truly."

"But treacherous, nonetheless," Father Colm broke in. "Never forget that about witches. Fair of face, foul of soul."

Dougie felt an all too familiar urge to throw the contents of his tankard into the holy man's face. As for Diarmuid, he wasn't in the least holy, merely too old to challenge to a fight. Dougie calmed himself with a long swallow of ale. Father Colm set his tankard down on the ground, then pulled the skirts of his brown cassock up to his knees, exposing hairy legs and sandaled feet.

"Hot today," the priest remarked.

"It is that, truly," Diarmuid said.

In the spring sun, the three of them were sitting outside the tumbledown shack that served the village as a tavern. Since most of the local people were crofters who lived out on the land, four slate-roofed stone cottages and a covered well made up the entire village. It was more green than gray, though, with kitchen gardens and a grassy commons for the long-horned shaggy milk cows. From where he sat, Dougie could see the only impressive building for miles around, Lord Douglas' dun, looming off to the west on a low hill.

"If this new fellow's not a demon," Diarmuid started in again, "then who is he, eh?"

"He doesn't remember much beyond his name," Dougie said. "It's as simple as that. Tirn, he calls himself. Some traveler who ended up in the lake, that's all."

"Burnt a fair bit, and him with unholy sigils all over his face? Hah!" Father Colm hauled himself up from the rickety bench. "Now, frankly, I don't think he's a demon. I think he's a warlock who was trying to raise a demon and paid for his sinful folly. Speaking of paying—" He laid a hand on the leather wallet hanging from his rope belt.

"Nah, nah, nah, Father," Diarmuid said. "Just say a prayer for me."

"I will do that." Colm fixed him with a gooseberry eye. "For a fair many reasons."

With a wave the priest waddled off down the dirt road in the direction of Lord Douglas' dun and chapel. Diarmuid leaned back against the wall of the shed and watched the chickens pecking around his feet. Dougie had stopped by the old man's on his way to Haen Marn to hear what the local gossips were saying—plenty, apparently. Diarmuid waited until the priest had gotten out of earshot before he spoke.

"Well, now, lad, you've seen this fellow, haven't you? Do you think he's a demon?"

"I do not, as indeed our priest said, too. He must be a foreigner, is all, and most likely from Angmar's home country."

"Imph." Diarmuid sucked the stumps that had once been his front teeth in thought. "Well, one of these days Father Colm's going to work his lordship around to burning these witches, and that will be that. I'm surprised he's not done it already." Diarmuid spoke casually, but he was looking sideways at Dougie out of one rheumy eye.

"It's Mic's hard coin," Dougie said. "Who else around here can pay his taxes in anything but kind? A silver penny a year the jeweler gives over, and that buys my gran a fine warhorse for one of his men."

"Well, now, you've got a point there. The village folk keep wondering, though, if his lordship holds his hand because of your mother."

"Are you implying that my mother's a witch?" Dougie rose from the bench and laid his free hand on his sword hilt.

"What?" Diarmuid nearly dropped his tankard. "Naught of the sort, lad! Now, hold your water, like! All I meant was that she's the lordship's daughter, and you're her son, and there's Berwynna, and uh, well, er . . ." He ran out of words and breath both.

Dougie put his half-full tankard down on the bench.

"I'll just be getting on," Dougie said. "You can finish that if you'd like."

Dougie strode out of the yard and slammed the rickety gate behind him for good measure. Although he owned a horse, he'd left him behind at the steading. Still glowering, he set out on foot for Haen Marn.

Dougie had good reason to be touchy on the subject of witchcraft. All his young life he'd overheard rumors about his mother and father. In the impoverished loch country of northern Alban, the steading of Domnal Breich and his wife, Jehan, had flourished into a marvel. Every spring their milk cows gave birth to healthy calves, and their ewes had twins more often than not. In the summer their oats and barley stood high; their apple trees bowed under the weight of fruit. When Domnal went fishing, he'd bring home a full net every single time.

Some neighbors grumbled that Domnal must have made a pact with the Devil. As those things will, the grumbling had spread, but not as far as you might think, because Jehan was the local lord's daughter. Lord Douglas, whose name Dougie bore, disliked nasty talk about his kin. No one cared to have their gossip silenced by a hangman's noose.

The gossip had transferred itself to the mysterious women on the island to the north of Lord Douglas' lands. Lady Angmar—everyone assumed she was of high birth because she had dwarves in her household—and her twin daughters had spawned ten times the gossip that Domnal and Jehan ever had. Partisan though he was,

Dougie could understand why the folk spoke of demons and witchery. The women and their island had turned up some seventeen winters ago, in the year before he'd been born. The older people around remembered its location as a wide spot in a burn, not a loch at all, but when the island arrived, one winter night, it brought its own water with it.

Witchcraft—a house, island, and loch appearing like that out of nowhere! "All the way from Cymru they came in the blink of an eye," the old people said, "and they must have come from Cymru, judging by the way they speak. Foreigners, that's what they are! What else could they be but witches, them and their flying house?"

The loch that harbored the island lay in a dip of land too shallow to be called a valley, but the dark blue water must have run deep, because the same beasts that dwelled in Loch Ness lived beneath its choppy waves. The small island rose out of the water like the crest of a rocky hill. At its highest point stood a square-built tall tower, surrounded by apple trees. At its lowest point, a sandy cove, stood a wooden pier and a boathouse. In between the two stood the manse, such a solid structure that it was hard to imagine it taking to the air like an enchanted swan from some old tale.

Solid, and yet, and yet—the buildings seemed to move around on the island, just now and then, when no one was looking. Whenever he visited, Dougie made sure to stand on the same spot to view it. Sometimes the manse appeared to be closer to the tower than on others, or the tower presented a corner rather than a flat side, or the entire island seemed a little nearer the shore or farther away. He'd once asked Lady Angmar about the shifting view. She'd scowled and told him he'd been drinking too much dark ale. He'd never gotten up the courage to ask again.

At the edge of the loch a big granite boulder sat among tall grass. An iron loop protruded from its side, and from the loop dangled a silver horn on a silver chain. Oddly enough, neither silver piece ever tarnished, no matter how wet the weather. This clear evidence of witchcraft—well, clear in the minds of the local folk—had kept them from being stolen. Dougie picked up the horn and blew three long notes, then let it swing free again. While he waited, he took off his boots and hitched up his plaid, tucking the ends into his heavy belt.

Not long after he saw the longboat set out from the pier under oars. He heard the bronze gong clanging, just in case the beasts in the lake were on the prowl for a meal. Fortunately, the water near shore ran too shallow for the beasts. When the boat pulled up, with the oarsmen backing water to hold her steady, Dougie waded out and with the help of the boatmaster, Lon, hauled himself aboard.

"And a good morrow to you," Dougie said.

"Same to you." Lon knew only a few words of the Alban language. "Take gong?"

"I will, and gladly." Dougie took the mallet from him.

While they rowed across, Dougie smacked the gong to keep it clanging and whistled for good measure. Once, when he looked over to the far side of the loch, he saw a tiny snakelike head on the end of a long neck lift itself out of the water, but at his shout the beast dove, disappearing without a ripple. As they approached the island, Berwynna walked out on the pier to meet the boat. His heart began pounding as loudly as the gong, or so it seemed to him.

A slender lass, she stood barely up to his chest. She wore her glossy raven-dark hair clasped back. Cornflower-blue eyes dominated her delicate face. To set off her coloring she wore a finely woven plaid in a blue-and-gray tartan—cloth that Mic the Dwarf had brought home from Din Edin, earned by his trade in gems and jewelry. When she saw Dougie, she smiled and hurried forward to help him onto the pier.

"I'd hoped to see you today," Berwynna said.

"Well, I truly came to see you," Dougie said, "but I told my mother that I need to see your Mic. I was wondering if he'll be traveling south soon."

"He will." Berwynna's smile disappeared. "I hate it when you go a-trading with Uncle Mic."

"He's got to have some kind of guard on the road." Dougie grinned at her. "Do you miss me when I'm gone?"

"That, too. Mostly I wish I could go with you. I want to see Din Edin, and I don't care how bad it smells."

"A journey like ours is no place for a lass."

"If you say that again, I'll kick you. You sound like Mam."

"Well, I'm sorry, but—"

"Oh, don't let's talk about it!"

Berwynna turned on her heel and strode down the pier to the island, leaving Dougie to hurry after, babbling apologies. By the time they reached the door of the manse, she'd forgiven him. Hand in hand, they walked into the great hall of Haen Marn.

On either side of the big square room stood stone hearths, one of them cold on this warm spring day. At the other an ancient maidservant stirred a big iron kettle over a slow fire. The smell and steam of a cauldron of porridge spread through the hall. The boatmen came trooping in and sat down at one of the plank tables scattered here and there on the floor. At the head table sat Angmar, her graying pale hair swept back and covered by the black headscarf of a widow. When Dougie and Berwynna joined her, she greeted them with a pleasant smile.

"Come to talk to Mic, Dougie?" Angmar spoke the Alban tongue not well but clearly.

"I have, my lady," Dougie said. "Will he be needing my sword soon?"

"Most likely. You can ask him after he's joining us."

One of the boatmen brought Dougie a tankard of ale, which he took with thanks. He had a long sip and looked around the great hall. In one corner a staircase led to the upper floors. In the opposite corner old Otho, a white-haired, stoop-shouldered, and generally frail dwarf, sat on his cushioned chair, glaring from under white bushy brows at nothing in particular. Berwynna's sister, Marnmara, stood near the old man while she studied the wall behind him.

The two young women had been born in the same hour, and they shared the same coloring. Marnmara, however, was even smaller than her sister, a mere wisp of a woman, or so Dougie thought of her. At times, he could have sworn that she floated above the floor by an inch or two, as if she weren't really in the room at all but a reflection, perhaps, in some invisible mirror. At others, she walked upon the ground like any lass, and he would chide himself for indulging in daft fancies about her.

Haen Marn's great hall tended to breed fancies. The dark oak panels lining the walls were as heavily decorated as the Holy Book in Lord Douglas' chapel. Great swags of carved interlacements, all tangled with animals, flowers, and vines, swooped down from each corner and almost touched the floor before sweeping up again. In among them were little designs that might have been letters or simply odd little fragments of some broken pattern. Berwynna had told him of her sister's belief that the decorations had some sort of meaning, just as if they'd been a book indeed. Since Dougie couldn't read a word in any language, it was all a great mystery to him.

"Think she'll ever puzzle it out?" Dougie said to Berwynna.

"She tells me she's very close. Tirn's been a great help to her. He knows what some of the sigils are."

"Sigils?"

"It means marks like those little ones." Berwynna shrugged. "That's all I know."

"The townsfolk are saying that Tirn's a demon."

"Are you surprised? They think we're all witches and demons, don't they?"

"Well, true enough, the ingrates! And after all the healing your sister's done for them, too!"

Tirn came in not long after. Like Dougie himself, he was an unusually tall man, and no doubt he'd once been a strong one, too, judging from his broad shoulders and long, heavily muscled arms, but at the moment he was still recovering from whatever accident had burned him so badly. He walked slowly, a little stooped, and held his damaged hands away from his body. Thin cloth, smelling heavily of Marnmara's herbal medicaments, wrapped his hands and arms up to the elbows. Peeling-pink scars cut into the tattoos on his narrow face and marbled his short brown hair. He nodded Dougie's way with a weary smile, then sat down across from him at the table.

Angmar asked him a question in the language that the locals took for Cymraeg, and Tirn answered her in the same. Berwynna leaned forward and joined the conversation. Here and there, Dougie could pick out a word or phrase—Berwynna had been teaching him a bit of her native tongue—but they spoke too quickly for him to follow. Tirn considered whatever it was she'd said, then smiled and nodded.

"Mam's asking him if Marnmara can take another look at this gem he brought with him," Berwynna told Dougie. "Uncle Mic says it's a bit of cut firestone. I've not seen anything like it before."

Angmar got up and went round to where Tirn sat. With his

burnt hands still so bad, he could touch nothing. She pulled a leather pouch on a chain free of Tirn's shirt. From the pouch, she took out a black glassy gem shaped into a pyramid about six inches tall. The tip had been lopped off at an angle.

"I've not seen anything like that before either." Dougie shook his head in bafflement. "It looks like glass, though."

"It's got no bubbles in it," Berwynna said. "So Uncle Mic said it can't be glass. It comes from fire mountains, whatever they are."

"Well, he's the one who'd know." Dougie turned to Angmar. "Could I have a look at that, my lady? I'm curious, is all."

"I don't see why not," Angmar said.

When Angmar set the pyramid down in front of him, Dougie picked it up and examined it, turning it around in his fingers. Tirn made a comment, which Angmar translated.

"Don't look into it too closely," she said. "It's a rather odd thing. You don't want to stare at it for too long."

Dougie glanced at it out of the corner of his eye and saw the ordinary daylight in the great hall shining through black crystal. *There's naught to this,* he thought, and looked directly down into the black depths through the squared-off tip. He heard Marnmara's voice, coming nearer, sounding annoyed at something. He wanted to look up and ask her what the matter was, but the stone had trapped his gaze. He simply could not look away. Inside the black glow something appeared, something moved—a man, a strange slender man with pale skin, hair of an impossibly bright yellow, eyes of paint-pot blue, and lips as red as cherries.

The fellow was standing in the kitchen garden of Dougie's family steading. He seemed to be staring right at Dougie, then turned and walked through the rows of cabbages till he reached the pair of apple trees by the stone wall, but the trees, Dougie realized, were young, barely strong enough to bear a couple of branches of fruit. The strange fellow stopped and pointed with his right hand at the ground between them. Over and over he gestured at the ground, then began to make a digging motion, using both hands like a hound's front paws.

"Dougie!" Marnmara shouted his name. She grabbed his shoulder with one hand and shook him.

The spell broke. He looked up, dazed, unsure of exactly where he might be for a few beats of a heart. Marnmara turned to her mother and Tirn, set her hands on her hips, and began to lecture them in their own tongue. Tirn spoke a few feeble-sounding words, then merely listened, staring at the table. Angmar, however, argued right back, waving a maternal finger in her daughter's face. When Dougie put the pyramid onto the table, Marnmara stopped arguing long enough to snatch up the gem.

"What did you see in it, Dougie?" Marnmara said.

"A strange-looking fellow standing between two apple trees. You might have warned me that the thing could work tricks like that."

"I didn't know it could." Marnmara smiled briefly, then spoke to Tirn in their language. He looked utterly surprised and spoke a few words in reply. "He says he told you not to look into it."

"That's true enough," Dougie said. "My apologies."

Dougie decided that he didn't like the way everyone was staring at him. He stood up and held out his hand to Berwynna.

"I'll be needing to go home soon."

Together, they walked down to the pier. Although he'd never seen the boatmen leave the great hall, there they were, manning the oars, ready to take him back across. Dougie shook his head hard. He felt drunk, but he'd only had half a tankard of Diarmuid's watered ale, and then another half of Angmar's decent brew—hardly any drink at all.

"Are you well?" Berwynna said. "You've gone pale."

"I saw the strangest damned thing in that stone of Tirn's. It was like a dream, some fellow pointing to the ground over and over. He seemed to think it was important, that bit of earth."

"Do you think it was a spirit?" Berwynna turned thoughtful. "They say that spirits know where treasures are buried."

"Well, so they do—in old wives' tales and suchlike. I wouldn't set your heart on me finding a bucketful of gold."

She laughed, then raised herself up on tiptoe and kissed him farewell.

The kiss kept Dougie warm during his long walk home, but the memory of his peculiar experience kept the kiss company. After he'd brooded on what he'd seen for a mile or two, the look of the fellow in the vision jogged his memory. He knew something about that fellow, he realized, but he'd forgotten the details.

Domnal Breich's steading lay in a narrow valley twixt wooded hills. Over the years he'd built his family a rambling stone house and barn, surrounded by kitchen gardens and set off from the fields by a stone wall. The two apple trees of Dougie's vision stood by the gate, at least twice as high as they'd appeared in the black gem. When he let himself in, he paused for a moment to look at the ground between them—ordinary enough dirt, as far as he could tell, soft from the recent rain and dusted with spring grass.

Domnal himself came out of the barn and hailed him. Although he still walked with a swagger, and his broad work-worn hands were as strong as ever, his dark brown hair sported gray streaks, and his moustache had gone gray as well.

"Been at the island?" Domnal said.

"I have," Dougie said. "Here, Da, a thing I want to ask you. Do you remember a tale you told me—it was on my saint's day, a fair many years ago now, and we went riding up to Haen Marn's loch?"

"The tale about Evandar, you mean, and how he saved my life?"

"That's the one! It was a snowy night, you said, and you were lost."

"Lost and doomed, I thought, truly. But he was a man of the Seelie Host. The cold meant naught to him. He took me to Haen Marn, where they kept me safe for the night."

"What did he look like? I can't remember."

"He was tall and thin with bright yellow hair and eyes of the strangest blue, more like the sky just at twilight than an ordinary color. A well-favored fellow, but there was somewhat odd about his ears. They were long and curled like the bud of a lily. Ye gods! It's been seventeen years now, but I can still see him as clear as clear in my memory."

"No doubt, since he saved your life."

"He did that, indeed, by getting me to Haen Marn and its hearth." Domnal paused to chew his moustache in thought. "You know, there's somewhat that I still don't understand. That night, I could have sworn that the island and its loch lay south of Ness. But the next time I saw it—in the spring, it was—it lay to the north, where it is now."

"If it could fly here from Cymru, why couldn't it move itself again? Maybe it didn't like its first nest."

Domnal shrugged. "Mayhap so," he said at last. "I can't explain it any other way."

"No doubt. My thanks, Da," Dougie said. "I was just wondering."

That's who I saw, Dougie thought, *Evandar!* He was frightened enough by the magical gem to consider avoiding Haen Marn from that day on, but he knew that he never could. For one thing, there was Mic and the profitable trips down to Din Edin. And, of course, for another, there was Berwynna.

That night, when his family lay asleep, Dougie was still awake, thinking over the vision in the gem. His curiosity had been well and truly roused. Through the narrow slit of window he could see the moon, full and bright in a clear sky, its light a further temptation. He wondered, in fact, if somehow Evandar had meant him to look into the gem at the full moon. The wondering prodded him to action. Although he shared a bed with his two younger brothers, Dougie as the eldest had the privilege of the spot on the edge. He slid out of bed without waking them, put his plaid on over his nightshirt, then climbed quietly down the ladder of their loft.

The dogs, asleep at the kitchen hearth, roused enough to sniff the air and recognize him. With a wag of tails they settled themselves again and went back to sleep. Dougie crept through the dark kitchen, barked his shins on a bench, stopped himself from swearing, and very carefully unbarred the door. It creaked, but no one called out at the sound. He slipped out into the moonlit farmyard, then took his boots from the doorstep and put them on.

A shovel stood leaning against the hen house. Dougie fetched it, then strode over to the apple trees. In the shadows cast by their branches, he found it hard to see, but he dug as carefully as he could to avoid damaging the tree roots. He'd not gone down more than a foot when the shovel clanked on metal. Dougie laid it aside, then dropped to his knees and felt around with one hand in the damp chilly dirt. His fingers touched something cold, hard, and dirt-encrusted. By feeling around, he found its edges, then dug with both hands. Finally, he managed to pull free a casket, about three feet long and two wide.

Behind him, lantern light bloomed. Dougie twisted around to see Domnal, dressed only in his long nightshirt, walking over, a candle lantern held high.

"What damned stupid thing are you—" Domnal said, then stopped, staring. "God's wounds! What's that?"

"I don't know, Da." Dougie scrambled up, carrying the casket. "I had a dream, you see, about Evandar. He was telling me to dig here between the trees. I tried to ignore it, but it kept gnawing at me, like."

"Oh." Domnal lowered the lantern. "Well, let's take it into the barn. I don't want to wake your mother."

His father's sudden meekness troubled Dougie's heart. He'd just lied to his da, he realized, but somehow he hadn't wanted to tell him about Tirn's strange gem on Haen Marn—he just hadn't, though he couldn't say why.

In the barn Domnal hung the lantern on a nail above a little bench. Dougie laid the casket on the bench, then found an old sack and used it to wipe away the dirt. Its long time buried in the wet earth had turned the casket so green and crusty that he couldn't tell if it were silver or pot metal. When he tried lifting it, the lid came away in his hands. Domnal took it from him.

"What's inside?" Domnal asked. "It looks like old rags."

"So it does," Dougie said. "I wonder if there's somewhat inside them?"

One at a time Dougie peeled away the swaddlings—wads of rotten cloth on the outside, then a layer of oiled cloth, then layers of stained but sound cloth, until finally he came to a sack of boiled leather. Inside lay something solid and flat. Another casket? But when he slid it out, he found a book, bound in white leather, stained here and there from its internment. A black dragon decorated the front cover.

Dougie was too disappointed to swear. "I was hoping for a bit of treasure, Da." He opened the book, but in the candlelight all he could see was page after page of writing.

"I wasn't," Domnal said. "When Evandar's involved, you never know what you'll get, but you can wager it'll be a strange thing." He took the empty casket and held it up to the light, twisting it this way and that as if he were looking for a maker's mark. "It's too filthy to see anything." He set the book down on the bench. "Put that book back in, lad, and we'll hide it under some straw for the morrow."

"Well and good, then. Do you think this belongs to Haen Marn?"

"I do. The night he saved me, Evandar told me that he needed a messenger, and it was going to be my son, when I had one. I'm supposing he meant someone to bring them this."

"And why couldn't he have taken it over himself?"

"Witches can't travel across water, nor the Folk of the Seelie Host, either, or so I've always heard."

"So he needed a man to do his ferrying for him. I suppose that makes sense of a sort."

"Naught about Haen Marn makes sense." Domnal smiled with a bare twitch of his mouth. "I think me it might be dangerous to forget that."

Dougie went back to bed. He woke just before sunrise, got up and dressed for the second time, then went out to the barn in the cold gray light to feed the cows. His brother Ian arrived soon after with his milking stool and pails. Dougie fed the horses, turned them out into pasture, then returned to the house to talk with Jehan. He found her in the kitchen, kneading a massive lump of bread dough.

Over the years she'd borne eight children and done plenty of farm work as well. She was stout and her hands were a mass of calluses, but despite the gray in her red hair and the lines around her green eyes, Dougie could see how beautiful she must have been when his father had won her.

"I was thinking of going back out to Haen Marn today," Dougie said. "Will you be needing me for aught?"

"Not truly," Jehan said. "But you know, it's time you married your Berwynna and brought her home."

"I'd like naught better, Mother. Berwynna says she wants to marry me as well. It's Lady Angmar who's dead set against it. She doesn't want Berwynna to ever leave the island, not for a single day. She keeps saying it's too dangerous."

"Is it the local folk she fears? Once you two were married by Father Colm in the chapel, then all this stupid talk about witches would stop."

"It's not that. She won't explain why."

"You're sure she has a real reason, then?" Jehan frowned at him. "Or does she look upon us with scorn?"

Dougie shrugged to show that he didn't know. He was suddenly afraid, wondering if his Wynni was a witch, after all. His father had told him that witches couldn't cross water, hadn't he? Jehan paused to push a stray lock of gray hair back behind her ear with her little finger.

"I'll tell you what," Dougie said. "This very day, I'll ask Lady Angmar about claiming my Berwynna. If she says me nay again, I'll keep after her and see if I can find out if she truly doesn't want the lass to leave the island or if she thinks I'm not worthy or suchlike."

"Well and good, then." Jehan looked up from the kneading. "You might as well know the truth."

Before he left, Dougie put a clean shirt on under his plaid, then fetched the mysterious book from the barn. Since he was going to Haen Marn anyway, he figured, he might as well run Evandar's errand for him.

Toward noon, Lon brought a bucket of fish into the kitchen hut behind the manse. Berwynna put on her oldest tunic, wrapped a fragment of stained, fraying plaid around her for a skirt, and set to work cleaning the catch. Marnmara's six cats rubbed round her ankles and whined. The orange brindle leaped up onto the workbench with its usual dirty paws. When she yelled and swatted the animal, it jumped down again. Berwynna chopped off the fish heads and tails with efficient strokes of her long knife, then tossed them down at varying distances to give every cat a chance at this bounty. She gutted the fish, then threw the innards to the mewling horde as well.

Feeding the island took hard work. Despite the presence of so many large beasts in its water, the loch supplied full nets of fish all year long. Berwynna suspected that some sort of dweomer made the loch unusually productive, but neither her mother nor her sister would confirm her suspicion nor deny it. Man and dwarf, however, do not live by fish alone, as old Otho was fond of saying. The local villagers and farmers paid for Marnmara's healing services with produce and what little grain they could spare. Mic's coin bought beef, oats, and barley from the farmers on the richer lands to the south. Occasionally the boatmen managed to kill a deer. As well as medicinal herbs, Marnmara raised vegetables in her garden, and apple trees grew around Avain's tower.

"Wynni!" Marnmara stood in the door of the kitchen hut. "Dougie's just come across to the pier."

"Oh, ye gods!" Berwynna said. "Here I stink of fish."

"That won't bother him. He's besotted."

Still, Berwynna scrubbed her hands with a scrap of soap and rinsed them in a bucket of well water. She wanted to change her filthy old clothes, but as she was hurrying toward the manse, she saw Dougie, just coming up the path, his tousled red hair gleaming in the sun. Under one arm he carried a bulky packet, wrapped in cloth.

"There you are!" Dougie said, smiling. "Ah, you look beautiful today, lass!"

"My thanks!" *He is besotted,* Berwynna thought. *Thank God!* "It gladdens my heart to see you, too."

"Good. I'm hoping to have a bit of a talk with you and your mother." He paused for a grin. "About us."

Berwynna's heart leaped and pounded. "Indeed?" she said. "Well, I'm sure I wouldn't know what there is to talk about."

He merely grinned and reached out to catch her hand.

They found Angmar in the great hall, where she was sitting at a window with mending spread out on the low table in front of her. Dougie laid his parcel on the table, then bowed to her.

"What's all this?" Angmar raised a questioning eyebrow. "Usually you just sit yourself down without so much as a by-your-leave."

"Uh, my apologies, my lady." Dougie's face turned a faint pink. "I've brought you a very strange gift, and I was hoping that we, I mean Wynni and I and you, could have a bit of a chat."

"If you're going to ask me if you may marry her, save your breath. I'll not agree."

Dougie winced.

"I don't want her living off the island," Angmar continued.

"Truly?" Dougie said. "Or is that me and my kin aren't grand enough for you?"

"What? Naught of the sort! Dougie, I know not how or why, but in my soul I do know that me and mine will cause you grief one day. I'd beg you to put my daughter out of your heart."

"Mam!" Berwynna could stay silent no longer. "But I love him. I want to marry Dougie."

He turned her way and grinned. When Berwynna held out her hand, he clasped it and drew her close.

"Wynni, heard you not one word of what I said?" Angmar flopped her mending onto the table and scowled at both of them. "Avain did see much grief—"

"What she sees in the water isn't always true," Berwynna said. "Sometimes it's wrong, or else it comes true in some odd way that's more of a jest than anything. Well, doesn't it?"

"True enough." Angmar paused for a long sigh. "But—"

"Besides," Berwynna hurried on before her mother could finish. "If you won't let me leave the island, why can't Dougie come live here?"

"And what would your family say to that, then?" Angmar glanced at Dougie. "With you the eldest son and all?"

"They'd take a bit of persuading," Dougie said. "But I'd keep at it and wear them down in the end."

"Still, most like it be too dangerous. The isle be a jealous place, and I doubt me if you belong to it the way we do."

Berwynna felt tears gathering just behind her eyes. She gave her mother the most piteous look she could manage and willed the tears to run. Her mother sighed with a shake of her head.

"Wynni, Wynni! You children don't understand, and there's no way I can make you understand, truly." Angmar hesitated for a long moment. "But whist, whist, child, don't weep so! Here, let me discuss this with Marnmara. But I'd not hope too much, either of you."

She picked up the mending again and frowned at it with such concentration that Berwynna knew they'd been dismissed. She snuffled back her tears and wiped her eyes on her sleeve while Dougie patted her shoulder to comfort her. Hand in hand, they went outside and sat down together on a wooden bench under an apple tree. Above them, the white flowers were just peeking from their pale green buds.

"Well, now," Dougie said at last. "So much for the grand speech I'd stored up in my mind. I never got a chance to speak any of it."

"It probably wouldn't have mattered. Mam's got one of her ideas, and my dear sisters are dead set against us, too, from what she said."

"I don't understand. What did she mean about Avain seeing things?"

"Oh, she sees visions in a bowl of water." Berwynna looked down, saw a pebble on the path, and kicked it viciously away. "Since she's a mooncalf, Mam and Marnmara say that the angels or the saints are sending her messages that way. I don't understand, and I don't agree, but you heard Mam."

"I did, and a nasty thing it was to hear. I'm willing to risk a fair lot of grief for you, but I don't want you sharing it."

"Bless you! But I'm willing to run the risk, too."

Dougie threw his arms around her, drew her close, and kissed her. She laughed in sheer pleasure and took another kiss, but just as he reached for a third, she heard a warning snarl of a cough behind her. Dougie let her go. Berwynna turned on the bench and saw old Lonna, arms akimbo, glaring at her. Dougie rose and bowed to the elderly dwarf.

"I'll just be leaving, then," he said with a sigh. "Fare thee well, my lady."

"I'll walk with you to the landing." She spoke to Lonna in Dwarvish. "Could you tell the boatmen to make ready?"

Lonna made a sound that might have been yes, then turned and stomped off toward the manse.

"Ye gods!" Dougie lowered his voice to a whisper. "I'm beginning to understand why you want to get out of this place, truly."

"Well, I don't want to leave it forever. I just want to see more of the world than Haen Marn." Berwynna paused, glancing around her. "There's not much of it, is there? Just one small island, and every now and then I get to go over to the mainland with Marnmara when she gathers wild herbs or if someone's ill in the village. Once we got to go to your grandfather's dun, too, when the groom's wife was so ill. That's all I've ever seen, and all I've ever known, and, oh, Dougie, I'm sick to my heart of it!"

"I can understand that." Dougie patted her hand, then raised it to his lips and kissed it, fish stains and all. "Let me think about this, lass. Mayhap I can come up with some scheme to get us married."

Berwynna walked him down to the jetty and saw him off. For a brief while she lingered on the pier and considered the boathouse, a roof and walls with lake water for a floor. A narrow walkway ran along one side to give the boatmen access to the ladder that led up to the loft where they slept. Besides the magnificent dragon boat, the island owned two coracles, a large one for the fishing, and a small craft that Marnmara and Berwynna used for their rare trips to the mainland. These hung out of the water from pegs on the boathouse walls.

The question, Berwynna decided, was whether she could creep into the boathouse at night, get the coracle down, and lower it into the water without making a splash or other noise that would wake the boatmen. *Not likely,* she thought. If only she could, she could row across and meet Dougie, and perhaps Father Colm would marry them before her family caught her. *Even less likely, since he thinks I'm a witch.* She picked up a stone and hurled it into the water as hard as she could, then turned on her heel and stalked back to the manse.

In the great hall the others had gathered around Marnmara, who had come over to Angmar's table to look at Dougie's gift. Angmar sat to her right, the mending unnoticed in her lap, while Tirn stood just behind Marnmara and peered over her shoulder. When no Mainlanders were around, the island folk talked in one of the two languages that Angmar called "our home tongues." Since Tirn knew no Dwarvish, they spoke the mountain dialect of Deverrian whenever he joined them. In fact, he seemed to know it oddly well, better than any of the rest of them. Berwynna sat down on a bench opposite her mother just as Marnmara opened the sack and slid out its contents: a book, bound in white leather, with a black leather piece in the shape of a dragon upon the cover.

Tirn gasped, tried to choke back the noise, then coughed. Marnmara twisted around to look up at him.

"My apologies," he said. "For a moment there I thought it was a book I used to own. That one had a black cover with a white dragon upon it."

"Indeed?" Marnmara said. "What sort of book might it be? A grammarie?"

"What's that?" Tirn looked puzzled. "I've never heard that word before."

"A book of spells." Marnmara was trying to suppress a grin.

"Ah." Tirn hesitated, caught, then shrugged. "Well, it was that, truly."

Marnmara allowed the grin to blossom. She opened the book randomly, then frowned at the page before her.

"Be somewhat wrong?" Angmar said.

"I did hope I could read this," Marnmara said, "but I've not seen these letters ever before." She turned round again and looked Tirn full in the face. "Except right there, tattooed on your skin. What language be they?"

"That of the Seelie Host," Tirn said.

Berwynna made the sign of the Holy Rood.

"Truly?" Angmar quirked one eyebrow. "Now, I myself have seen such letters before, and they were made by someone as much flesh and blood as you are."

Tirn face's turned scarlet between his tattoos and scars.

"My apologies," he said. "You must know about the Ancients, then. Some call them the Westfolk, others the Ancients. Do they dwell in this country, too?"

"I know not," Angmar said, "but they do dwell in my homeland. Indeed, the father of my daughters did have Westfolk blood in his veins." She leaned back to study his face. "I think me that you come from the place the Deverry folk call Annwn, not from Alban, no, nor Cymru nor Lloegr, either."

"You've caught me out, my lady." Tirn smiled and ducked his head in apology. "I didn't want to say anything at first because I thought you'd never believe me. I didn't realize that you, too, hail from Deverry."

"I come not from Deverry proper, but from the north of it, in the country known as Dwarveholt. Now, can you read that book?"

"Alas, I cannot in any true sense. I can read well enough in three languages, but that of the Ancients isn't one of them." Tirn raised his bandaged hand and pointed at the tattoo on his left cheek. "These marks? Among my kin they're thought to bring good luck or the favor of the gods. They're very old, and their meaning's been long forgotten."

Angmar continued studying his face, while Marnmara paged through the book, frowning at a bit of writing here and there and shaking her head over the lot.

"What I can do," Tirn went on, "is sound out the letters, though I don't know what many words mean. Well, truly, they're not letters in the way that the Holy Book of this country is writ in letters. Each one stands for a full sound, what mayhap would take two or three letters in some other tongue."

Everyone stared, puzzled, except Marnmara, who laid a finger on one mark. "This one?" she said.

"La," Tirn said, "and the next is sounded drah."

"Be you a scholar, then, Tirn?" Berwynna said. "Father Colm does warn against the studying of books, saying it leads to sorcery."

"Does he?" Tirn grinned at her. "He may be right, then, for the first time in his fat life."

Berwynna began to laugh, then stifled the sound when Angmar glared at her. Tirn shifted his weight from foot to foot, then walked round to sit down on the same bench as Berwynna. She moved over to give him plenty of room. Angmar gave both of them a sour look.

"Is somewhat wrong, my lady?" Tirn said to Angmar.

"There be Horsekin blood in your veins, bain't?" Angmar said.

Tirn blushed again, then nodded.

"Mam, Mam!" Marnmara looked up from the book with a sigh. "Matters it to you, with all of us so far from home?"

"Not truly," Angmar said. "I find truth sweeter than lies, is all."

"It is, and I owe you an apology," Tirn said, "but I feared you'd have me killed or suchlike if you knew about the Horsekin."

"If you realized not that we be from Annwn like you," Angmar said with some asperity, "why did you think we might know about the Horsekin?"

Tirn blushed again, then spoke hurriedly. "I'm an outlaw among them, you see, and I'll swear to the truth of that. They'd kill me if they ever got hold of me."

"Now, that I do believe," Angmar said, "because of the fear in your voice."

Her mother and old Lonna had told Berwynna tales of the Horsekin, vicious killers who worshiped an evil demon named Alshandra. Now here was one of them, sitting next to her, a very ordinary man by the look of him, and badly injured to boot.

"Do you believe in Alshandra, then?" Berwynna said to him.

"I don't," Tirn said, "and that's why I'm an outlaw."

"I see." Angmar rose and began to collect the mending in a basket. "Well and good, then."

Berwynna followed her mother out of the great hall and up the stairs to Angmar's room. She'd been planning on badgering Angmar about Dougie, but her mother's mood had turned so grim that she thought better of the plan. Alone, they spoke in Dwarvish.

"Mama, do you trust Tirn?" Berwynna asked instead.

"I don't," Angmar said. "There's somewhat more than a bit shifty about him beyond his Horsekin blood. I do believe him about being an outlaw, mind. I wonder, in fact, if his own kind gave him those burns and scars, a-torturing him somehow."

"Ych!"

"Truly, they're a cruel lot, the Horsekin. But be that as it may, Tirn knows lore that Marnmara needs if she's to get us home again."

"Will we ever really go home," Berwynna said, "wherever that is?"

"I have my hopes. It may not mean much to you, but I long to see your father again."

"Well, of course. I wish I knew him, too. My father. It has such a distant ring to it, doesn't it? Even though you've told me about him, it's not the same as knowing him."

"It's not." Angmar allowed herself a long sigh. "I've tried to think of myself as a widow and stop longing for him, but deep in my heart I'm sure he's still alive back home, if we could only get there. And I miss my homeland, too, the Dwarveholt."

"Mam, I'm sorry, I don't mean to slight what you treasure, but the land means naught to me. This is the only home I've ever had."

"I do understand that. But I have hopes that someday you'll have better and find a better man, too."

This last was too much to bear. "Please, please, tell me why I mayn't marry Dougie?" Berwynna said. "I love him ever so much."

"I know, but ye gods, it would ache my heart to go home but leave you here with your Dougie. You're young, child. There will be other men—"

"I don't want any of them."

"Dougie's the only handsome lad you've ever known." Angmar managed a smile. "First love is the love that stings, or so they always say. But answer me this. Suppose you did marry your lad and go to live with him, and then we all disappeared without you. How would that feel?"

Berwynna felt the blood drain from her face. The thought of losing her family—

"I see it doesn't sit well with you," Angmar said. "Well, it could happen, were you to go live on Alban land. Haen Marn goes where it wills when it wills, and it doesn't bother with giving fair warning."

"Then how come you let Marnmara go over to the mainland to heal the folk and suchlike?"

"Because the island's not going to go anywhere without her. That I know as surely as I know my own name."

Berwynna bit back the bitter words that threatened to break free of her mouth. *It's always Mara, isn't it?* she thought. *She's the important one, never me.*

Laz had told the truth when he'd told Angmar that he couldn't read the Westfolk language. He regretted it bitterly, too, thanks to that book of spells. So much dweomer so near—but the book might as well lie on a table in Deverry for all the good it would do him. Wildfolk hunkered down on the table around the book, slender green gnomes, each with a cap made of rose petals. Now and then one of them would stretch out a timid finger and touch the edges of the page. When Marnmara threatened to swat them, they disappeared. For some while Laz watched Marnmara turn pages, her stare as fierce as a warrior's, as if she could force the meaning from the alien letters by sheer will.

"Not one word can I read," she announced. "And the whole thing be writ in the same markings."

"So it looked to me," Laz said, "and it aches my heart, I tell you."

"No doubt. Here." She pushed the heavy book across the table toward him. "Mayhap if you sound out more of the marks, you might find a word or two you know. I do hope that somehow this book holds the dweomer to take us all home again, though I do have this strange feeling in my heart that it be naught of the sort."

"Let me take a look, then."

Using his wrists rather than his damaged hands, Laz managed to turn the book right side up in front of him. Marnmara moved to sit next to him and turn the pages when he asked. As he sounded out letters from the syllabary, he did come across words he knew, most of them useless, such as "next," "then," "and," "is," and the like. Still, Marnmara watched him so admiringly that he kept going.

"Turn all the way back to the first page," Laz said finally. "If you'd be so kind."

Marnmara did as he asked.

On the top of that first page a line of symbols, larger than the rest, had been carefully painted in red. Laz sounded them out several times. Thanks to the Westfolk custom of putting dots between words to set them apart, he managed to form them up into something he could guess at.

"Now this first word," he said, "is a verb of some kind. That is, it's the name of an act, a thing you do. I can tell by this sound at the beginning. It stands for keh-, and that means an action follows."

A wide-eyed Mara nodded, taking it all in.

"And this sound at the end," he continued, "means 'how' or 'why' one does this action. Alas! I don't know what the action is. However, I'm fairly sure this next word means 'a dragon' because that name sounds much the same in several tongues, drahkanonen among the Westfolk, draeg in Deverrian, and drakonis among the Bardekians."

"You most certainly be a scholar, Tirn. Here, I think me you should study this book for all of us. Maybe more will come to you if you do contemplate it."

"Mayhap. We can hope."

"I—" Mara paused, then turned around. "Be it that you wish somewhat, Wynni?"

Berwynna stood in the doorway, where, Laz realized, she'd been listening for some while, not that he saw anything wrong with her doing so. Marnmara, however, rose, shutting the book with a puff of dust.

"Come take this upstairs to Tirn's chamber," Marnmara said. "He can carry it not himself."

"You might say please, truly, once in a while." Berwynna walked over to the table.

"Oh, don't be tedious!" Mara shoved the book at her. "Here!"

With a scowl Berwynna took the book—clasping it to her chest with both arms—and trotted over to the stairs. She hesitated, glancing back, at the foot of them as if she might speak further, then shrugged and went on up.

"Little sneak!" Mara said. "She always be listening and prowling around. Now. We'd best work on your hands before dinner. Rest here a moment. I be going to fetch the medicaments."

Laz suppressed a sigh. He needed more than a moment to brace himself for what lay ahead. Before Marnmara went upstairs, she spoke briefly to Lonna, the aged maidservant, who merely nodded for answer. Lonna went to the hearth, poured water from a big clay jar into an iron pot, then set the pot in the coals to heat. By the time Marnmara returned, carrying a small cloth sack, the water was steaming. Lonna set it on to the table in front of Laz, then stomped off, muttering to herself. Marnmara took a handful of herbs out of the sack and dropped them into the water.

"Let that cool for a moment," she said.

"Indeed," he said. "May I ask you somewhat?"

"You may, though I might not answer."

"Fair enough. Where did you learn so much about healing?"

"I don't know." She paused for a smile at his surprise. "When I were but a child, old Lonna did tell me of a few simples. She did know how to bind a small wound and such crude lore, too. But then, once I did grow into a woman, I did have a dream." She hesitated, considering him. "Here, Tirn, since you be a scholar, tell me what you do think of this. In the dream I did find a door dug into the dirt of Haen Marn, out among the apple trees, that were. I did open the door and go down the stairs within. At the bottom was another door. I did open that. Herbs came pouring out, a great flood of dried herbs. I did scream, thinking they would smother me, but I woke to find the blanket over my face." She laughed with a toss of her head. "But here be the strange thing. From that day on, I did know herblore."

"I'd say you remembered it. The door led to your memory of such things."

"From a life lived before, mean you? It could well be. I remember naught of this, but my mother does assure me that I was the lady of this isle once before. Avain did recognize me, Mam tells me, on the very day I was born." She looked at him with her head cocked a little to one side, and her eyes wide, as if she were expecting him to challenge or dismiss her tale.

"I'd believe it of Avain," Laz said. "She's got a dweomer air about her."

Marnmara smiled, perhaps relieved that he'd accepted her tale so easily.

"It's a great honor," Laz said, "to have such gifts."

"That's what my mam does say. I get a-weary of it."

"What? Why?"

"The gods have blessed you, she does say, so you must repay them and use your gifts as they wish. If I be the Lady of Haen Marn, then I have many a burden to take up." Her voice turned unsteady. "Whether I wish to lift them or no."

"I see. Well, no doubt you'll be given the strength when you need it."

She scowled at the surface of the water, then shrugged, as if she'd hoped for a different answer. Laz wanted to ask more, but he hesitated, afraid she'd resent his prying. She touched the surface of the water in the kettle with one finger, then dipped her hand in.

"Just cool enough," she said. "Here, stretch out your hands, Tirn. We'll have the bandages off."

Laz gritted his teeth and did as she asked. Her touch was so light that pulling off the thin cloth caused him no pain, but the sight—both his hands were a mass of shiny pink scars. On his left hand the little finger had burned down to a stub of scar tissue, permanently fastened to the finger next to it, both of them useless. On the right hand the last three fingers formed one throbbing mass that he'd lost the power to move. In between the remaining fingers, and between each thumb and the meat of his hands, the flesh oozed a clear fluid as if it wept for its loss.

"They heal, they heal," Marnmara said. "But not yet can we leave them be. We'll do the left hand first."

Laz plunged his hand into the water. The herb brew stung the oozing wounds like a liquid fire at first, then numbed them, though not quite enough. Marnmara put her own hands in the kettle, caught his, and pried the good fingers apart, one pair at a time, deliberately cracking open the scars to keep the fingers free and usable. As he always did, he swore under his breath the entire time, running through every foul oath he knew in the Gel da'Thae language to keep from fainting and disgracing himself. The right hand took less time and caused him less pain than the left, but by the time she finished, his head was swimming, and the skin of his face felt ice-cold and damp, especially around his mouth.

Marnmara laid his hands on top of the bandages and considered them. A trace of blood oozed between each treated pair of fingers.

"Not much blood," she announced. "We'll leave these open to the air for now." She patted his right arm just above the wrist. "Go rest."

"Gladly." Laz got up, steadied himself, and forced out a smile. "My thanks."

He felt like an old man, hunched and staggering, as he made his way across the hall and up the stairs. His small chamber, bare except for a mattress on the floor and a basket for the extra pieces of clothing the women had made him, stood near the head of the stairs. The dragon book lay on the floor by the basket. He went in, shut the door with a nudge of his foot, then lay down and crossed his arms at the wrist over his chest.

"That's done for another day," he remarked to the hands. "Ye gods, I should have listened to Sidro. 'Don't,' she said, 'don't touch the crystals together.' Sound advice, but did I listen? Oh, no! Not that I should complain, I suppose. What was that my charming mother used to say? Walk behind a mule, and you deserve to get kicked, that's it."

The worst thing, he decided, was that he could no longer remember why he'd wanted to bring the crystals together. Obviously, it had been a stupid idea, yet he'd felt compelled—the word caught his attention. Compelled. Had some wyrd-dweomer lain inside the pair, waiting for a victim to bring their tips together so they could transport themselves and victim both to this island?

If so, one of them had made the trip safely, though he'd lost the other. He wondered if they might transport him back if he brought them together. They might take him elsewhere, of course, somewhere far less hospitable than Haen Marn, or burn off the rest of his hands even if he did end up back in the Northlands. He sat up and considered his maimed hands. The idea of trusting himself to the crystals again terrified him. Yet curiosity nagged. Where was the white one, anyway?

After Dougie's strange vision of the other day, he'd had Marnmara remove the pouch with the crystal from around his neck and put it under the clothing in the basket, hidden from curious eyes. When he tried moving his fingers, he found that he could control them, though it hurt whenever they rubbed against one another. He was healing, indeed, and the thought made him almost cheerful. Carefully, slowly, painfully, he managed to tip the basket over, find the pouch, and shake the black crystal out onto his pillow. In the sunlight coming through the tiny window, it gleamed, but sullenly, or so it seemed to him.

"I'll wager you can tell me where your brother lies," Laz said.

Laz set the crystal upright and looked down into its tip. He saw nothing at first, then murky images formed—an expanse of brownish gray, a lump of something that might have been wood. Ripples shimmered in the murk. A long narrow head appeared, two tiny eyes, a row of teeth, a neck. The head drew back. A spray of bubbles covered everything. Laz could draw only one conclusion: the white crystal sat at the bottom of the lake, far and forever out of his reach.

"Good! Rot, for all I care!"

Getting the obsidian crystal back into its pouch, and the pouch into the basket, made his hands throb. Throb or no, he decided to put the dragon book somewhere safe rather than leaving it on the floor where Berwynna had placed it. Lifting such a heavy thing—the thought itself pained him. He glanced at the book, then swore aloud.

Just above the cover hovered a thickening in the air. A sprite, perhaps, only half-materialized? Yet the thing had a glow to it that sprites lacked, and an abstract shape. He could discern a disk of some color that lay just beyond the ordinary colors of the world, an icy lavender? No, stranger still. Was it a spirit at all or some odd vortex of force? He lay down on the mattress to consider it at eye level. As if it knew he studied it, the glow sank into the book and was gone.

Once, perhaps, Laz might have called to that spirit and inquired about its nature. Now he was afraid, quite simply afraid, to attempt even the most basic dweomer. What if he failed, what if he learned that the enormous power he'd treasured had deserted him? He'd been wounded by the pair of crystals, he realized, his confidence broken as badly as his hands. He'd done a rash, stupid thing that had resulted in the worst pain he'd ever suffered. Worse yet, though, was thinking that the crystals had somehow compelled him, had gained power over him. *A sorcerer, are you?* he told himself. *A pitiful fool, more like!* On a tide of such dark thoughts he eventually fell asleep.

Laz woke long after the dinner hour, when the manor of Haen Marn already lay wrapped in silence for the night. During his convalescence, hunger had deserted him, not that he'd ever eaten much in any given day. When he sat up, he noticed that the dragon book was glowing again. Ice-white flames, tipped in a peculiar blue, danced on its surface. Spirits. He had to be seeing spirits of Aethyr, he realized, and of a rank far more powerful than any Wildfolk.

"I want that thing out of here!"

The glow disappeared. They had heard him. He felt sick, not with physical pain, but with shame that he'd turned into a coward. He got up and walked over to the window. Outside, the night lay clear and still. Moonlight streaked the water of the loch with an illusionary road, heading west. *If only I could run along that back to the Northlands!* Laz thought. *Or if I could fly.* He decided that the time had come for him to cast his cowardice aside and see what he could—or could not—do. *It's the only way you'll ever heal,* he told himself.

He stripped off his clothes with some difficulty, then stood naked at the window. When he called it forth, the mental image of the raven came to him. He worked with it, imagining the details of wing and head, until it seemed to live apart from his working as it stood on the windowsill. With a snap of will, he transferred his consciousness over to it. There he had an unexpected struggle, but at last it seemed that he looked out from the bird's eyes at his body, slumped as if asleep on the floor.

Now came the hardest step, drawing the physical substance of his body into this new form. Once, the process had come easily to him. That night he tried three times and failed at every attempt. No matter how hard he concentrated, how carefully he recited the working, his stubborn lump of flesh stayed where it was, and the raven remained an image, a body of light, only. His mind kept slipping back, as well. At one moment he would be looking out of the raven's eyes; at the next, he'd be seeing the strip of wall in front of his body. Finally, he realized that his body was panting for breath and dripping with sweat. He withdrew the raven image from the windowsill, banished it with the proper seal, and sat up, turning to lean against the wall while he let his breathing slow to normal.

"Squittering shits!" he said in the Gel da'Thae tongue. They were the only words that seemed appropriate.

Once he felt steady again, he got up and struggled back into his clothes. *Why, oh, why, didn't I listen to Sisi?* The question was going to torment him for the rest of his life.

Moving as quietly as he could, he went downstairs and out to the cooler air of the apple grove. White blossoms hung thick on the branches like trapped moonlight. That morning the trees had barely begun to bud. He stared at the blossoms while his heart pounded in terror.

"How long did I sleep?" he whispered.

"Naught but a few hours," Marnmara said from behind him. "Time on Haen Marn runs at its own pace."

Laz spun around to find her holding up a pierced tin lantern. He could see her smiling in its dappled light.

"You've not been here long, Tirn," Marnmara continued. "The island still has tricks to show you."

"So it seems. No wonder my hands are healing so quickly."

"That may be so, indeed."

"May I ask you a question? Where are we? How does this island move itself?"

"As to the first, we be in a land called Alban. As to the second, I know not, nor do I know which is its true dwelling place. If we could return to the land that you and my mam call home, then mayhap I would know. My own dweomer should kindle then, like a flame shielded from the wind." She shrugged her shoulders. "It be weak here."

"What makes you think I have dweomer?"

"Oh, come now!" She laughed aloud. "Did you not send the dragon book to my chamber just now?"

"I—uh—" Laz felt his face burn with a blush that, he hoped, the darkness would cover. Had the spirits taken his words as a command? Or had he merely hurt their tender feelings? Spirits could be extremely touchy. He had no idea which it was, although he wasn't about to admit his ignorance. "So, the spell worked, did it?"

"It did. The book did appear on white wings and settle onto a coffer in my chamber. So I did put it safely away inside."

"I thought it would be best if you kept it with you."

"Well and good, then." She hesitated briefly. "Oft have you told me you wished to make some repayment for my healing."

"I do, truly, if there's aught of mine that you'd want."

"You know dweomer, don't you? Teach me some."

"I could do that, certainly. But you must have knowledge of your own."

Marnmara shook her head. "I have bits and shreds of such knowledge only. It comes to me in dreams or now and again in memory. I do feel—nay, I do know in my heart that if I did know the first steps of the dweomer way, then I might walk far. But I know them not."

"Well and good, then. I can certainly teach you those."

In the lantern light her smile turned soft, flickering, it seemed, like the candle flame itself. Although he'd always thought of her as beautiful, that night the thought carried a sexual interest that had escaped him when he'd been weak and in constant pain. He realized that he had started emitting the betraying scent of his interest, too, but he could take comfort in knowing that she'd not understand it, if indeed she could smell it at all.

Perhaps the look in his eyes had told her enough.

"Tirn," she said, "there's somewhat you need to know about me. I wear this body the way you wear a shirt. Don't be taken in by it."

She patted him on the shoulder with the same affection with

which she'd pat one of her cats, then walked away, disappearing into the manse.

And what, by the gods, does she mean by that?

As he followed her inside, Laz felt both sad and profoundly weary in a way he'd never experienced before. At last he identified the sensation. He wanted to go home.

PART 1

THE WESTLANDS
SPRING, 1160

Some say that the ancient mages of the Seven Cities, those long-dead fortresses of beauty and magic, left a record of their secret work not in words or images but in stones and earth. Yet I, for one, call such a foolish tale because I see not how it may be possible, no, not in the least.

—*The Pseudo-Iamblichos Scroll*

"The crux of the problem," Valandario said, "is Laz. We want the pair of crystals. As far as we know, he still has them. Finding them means finding him."

"You're right, of course," Dallandra said. "I wish I knew whether or not he's worth the effort of finding."

"Sidro says he is."

"Sidro loves him or thinks she does. She's not a reliable advocate. From everything she's told me about him, I certainly don't understand how she could care so much about him."

Valandario managed to shield her thought just in time. *You're a fine one to talk about her, Dalla, running off with that awful Evandar the way you did!* They were communicating through the fire, Valandario in her chamber in Mandra, Dallandra in her tent some miles east.

"So you're convinced he's still alive," Valandario said.

"Not I." Dallandra's image, floating above the bed of coals in the brazier, paused for a wry smile. "My guess would be that he's dwelling on the spirit plane, waiting to be reborn. It's Vek who's convinced he's still alive."

"Vek? Oh, yes, that Horsekin boy prophet."

"A Gel da'Thae boy prophet. There really is a difference."

"Very well, if you say so. Now, consider the vision Ebañy saw in the crystal, Evandar standing on Haen Marn. Do you think that means the crystal's linked to the island?"

"It might, but you can't trust Evandar's riddles to be logical. It certainly indicates that the book he was holding is linked to Haen Marn. But the crystal—I can't say either way."

"Blast! I was afraid of that. Can we definitely say that wherever Haen Marn may be, it's not the physical plane?"

"Again, maybe. It's surrounded by water, after all. Maybe it's enough water to make scrying impossible."

"If it's surrounded by water, how could Evandar even reach it? The play of forces in the water veil should have torn him apart."

"That's a very good question. He probably couldn't, and the view of Haen Marn that Salamander saw is just an image of the place. Probably. I don't really know."

"In short, we can't say anything useful about the wretched island at all, and I'm starting to think the beastly thing should just stay gone."

Dallandra laughed. "Val, your image looks so sour! Not that I blame you, mind."

"Thank you, I suppose. The omens are so tangled! It's enough to drive one daft."

"I couldn't agree more about that. But tell me, how are you surviving the winter?"

"Well, I miss everyone in the alar, but I have to admit that I've never been so comfortable in my life."

For a while they spoke of trivial things, then broke the link between them. Valandario leaned back in her chair and considered the set of rough shelves across from her, a precious library of some fifty books protected by the solid walls of her chamber. For the first time in her life, Valandario had spent the winter inside a house rather than a tent.

In the winter the Westfolk and their herds usually moved south, until, by the shortest day in the year, they camped along the seacoast. Although it snowed only rarely that far south, it did rain three or four days out of every five. In a Westfolk tent, Grallezar's library of dweomer books would have stood in as much danger as it had faced from the devotees of Alshandra back in Braemel, its original home, although the danger would have come from water, not fire.

Another place, however, had offered it shelter—Linalavenmandra, the new town that returning elven refugees had built at a natural harbor near the Deverry border. Although the name meant "sorrow but new hope," its eight hundred inhabitants generally called it Mandra, simply "hope." They were young people, by and large, fleeing the minutely structured life of the far distant Southern Isles where they'd been born. To them, having a Wise One, as the Westfolk term their dweomermasters, among them was not merely an honor, but a sign that their town had achieved the same status as the ancient cities they'd left behind.

So, when Valandario had volunteered to live in Mandra and tend Grallezar's library, the townsfolk had responded by finding a house with room for her and the books both. She had moved all her belongings into a big upstairs chamber with a view of the sea from its window. Elaborately patterned Bardekian rugs covered the floor, her red-and-blue tent bags hung along the walls, embroidered cushions of green and purple lay piled on the narrow bed. The townsfolk had added a wooden table and chair so the Wise One could study her books in comfort and a small wooden coffer to keep her supply of oil, wicks, and clay lamps handy.

"Wise One?" Lara, the woman who owned the house with her husband, appeared in the doorway to the chamber. "We're preparing dinner. Would you like some meat with your bread and soup?"

"No, thank you. I'm not very hungry."

Lara smiled, made a little bow, then silently shut the door again. Laradalpancora, to give her her full name, and her husband, Jinsavadelan, insisted on acting as if they were servants in Valandario's house rather than the owners of the house in question, cooking, cleaning, mending her clothes, and generally fussing over her. They also fussed over each other.

"They never would have let us marry back home," Lara told her one evening. "Even though we'd loved each other for years. So we had to come here."

"I don't understand," Val said. "Who's they, and why would they forbid it?"

"The Council, of course. Jin's birth-clan was too far above mine in rank." She held her head high with a defiant lift to her chin. "That doesn't matter here."

Jin smiled at her with such a depth of feeling that Val quietly got up and left the room. Seeing them so happy had woken an old grief. At times after that conversation, she missed Jav as badly as if he'd been murdered only a few years past.

Val used her work to blot her memories from her mind, reading for hours on end by pale sun or flickering candlelight until her eyes watered and ached. She was searching for information concerning a particularly powerful act of dweomer, one beyond the capabilities of any living dweomermaster, elven or human. Any one of Grallezar's books might have held a clue. Fortunately, most of them were bilingual, with a roughly-translated elven text on one page and the Gel da'Thae text facing it. Grallezar had wanted to make the knowledge they contained accessible to Westfolk dweomermasters as well her own people.

As Valandario read through each book, she copied any relevant passages onto a scroll made of pabrus, a writing material that had come over from the islands with the new settlers. One book in particular she kept on the table near her, but not for its information. Bound in black leather, decorated with a white applique of a dragon, it contained a translation into Gel da'Thae of a familiar work on dweomer, one she knew practically by heart. Its importance lay in its links to its previous owner, Laz Moj. According to Sidro, he'd made the translation and written it out in the book as well. Now and then Val would lay a hand upon it and try to pick up some impression of its absent scribe. Very slowly, an insight grew in her mind. Once she could articulate it, she presented it to Dallandra.

"It's about Laz's book. It's the antithesis of the one Evandar showed Ebañy in the vision crystal. The binding's in the opposite colors, and the information inside it is well-known, while we don't have any idea what may be in Evandar's."

"That's all true," Dallandra said.

"So if the two books are linked by antithesis, they might echo the pair of crystals, the black and the white."

"In which case," Dalla continued the thought, "the missing book might also tell us about the crystals."

"Exactly! Furthermore, both the crystals and the island are

shadows from some higher plane. Could it be that Haen Marn's their real home, and they wanted to take Laz there for some reason?"

"Or else they used him to get there. Salamander was planning on smashing the black one. I wonder if it was trying to escape."

"How would it have known?" Val asked. "You don't think it had some kind of consciousness, do you?"

"I can't say either way. I didn't get to study it for very long."

"That's not exactly helpful."

Dallandra's image grinned at her. "Sorry," she said. "I'm not thinking very clearly these days. It's the baby, I suppose. I'm sinking to the level of a pregnant animal, all warm and broody like a mother dog." Her smile disappeared. "I hate it."

"At least it's only temporary."

"That's very true, and I thank the Star Goddesses for it."

Dallandra's image, floating over the glowing coals, suddenly wavered, faded, then returned to clarity.

"Val, I have to leave," Dallandra said. "Someone's calling for me, and they sound panicked."

"Dalla! Dalla!" Branna was standing right outside the tent. "Vek's having a seizure, and it's a bad one."

Dallandra grabbed the tent bag of medicinals she kept ready for these occasions and hurried outside. Wrapped in a heavy cloak, Branna stood waiting for her. A mist that fell just short of rain swirled around her in the gray light and beaded her blonde hair. Her gray gnome hunkered down next to her and squeezed handfuls of mud through its twiggy fingers.

"He's in Sidro and Pir's tent," Branna said. "Over this way."

The gnome dematerialized as they hurried through the maze of round tents, as strangely silent as winter camps always were, with life moved so resolutely inside. As usual, the winter rains had washed off their painted decorations, leaving strange ghostly stains on the leather, outlines to be repainted once the weather turned toward summer. In the gray light it seemed that the camp lay caught between two worlds of water and earth, scarcely there.

Since Branna was striding along just ahead of her, Dallandra noticed that the girl's dress hung thick with yellow-brown mud about her ankles. Her clogs sank into the ground with every step.

"You really need to wear leggings and boots," Dallandra said. "I'll get the women to make you some."

"I suppose so," Branna said. "I'm just so used to dresses, but truly, it's impossible to keep them clean out here." She paused for a sigh. "It sounded so exciting, coming to live among the Westfolk. I didn't realize what the winters would be like."

"They can be a bit grim, truly."

"I understand now why Salamander wintered with my uncle. I thought he was daft for it, until the rains started."

"Do you want to go home?"

"I don't. There's too much to learn here. I just wish I could get really dry and warm."

"Well, it's almost spring. Things will be better then."

"The days are getting longer, truly." Branna paused to extricate a clog from a particularly sticky lump of mud.

"And in a few days we'll move camp," Dallandra continued. "The ground will be cleaner in the new site."

Sidro and Pir had pitched their newly-made tent on the edge of the camp, not far from the horse herd. When Dallandra ducked inside, she saw Vek kneeling on the floor cloth and leaning, face forward, onto a supporting heap of leather cushions. He'd come of age the summer past, and as was usual among the Horsekin, he'd been bald until that point in his life. Still short and straight, his hair clung to his dead-white skin. Sidro knelt beside him and wiped his sweaty face with a damp rag. Drool laced with pink stained the neckline of his dirty linen tunic.

"I do think the worst be done with," Sidro said. "But he did bite his tongue afore I could get him turned over and sitting up like this."

Branna hovered back in the curve of the wall to watch. Dallandra set her bag down, then knelt at Vek's other side. When she laid her hand on his face, she found it cold and clammy. He looked at her out of one dark eye.

"I've brought your drops," Dallandra said. "Let me just get them out."

In response he let his mouth hang open. She rummaged through the tent bag and found the tiny glass vial, filled with an extremely potent tincture of valerian. It smelled horrible and must have tasted worse, but Vek neither squirmed nor made a face when she used the glass stopper to drip a small quantity into his mouth. She could see the cut on the side of his tongue—not big enough to worry about, she decided.

"You know this will help. Good lad!" Dallandra made her voice soothing and soft, as if she were speaking to a small child instead of a boy who was at least thirteen summers old. She was never sure how much he understood when he was in this condition. Afterward he could never remember.

Sidro handed her a cup of spiced honey-water. Dallandra helped Vek drink a few sips to wash the medicine down and the taste out of his mouth. She gave the cup back to Sidro, then patted him on the shoulder.

"You just rest now," Dallandra said. "Sidro, will it be all right if he stays here with you?"

"Of course. Help me lie him down on those blankets over there. Pir be out with the horses, but he'd not mind anyway were he here."

"I'll help." Branna stepped forward. "Dalla, you shouldn't lift anything heavy."

"Perhaps not." Dallandra laid her hands on her swollen stomach, hanging over the waist of her leather leggings—she no longer bothered to lace them up in front. "This is the part about being with child that I hated before, feeling so bloated and awkward."

"True spoken," Sidro said. "But I'd put up with that again gladly to give Pir a child. He does so want one." She smiled. "He's not like Laz."

"I've no doubt you'll get your wish soon. You're both in good health."

"So did Exalted Mother Grallezar say. She did tell me that when one woman in a circle be with child, the rest be sure to follow. The smell in the air does induce fertility." Sidro grinned and took a deep breath. "I do hope she be right."

"She generally is," Dalla said.

As if she'd heard, the female child in Dallandra's womb kicked her, an unpleasant sensation though not precisely a pain, as she'd missed the kidneys—this time. *Soon, little one,* Dallandra thought, *soon you'll be out, and we'll both be free of this.*

Between them, Branna and Sidro hauled Vek to his feet. He threw an arm over each of their shoulders and let them drag him to the heap of blankets over by the wall of the tent. Once he was lying down comfortably, the two women came back to distribute the leather cushions and sit with Dallandra. Sidro ran both hands through her raven-dark hair, still too short to braid thanks to her humiliation of the summer before, and pushed it back from her face.

"And what about you, Branna?" Sidro said. "Do you, too, long for a child?"

Branna's gray gnome popped into materialization and shook its head in a resounding no.

"What's this?" Branna said to the gnome. "You'd be jealous, I suppose." She brought her attention back to Sidro. "I hope this doesn't mean I'm an awful unnatural woman, but I don't really want a child just now. I want to keep studying dweomer. A baby would be a nuisance."

"Not here," Dallandra said, "not among the Westfolk. We prize our children so much that you'll have plenty of help when you do give birth."

"Good. If he got me with child, Neb doubtless would gloat over it, but I'll wager he wouldn't be any help with the baby. Although I might be doing him a disservice. He's not like the men I grew up with."

"I'm glad you can see that." Dallandra smiled at her. "An honor-bound warrior he's not."

Over on the blankets, Vek let out a long snore, then turned over on his side and nestled down, his back to the women.

"Good, he's asleep," Dallandra said. "That's the best thing for him."

"So it is," Sidro said, then lowered her voice to a murmur. "He had one of his visions during the fit."

"Did he see Laz or the black stone?" Dallandra leaned closer and spoke softly.

"Alas, he did not. He spoke of a tower that reached to the sky, but it turned to smoke."

"The tower did?"

"It turned to a pillar of smoke whilst it sent out flames, he did say. Do you think his mind did fasten on the burning of Zakh Gral? The men here have talked of little else all winter long."

"It seems likely, truly. Did he say anything about where this tower was?"

"He did not, but many of our people—the Gel da'Thae, that be—did die in the flames. He wept to see it. Then spirits came down from heaven and spread snow upon the burning, and the snow did fall everywhere and ruin a harvest. 'The oats and barley in the field do die,' he cried out. The snow were ashes, I suppose." Sidro frowned, thinking. "But there were no tilled fields near Zakh Gral. The rakzanir did speak of settling slave farmers around it to feed the soldiers stationed there, but that were to happen the next year. Our food did come from the cities."

"Well, I don't think we can expect every detail of his visions to make perfect sense." Dallandra glanced at Vek to make sure that he was still sound asleep. "This one seems clearer than the others, though, so I can see why you're trying to puzzle it out.

"So it be." Sidro paused for a sigh. "I think me, Wise One, that we'll be having a harvest of omens this summer."

"And few of them good." Dallandra had meant to speak lightly, but her words sprang to life in her mouth and burned.

Branna and Sidro both turned toward her and waited, studying her face. "More trouble, I suppose," Dallandra said. "The Star Goddesses only know what, though I've no doubt we'll find out for ourselves soon enough."

"True spoken," Branna said, "or too soon."

Branna's gray gnome grinned and nodded, then slowly, one bit at a time, disappeared.

On the morrow the rain slacked. A wind sprang up from the south and brought not warmth but the promise of it as it drove the clouds from the sky. Prince Daralanteriel gave the order to his royal alar to break camp. Besides his wife, Carra, and their children, the prince traveled with his banadar or warleader, his bard, his dweomermasters, and a hundred warriors, most of them archers, along with their wives and children, or in the case of the women archers, their husbands and children. Getting this mob on the road took time.

Besides the crowd of Westfolk, the alar traveled with herds of horses, flocks of sheep, and packs of dogs, trained for herding or hunting. Although the People were adept at packing up their goods, their livestock, and their tents, by the time they got moving along the predetermined route, the sun would be well on its way to midday. They'd travel until some hours before sunset, when everyone would stop to allow the stock to graze before nightfall. In the short days of winter's end, they managed perhaps ten miles a day.

Dallandra thanked the Star Goddesses for the slow pace. She was too pregnant to ride astride. Walking would have tired her after a few miles, and sitting on a travois to be dragged along would have shaken her bones and the baby both. With the ground still saturated from the winter rains, using a wagon would have been out of the question even if the Westfolk had possessed such a thing. Fortunately, Grallezar had a solution.

"Among my people," the Gel da'Thae said, "we have a thing called a mother's saddle. It be long from pommel to cantle, and both stirrups, they hang on one side."

"I saw something similar in Deverry," Dallandra said. "I'd be afraid to use one. What if something frightens my horse, and it tries to throw me? I couldn't get free in time to save myself and the child."

"With Pir leading your horse, think you it will spook at shadows?"

Dallandra grinned at her. "I'd forgotten about Pir. Do you think we can put together one of those saddles?"

"Somewhat like it at the least."

It took Dallandra some days to grow used to the new saddle. She had to sit extremely straight to keep her back from hurting, which meant counterbalancing the weight of her pregnancy. She felt her posture as awkward and ugly both. By the afternoons, she wanted nothing more than to call an early halt, but with the memory of omens burning in her mouth, she set her teeth against the discomfort and said nothing. At least with the horse mage walking along beside her, she knew that she could trust her mount, who seemed to view Pir as a wiser sort of horse. A tall, lean fellow, Pir's dark hair hung in an odd style all his own. He'd cropped most of it off short but left a wide stripe down the middle of his head from brow to neck that was long enough to braid like a horse's mane. At moments, Dallandra's mare would snuffle into the mane or onto Pir's shoulder, as if reassuring herself that he was still there.

The royal alar made its last camp before reaching Mandra late on a day that most definitely felt like spring. Dallandra contacted Valandario while her apprentice and some of Calonderiel's men set up her tent.

"We'll arrive just after noon, I think," Dallandra told her.

"Very well," Val said. "I'll tell the mayor. The townsfolk will want to greet the prince properly."

"What does properly mean to them?"

"Lots of speeches. Tell Dar to have one ready."

"Devaberiel's traveling with us. The two of them can work something up."

"Excellent! It would be a good idea for Dar to ride into town with some sort of ceremony around him, banners, pennants that kind of thing. Does he have more than that old shabby one he took to the war?"

"He does. Carra and some of the women have been stitching all winter long."

"Good. The town will like that."

On the morrow, the alar set out with the prince and his banadar in the lead, dressed in their best clothes and riding golden horses. Behind them came Dallandra and the royal bard, Devaberiel, also wearing what finery they owned. Next rode the archers and swordsmen, with the rest of the alar bringing up the rear with the flocks and herds. Some of the older children rode in front of the warriors and carried the banners and pennants of Daralanteriel's royal line, embroidered and appliqued with the red rose and the seven stars of the cities of the far western mountains.

For those last few miles, the road, a rough affair of mud and gravel, ran along the tops of the sea-cliffs. Long before they reached its walls, they came to fields of sprouting grain and orchards of young apple trees, spindly and doubtless still barren, but a promise of fruit to come. The farmers working in the fields rushed to the stone fences to call out, "The prince! The prince! Here's to our prince!" as the alar rode on by. Daralanteriel bowed from the saddle and waved to acknowledge them all.

At last they saw the roofs of Mandra in the distance. All around the town the wild grass still waved, a common ground for milk cows at most times, but the townsfolk had put up a temporary enclosure to keep the royal alar's herds and flocks from wandering too close to the cliff edge. Herdsmen were waiting to help turn the stock inside the rough walls, thrown together of driftwood and stones, broken planks and branches. At the sight of the prince, the herdsmen rode out, cheering. Dar waved and smiled.

Everything seemed to be going splendidly, in fact, until the town herdsmen began to help round up the flocks and herds following the procession. Up near the front as she was, Dallandra heard angry shouts, yells, cries of fear and alarm, but she could see nothing. Everyone halted except for the dogs, who rushed back and forth, barking. The archers and swordsmen in the middle of the line of march began to turn their horses to ride back. The entire line broke apart as riders drifted into the meadows lining the road.

"Ye gods!" Pir said. "Those shouts—some of them be Gel da'Thae."

Too late, Dallandra remembered just how many Gel da'Thae rode with the alar—the men Pir had brought with him, the remnant of Grallezar's bodyguard, and Grallezar herself. Over the winter they'd become loyal friends to the other members of the alar, but in the eyes of the refugees who'd settled Mandra, they'd be Meradan, demons, and little else. Swearing under his breath, Calonderiel turned his horse out of line and galloped back. As he passed the squads of swordsmen, he called to them to follow.

Dallandra's dappled gray mare danced nervously in the road and pulled at the reins. Pir laid a hand on the horse's neck, up under her mane, and she quieted.

"My thanks," Dallandra said. "Can you see what's happening back there?"

"I can't," Pir said. "But the shouting's died down."

Calonderiel returned shortly after with Grallezar riding beside him. Grallezar guided her stolid chestnut gelding up to Dallandra and leaned over to speak to her while Calonderiel went on to confer with Dar.

"We Gel da'Thae," Grallezar said, "had best avoid strife. I did tell the banadar that we be willing to camp elsewhere, up the north-running road a fair piece, say. Then when you all leave Mandra, we shall rejoin you as you pass by."

"I'm so sorry," Dallandra said, "I should have thought—"

"Nah, nah, nah, we all should have thought! Be not so apologetic, my friend." Grallezar smiled, revealing her pointed teeth. "It be no great difficulty for us to all turn out of line. Sidro, though, I would leave with you. She does look much like a Deverry woman, and she does take good care of you."

"True, and Vek had best stay with her in case he has another seizure."

"Just so." Grallezar turned to Pir. "The mare that the Wise One rides, will she be calm enough now?"

"I'd best walk beside her into town," Pir said. "When she dismounts, then will I head north to join you. None will notice a mere one of us."

"True enough," Grallezar said. "What is that they say in Deverry? Done, then!"

Daralanteriel rode back along the line of march to reassure the townsfolk while Calonderiel restored order to the alar itself. The Gel da'Thae contingent sorted out their packhorses and tents, then headed north under the grim eyes of the local herdsmen.

When Daralanteriel rode back to his place at the head of the line, his face showed no trace of emotion, a sure sign that he was hiding some strong feeling—worry, Dalla assumed. No one had ever taught him how to rule even a small territory, since no one had ever guessed that some day he would have actual subjects in an actual town. As the procession moved forward again, Carra, his wife, urged her horse up next to his and took over the job of acknowledging his admirers. His children followed, aping their mother's smiles and waves. Judging from the cheers, the townspeople and farmfolk lining the road were well pleased.

At the edge of town Valandario waited. Beside her stood a tall, pale-haired man, dressed in a long tunic clasped with a distinctive broad belt, beaded in a pattern of blue circles and triangles. Valandario introduced him to the prince as the town mayor. When Daralanteriel dismounted, the mayor knelt to him.

"Please get up," Dar said. "There's no use in you kneeling in cold mud."

The mayor laughed, then rose and launched into a speech of welcome. Other townsfolk came running to usher the prince's retinue inside with speeches of their own. In the resulting confusion, Dallandra managed to slip away and join Valandario.

"Let's go to my chamber," Val said. "It'll be quiet there."

As they walked through the muddy streets, Dallandra marveled at the town around them. Out in the grass few trees grew. Traders had hauled in some timber in return for the salt that the townsfolk harvested from the sea. The farmers had dug stones from their new fields and collected driftwood from the beaches to build a strange collection of squat, thatch-roofed cottages. Most of the walls stood at odd angles; some bristled with assemblages of random driftwood. Smoke from the hearths and lime from the sea birds stained roofs and walls. Behind most houses, cows and chickens lived in shelters built of blocks of cut sod. A whiff of sewage hung in the air. Still, the men and women who lived in those houses weren't Roundears, a marvel in itself. *They're my people,* Dallandra thought, *but they know things we've forgotten for a thousand years.*

"It's still small," Valandario said, "but we're expecting several boatloads of new settlers by the autumn."

"We?" Dallandra asked, smiling.

"I've become part of the town, yes, at least for the winters."

"I'm going to need you to come with us when we leave."

"And I'm ready to ride, or at least, I will be once I finish packing up my things. Don't worry about that." Val paused for a glance around. "But I'm hoping to come back in the autumn."

The house in which Valandario was staying was a grander affair than most, two stories high, the lower of stone, the upper of timber planks, with proper wooden shutters at every window and a slate roof. Inside the fenced yard, chickens pecked and squawked in the spring greenery. Although she couldn't see it, Dallandra could smell a cow as well.

"Your hosts must be prosperous people," Dallandra said.

"Yes, they're the town potters," Valandario said. "The kiln's round back, and their shop's on the ground floor. And Jin's teaching some apprentices how to make pabrus, too, as well as how to throw pots." She pointed to the side of the house. "We'll go up the side stairs here."

The creaky wooden stairs led to an off-kilter door of planks laced together with rope. Val opened it and ushered Dallandra inside to the kitchen, a big room with a brick hearth at one end, a long table in the middle, and crates and barrels along a side wall. Doorways led to various rooms, including the Wise One's. Just like her old tent, Valandario's chamber gleamed with bright colors on the walls and on the floor. Blankets and a pile of cushions lay on the narrow bed jammed against one wall.

"Do sit down." Valandario waved at the bed. "You look like you could use a rest. Is the baby due soon?"

"A pair of months." Dallandra sat down with a sigh of gratitude. "About. I'm not sure when exactly. Probably she'll come at the most inconvenient moment."

"Babies seem to, yes. I know this is practically treason to our kind, but I'm glad I never had one."

"Well, I'm hoping that things work out better for this soul than they did the last time he was born. I won't abandon him this time, for one thing."

Valandario stared at her with abruptly cold eyes. "Are you saying that it's Loddlaen?" Her voice dwindled to a whisper on the name.

Too late, Dallandra remembered who had murdered Valandario's only lover. Val stood so still that it seemed she'd stopped breathing, waiting for the answer. From outside came the noise of the inhabitants returning to their town after greeting the prince—laughter, chatter, snatches of song, the barking of dogs and the high-pitched shrieks of children.

"I won't lie to you," Dallandra said at last. "Yes, it is, but she—and notice that I said she—she'll wear a different personality this time around."

"Of course." Val turned away and walked over to the window. "Forgive me!" She paused again, while the everyday noises from outside seemed to mock old griefs. "It would be a terrible thing to carry grudges from life to life," Val said at last. "Maybe that's one reason we don't remember lives, so we can let old hatreds die."

Again a long pause, until the laughter and shouting had moved on. "I won't revive mine, I promise you. The news just took me by surprise, that's all."

"I'm sorry I let it slip like that. I should have prepared you—"

"It doesn't matter." Yet Valandario continued staring out the window. "You were gone when the murder happened. I can't expect you to remember the particulars." Her voice nearly broke on the word "particulars." "It's just that all sorts of little things have happened, just lately, to remind me of Jav." She turned around at last. Her eyes glistened with tears. "And I still miss him. Elven lives are so long, no one stays together forever, but for us, everything ended too soon."

"Very much too soon, yes."

Val went back to her worktable. For a moment she stood, letting her fingers trail across the tooled leather cover of a volume lying there; then with a sigh she sat down in one of the two chairs standing behind it.

"I've put together some interesting information about crystals." Val's voice was steady again. "I've compiled a set of notes for you. Grallezar brought us some immensely valuable books."

For some hours they discussed Valandario's findings. When the light in the chamber faded, Val lit candles. Sidro came and went, bringing food and news. With warm bread came the information that Branna had gone with Grallezar and the Gel da'Thae. Chunks of roast lamb accompanied the welcome bulletin that thanks to a speech that Devaberiel had composed, Prince Daralanteriel had impressed everyone at the banquet. Along with a flask of Bardek wine for Val, Sidro reported that Calonderiel was discussing the town's defense with the mayor and the leader of its ill-armed militia.

Dallandra was resting on the bed in Valandario's chamber when Sidro came in for the last time, carrying a pottery cup of boiled milk with honey for Dalla to drink. At her table Valandario had spread out her scrying cloths. Sidro noticed them and lingered for a moment.

"I did want to ask you, Wise One," Sidro said to Val, "if there be aught I may do to help you find Laz. I know but a little dweomer, though it would gladden my heart to learn more, but what I have I'll happily use if it would give you any aid."

"Thank you," Val said, "but I don't know—"

"Val," Dallandra interrupted in Elvish, "did you know that Sidro can read and write?"

"I didn't, no," Val answered in the same. "That might be useful."

"It's time to record your gem scrying." Dallandra gave her a stern look over the rim of the cup. "The lore's too valuable to risk losing."

"Oh." Valandario looked surprised, then nodded. "Sidro," she said in Deverrian, "there's indeed somewhat you can do for me. How would you like to learn how to use these cloths and gems to search for omens?"

"That would gladden my heart indeed."

"Good. I'd like you to write down what I teach you, too. Could you do that?"

"I can, though the only letters I know be Horsekin ones."

"It won't take you long to learn the Deverrian letters," Dallandra said. "I can teach you. There's only thirty of them."

"Oh, well, then!" Sidro smiled at her. "It be easy, truly."

"Splendid!" Valandario said. "We'll start on the morrow, but for now, why don't you just sit down and watch, to get an idea of the process, I mean."

Sidro pulled a chair up to the table and sat down while Valandario went to a hanging tent bag and brought out a leather pouch of gems. Dallandra meant to watch the lesson, but the hot milk combined with her weariness from traveling, and she fell asleep with the empty cup clasped in her hands.

Valandario took the cup from Dallandra without waking her, set it down outside the door, then seated herself at the table next to an eager Sidro. She poured out her pouch of gems, then chose twenty for a simple reading. In the candlelight they glittered, a chaotic rainbow. A crowd of sprites appeared to dart among the glints of colored light. One settled briefly on Sidro's hair, then darted away again.

"We want four gems each of the five colors," Val told her new apprentice. "They represent the elements and the Aethyr, of course." She put the rest of the gems away. "Now, if we were considering an important matter, we'd add other colors, but this will do for now."

Valandario spread out the scrying cloth, a patchwork of Bardek silks, some squares embroidered with symbols, others plain. Sidro listened carefully as Val explained each symbol.

"I'll repeat this on the morrow," Val said, "so you can write it down. At the simplest level, a gem that falls upon its own color represents what most people would call good fortune. It's all based on the compatibility or incompatibility of the elements."

"I see." Sidro leaned a little closer to study the cloth. "So if a blue stone, it do fall upon a fire square, then that be a dangerous sign?"

"Exactly. Very good!"

Valandario shook the gems in her cupped hands like elven dice, then strewed them out with a careful motion of her wrist. For a moment she studied the pattern formed.

"What do you think this means?" Val said. "I know you don't know all of the system yet. Just give me an impression."

Sidro frowned, tilting her head this way and that as she studied the layout from different angles. "Forgive me," she said at last, "but I can see naught in it."

"Then you're going to do well at this." Val grinned at her. "I can't either. This is the most confused reading I've ever seen, probably because we're doing it just as a lesson." She let the grin fade. "I hope, anyway."

"What would it mean if you were asking it about the future? Aught?"

"I'd have to say that it signified some sort of standoff, a balance of forces that were locked together like this." Val held up her hands, hooked her fingers together, and made a pulling motion. "I couldn't say between what or whom, since we never focused our minds on a particular question." She felt a sudden irritation, as if a stinging insect were flying around and around her head. The feeling was so strong that she lifted a hand to brush it away but found nothing. "Let's put these back in their pouch. I must be more tired than I thought."

"It were a long day, truly," Sidro said. "I'll fetch the banadar so he can carry his lady to their tent."

That night Valandario dreamt about Jav and the black crystal pyramid. They stood together on a sea-cliff and looked down at a heap of stones on the beach below. He was trying to tell her something, but she couldn't hear him over the sound of the waves. Finally she woke to a sudden understanding.

"The place where he found the crystal. That's what he was trying to show me."

The gray light of dawn filled the room. Valandario got up and dressed while she considered the meaning of the dream. Could there be another crystal at the tower? But Aderyn had told her, all those years ago, that Evandar must have found the black stone elsewhere and merely placed it in the ruin. She left the house on the chance that walking along the cliffs might clear her mind and allow her to delve further into what the dream-cliffs had signified.

To her surprise, she found Prince Daralanteriel there ahead of her. He was standing and looking out to sea with his arms folded across his chest. As she walked up to him, her footsteps crunched on the sand among the beach grasses, and he turned to greet her with a wave of one hand.

"Dar?" Valandario said. "Is something wrong?"

"No, not really," Dar said. "Just thinking about the road ahead."

"Will we be going to the trading grounds?"

"No, we'll be traveling north along the Cantariel. There's a Roundear lord—Samyc's his name—who's my vassal now. We should make sure that he's safe. I'm thinking of asking for volunteer archers to spend the summer in his dun, just in case Horsekin raiders come his way."

"Do you think the Horsekin will dare?"

"No, but I'd rather not be proved wrong. And then we need to cut east to visit Tieryn Cadryc."

"That's a long ride away."

"Yes, it certainly is." Dar got a harried look about the eyes. "I'm thinking that I need to build a winter residence up north. Not exactly a palace, though I suppose it amounts to one. The gods only know where I'll get the stone to build it or the craftsmen, either.

And then there's Lord Gerran. I owe him a new dun as well." Dar paused to look miserably away. "I never wanted to be tied down to a town. Everything's changing, Val. I don't know what to do!"

"That's why you have us. Wise Ones, I mean. When Gavantar comes back from the Southern Isles he'll bring new settlers with him, and they know all about building towns. Look at Mandra."

"Just so." He smiled, sunny again. "We'll have one last summer of freedom, anyway."

Is that what this is? Val thought. *Our last summer as wandering Westfolk?* Their lives would pass into legend, she supposed, a time wrapped in wistful mist that hid the mud and chill of winter, the black flies of summer, the constant search for wood or the collecting of dried dung from their horses and sheep for meager fires, the endless striking of tents only to raise them again. She turned and looked out over the farmland around Mandra. In some of the fields the winter wheat stood a couple of feet high, bowing and rising like ocean waves under the south wind. No one would have to trade with Deverry men for the bread and porridge it represented.

"To be honest, Dar," Valandario said. "I, for one, won't miss the wandering."

"Carra said the same thing. So have a lot of the other women."

"But the men agree with you? Will they miss it?"

"Mostly, yes. Well, maybe in the summers, those who love to wander can take the herds out, while the rest stay behind in wherever it is, town, farms, whatever we eventually have." He shook himself like a wet dog, then repeated himself. "We'll have our last summer of freedom, anyway."

"So we will. Are we leaving today?"

"On the morrow. It's time for the Day of Remembrance, and I thought we should hold it here with the townsfolk."

"Yes, that's an excellent idea. The more you can do to remind the townsfolk you're their prince, the better."

"So Devaberiel said, too. He's composing a special poem for the occasion. I'm not sure where to hold the gathering, though. There isn't any town square or the like."

"I know!" Val smiled at her own idea. "About a mile to the west there's a ruined tower. Some Deverry lord built a dun out here, back when Calonderiel was a young man, I think it was. I wasn't born yet, of course. Anyway, the People drove him out again. The ruin would be an interesting reminder in itself."

"Splendid! We'll do that. I'll just go tell the mayor."

Some hours before sunset, the townsfolk and the alar, minus a few herdsmen who'd volunteered to watch over the herds and flocks, gathered at the ruined dun. Over the past few years, the People in Mandra had pulled down much of the outer wall to use the stone for their town, but the tower still stood inside the fragment of arc left. Brambles, ivy, and weeds grew thick inside what had once been the ward. The wooden doors and outbuildings had long since rotted away, as had the floors inside the broch tower itself, or so Calonderiel told her.

"We had a couple of stiff fights at this dun," the banadar said. "The first one was when we cleaned out the rats that had infested it."

"I take it you mean the Deverry lord and his men," Val said.

"Just that." He smiled at the memory. "And then—not long ago, really, maybe ninety summers ago or suchlike—another Deverry lord had the gall to try to kill Aderyn here. That was because of—" He stopped in mid-sentence.

"Loddlaen. I know. I heard the tale from Aderyn."

"Um, well, my apologies anyway. Here, I'd better go help the mayor."

Wrapped in embarrassment like a cloak, Calonderiel hurried off. Valandario watched him go and thought about Aderyn, dead for so many years now. He'd had the courage to kill his own son, something that made her shake her head in wonder. And now that son was about to be reborn—*No!* she told herself. *Not Loddlaen. Someone new, and a girl child at that!*

A few big blocks of stone stood at one edge of the remains of wall. Devaberiel climbed onto the highest stone. When he raised his arms into the air, the murmuring crowd quieted. Mothers collared children and made them sit down in a little chorus of "Hush, now, hush."

Devaberiel called out with the ancient words of the ritual.

"We are here to remember."

"To remember," the crowd chanted, "to remember the West."

"We are here to remember the cities," Devaberiel continued, "Rinbaladelan of the Fair Towers, Tanbalapalim of the Wide River,

Bravelmelim of the Rainbow Bridges, yea! all of the cities, and the towns, and the marvels of the Far West." He paused, smiling at the assembly in front of him. "But while we mourn what we have lost, let us remember new marvels. Mandra rises amid fertile fields. Ranadar's heir lives and walks among us."

The listeners cheered, a sound like the roar of a high sea breaking on the graveled beach. Some clapped, some stood, all called out. When Devaberiel raised his arms again, the crowd quieted, but slowly.

"The cities of the Far West lie in ruins," the bard went on, "but Mandra grows and prospers. I see what comes to us on the wings of destiny. Some day the West will be ours again."

More cheers, more clapping, and despite all her careful self-control, despite her dweomer and her power, Valandario realized that she hovered on the edge of tears.

Since Devaberiel was the only bard in attendance, the ceremony that day was a short one. He retold the ancient tale of the Hordes, riding out of the north to destroy the elven civilization of the mountains, but he'd shortened the story, Val noticed. All of the adults among the listeners sat politely, attentively, making the ancient responses when the ritual demanded, yet it seemed to her that few truly mourned. The children fussed and fidgeted, unentranced by the telling.

Once Devaberiel had finished, however, and the music and the feasting got underway, everyone grew lively again. Valandario walked through the celebration, nodding and smiling, since it was impossible to hear what anyone said or for them to have heard her answer had she given one. At last she found Daralanteriel, standing in the midst of admirers. When he waved her over, the townsfolk all stepped back to allow the Wise One access to the prince.

"It went very well, I thought," Val said.

"So did I," Dar said. "Dev is a marvel in his own way."

"Just so. Is Dalla still here?"

"No, Cal insisted on taking her back to the tents to rest. You look like you're ready to leave, too."

"I am. I need to pack if we're leaving on the morrow."

"And we are—early." Dar sighed and looked away, perhaps considering that last summer of freedom. "It's time we got on the road."

Rather than risk them on the road, Valandario left the books in the care of Lara and Jin. The only exception was the book that had belonged to Laz, which Sidro wanted back. She packed up her personal possessions, putting them and the scrying cloths and gems into tent bags and leather sacks. Some of the alar's young men were waiting to carry them over to the camp for her. They all trooped upstairs to collect them, while Lara and Val stood to one side to watch.

"Wise One, will you come back to us in the fall?" Lara said.

"If it's not an imposition—"

"What?" Lara gave her a brilliant smile. "Not in the least! It's an honor we've reveled in having."

"In that case, I'll come back, yes. And you have my thanks for your hospitality."

Valandario followed her belongings out of town in an odd sort of procession. As they walked through the streets, every person they passed ran up to bid her farewell and to urge her to return. "I'll come back," she told them all, "and this time, I'll stay." *If naught else,* she told herself, *I won't have to watch Loddlaen grow up if I'm here.*

Next to the north-running road, the alar was striking tents and loading them onto travois and packhorses. Children ran back and forth; dogs barked; adults yelled at each other and bickered. Out in the wild grass the men were rounding up the horses, and the sheep dogs were forming up the bleating flocks. It was all so familiar that Val had a moment of thinking she might miss it; then she reminded herself of the smoky dung fires, the black flies, and down near the coast, the mosquitoes.

As she made her way through the crowd, Valandario came across Neb, kneeling beside a travois and tying down some sacks of gear. He worked slowly, methodically, with an odd set to his shoulders, as if perhaps his neck or arms pained him. His yellow gnome stood nearby, hands on its hips, and watched with a frown. Val stopped beside him.

"Neb," she said in Deverrian, "are you all right?"

He looked up at her, but for a moment he didn't recognize her—

she could see the lack in his ice-blue eyes, cold, narrowing, suddenly affronted. The yellow gnome reached over and pinched him. Neb laughed and shook his head in self-mockery.

"My apologies, Wise One," Neb said, "I was thinking somewhat through."

"Well and good, then, but you know, you need to close down your dweomer practices when it's time to do mundane things."

"I do know that!" He'd snapped at her, then once again covered it with a smile. "But you speak true, of course. Actually, I was only thinking about herblore, what plants will help wounds heal cleanly and the like."

"Oh, well, then, that shouldn't harm you. But do try to strike a balance, Neb, between this world and the ones beyond."

"I'll try harder to do just that." But his tone of voice implied that he had no intention of following her advice.

As Valandario walked on, she was thinking that she was glad he was Dallandra's apprentice, not hers.

Branna had already noticed the problem that Valandario had seen in Neb's eyes. Even as the alar journeyed north, the two apprentices kept up the practices their teachers had set them. Every morning and evening, they found time for their work while the camp packed up from the night's stop or set back up again in the sunset light. When it rained, the alar stayed in camp, giving them a day or two to catch up on anything they might have missed.

After the simplest dweomer exercise, even so little as tracing a pentagram in the air with his hand, Neb's ice-blue glance turned cold and penetrating. He would seem to be looking at the view or whatever lay in front of him from a great distance away, as if he were unsure of its reasons for existing. Yet when he turned away and looked at Branna, he would smile, and the expression in his eyes became soft and warm again. This pronounced change made her feel that she was watching a shapechanger, not an apprentice.

On a morning when the rain kept the alar in camp, Neb spent some hours working through the steps of a simple ritual, tracing out a circle around him, then visualizing blue fire springing up at his command. Branna, who'd been doing some memory work, looked up from her book to watch him as he finished the exercise. This time the look in his eyes made her think of an honor-bound warrior who sees his worst enemy. Then he glanced her way and grinned.

"This is harder than I thought," Neb said.

He's back. The words formed themselves in Branna's mind so clearly that she laid a hand over her mouth as if to keep them in. She covered the gesture with a cough.

"It is, truly," Branna said. "My mind keeps wandering when I try to see the flames."

"Mine, too. I keep thinking about that wretched plague back in Trev Hael." Neb paused, frowning at the floor cloth. "I keep wondering how it spread so fast, and why it spread at all."

"Well, my poor beloved, it was a truly ghastly horrid experience. I'm not surprised you can't forget it."

"It's not a question of forgetting, but of understanding it." He looked up, his eyes so grim and cold that she flinched. "Is somewhat wrong?"

"I'm not sure," Branna said. "It's like you become someone else at times. When you work dweomer, you turn into Nevyn, don't you?"

"Well, so what if I do? I mean, I am Nevyn, really, when you think about it. I was him, and if we're talking about the long view of things, I am him still."

"You're not, though. You've got a new life now."

His look turned murderous, but only briefly. "Well, I suppose so," he said. "Of course that's true. On some level, anyway."

"On all levels. You should tell Dalla about this."

"You're right. I will, then."

Yet she didn't believe him, not for a moment. Although she considered telling Dallandra herself, she knew that such would be an interference between him and his master in the craft, to say naught of going behind his back and risking a hellish argument if he found out.

They did argue, these days, in a way they never had during the first idyllic months of their marriage. Branna wanted to think that they were both uncomfortable from the damp and the cold, to say naught of the utter strangeness of their new home, but at heart she was too honest to dismiss the problem so easily.

"He wants me to be Jill," she told Grallezar. "And I won't. At times he even calls me Jill, and I refuse to answer until he uses my real name. Then he gets angry with me."

Her teacher considered, sucking a thoughtful fang. Since Grallezar shaved her head, she was wearing a knitted wool cap, striped in gray and blackish brown, that came down low over her ears and forehead. She'd also bundled herself in a heavy wool cloak and wore fur-lined boots against the cold. Back in her home country, she'd spent winters in a heated house, not a drafty tent.

"Well, he be not my student," Grallezar said at last. "So this be but a guess. I think me that Nevyn's life, it were so long that Neb be unable to remember past it. From our work I know that you do see bits and pieces of many lives and deaths."

"That's true. Jill's life is only one of them. I'm not Jill any more than Jill was Morwen or Branoic."

"True spoken. But Neb, the only memory that lives for him is Nevyn, and by all that I have heard, he were a mighty dweomer-master indeed. Neb does covet all that power. To earn it all again, to do the work, it be burdensome, but needful."

"I see. There's another thing, too. He keeps thinking about the plague in Trev Hael that killed his father and sister. He talks about it a lot. It's so morbid! It can't be good for him."

"Well, mayhap, mayhap not. There may be a riddle there for him to answer." Grallezar held up a warning forefinger. "Not one word of this to Neb, mind, and no more may you tell Dallandra of your fears. For a student to interfere with another master's student be a baleful thing."

"I promise I won't."

"Good. It would go ill for you were you to throw my words in Neb's face." Grallezar suddenly smiled. "But of course, I be a master myself, and if I should speak to Dallandra, well, who's to say me nay?"

Branna felt so relieved that she nearly wept. *I've been frightened,* she thought, *not just worried.*

Over the next few weeks, Branna found herself hard-pressed to keep her promise to Grallezar, but every time she was tempted to break it, her own mind distracted her by raising the enormous question that lay just beyond her worries about Neb. If he wasn't Nevyn, then who was Neb? Worse yet, if she wasn't Jill, was she truly Branna? Who was any person, then, whether Westfolk or Gel da'Thae or human being, if their body and their personality were only masks they wore for a little while, masks that they'd toss aside at their death only to don new ones at birth?

Contemplating such matters made her turn cold with terror, as if she stood on the very edge of a high cliff and felt the soil under her feet begin to crumble away. She would jump back from that edge and take refuge in any distraction she could find. In a traveling alar, distractions lay thick on the ground, most of them trivial, though now and again Branna found something that hinted at her future role of Wise One.

One evening, just at sunset, she was walking back to her tent when she heard someone weeping, a soft little sound, half-suppressed, unlike the usual loud sobs of one of the Westfolk. She followed the sound and discovered Sidro, standing alone out in the wild grass. Overhead the sky hung low with clouds, dark and gathering.

"What's wrong?" Branna said from behind her. "Can I help?"

Sidro swirled around, her eyes wide and tear-wet, her hand at her throat.

"A thousand apologies!" Branna said. "I didn't mean to startle you."

Sidro tried to smile, sniffed back tears, and finally wiped her eyes on her sleeve. "Oh, 'tis naught," she said at last. "Just a silly moment."

"Oh, now, here, if somewhat's made you cry, it can't be naught." Branna laid a gentle hand on Sidro's shoulder. "Tell me. Is it about Laz?"

"Him, too, but missing my old home in Taenalapan is the most of it. Which be a strange thing, since I was but a slave lass there. It were always warm and dry in the house, and there were warm food and laughter. I think me that be what I miss the most."

"I can certainly understand that! But truly, I don't see how the comfort would make being a slave tolerable. Didn't you long to get away and be free?"

"And how was I to know what being free did mean?" Sidro smiled with a rueful twist of her mouth. "Laz, he did say somewhat about that to me once, that all I did know was slavery, whether slave to his mother or to Alshandra. He were right about that, too. Now, being here among the Westfolk and having Pir, too, for my man, I do begin to see what freedom is, but truly, I see it with my mind, not my heart."

"Is that why you're always waiting on everyone?"

Sidro started to answer, then hesitated, visibly thinking. "I suppose it be so," she said at last. "What we always knew before, it be comforting, somehow. My thanks, Branna! I'll be thinking on that, I truly will. Though the Wise Ones, they do deserve what service we can pay them."

"That's true." *I just wish Neb could see it,* Branna thought. *Well, mayhap someday he will.*

Yet, when she returned to their tent she found Neb sitting under a silver dweomer light, studying the book of herblore that she'd compiled back in her life as Jill. He looked up at her with watery eyes.

"Is the moldy smell bothering you?" she asked.

"Not truly." He laid the book down, stretched, and yawned. "My eyes are just tired, that's all. I'll brew up some eyebright water on the morrow."

"You told me that Dallandra wanted you to study less."

"So?" He spat out the word. "She doesn't know everything."

"She knows more than you do."

Branna regretted the words the moment she'd said them. She braced herself for one of their fights, but Neb merely shrugged and looked away.

"So she does," he said at last. "For now."

Branna said nothing. Outside, the storm suddenly broke with a patter of rain on the tent roof.

As the alar continued making its slow way north, the rain followed. On the few dry days the alar set up only a few tents, but a day or two out of every four it needed to make a full camp and wait out the storm, no matter how impatient its Wise One was. At least, Dallandra reminded herself, they never came upon any lingering snow.

"A blessing," Dallandra remarked to Valandario. "I lived with snow for one whole winter, up in Cengarn, and I swear to all the gods I never ever want to see the stuff again."

"I don't think I ever have." Val considered for a moment. "I'm glad, too."

Dallandra glanced around the camp. Under a gray sky, streaked with near-black, the men were bustling around, setting up the tents for the night, while the women worked with the herds, hobbling the horses in case the coming storm broke with thunder and lightning. Wildfolk, children, and dogs raced through the camp in unruly packs, always in everyone's way.

"We'd better get inside," Dallandra said.

"Yes, come to my tent, will you?" Val said. "I keep thinking about Haen Marn, and we need to scry."

Now that she was Val's apprentice, Sidro had already brought her teacher's possessions into the tent. Most lay piled neatly in the curve of the wall, since the alar would stay in this camp for a short time only, but her blankets and scrying materials lay spread out and ready. Sidro herself was hooking tent bags onto the wall near Val's pillow.

"Be there a want upon you to eat dinner now, Wise Ones?" she said.

"Not now, but soon," Valandario said. "My thanks, but I'll call you when we're ready."

With a curtsy, Sidro hurried out to leave them their privacy. Dallandra made a golden dweomer light and tossed it up to the tent roof, then sat down on a cushion opposite Valandario with the scrying cloth between them.

"The thing is," Dallandra said, "no one's been able to see the beastly island in any sort of vision. It may be impossible, because after all, it has to be surrounded by water, since it's an island. But I keep wondering if there might be some way to reach it somehow."

Val nodded, then assembled a handful of gems, picking and choosing from various pouches.

"We wish to know about Haen Marn," Val said. "How may we

see it for ourselves?" She scattered the gems over her scrying cloth. For some while she studied the layout, whispering a word or two at moments. "Ah," she said at last, "something needs completing, something unfinished lingers in the question."

"Well, we rather knew that," Dallandra said.

Val frowned, then laid a finger on a topaz ovoid that lay on the seam between a red square and a black.

"No, no, not just the question itself," Val said. "It's some small thing, a step toward finding the answer."

Dallandra reminded herself to hold her tongue and let her colleague do things her own way. Finally Val pointed out a gold bead that gleamed against a misty lavender square in one corner of the patchwork.

"Treasure in the past," Val announced. "Or from the past." She raised her head and looked off into space, her mouth slack, her eyes expressionless as she waited for some thought or omen to rise into her mind. "The scroll." She smiled, herself again. "Dalla, Aderyn had a scroll that Evandar left for him. It was a set of evocations in the strangest language I've ever heard or seen. Do you know what happened to it?"

"It's in my tent," Dallandra said. "Gavantar gave it to me before he set sail for the southern islands. Aderyn had wanted me to have it, he said."

"Splendid! I had the privilege of working with the thing with Aderyn and Nevyn when I was just out of my apprenticeship. Evandar made sure that it was found at the same time as the obsidian pyramid. They didn't seem to be connected back then, but he might have had some reason to leave them together."

"Evandar always had a reason." Dallandra got to her feet. "I'll fetch it right now."

The men of the alar had finished raising Dallandra's tent. She ducked inside and found Neb arranging her bedding and goods.

"Have you seen the gray tent bag with the symbols of Aethyr on it?" Dallandra said. "They're embroidered with purple yarn."

"I have indeed." Neb unpiled a few things, rummaged around in a heap of bags, and at last brought out the correct one. "Here we are. Why do you want it?"

"It doesn't concern you."

He winced but said nothing more.

As she walked back to Valandario's tent, Dallandra was thinking more about Neb than the scroll. He was not exactly disrespectful around her, his master in dweomer, but still, at moments his behavior was a little too free and familiar, as if he'd known her for a long time. In a way, he had, of course, in his previous life, when as a young woman she'd been very much his inferior in dweomer workings. *That was a long time ago,* she reminded herself. *I'd better make that clear to him.* At these moments she was grateful to Grallezar all over again, for warning her about his wish that he was Nevyn still.

Inside her tent, Val had put away her scrying gems and cloth. Dallandra knelt under the dweomer light and brought out the wooden box holding the scroll. She laid the bag down, sketched out a circle of warding around it, then opened the box and brought out the scroll. The pabrus had turned brown over the years, and it threatened to split along the creases where it had been first rolled, then squashed into a box. Very carefully indeed she unrolled it and laid it down on the tent bag.

"I should have left this in Mandra with Grallezar's books," Dallandra said. "To be honest, I'd forgotten I had it."

"It's just as well you did," Val said, smiling. "Since we need it."

They leaned closer, nearly head to head, to look it over.

"As I remember," Valandario said, "there's one invocation that's incomplete. That may be what the scrying meant. So let's start there. Ah, here it is!"

Valandario cleared her throat, then read the call aloud in a deliberately colorless voice. "Olduh umd nonci do a dooain de Iaida, O gah de poamal ca a nothoa ah avabh. Acare, ca, od zamran, lap ol zirdo noco olpirt de olpirt."

"Is that supposed to mean something?" Dallandra said.

"Oh, yes. Although—" Valandario frowned at the scroll. "Master Aderyn read these out in an odd way. He sounded every letter as the syllable it represents. Ol-de oo-me-deh deh-oh—like that."

"It doesn't make any sense that way either."

"It's not in Elvish, that's why. There's a translation of everything down at the bottom—"

Dallandra looked where Val was pointing. "Right! Here it is!"

Dallandra read from the scroll. "I do call you in the name of the Highest, O spirit of the palace on the in the midst of hyacinth seas. Come, therefore, and show yourself to me for I serve the same Light of Lights."

"I'd say that the missing word has to come right here, 'palace on the in the midst of hyacinth seas.' " Valandario laid a delicate finger on the fragile scroll. "The palace on what? Could it be an island?"

"It certainly could, and look! right here in the gloss, it says: 'some say that the spirit word for island is hanmara.' " Dallandra nearly choked on the name. "Hanmara," she repeated. "But Rori told me once that haen marn means black stone in the Dwarvish tongue."

"Oh, does it?" Valandario broke into a grin. "Well, why can't hanmara mean both? The island might appear to be made of black stone if we saw it on the spirit plane."

"Yes, that's plausible."

"The palace on the black stone in the midst of hyacinth seas. I like the way that echoes in my mind."

"One of us needs to vibrate this call."

"I don't want you to risk the child."

The generosity of this simple statement—considering who that child had been in her previous life—left Dallandra speechless. Valandario misunderstood the silence.

"Something nasty might answer, you know," Val said. "Aderyn was very careful about that, when he first had the scroll. So it had best be me."

"You're probably right, but I'm going to come along when you do the working. Just in case."

"Good. I had no intentions of keeping you away, mind. Just stay outside the circle." Valandario paused, listening to the noise filtering through the tent walls. "We're going to have to get away from camp, so we need to wait for a break in the rain."

The rain fell all the next day, keeping everyone in camp. Dallandra took the opportunity to bring Neb into her tent for a private talk. She spoke in Deverrian to make sure that he understood her. When his yellow gnome followed him in, Dallandra shooed it out again. Even though the gnome lacked a true consciousness, she wanted no witnesses to what Neb might well find shaming.

"Neb," she began, "there's a common problem with dweomer apprentices, that they don't work hard enough at their studies." She paused for a smile. "But I'd say you have the opposite problem. You need to work a little less and do more of the physical work around the camp, like helping with the horses."

"Indeed?" Neb's eyes flared rebellion. "But I've got so much work to do already."

"Are the exercises I set you too much to finish in a day?"

"They're not. I'm studying herbcraft, too, is all, and I want time for that."

"You've got years ahead of you for all of that."

"You know, I'm human. I'll only have a short life this time. I don't see why I should waste any of it when I've got so much to learn."

"Why are you so sure your life will be short?"

"Well, because—" Neb stopped, startled. "Well, won't it be? Compared to a Westfolk life, I mean."

"Maybe, maybe not. I don't know. But those who give their heart to dweomer, and you obviously have, tend to live a fair bit longer than ordinary folk. You of all people should know that."

"True spoken." He ducked his head and looked only at the floor cloth.

"Now, I've taught several apprentices in my day, and for that matter, I was an apprentice myself once. I know how hard it is to hold back when you're so eager to learn." She paused, as if thinking. "That was so long ago, truly. Nevyn only knew me as an apprentice, you know. Why, it must have been over four hundred years ago, now."

"I take your point." Neb looked up, and the rebellion came back into his eyes. "You've lived a cursed lot longer than I have, and you know a cursed lot more, too."

"Then why don't you listen to what I say?" Dallandra dropped any pretense of jollying him along. "I'm your master in dweomer now. You refused to listen to the last one, too, Rhegor that was, so long ago. Do you remember what came of that?"

Neb turned white around the mouth, and his hands clenched hard into fists.

"I see you do," Dalla went on. "Well?"

Their gazes met and locked. The drip and patter of the rain outside sounded as loud as drumbeats until at last, he looked away.

"I'll help with the horses," Neb whispered. "Morning and night."

"Splendid!" Dallandra arranged a friendly smile. "That gladdens my heart to hear."

"May I leave now?" He was staring at the floor cloth.

"You may, certainly."

Neb got up and rushed out without looking her way. *Stubborn colt!* she thought. *But he'll grow into a splendid stallion one day.*

In the late afternoon the rain slacked. A strong south wind sprang up, chivying the fading storm and driving it off. Dallandra and Valandario walked to the edge of the camp and stood studying the sky. The damp wind felt pleasantly cool, not biting or chilly, and it carried the scent of new grass.

"We could go out now, I suppose," Dallandra said. "I do love the feel of a spring wind."

"So did I," Val said, "but the ground's still too wet. The grass will be soaked."

"Well, if this wind keeps up, it will dry out quickly. We should be able to do the ritual just at sunrise, once the astral tide turns toward Aethyr. We'll probably travel all day tomorrow, and I'd like to experiment with that evocation before too long."

"Me, too." Val grinned at her. "Sunrise it is. I'll memorize the words tonight."

In the chilly dawn, Valandario left her tent and met Dallandra out by the horse herd. Both of them carried their ritual swords, wrapped in bits of cloth to keep off the damp. They were blunt blades of cheap metal to look at, but charged with a very different kind of power than that in a warrior's muscles. For privacy's sake they walked a good mile from the camp, then chose a spot suitable for the working. A gaggle of gnomes trailed after them, but as soon as Val unwrapped her sword, they rushed away to disappear.

Together, Val and Dallandra trod down a rough circle in the grass. After the proper invocations Val evened up its perimeter into a proper circle by marking the damp sod with the point of the sword. As the sun rose, she greeted the powers behind this visible symbol of warmth and light. To them, she consecrated the ceremony.

"Are you ready, sentinel?" Val said.

"I am." Dallandra raised her own sword. "Let the ritual begin." She brought the sword down sharply.

Valandario stood in the center of the circle, lifted her arms over her head, and vibrated the words from the scroll, drawing breath from deep within herself, breaking each word into syllables as Aderyn had taught her, all those years before.

"Ol-duh um-duh non-ci do a doh-oh-ah-een day Iah-ee-da, O gah day poh-ah-mal ca a no-tay-hay-oh-a ah av-ah-bay-hay. Hana-ma-rah ha-na-ma-rah! Ah-ca-ray, ca, od zah-meh-rah-nah, lapay ol zee-air-do noo-coh ol-pay-ee-air-tay de ol-pay-ee-air-tay."

For a moment nothing whatever happened. Valandario took another deep breath—and flew, or so it seemed to her, darted up through the air and the brightening sunlight, up ever upward, until she stood on an island, a perfect circle in the midst of hyacinth-colored seas. All around it, purple waves rose stiffly, then subsided without a trace of foam. A greenish sunlight shimmered on the sea and glinted from the island's glass-smooth surface. In the island's center a circular dimple formed. Out of it rose a silver pillar, a mere stump at first, then growing higher and higher, until at last Val stood before a translucent tower.

"Ah-ca-ray, O Servant of the Light!" Valandario said.

Within the pillar a point of violet light bloomed, grew larger, and stretched into a vertical line of violet light. The line thickened, swirled, and formed at last into the tenuous shape of a woman.

"Why do you call upon me?" the spirit said. "What do you wish to know?"

"I wish to know about Haen Marn, the island in the planes of form that's a shadow of this island."

"Not of this island, but of another. I know not where that lies."

"If you do not know, how may I find out?"

"I know not that, either. You must ask the Lady of the Black Stone Isle, she who dwells on the plane of matter and death."

"How may I find her?"

"Go to the island." A trace of annoyance crept into the spirit's voice. "Even a fleshly creature such as you should know this. Go to the island and ask her."

"The island has fled. I don't know where it lies."

"Then summon it."

"I don't know how to summon it."

"The island has its own summons. You need not ask me. Mospleh, mospleh, mospleh."

"I don't know what mospleh means."

Inside her pillar, the spirit frowned. "Look to the metal of the moon and to the moon herself at her first waxing."

"What—"

But the spirit was growing thin, fading, turning back into a strand of violet light, gleaming against silver. The pillar swirled once, then sank slowly back into the island. Valandario felt herself take flight, swooped down, circled round, saw below her the ritual sword, gleaming in the rising sun. She let herself drop, then settled feet first onto the hard metal.

The vision disappeared. She was back, slipping a little on the wet grass as she stepped off the sword blade. She stamped thrice on the ground, then picked up the sword and cut through the circle.

"May any Wildfolk bound by this ceremony go free! It is over!" Val called out and stamped again for good measure. With a sigh she wiped the mud on the point of her sword off on the side of her boots.

"I gather the evocation called something forth," Dallandra said. "I could hear your questions. Did the spirit ever answer?"

"Oh, yes, but we're not much farther along than we were before. You know, there are times when I get really tired of spirits and their blasted riddles."

"So do I," Dallandra paused and glanced back to the spot where the camp had stood. "It looks like the alar's ready to ride out. Tell me what you saw while we walk back, will you? I can't bear to wait till we make camp again."

Branna had seen Valandario and Dallandra leave camp for a dweomer working. During that day's ride she burned with curiosity, but she knew that she had no right to pry. She could only hope that Dallandra would choose to tell her at the evening meal.

As dweomer apprentices, Branna and Neb generally ate with their masters rather than cooking for themselves. The various members of the royal alar took turns feeding the Wise Ones—a good thing, since Branna had never cooked a meal in her life. Calonderiel usually joined them as well. While Branna was expecting Neb as usual that evening, he never arrived.

"I don't know where he went," she told Dallandra. "Do you?"

"I don't." Dallandra glanced at Calonderiel. "Have you seen him?"

His mouth full of herbed greens, Cal nodded and hastily swallowed. "I did," the banadar said. "He told me he was fasting, but he didn't say why. I assumed you'd set him some practice."

"Naught of the sort!" Dallandra briefly looked sour. "Mayhap he doesn't feel well or suchlike."

"Starve a cold, feed a fever," Cal said. "Or is it the other way round?"

Dallandra mugged disgust, then handed him a piece of soda bread, which he took with a grin.

For the rest of the meal, Dallandra said little. Branna went back to her own tent with her curiosity still burning. Neb returned much later in the evening. Under a pale dweomer light Branna was laying out their blankets when Neb strode into the tent.

"You've been talking to Dallandra about me, haven't you?" Neb said.

"I haven't." Branna looked up in some surprise. "What—"

"Well, someone told her I was fasting."

"It was Calonderiel, not me. It happened at dinner tonight."

"Oh."

"Did she tell you not to?"

"She did. I was only trying to sharpen my second sight, but she told me it was dangerous at my stage of development."

Branna made a noncommittal noise.

"And another thing." Neb folded his arms tightly across his chest and glared at her. "If it wasn't you, why did she bring up Nevyn, then?"

"When?" Branna rose to face him.

"Yesterday afternoon. And then tonight she mentioned somewhat again. It must have come from you."

"I don't even know what she said to you."

"Yesterday she mentioned Rhegor."

"I—who?"

Neb's expression suddenly changed to something slack and exhausted. The silver light directly above him filled the hollows of his face with dark shadows. He turned away and shoved his hands in the pockets of his brigga. "I don't suppose you would remember him," Neb said. "My apologies."

"Neb, I don't understand what you're going on about."

He gave her one brief look, then turned and ducked out of the tent. It was some while before he returned, and by then Branna had given up waiting for him and gone to bed. For a few moments he stumbled around in the dark tent.

"You could make a light," she said. "Or I could."

He spoke not a word, merely sat down on the edge of their blankets and began to pull off his boots. The smell of mead hung around him. If he'd been drinking with the other men, she knew, conversation would prove frustrating and little more. Branna turned over and pretended to sleep. Eventually he managed to undress and slip into the blankets beside her, only to fall asleep with a loud snore.

Branna lay awake, wondering if she was sorry she'd married him. She found herself missing Aunt Galla and Cousin Adranna with a real longing to see them again, to sit down and ask them what they would have done, married to a man like Neb. *I can never tell them,* she reminded herself, *not without mentioning dweomer.*

With the morning Neb became perfectly pleasant again, charming, even. When he went out to help with the horses, he was whistling. Still, the farther north the alar traveled, the more thoughts of her kinfolk came to Branna's mind. When by Prince Dar's reckoning they reached the border of Pyrdon, she found herself wondering how the winter had treated them.

"I've been doing those exercises on farseeing that you gave me," Branna told Grallezar. "Do you think I could practice by trying to see the Red Wolf dun? I do worry about my aunt, up there in the snow for months, and the army took so much food away, too."

"That would be a good practice, I do think," Grallezar said. "You be very familiar with the place, and your worry does lend strength to the seeing. But spend only a short while at each attempt, and bring yourself back to the earth plane when you be finished." Grallezar glanced around the tent. "In that wood box there on the floor, below the red bag, there be a time glass. Take it. You may practice for as long as it takes the sand to run half out of the upper glass."

Branna found the box and opened it, then took the glass out with great care. She'd never seen anything as fine as the pale green glass cones in their polished wood stand, about six inches high overall. She turned it over and watched the sand drip from one cone to the other at a slow, steady pace. Her gnome stared at it openmouthed.

"Take the box, too," Grallezar said, "to keep it safe, like."

"I will, then, and my thanks!"

During her first few practices, Branna saw nothing but her memories of the Red Wolf dun. Yet finally, early one morning when Neb was off studying with Dallandra, she received a very brief, very misty impression of the great hall. Aunt Galla was just coming down the stairs, and she looked well and happy, if somewhat thinner. Branna's pleasure at seeing this vision broke it. It was another four practices before at last she saw the dun again and the fields roundabout, all muddy from spring rain. From then on, Branna managed to catch regular glimpses of the dun, although she couldn't control which part of it she was seeing.

"Everyone looks well," she told Grallezar. "It gladdens my heart to see them. I wonder, though, about Solla. I told you about her, didn't I? Gerran's wife? I have this feeling that she's with child, but I can't really be sure. It's too bad you can't smell things when you scry."

Grallezar laughed aloud at that. "From what the prince do say," Grallezar said, "we should be there in some while. And then we'll know if she be so or not."

Up north in the Red Wolf dun, its women had been worrying about Branna as much as she'd been worrying about them. Not an evening meal went by, Gerran noticed, without the dun's lady, Galla, or the widowed Lady Adranna mentioning her.

"Out there with the Westfolk!" Galla would say. "I just can't believe it sometimes, that a niece of mine would be off with the Westfolk!"

"Well, Mama," Adranna generally answered. "I can believe it of Branna. She always had a wild streak, and look at the way she spoke to that dragon, as bold as brass!"

Gerran would glance his wife's way and see her trying not to smile. Only he and Solla knew exactly how deep Branna's wildness ran.

As the days slipped by, each a little longer than the last, the spring air became warm enough for the womenfolk to carry their sewing outside to take the sun. Servants put chairs out in the dun's kitchen garden and carried the ladies' sewing. Gerran escorted them and saw his wife settled in a chair near the dun's lady. The sunlight caught auburn highlights in Solla's brown hair, and her hazel eyes had turned a beautiful green.

"Shall I bring you a cushion?" Gerran said. "Or a footstool?"

"I'm fine like this, my love," Solla said.

"Are you sure? Do you need a shawl?"

"Gerro!" Lady Galla leaned forward in her chair and laughed. "She's with child, not ill!"

"Lady Galla's right." Solla laid a soft hand on his arm. "We northern lasses are a tough lot."

Gerran smiled; she'd been repeating that sentiment often in the last few months. "Still," he said, "I'll send one of the pages out to sit here with you. If you need somewhat, he'll fetch it."

"Penna's right here." Solla sounded puzzled.

Gerran had simply not noticed her young maid, who sat on the ground right beside her mistress' chair. Penna looked up at him with wide dark eyes that revealed no trace of any emotion under their plumed brown brows. She was a peculiar lass in his opinion, a skinny little thing with slick brown hair that she wore as short as a lad's. Solla had given her a place in the dun, but the lady took as much care of the maid as the maid did of the lady.

"It's the pages' duty to run messages," Gerran said. "Penna's duty is to sew."

"Whatever you say, my love." Solla rolled her eyes heavenward at this precision.

Penna managed a brief smile.

Gerran went off to hunt for pages. Eventually he found Ynedd, the youngest of the three, leaning against the wall of the stable. His hands were in his pockets, and he seemed to be studying the ground between his feet. Dirt and bits of straw clung to his blond hair, cropped off but curly.

"What's wrong?" Gerran said. "Have Clae and Coryn been tormenting you again?"

Ynedd looked up with red-rimmed eyes. A fresh purple bruise mottled his cheek.

"I see," Gerran said. "They won't stop until you fight back."

"I tried to, my lord," Ynedd said, "but there's two of them."

"What? They both jumped you at once, did they?"

Ynedd mumbled something so softly that Gerran could barely hear him. He took it to mean "I'm not supposed to tell."

"Where are they, do you know?"

"I don't, my lord."

"Well, I'll find them sooner or later, and I'll have a bit of a chat with them. Two against one? Not among the lads I'm training!"

Ynedd managed to smile at that, a little smirk of anticipated revenge. "Are you going to beat them?"

"I'm not. The grooms need help mucking out the stables, and Clae and Coryn can provide it. As for you, go join the women out in the garden. My lady might need to send me a message."

"Well and good, my lord." Ynedd grinned at him. "My thanks."

The boy peeled himself off the wall and hurried off, so pleased with the order that Gerran followed for some yards, then stood watching as the womenfolk exclaimed over Ynedd's bruise and sat him down among them. Lady Galla even gave him some sort of sweetmeat. *What's next?* Gerran thought sourly. *Will they be teaching him how to sew?* Since he couldn't argue with her ladyship, he turned back and went inside the broch to the great hall.

The warband had gathered around one table and was wagering furiously on a game of carnoic between Daumyr, one of the tieryn's riders, and Salamander, the gerthddyn who'd spent the winter at the tieryn's table. Gerran dipped himself a tankard of ale from an open barrel near the honor hearth and wandered over to watch. He was planning on sitting in his usual chair at the head of the table nearest the servants' hearth, but he found it already occupied by Lord Mirryn.

"And what are you doing here?" Gerran said.

"I could ask the same of you, my lord." Mirryn paused for a grin in his general direction. "You've got a higher rank than me now, married as you are, and here your wife's with child already. I figure that from now on, I'm the captain of my father's warband and little more."

"If Solla has a son, I'll gloat then and not before." Gerran felt his usual pang of cold fear at the mention of Solla's pregnancy. *What if she dies?* He shoved the thought away with a toss of his head. "But anyway, it doesn't matter if you or I or the Lord of Hell call you the captain. What counts is what your father thinks of the matter."

Not long after they learned exactly that, when Cadryc strode into the great hall. He pulled off his yellow-and-red plaid cloak, tossed it over the back of his chair at the head of the honor table, then stood looking around him with a puzzled frown. When he spotted Mirryn, he walked across to join them. Mirryn got up and turned to face his father. The men gathered around the carnoic game fell silent; those who'd been standing hurriedly knelt. Cadryc waved his hand in their direction to allow them to stand up again, then turned his attention to his son.

"Well, Mirro," Cadryc said, "what are you doing over here?"

"The Falcon's going to have a dun of his own soon enough," Mirryn said. "So I'm the captain of your warband now."

"Ah." Cadryc paused for a long moment. "So you are. Carry on with your game, men." He turned and walked away, leaving Mirryn openmouthed but speechless behind him.

The men of the warband looked as stunned as their new captain. They said nothing, but they kept glancing at one another. *And what will they think of him?* Gerran wondered. *He's never ridden to war.*

Their carefully arranged faces revealed nothing. Mirryn sat down to a profound silence.

"That was easy enough," Gerran said.

Mirryn nodded and picked up his tankard from the table. The conversation and the wagering resumed, slowly at first, then erupted into cheers from Daumyr's supporters when his next move won the game.

"Ai!" Salamander said. "I am vanquished, well and truly conquered, routed, and driven from the field!"

"I take it that means you don't want another game," Daumyr said.

"Quite right. You've beaten me thrice, and my vanity won't take another blow." Salamander got up with a grin. "I think I'll drown my sorrows in some of our lord's ale."

Daumyr turned on the bench and made a sketchy bob that might have signified a bow to the two lords.

"Here, Captain," Daumyr said to Mirryn, "care to give me a game, my lord?"

"I do, indeed," Mirryn said. "Bring the board up here, will you?"

Good man, Daumyr! Gerran thought. He decided that he didn't dare risk acting as if he thought Mirryn needed his backing on his new authority. He went to the honor table and sat down at Cadryc's left. The tieryn was obviously trying to suppress a grin at the effect he'd just had on his son. Gerran waited until a servant lass had brought Cadryc ale and left again. Carrying his own tankard, Salamander joined them.

"I don't know if you want my opinion, Your Grace," Gerran said, "but you made the right choice for your new captain."

"Good. It gladdens my heart that you agree." Cadryc frowned into his tankard. "No doubt the lad will have plenty of chances to prove himself, with the cursed Horsekin prowling around." He reached into the tankard and pulled out a bit of straw, which he tossed onto the floor before continuing. "I just hope it's not too soon."

The tieryn and the gerthddyn exchanged a significant glance.

"Um, well, Your Grace," Gerran said, puzzled, "the sooner he gets a chance to draw his first blood, the better."

"I know that. Wasn't what I meant." Cadryc glared at his ale again, as if suspecting it of harboring dark secrets.

"If there's more straw in that, we should send one of the lasses to tell Cook."

"Um? Oh, true spoken, but it should be all right." Cadryc took a long swallow. "Naught wrong with it now."

"If you don't mind me shoving an oar in," Salamander said, "Mirryn needs to marry, and soon."

"True spoken," Cadryc said. "And I hope to the gods he sires more sons than I did!"

"Does Lady Galla have a match in mind?" Salamander asked.

"She's doing her best to find one. That's the trouble with being out here on the wretched border, with the noble-born so thin on the ground. I don't particularly want him marrying a common-born lass, but who else is there, eh?"

"Admittedly the choice is limited." Salamander glanced at Gerran, as if inviting him to comment.

Gerran shrugged. He had no ideas on the subject.

"Might as well leave all that to the womenfolk," the tieryn said. "Now, Gerro, I've been meaning to talk with you about the Falcon clan's new dun. Cursed if I know who's going to pay for it. You can't just throw a few stones together like a farmer, eh? You'll need a proper master mason from Trev Hael to plan the thing."

"Well," Gerran said, "my wife tells me that her brother owes her a fair amount of hard coin—an inheritance from an uncle, I think she said—but I'd hate to use that."

"You may have to. We don't live in the best of times, lad." Cadryc paused for a long swallow of his ale. "We've got to get men and defenses out into the Melyn Valley as soon as we can. I doubt me if the Horsekin will have the stomach for raiding this summer, but sooner or later, they'll come back. I've been thinking about our new overlord. The coin should come from him."

"Do you think he has it?"

It was Cadryc's turn for the shrug. Salamander heaved a mournful sigh.

"Do we even know where he is?" Gerran went on. "I swore to Prince Dar gladly, but ye gods, the Westfolk could be anywhere out in the grasslands. All I've ever heard is that they ride north every summer."

"That will have to do, then, eh? Sooner or later he's bound to ask us for dues and taxes, and we'll find out then."

Gerran looked at Salamander and raised an eyebrow, but the gerthddyn merely buried his nose in his tankard. Since they couldn't speak openly of dweomer in front of the tieryn, Gerran let the matter drop.

Cadryc and Gerran weren't the only men wondering where Prince Daralanteriel of the Westlands might be. A few days later messengers turned up at Cadryc's gates, two road-dusty men riding matched grays and leading two more mounts behind them. The extra horses identified them as speeded couriers, and their tabards sported the royal gold wyvern of Dun Deverry.

One-armed Tarro, who'd been watching the gates that afternoon, showed them directly into the great hall. When Gerran realized who they were, he sent a page off to find his wife, one of the only two people in the dun who could read. The messengers knelt at Tieryn Cadryc's side. One of them proffered a silver tube, sealed at both ends with gold-colored wax.

"From Prince Voran of Dun Deverry, Your Grace," he said. "Humbly requesting a favor should Your Grace be willing."

"Very well." Cadryc took the message tube from him. "Go sit with my men. A lass will bring you ale, and tell her if you'd like a meal to go with it."

"Our humble thanks, Your Grace."

Both men rose and strode away to the far side of the hall. Cadryc scowled at the messages in his hand.

"You know, Gerro," he said, "there was somewhat about the way that fellow spoke to me, so carefully, like, that troubled my heart. I was cursed glad to get out from under Gwerbret Ridvar's overlordship last autumn. It was leave or rebel, truly. I know you agreed. It was good of Prince Dar to take us on. But—" He hesitated, groping for words. "Ah, by the black hairy arse of the Lord of Hell! I don't know what I mean."

"I think I do," Gerran said. "We live outside of Deverry now, don't we? We're not vassals of the high king and the princes any more, so Voran has to ask, not demand. We might as well be West-folk ourselves."

"That's it!" Cadryc grinned, then let the grin fade. "I knew that, of course, when we swore to Dar. But somehow I hadn't quite grasped it. I have now."

"I still wonder why he got the gwerbret to let us go. You'd think the royal line would want as many vassals as it can hold."

"Ah, that's the issue, lad! As they can hold, but they can't hold a blasted one of us if we can't hold our land for them. The Melyn Valley's too far west. I'll wager the high king knows it'd just be a wound on the kingdom, bleeding coin and men."

"So he'll let Prince Dar do the bleeding instead."

"Just that." Cadryc saluted him with his tankard. "But with all those archers he has, the wound won't be a big one."

When Solla arrived at the table of honor, Cadryc broke the seals on the tube and pulled out the letter inside, then handed it to her. She sat down in the chair to his right and unrolled the parchment to look it over.

"Just read it out," Cadryc snapped, then ducked his head in apology. "Well, if you would, my lady."

"Of course." Solla began: "To his grace, Tieryn Cadryc of the Westlands, and his lords of the Melyn Valley, I, Prince Voran of Dun Deverry, send greetings. I have news of some import for your overlord, Prince Daralanteriel of the Westlands. Alas, I know not where he might be or where I might meet with him. If Your Grace should know, would he be so kind as to send me an answer by the messengers who have brought him this letter? I am currently residing at Gwingedd in Cerrgonney, but I plan to continue on to Arcodd as the spring progresses. I will be residing there for some while, as I have every intention of demanding some legal redress against Govvin, priest of Bel, for the insults he tendered me during last summer's campaigns. If his highness Daralanteriel could join me there, I should be most gratified." Solla glanced up. "The rest is all a formal farewell. He never says what this thing of great import is."

"Blast him!" Cadryc muttered. "No doubt we won't be able to pry anything out of those messengers, either."

"They may not know," Gerran said. "I doubt if it's his action against Govvin. He wouldn't need to consult Prince Dar about that."

"Huh!" Cadryc said with a snort. "I wonder what the high priest down in Dun Deverry will think?"

"Knowing the prince, Your Grace," Solla said, "I'd wager that he's already brought the high priest round to his side."

"Most like. Well, I don't know where our Prince Dar is, and I don't know how in the hells we're going to find him, either."

Gerran glanced around and saw Salamander, lurking behind a nearby pillar, convenient for eavesdropping.

"Leave it to me." Gerran got up from his chair. "I've got an idea."

When Salamander saw Gerran walking his way, he headed for the back door of the great hall. He knew that Gerran would follow him down to the dun wall, where they could have a little privacy away from the clutter of the ward. It was odd, he reflected, that Gerran would have so few qualms about calling upon dweomer, when most Deverry lords refused to admit that such a thing could even exist. Odd or not, he was glad to dispense with the usual verbal fencing and insinuations.

"I take it you want me to find out where Daralanteriel is," Salamander said.

"Just that," Gerran said. "Can you?"

"Easily."

Salamander glanced up at the sky, where toward the west a few clouds drifted against the crystalline blue, and let his Sight shift to thoughts of Dar and the royal alar. He saw them immediately, a long line of riders followed by herds of horses, flocks of sheep, horses laden with packs and more dragging travois, dogs, children on ponies—all the usual straggling untidiness of Westfolk on the move. All around them stretched grassland.

"Somewhere west of Eldidd," Salamander said. "I can't tell exactly where, I'm afraid, because they're out in open country."

"Is there anything but open country west of Eldidd?" Gerran said.

"There's not, and that, indeed, is the problem. Here, give me a while, and I may be able to tell you more."

"Well and good, then, and my thanks."

They walked back inside together, but Salamander left the lord at the table of honor and hurried upstairs to his wedge-shaped chamber high up in the broch. He barred the door, then sat down on the wide stone sill of the window. The sharp west wind drifted in, bringing with it the scent of the stables below. Salamander rummaged under his shirt, brought out a pomander, made of an apple dried with Bardek spices, and inhaled the scent.

From his perch he could see over the stables and the dun wall both to the meadows beyond, pale green with the first grass. The clouds had drifted a little farther toward zenith and grown larger as well. He focused on the white billows and thought of Dallandra. He saw the royal alar again, stopped in a swirl of riders and animals. Some of the men had dismounted and were strolling toward the various travois. Apparently they were going to set up the tents. In the vision Salamander realized that the western sky had already clouded over. Some distance from the alar ran a river. It looked to him like the Cantariel, but since it wound through flat meadowland as so many rivers did, out in the grasslands, he couldn't be sure. Dallandra was standing at the riverbank and watching muddy water flow. He sent his mind out toward hers.

It took her some moments to respond. He could pick up her emotional state, a blend of annoyance and physical discomfort. Finally, she acknowledged him with a wordless sense of welcome and a wave of one hand.

"Are you ill?" Salamander thought to her. "Have you been hurt?"

He focused in on the image of her face. She looked pale, and dark smudges marred the skin under her eyes. "I'm fine," she said. "I'm merely pregnant, and I spent the day on horseback. It's not a happy combination."

"I can easily contact you later—"

"No, no, I've been meaning to speak with you. I need to ask you something. It's about Nevyn. You knew him well, didn't you?"

"I certainly did, ofttimes to my severe distress and humiliation. The old man had the horrid habit of always being right, especially when it came to my faults, flaws, mistakes, and general ill-doings."

He could feel Dallandra's amusement as clearly as he would have heard her laughter had they been together. "Was he stubborn?" she said.

"Very. Like the proverbial bull in a warm stable. Getting him outside on a winter's day is a most formidable task. Is Neb giving you trouble?"

"Aha, you guessed! I'm worried, really. He seems to want to shed his current personality and just turn back into Nevyn. Yet when I try to speak with him about it, I can feel his mind close up."

"This sounds dangerous."

"It is. Once the child's born, my attention's bound to be divided. I should have apprenticed him to Grallezar, I suppose, and taken Branna on myself, but at the time it seemed a better match this way."

"I thought you made the right decision then, and I still do."

"Thank you. At times I have trouble remembering why I made it." She paused, and he received the general impression of a jumble of thoughts. "It was because of the healing lore, I think. He seemed to want to learn that as well, and Grallezar has none."

"Is there anything I can do to help? I can easily take him through some of the work."

"If he'll listen to you, and he'd blasted well better!" Her image smiled in relief. "If nothing else, you can keep an eye on him for me."

"Gladly, and if he won't listen to me, I'll smack him a good one." He flexed one arm. "We mountebanks and jugglers have strong muscles, you know."

Dallandra laughed, and the sense of relief strengthened.

"I may hold you to that," she said. "But how are you? You sound well."

"I am indeed, having survived another miserable winter. I was wondering, O Princess of Powers Perilous, where you and the royal alar might be."

"Still in the Westlands, but ultimately we're heading for the Red Wolf dun."

"Splendid! I've got news for our prince. There's a message waiting for him here from Prince Voran. His royal self sounded more than a little put out that he didn't know where to send the message, too. He wants Dar to meet him in Cengarn to discuss some mysterious matter."

"How odd! I'll tell Dar, certainly, but we're going to stop along the way. He wants to visit Lord Samyc, since he's Samyc's overlord now."

"Ah, I see. However, if he could send Cadryc a letter, announcing his most regal plans, it would set at rest both Cadryc's mind and that of Prince Voran."

"I'll have him do that. Neb can write it, and it'll do him good to earn his keep."

Salamander laughed under his breath. "How far away are you?"

"A good long way. We're traveling up the Cantariel." Dalla paused briefly, calculating. "We're maybe a couple hundred miles from the coast. Well, maybe a little more, closer to two hundred and a half, say. I can't be any more sure than that."

"Of course. In vision it looks like you're west of Eldidd."

"We are. The traveling seems to drag on and on, somehow, but perhaps I'm just tired. It's a good thing we started as early in the year as we did, or we wouldn't reach you till high summer. As it is, we should get there some while before. Curse it all, at moments I wish Meranaldar were still riding with us! He could be a bore, but he knew how to mark out time."

"Eventually we all will, O Mistress of Mighty Magics, whether we want to or not. Such things always seem to matter in towns, and towns, alas, lie in our Destiny. If naught else, having a royal dun would let his peers know where to send Dar letters."

While the absent Meranaldar might have known how to mark out time, someone arrived at the Westfolk camp not long after who understood space and distances. Just as the alar was pitching the tents for a night's rest, the silver wyrm flew in, circling high over the camp, then landing a good half a mile off to avoid panicking the horses. Dalla took her sack of medicinals and hurried out to meet him.

The dragon lay down to allow Dallandra to examine his wound, a thin pink stripe on his silvery-blue side. When she'd first been treating it, she'd cut a piece of leather, boiled it with wax to keep it from stretching, and marked the length of the cut upon it. When she measured the cut against the marked strip, she found the wound the same length as before. Although it looked pink and clean, it still opened into flesh, not scar tissue.

"Rori, you've been licking it!" Dallandra said.

"I have not!"

"Then why hasn't it healed up?"

"Arzosah tells me that dragons heal as slowly as they grow, but truly, she's as puzzled as you are."

"Especially slowly, I imagine, when the dragon's not done what the healer asked of him."

"I swear it, Dalla, I've not licked it or scratched it or rubbed it against anything. Well, once by accident I did rub it against a rock, but it hurt so much I made sure I'd never do it again."

Dallandra set her hands on her hips and glared at him. He raised his head and glared right back.

"At least it's not bleeding," Dallandra said. "Does it ever?"

"No," Rori said. "But it's driving me daft, itching itching itching! Ye gods, sometimes I'm tempted to lick it, I have to admit. It's worse to itch than to ache, I swear it."

"I can wash it with willow water for a little relief now that you're here. It might sting at first."

"Stinging's better than itching."

Rori sat up while Dallandra got together a leather glove, a little heap of dry horse dung, a kettle of water, and the strips of dried willow bark. She lit the dung for a fire, brought the water to a simmer, tossed in a good handful of bark, then took the kettle off the fire and allowed the mixture to steep. While they were waiting, Valandario came walking out from camp to join them. She was carrying something clasped in her right hand.

"I was wondering if you could answer me a few questions," Val said to the dragon, "about this." She opened her hand to reveal a chunk of lapis lazuli the size of a crab apple, carved into an egg shape. A fine gold chain ran through a hole drilled into the smaller end. "Dalla told me it belongs to you."

"So it does," Rori said. "Or it did, once. I wondered what had happened to it."

"I found it on the ground with your clothes," Dallandra said, "after the transformation."

"Ah, I see." He sighed in a long hiss. "It's of little use to me now. Val, it's yours if you want it."

"That's very generous," Valandario said, "but I assure you that I wasn't trying to get it away from you. I was just wondering what it is. It's got dweomer upon it, doesn't it?"

"Yes. An old dwarven woman gave it to me—Otho's mother, in fact." He turned his massive head Dallandra's way. "Otho the dwarf, the silver daggers' smith—I doubt me if you knew him. He's the one who got me to Haen Marn, in fact, for all the good it did the poor old bastard. I never met a man more sour than Otho, and I hope to all the gods that I never do, either. Be that as it may," he turned back to Valandario, "his mother told me that no one could scry me out as long as I was wearing that talisman. She may well have been right, too. I know that Raena couldn't find me when I was wearing it."

"No more could Jill," Dallandra said.

"Very powerful, then." Val considered the lapis egg with a small frown of concentration. "Are you telling me that the Mountain Folk have dweomer? Here I always thought they mocked it."

"The men do," Rori said. "The women don't. What their men think doesn't matter a cursed lot to dwarven women."

"Good for them," Val said. "But are you sure that the women used dweomer on this stone? They could have come by this some other way, traded for it or the like."

"That's true, but I'd wager it was made right in Lin Serr. When I met her, Othara was ill and blind with sheer old age, but she still reminded me of Jill. You could feel power around her. And the trip down—" The dragon paused, looking away as he remembered. "She lived in the deep city, you see, where visitors weren't supposed to go. I was still in human form then, of course. So a friend—Garin, it was—led me down hooded like a hawk. Once I was good and confused, he let me take off the hood. We went into a cavern where it was lit with blue light, oozing out of the walls. There were some women standing there, waiting to look me over and make sure it was safe to let me through the next doorway. Garin told me that the name of the cavern was the Hall of the Mothers." The dragon shuddered. "I went cold all over, just hearing it."

"That makes me shiver even now," Dallandra said.

Valandario nodded her agreement and went on studying the talisman. Dallandra tested the willow water and found it pleasantly warm. She put on her glove, picked up a linen bandage, wrapped it around a big handful of lamb's wool, then dipped the lump into the water to soak.

"Lie down again," Dalla said to Rori. "And remember, it might sting."

The dragon flopped onto his side, making the ground shudder and the water in the kettle slop back and forth. With her gloved hand, Dallandra laid the wet bandage over the wound and squeezed to let the medicinal seep into the cut. He flinched, then relaxed with a ripple of scales.

"Much better than itching," he said.

"Good." Dallandra glanced at Valandario, who had closed her hand over the talisman and was staring off at the horizon. "Val? Are you still with us?"

"Hmm?" Valandario looked at her. "My apologies. Now, about Haen Marn. Rori, I know that it disappeared. Do you know why, exactly?"

"It had the best reason in the world. Horsekin. One of their armies was marching straight for it."

"I just thought of something." Dallandra put the lump of cloth back into the herbwater to refresh. "At the time I assumed that the army was heading for Cengarn and that Haen Marn was merely on the way. Do you think they could have been planning to attack the island?"

"I have no idea," Rori said. "I never saw them, only the trail they left behind. The tracks started and stopped by dweomer, Raena's dweomer, or so you told me."

"Why bring an army up to the Northlands and then take it away again?" Valandario sounded puzzled. "If they were actually going somewhere else?"

"No reason at all," Rori said. "I wonder why Alshandra wanted to destroy Haen Marn?"

"She may have simply wanted to capture it," Dallandra said, "though she did tend to destroy the things she coveted. I wonder if Evandar made some prophecy about the island that had to do with Elessario? She was determined to get Elessi back before she could be born."

"That was the whole point of the wretched war." Rori moved uneasily. "Could you put a bit more of that water on the cut? It's better, but I can feel it still."

Dallandra fished the sop out of the kettle and went back to work.

"You're missing something," Valandario said suddenly. "Evandar made a prophecy about the island, most assuredly, but it didn't have anything to do with Elessi. It was about Rori, and the spell book—the vision Ebañy saw in the black crystal."

"Of course." Dallandra tossed the sop back into the bucket again—the medicinal water had soaked through the glove and her fingertips were turning numb. "It's another hint that the crystal somehow belongs to the island."

"More than a hint," Val hesitated, then spoke calmly of what must have been painful things. "After Jav was murdered, Alshandra appeared to me. She was party to the theft, and that means she must have seen the message in the crystal."

"Maybe not." Dallandra paused to pull off the wet glove. "Evandar most likely locked it against her. Although, for all we know, Loddlaen may have been able to see it and tell her."

"It seems more and more likely that the crystal's on that island. So what we need to do, obviously, is bring Haen Marn back."

"Obviously, she says." Rori's voice hovered near a growl. "And how, my dear Valandario, do you propose to bring it back?"

"Dweomer, of course."

"Of course." Rori slapped his tail hard on the ground. "Just like that, eh?"

"Will you stop that?" Dallandra snapped. "The tail banging, I mean. It makes the water in the kettle slop around." She knelt down to rummage through her supplies, then brought out a pair of tongs to use instead of the glove.

"My apologies." The dragon sounded less than apologetic.

Valandario once again gazed off at the distant horizon, using the lapis talisman for some sort of scrying or so Dallandra assumed.

She used the tongs to fish the sop out of the herbwater and apply it to Rori's wound. The dragon hissed with a long sigh of relief.

"The itch is gone, and the sting's easing up. You're a marvel with your medicaments, Dalla, you truly are."

"My thanks."

Valandario abruptly turned back to face them again. "But about Haen Marn," Val said. "Is there any chance that this lapis talisman came from there?"

"No," Rori said. "I wore it there, and no one remarked upon it. They would have had it been theirs."

"I was afraid of that." She looked Dallandra's way. "I was hoping that it might be linked to Haen Marn. All I get from it is a very dim impression of a rock vein, probably the one this thing was mined from."

"Life's never that convenient, is it?" Dallandra shared her regret. A dweomer talisman from the island might have given off a far more useful impression. "Rori, you didn't happen to bring a trinket or suchlike away with you, did you?"

"I didn't. Naught except painful memories." He began to speak in Deverrian, as he often did when talking of the past. "And since it's gone, I can't fly off and fetch—hold a moment! I've just remembered somewhat. There was a silver horn chained to a rock outside Haen Marn. You could blow it, and it would summon the boatmen. Well, it would if you were meant to visit the island. Now, after the place disappeared, the horn was left behind, but all smashed and tarnished. Still, it must have had some dweomer upon it."

"It summoned," Valandario pronounced the words carefully. "Dalla, its function is to summon."

"The moon has horns when it's new," Dallandra said.

"And silver's the metal of the moon!" Val threw both hands in the air and jigged a few dance steps.

Rori growled long and hard. "What by the pink arses of the gods are you two talking about?"

"Some omens, naught more." Dallandra turned to him. "Where is this horn?"

"Enj has it, I think."

"Enj?" Dallandra knew she'd heard the name before, but she failed to place it. "Who's Enj?"

"Angmar's son, born on Haen Marn. His father was one of the Mountain Folk, but Enj is a fair strange example of them, I'll tell you. He lives most of the year in the wilderness, out under the sun, and only goes back to Lin Serr for the winter snows."

"Very strange, then," Valandario said.

"Well, only half of his mother's blood came from the Mountain Folk," Rori went on. "And he was raised above ground on the island."

"But he didn't disappear along with the rest of them?"

"He wasn't on the island at the time, Val. He was helping me find Arzosah."

"I remember that bit," Dallandra said. "Rori, can you bring Val that horn?"

"That depends on Enj. If he'll part with it, I suppose I could fly hundreds of miles north and figure out a way to carry it and then fly all the way back again."

"Well, by the Black Sun!" Val said. "It's not like you've got anything better to do."

"Naught but scout for our mortal enemies." The dragon raised his tail as if to slap the ground, then gently laid it back down. "Or have you forgotten the Horsekin?"

"They're to the north, aren't they?" Val said. "Why can't you do both at once?"

The dragon raised his head and glared at her. Val set her hands on her hips and stared into his eyes until, with a sigh, Rori looked away. "Flames and fumes!" he said. "Living around dweomerfolk could drive a man daft and a dragon even dafter."

"There, there." Dallandra patted his massive jaw. "Don't forget, we're discussing this in hopes of turning you back into your true form."

"Just so," Valandario said. "Now, if you could fetch me that horn, and if I can heal it so it sounds the dweomer spell again, and if Dalla and I can figure out the correct workings, well, then, we might be able to summon the island."

"Exactly." Dalla said. "And if we actually manage to do all that, then let's hope that the book does have the instructions for the dragon working in it. You never know with Evandar's schemes."

"True spoken." The dragon heaved himself to his feet. "That's the Guardians for you! But well and good then, I'm off to the Northlands. If Arzosah comes looking for me, you'd best not tell her where I've gone. I doubt me if she'll take kindly to the idea of my turning back into a man."

"I hadn't thought of that." Dallandra felt her stomach clench at the thought of Arzosah in a rage. "Um, we'll ford that river when it's time to cross. What else can we do?"

With a shrug of wing, the silver dragon waddled off, ridiculously clumsy in the grass. He waddled faster, bunched his muscles, and leaped into the air with a rush of wings like thunder booming, all grace, suddenly, and power, as he soared high and disappeared into the glare of the sun.

As he flew off, Rori was grumbling to himself about the arrogance of dweomerfolk, but soon enough the flying itself soothed him. He loved the feeling of soaring high above the earth, rising on the wind in splendid freedom, or swooping down only to spiral skyward again. At times, when he glided upon a favoring wind, it seemed to him that the world below was moving while he rested, master of the air.

If he returned to human form, he'd be giving up the power and the freedom of flight. That thought nagged him worse than his wound. And what would he get in return? *Hands,* he thought. *It would be splendid to have hands again, and cooked food, and other such comforts.* But those puny comforts could never compensate for the loss.

As he flew over the Melyn River, he considered turning back and telling Dallandra that the effort she would have to make was simply not worth it, that she and Valandario doubtless had more important work to do. What stopped him was the thought of Enj. If naught else, perhaps the two dweomermasters could bring the island back and Enj's clan with it.

And what of Angmar? Rori asked himself. He'd longed for her return himself, once, a very long time ago now, it seemed to him when he thought about it. He could remember her so clearly, and remember his grief at losing her, but the grief had lost its sting. Missing Angmar, flying north each spring to see if Haen Marn had returned, stopping to speak with Enj—he'd performed these actions faithfully each year for over forty years now, until they'd taken on a distant quality, like a ritual performed by a priest while he merely watched.

Yet, for Enj the grief still lived. For the sake of his friend, Rori flew north on Valandario's errand. He'd bring the horn back, he decided, then return to his scouting. As for the other matter, he would wait and see if it were even possible to walk the earth as a man instead flying so far above it. If it turned out to be possible, he'd make his decision then.

The river that flows through Lin Serr's parkland seems to emerge like dweomer from under the dwarven city, but in truth, it runs above ground for most of its course. At the time of which we speak, few people knew its secret, but Enj was one of them. About twenty miles north of Lin Serr, an ordinary-looking river flowed into a canyon gouged from the limestone of an ancient sea floor, only to disappear under the cliff blocking the canyon's southern end. It ran through caverns until it reached the city, and from there at last regained the sunlight.

Every spring, Enj left Lin Serr and hiked to that canyon, then followed the river north. It led after many windings to the general area in which Haen Marn had existed during its sojourn on the Roof of the World. At times Haen Marn's own river had joined up with it, though at other times, it hadn't. No one knew why or how the changes occurred; they followed, like everything about Haen Marn, some unknowable fluctuation within the inner planes of the universe.

Over the past forty years Enj had built himself a cabin in a mountain meadow near the previous location of his old home. Every spring he returned there, planted a vegetable garden, and spent the summer waiting just in case the island decided to return. As Rori had guessed, Enj did have the remains of the horn that had summoned the dragon boat from the island. Occasionally he would sit on the front steps of his cabin, hold the crushed lump of silver, green with tarnish, and weep over it while he wondered if he'd ever see the island again. At times he felt profoundly foolish for doing so, but the ritual gave him a certain amount of satisfaction, rather like biting on a sore tooth.

Enj had just finished one of these sessions and was putting the horn back into its leather storage pouch when he heard the thunder of approaching wings. He hung the pouch from a nail on the cabin wall, then strolled outside as the silver dragon landed. Rori waddled over to greet him.

"I did wonder when you'd be turning up," Enj spoke the Mountain dialect of Deverrian. "The weather be about right for dragons."

"It's spring, truly," Rori said. "Did you fare well over the winter?"

"Well enough. Lin Serr does weigh upon me after but a month or so, all that stone and short views." Enj glanced around the broad meadow, dusted with the first pale green grass, ringed with distant pine forest. To the north, beyond the trees mountains rose, glittering with snow at the peaks. "This does suit me far better."

"Me, too." The dragon folded his enormous wings with a long rustle like collapsing canvas tents. "I've brought you some news. Two Westfolk dweomerworkers have taken up the task of bringing Haen Marn back."

Enj tried to speak, couldn't, felt tears gathering in his eyes. Irritably, he brushed them away with the back of his hand. "That does gladden my heart," he said at last. "Think you that they'll succeed?"

"If anyone can, they will."

"If anyone can."

Rori shrugged with a ripple of massive muscles. "If not, then we'll have to go on hoping that the island makes its own way back."

"True spoken, that."

"They need somewhat of yours, though, the silver horn. They think that if they can heal it with dweomer, then it might help them summon the island."

"I'll give it over gladly in the hopes of seeing my mam and my home again. Will you carry it back?"

"I will, if you can fix up some sort of pouch that you can tie around my neck. That would be the safest way, I think."

"I do have the pouch." Enj paused, estimating the circumference of the dragon's massive neck. "We'll need a long fastening for it. I did kill a deer some weeks past, and I've been tanning the hide. 'Twill do to cut some strips for braiding, but the work will take some time."

"We've waited forty years. We can wait a day or two more."

They shared a laugh.

While Enj worked on cutting and braiding straps for the leather pouch, Rori flew off again to hunt. He returned two days later, bringing another dead deer with him—his dinner, though he had Enj butcher a haunch for himself. After Enj had put the haunch on a hook in a shady corner of the cabin to hang, and Rori had eaten the rest of the deer, Enj came back outside to join him.

"My thanks for the venison," Enj remarked. "You were always a generous man, Rori."

"A man, truly," Rori said. "Once. Well, we'll see what these dweomermasters can do. They have a plan, you see, to turn me back again, should I want."

"Do you want?"

"I don't know. At times I do, at times I don't. Who knows if their plan will work, anyway? Dweomer's like that. It always seems to be able to do what you don't want, then fail on the things you do."

"Bitter, bitter, eh? Still?"

The dragon growled under his breath, but Enj laughed, and the dragon eventually joined him.

"One thing I wonder about," Rori said. "For as long as I've known you, you've not had the slightest trouble believing that dweomer exists and works in the world, yet other dwarven men I've met deny it. Deny it? They mock it."

"That be so," Enj said. "But I was born and raised on Haen Marn. They weren't."

"Of course. I should have thought of that. Although you know, I once met a band of Mountain Folk who had a dweomermaster of their own, and he was a man, not a woman. They lived a fair bit differently than your folk, though. Their women walked around in the sunlight just like the men."

Enj nearly choked on the thought. For a moment he could only goggle at the dragon like a half-wit. "Worms and slimes," he said feebly. "And where did this marvel lie?"

"Down in Deverry proper. There's some hills there—I would have called them mountains once, but now I've seen true mountains—so, hills on the border twixt Cantrae and Cwm Pecl. And some of your folk live inside them and farm above."

Enj's thoughts began to sort themselves out at last. "Another band of Mountain Folk?" he said. "This be the most interesting bit of news I've had in years, Rori. Now, I did hear about one other group of our brethren in an old tale about the ancient days. They did survive the first Horsekin attacks and tried to shelter with the Westfolk, but the Westfolk turned them away, and they were all slain."

"I've heard that tale, too," the dragon said, "but what if they weren't killed? What if they fled east—east and south, that would be?"

Enj suddenly laughed. "Makes sense, truly. If so, that be one up on the old men like Otho, eh? For centuries they've clung to that bitter tale, pouring vinegar in their wounds over it, and now, by all the gods! It might not even be true."

"When you go back to Lin Serr this winter, tell your loremasters, will you?"

"I will. You may rest assured about that."

Enj brought out the remains of the silver horn and tied the pouch securely around the dragon's neck. With a last call of farewell, Rori launched himself and flew off to the west. Enj stood in the cabin door and watched the dragon disappear into the sunny sky. For the first time in over forty years, he felt honest hope.

"Mam?" Mara said. "Be you busy just now?"

"Not truly, my sweet," Angmar said. "Why?"

"I did wish to talk with you."

Angmar nodded at the bench near her chair. Mara sat down, smoothing her skirts under her. They were sitting in the great hall of Haen Marn's manse, near a window where sun streamed in with the promise of summer. In the chair opposite Angmar's, Laz had been basking in the heat like the cats, who lay scattered on the floor, each in a patch of sun.

"Should I leave you?" Laz said to Mara.

"Nah, nah, nah, for I would hear your advice about this." Mara hesitated briefly. "I did have the strangest sensation just now. It were hope, a sudden hope, like the sun coming in the window here. And I thought, mayhap we'll go home soon."

"Be you sure?" Angmar leaned forward a little in her chair.

"I be not, Mam, and I'd not have you put too much upon it. But then, I'd not dismiss it, either. I did think, mayhap my teacher here might tell us somewhat about it."

"I'm not sure there's much to tell," Laz said. "Was this like a dream, or even a daydream?"

"It were not, just a sudden flood of feeling. I did go tell Avain about it, but she did make me no answer."

"My sweet," Angmar said, "Avain understands little unless it come to her as pictures in the water."

"Then her silence means naught." Mara glanced at Laz. "It were for that moment or two a glorious feeling."

"Did you feel that it came from outside your self?" Laz said.

"I did, truly, but I did see no spirits about or suchlike."

"Then it might have come from far away, through some powerful dweomer." Laz raised a quick hand. "Note, however, that I said 'might have,' not 'it most assuredly did.' "

"Very well. I'll think on't."

Angmar sighed and settled back in her chair. The bright sun picked out the fine lines around her mouth and turned the gray in her hair to silver. She glanced out the window, then pursed her lips and narrowed her eyes. When Laz followed her glance, he saw Berwynna and Dougie walking among the apple trees, holding hands, laughing together.

"Huh!" Mara snapped. "Wynni's lout be here again!"

"So he is," Angmar said. "I do like the lad, mind, but truly, he belongs not here. Ai, when I were young, never did I heed the warnings of my elders, and so I do suppose he be much the same."

"Wynni should be sending him away because you did ask her to," Mara said. "Not just because of what Avain did tell you."

"Well, now, she does deserve a bit of merriment. She does work so hard for all of us. I think me you understand not just how much we do depend upon her labors."

Mara wrinkled her nose at her mother, who ignored the sneer.

"My poor Wynni!" Angmar went on. "It does ache her heart, shut up here like she be."

"Why not let her marry, then, and go live among the pigs and dogs on the mainland?" Mara said. "Since she does seem to like them so much."

Angmar swung her head around and glared. Mara started to speak, but Angmar got in before her, letting fly with a stream of Dwarvish. Although Laz couldn't understand a word, he could hear anger easily enough. Mara, in turn, snarled out a few sullen words, also in Dwarvish, which only made Angmar angrier. With a muttered excuse that neither woman bothered to acknowledge, Laz got up and slunk away.

He made his way through the apple trees to the lakeshore. Out behind the manse, he'd found a tiny beach that had become his favorite spot on the island. A willow tree, pruned into a canopy, overhung a stone bench. When he sat down, he could watch the water through the slender branches, just budding with green. Across the rippled lake rose the dark, stone-streaked hills of Alban—whatever or wherever that name might have meant.

Over the past few weeks, as his hands had continued to heal, and his strength continued to build, Laz had attempted simple dweomer workings, only to fail at all of them. All around the island rose a water veil of etheric force that made scrying beyond it impossible. He'd expected that. Another difference in the feel of the etheric, however, troubled him far more.

Back home in the Northlands, he'd sensed the etheric plane as a constant presence, hovering close to the physical, or perhaps even merging into the physical in some unclear way. He'd always been able to exploit that sense of proximity, transferring his consciousness and even his physical substance back and forth between them as easily as he might pour water from one bowl to another. Sidro had often remarked on his ability to shift levels of consciousness or shapechange as easily as most men could change the subject of a conversation. Her amazement at his skill had fed his confidence, which in turn had fed his abilities.

Here in Alban, he felt a rift or a discontinuity, as he decided to call it, between the two planes. Rising to the etheric to work dweomer—to say nothing of the astral plane beyond—cost him an enormous expenditure of energy and a careful attention to all the details of the dweomer craft. So far, he'd failed to elevate his consciousness to the higher planes for more than a few brief moments. He'd not managed to transform his physical body at all. Every attempt brought the dead, ugly, certain feeling that in this place he would never succeed.

And Sidro, of course, was far away. *I'm only half the man I was,* he thought, *without her.* His one hope lay in the possibility that it was Alban—or Alban's world in general—that was to blame, not his damaged self. But would he ever see the Northlands again? Hearing Mara speak of her odd sensation of hope had roused hope in him, but only briefly, a mere spark of light in the night that lived inside him these days, or so he thought of it, a constant gloom of self-appraisal and loneliness.

If Sisi were here, he berated himself, *she'd tell me to stop feeling sorry for myself. And she'd be right.* It was such a tedious old story, the man who didn't realize how much he loved a woman until he'd lost her. If there was anything Laz hated, it was tedious old stories, such as the little moral lessons his mother had been so fond of preaching to her brood of children and slaves. He got up from the bench and started back to the manse to see if Mara and Angmar had stopped arguing.

Mara, however, met him on the path. She walked up to him without looking him in the face, and her pretty mouth, normally so soft, stuck out in a pout.

"What's wrong?" Laz said.

"Mam does say there be a need on me to apologize to you," Mara said, "for I did say mean things about my sister in front of you."

"Well, you weren't saying them about me, so no apology needed."

Mara looked up and smiled with the life flashing back into her eyes, a touch of harmless malice. Briefly he was tempted to kiss her, but he remembered her warning: I wear this body like you wear a shirt. Did she feel a closeness to the etheric? Did she feel now what he'd once felt, the ease of slipping back and forth between the flesh and the etheric? He would have to teach her far more lore before he could even discuss the subject with her. He was also afraid, he realized, afraid that if she did feel a continuity with the etheric, then Alban's world was much like his own, and that fault lay deep within himself, not outside in the world around him.

"You do look troubled, Tirn," Mara said.

"Oh, it's just my hands. They ache, even in the sun."

"We'd best go in, and I'll brew up some herbwater to treat them."

Laz allowed himself a sigh at the pain ahead of him. It would divert his mind from memories of Sidro, he realized, and as he followed Mara back to the manse, he was almost cheerful at the thought.

"Sidro?" Pir said in the Gel da'Thae language. "What's wrong?"

"Nothing." Sidro pushed out a bright smile. "Just thinking."

"About Laz?"

She hesitated, unsure of how to answer, and concentrated on tying off a thread on her needlework. He waited, as patient as always, standing with his hands shoved into his brigga pockets. She was sitting outside their tent to take advantage of the clear light from the spring sun while she embroidered a horse-head design on the sleeve of the new tunic she was making for him. With a sigh he hunkered down in front of her.

"If you don't want to tell me," Pir said, "that's well, um, understandable."

If Laz had been the one to ask, he would have goaded her into telling him exactly what she'd been thinking, she realized.

"I was just wondering if I'd ever see Laz again," Sidro said. "That's all."

"Ah. I do wonder that myself." He glanced at her embroidery. "That's a splendid little horse. I didn't know you could draw pictures."

"I can't. One of the other women did it for me. Now all I have to do is fill it in."

He smiled, nodding, then stood back up.

"Pir?" she said. "Are you happy here among the Westfolk?"

"I don't know. The horses the prince gave me are splendid, but well, um, er, they're not our people, are they? The People themselves, I mean."

"That's true, but frankly, I'm glad of it. I'll never be a slave again as long as I stay here."

"Ah." He considered this in his slow, careful way. "I hadn't thought of that. But then, I wouldn't, would I?"

"You were free born, after all."

"Yes. Huh. I'll have to think about that."

"I'm coming to like it here, you see, so I wondered."

"Oh. I'll think about that, too." He smiled at her, then turned and walked off through the tents.

Had he been Laz, Sidro would have worried for hours about his reaction to her statement. With Pir, she knew that he would tell her in his own time, if indeed, his reaction concerned her at all.

Why do I care if Laz returns or not? She sat with her sewing in her lap for some while, that afternoon, amazed at her own thought.

By the time Rori returned, the royal alar had traveled a long way north. The spring days had grown longer and warmer, and as the land dried out and the grass sprang up, the horses and sheep had easier walking and better fodder, which meant that their herders could keep them moving for more hours a day.

Since Dallandra had been scrying for him, she saw Rori nearing the camp before he landed, and she met him out in the open meadows, far away from the horses and other animals, who had no way of knowing that this enormous predator had a human soul—not that they would have trusted it if they had.

"I thought Pir was going to train your horses to ignore dragons," Rori said by way of greeting.

"He is," Dallandra said, "but he needs somewhat with your scent upon it. He'd like you to lair upon old blankets for a while. It shouldn't take long for them to soak up the wyrm odor."

"Not with the way I stink! I'll do it gladly. Ye gods, it's been years since I've slept upon a blanket." Rori turned his head and contemplated his scaly stomach. "Not that I'll be able to feel the difference, I suppose. Here, untie this pouch, will you? I'm sick of the thing banging against me."

"You've got the horn, then?"

"What's left of it. Enj sends his thanks for any aid you can give him and his people on the island. He's longing to see them again. Oh, and by the by, I've bad news to give our prince. I saw Horsekin up in the Northlands when I was flying back." He rumbled with brief laughter. "I gave them and their horses a good scare, but it wasn't enough to send them home again."

Dallandra felt as if she might faint. She steadied herself quickly, but her hands still shook enough to make untying the pouch difficult. At last she got it free.

"I'll fetch Dar right now," she said, "and give this to Val while I'm about it. Will you wait?"

"Of course. And have Pir bring me out those blankets. I can lair here tonight and sleep on them."

When Daralanteriel went out to speak with the dragon, Calonderiel went with him. Dallandra gave Valandario the pouch with the horn, then sat down with her colleague to examine the remains. As well as the pouch, Enj had wrapped them in straw to cushion them during the long flight. Once freed of the wrapping, the horn looked a pitiful thing, all crushed and folded upon itself, filthy with tarnish. Yet as Val held it in her hands, it shone with a glimmer of silver, just for a brief moment before returning to its old color. Valandario caught her breath with a gasp.

"There's dweomer upon it, all right," Val said. "A very great dweomer."

"It seems to have recognized you for what you are," Dallandra said. "That gives me hope. It'll work with you rather than against you."

"Yes. I wish I could go to Haen Marn's old location. I'd like to meet Enj, too."

"Rori saw Horsekin prowling around—"

"I heard you tell Dar. Don't worry. I'm not going to do anything stupid." Val paused for a grin. "Not that stupid, anyway."

"Good. I'll be glad to help with the horn if you need me, but you're the gem master. I'm assuming that silver objects count as gems, anyway."

"I think they might. The poor thing! It's certainly been ill-treated somehow. I wonder if this damage is part of the dweomer that sent the island away, or if Alshandra got hold of it. I feel like I'm holding an ill child or suchlike." Val paused to wipe a tear from her eye. When she laid the damp finger onto the metal, a fleck of tarnish disappeared with a hiss. Val flinched and nearly dropped the horn.

"They might count as gems?" Dallandra said. "The question's been answered, in my opinion. This one most assuredly does."

"Well, I've seen enough sorrow in my life to work myself up into a fit of weeping," Val said. "If nothing else, I can clean it off."

All that night the silver dragon slept upon a spread of old blankets. In the morning, when Dallandra went out to say farewell, she found Pir gathering up the thick wool cloths. They most definitely stank of wyrm.

"You're not going to keep those in your tent, are you?" Dalla said. "I pity poor Sidro if you are."

"I'll be wrapping them in somewhat else," Pir said. "But it will do us no good if they wash clean in the rain."

"What will you do with them?"

"Put one on the ground, then calm the horses whilst they have the smell of it in their nostrils." He turned to the dragon. "My thanks, Rori."

"You're welcome," the dragon said. "I'll be back to report to Prince Dar, and I can renew the scent then."

"Very well, then," Dallandra said. "Maybe we'll have some good news for you by the time you return."

Rori stayed silent, looking off at the distant horizon.

"Is something wrong?" Dallandra said.

"Naught, naught. It's just that at moments I wonder if I do want to be a man again. Wouldn't it be deserting my post?"

"Your what?"

"Because of the Horsekin." Rori swung his head around to look at her. "I can do a fair bit more damage in this form than I could as a single rider, if I'd even be fit enough to fight, that is. Ye gods, I'll be an old man!"

"That's certainly true. But why do you think it's your duty to go on fighting? It's not like there isn't a willing army between us and the Horsekin."

"That's true, too. Oh, I don't know, Dalla! Here, we can talk more later." Rori turned away and waddled off.

"We should talk more now." Dallandra ran after him. "Do you want to be transformed or not? You're asking us to do a huge working—"

"I know." He hesitated, but only for a brief moment. "There's the matter of my son, you see." With a rustle as loud as a storm he began spreading his wings, an enormous stretch of skin and bone that shoved her back and away.

"Your son?" she yelled at the top of her lungs. "What? Rori, wait!"

He bunched his muscles and sprang into the air. The rush of air from his wingbeats knocked her over into the grass—a lot of very soft grass, fortunately. He'd flown off, heading north, by the time that Pir had helped Dallandra pick herself up.

"You bastard!" She shouted it after the dragon.

"Here now!" Pir said. "It be a hard choice for a soul like that to make."

"Oh, I know!" Dallandra said. "But he's still a bastard."

Dallandra returned to camp to find Calonderiel pacing back and forth in front of their tent. A pair of purple gnomes swaggered just behind him, mimicking his every move. When he saw her, he stopped and crossed his arms over his chest with a scowl. The gnomes did the same.

"What is it?" Dallandra said.

"Rori tells me you're going to try to turn him back."

"If he wants us to, yes."

"I don't want you to."

"What? Why not? Because of the Horsekin?"

"Naught of the sort! Don't you remember what happened to Evandar? Working that transformation killed him. I don't want you dead from working it backward or whatever it is you dweomerfolk do with spells."

Astounded, Dallandra could only stare at him. His scowl deepened. With a visible effort he looked away, only to notice the pair of mocking gnomes. When he swore at them, they vanished.

"That's not what killed Evandar, exactly," Dallandra said. "For one thing, he wasn't truly alive."

It was Cal's turn for the astounded stare. "Are you telling me," he said, "that you ran off with a dead—"

"I'm telling you naught of the sort. He was a spirit, not a ghost." She could tell that one of their pointless arguments was beginning to build and decided to end it early. "Cal, I've got to sit down. I'm so exhausted these days because of the baby."

"I know, I'm sorry." He became instantly contrite. "Here, let me pull back the tent flap for you."

He followed her inside and helped her settle herself on their blankets, then knelt beside her on the floor cloth. "I don't care if Evandar was a spirit or a slab of dead mutton," he said, "I don't want you risking your life with some dangerous dweomer working."

Dallandra sighed and tried again. "I never want you to ride to battle, either," she said. "Does that stop you?"

"Well, no." He glanced away. "We've had this argument before, haven't we?"

"Too many times."

"All right, I'll hold my tongue now." He rose, then stood smiling down at her. "You rest. We can argue after the baby's born."

A pair of boots lay on the floor cloth close at hand. Dallandra was tempted to pick one up and throw it at him as he walked away, but she decided that the effort wouldn't be worth the effect.

Valandario was surprised to find how easy it was for her to weep for Javanateriel despite the passage of so many years. She remembered how she'd wept the night of his murder, then realized that after the day of his cremation she'd kept her grief locked inside herself—and her self locked inside the grief. Flooded by old mourning, the remnants of the broken horn washed clean. She wiped her tears away from her face and the pieces of the silver horn and realized that she felt as if she could float away, released from the weight of dead sorrow.

When she inspected the gleaming silver, she saw that the horn had been shaped from thin sheets of beaten metal. The original craftsman had decorated the pieces with delicate lines of engraved knotwork, then soldered them together, finally adding a lipped mouthpiece. The passing of Haen Marn from the world had smashed the horn to pieces, then squashed the pieces together. Now that she'd freed and cleaned them, she needed to get them back together before she could restore any kind of enchantment.

Valandario went from tent to tent of the royal alar to ask about jewelers. Everyone knew someone—someone in Aberwyn, someone riding with another alar, someone who had died a few years back, someone who had a cousin who did silver work, and so on.

"You'd think that there'd be a few craftsmen riding with the prince," Valandario said to Dallandra.

"So you would," Dalla said. "Unfortunately, there's not."

"Though you know, since Haen Marn seems to be linked to the Mountain Folk, perhaps we should try to find a dwarven smith to repair the horn."

"Out here? Where? On the other hand, I just thought of something. Dwarven merchants do come to Cengarn. They might bring a jeweler with them or know of one they trust."

"Very well, I suppose I can wait till we reach it."

"You look disappointed, Val."

"Oddly enough, I am, but I think that's the horn's own feelings affecting me. It wants to be healed. That's the only explanation I can come up with. The horn wants to be healed as soon as possible."

Dallandra considered this remark while Valandario waited. They were sitting in Dallandra's tent, or at least, Val was sitting, decorously cross-legged on a leather cushion. Dallandra half-sat, half-sprawled across a pile of them. Now and then she laid her hands on her swollen stomach as if patting the child within.

"Well," Dalla said at last, "if we only knew what part of the inner planes Haen Marn really belongs to, we could perhaps fix it by dweomer."

"If," Val said. "We don't, however. Not even the spirit of the evocation knew it."

"That, alas, is true. I'll try to think of some way to find out. For now, you might meditate upon it."

In the event, finding the jeweler turned out to be easier than either Dallandra or Valandario anticipated. The route that the royal alar was taking to Cengarn ran west of Pyrdon and led eventually to the trading ground by the Lake of the Leaping Trout. By the time that the alar reached it, a number of Deverry merchants had arrived for the spring horse fairs. A good number of alarli had joined them. This time when Valandario asked around, she found a Westfolk jeweler, a slight man with the longest, most delicate fingers she'd ever seen, and emerald-green eyes that gleamed like gems themselves.

He sighed over the beauty of the pieces, then laid them on a cloth and began to fit them together, a few at a time, his fingers moving like spiders over the silver, until he could tell her that they would form a complete horn except for the mouthpiece, irrevocably broken and deformed.

"I'm not one of the Mountain Folk," he said. "I couldn't have done work like this, but I can repair it. I'll make a new mouthpiece, too, so it'll sound some notes again. Now, I can't guarantee that they'll be the original notes, of course."

Val's heart sank. "Of course," she said, and she managed a smile. "How much will you want for that?"

"Nothing but the Wise One's good wishes."

"Those you'll have, certainly, and my thanks."

As she walked back to her own tent, Val was cursing her ill luck. She should have realized that the sound of the horn might be different once mended. Would it still summon Haen Marn? She could only hope. Perhaps the summoning dweomer lay elsewhere in the horn, she reminded herself. It would be part of her working to find out.

When the jeweler returned the repaired horn, she decided that she'd best pay him something, no matter how he protested. Dweomer workings always require a price. She preferred it to be a gemstone, not some subtle personal sacrifice that would only appear when she least expected it. She reached into her bag of divination gems and pulled out one randomly—a chunk of lapis lazuli that made his eyes grow wide and greedy.

"My thanks." She dropped the chunk into his outstretched palm. "You've done a splendid job."

"My thanks to you, Wise One! This stone will make a splendid brooch to tempt a merchant with."

As the alar made its slow way north, Valandario kept the horn with her at all times. While she was riding, she hung it from a chain around her neck and tucked it inside her tunic. At night it slept on a pillow next to hers. She began to see it in her dreams, and finally it was a dream that gave her the secret of its healing. She saw a dwarven woman holding the horn in her arms and singing a lullaby while she rocked it like a baby.

"Of course!" Val woke suddenly and found herself sitting up in the dawn gloom inside her tent. "It's born of Earth, so I'll ask the Lords of Earth."

That evening, when the alar was making its night camp, Valandario found Dallandra outside her folded tent, waiting for the alar to put it together. Dalla sat slumped on a high pile of cushions, her knees spread, her hands dangling between them.

"You look pale," Val said. "You need to eat and rest."

"Rest, certainly," Dalla said. "I'm not so sure about eating. Did you want to ask me something?"

"I was going to ask you to be the sentinel for a working, but not after seeing you!"

"I'd better not, no. How about Grallezar?"

"Excellent idea!"

Grallezar was not only willing to come along and stand guard, she brought her apprentice with her so that Branna might see a ritual of evocation. The women walked about a mile away into the grassland. In the red-gold light of sunset they found a reasonably flat area where the new grass grew short and even.

As she had before, Valandario cleared her place of working, drew and consecrated a circle, and invoked the light. This time, however, she laid the newly restored silver horn down in the circle's center, then drew a pentagram around it. Once the star burned with blue astral fire, she called upon the Lords of Earth.

From where she stood, facing north, she could look past the fiery pentagram into the gathering twilight. At first she saw only the grass, burgeoning with reddish etheric force, waving gently in the sunset wind. The wind itself streamed blue and silver. The color told her that she was seeing on the etheric. An instant later, she saw a point of light form just inside the circle. The point stretched, became a line, then swelled into a towering pillar of multicolored light, shot through with swirls and rays of russet, olive, and citrine. The tower solidified upon a glittering black base.

"Child of Air, why do you summon us?" The voices came from inside the pillar, but she heard them as thought, not sound, a chorus of voices speaking as one. "Where did you get this talisman you lay before us?"

"It was given to me as a dead and broken thing," Val said aloud. "I have tried to heal it, but I know not how to give it power."

"Do you know from whence it came?"

"It came from Haen Marn."

The voices sighed and chattered. One strong voice, female, sang out from their midst. "You speak the truth," she said. "And it be well for you that you do so."

"Never would I lie to the great Lady of the North upon Earth."

"You know my name, and thus you have the right to summon me. Why do you wish to heal this horn?"

"To bring Haen Marn back to its rightful place. I was told this horn might do so."

"Very well. Lift up the horn."

Valandario picked up the horn and held it out, flat on both palms. Inside the pillar the multicolored lights swirled, brightened, turned into a blaze of colors, as russet as apples in the autumn, as olive as new leaves upon the trees in spring, shot through with the clear citrine of gemstones. The light swelled into a sphere that enveloped Valandario and the horn both. For what seemed a timeless space of time she could see nothing but the dance of colored light.

It vanished, leaving her blind and blinking in an afterglow of gold. When she heard Grallezar shouting the ritual words, "It is finished!" Val stamped three times upon the ground. Slowly her sight eased back to normal. The tower had vanished with the fading of the light. The astral fire had disappeared and taken the etheric silver with it. Night lay heavy on the grasslands. The horn in her hands glowed like a candle lantern.

"Well, well," Grallezar said briskly. "No doubt the Lady did somewhat, I'd say. We'd best consult with Dalla. That bit of silver you hold will light our way back to camp well enough."

Branna was staring at the horn with her mouth open like a fish's gape. She shut it and shook her head.

"I could hear her," she said in a trembling voice. "When she spoke, I could hear her."

"Splendid!" Val said, with a glance at Grallezar. "Your apprentice seems to be doing well."

"I'd say so." Grallezar was suppressing a grin. "But she'd best not be getting above herself. Let's go back now."

By the time they returned, Dallandra had woken from her nap. Valandario found her in her tent, where Calonderiel and Neb were finishing their dinner.

"I could use your advice," Valandario said. "But I don't mean to interrupt."

"I've eaten all I can choke down," Dalla said. "Let's go to your tent. I'd like to see the horn now."

"May I come, too?" Neb got to his feet fast.

Dallandra hesitated. Val shook her head no, ever so slightly.

"Not this time," Dallandra said.

"But Branna was allowed—"

"That doesn't concern you, Neb." Dallandra fixed him with a cold look that silenced him. "Finish your dinner."

"I will, then." Neb sat down opposite Calonderiel, who gave Valandario a broad wink. Fortunately, Neb seemed not to notice.

Valandario and Dallandra went to Val's tent, where Branna and Grallezar were waiting. When Val made a silver dweomer light, Dalla held the horn under it and examined it with a little gasp of surprise.

"It looks new," Dallandra said at last, "and I can feel the dweomer quivering upon it. You've done a splendid job, Val."

"My thanks," Valandario said. "But it wasn't me. The Lady of the North upon Earth did the working. I'm not even sure what she did, but she did seem to want Haen Marn back again."

"May I ask somewhat?" Branna said.

"Of course." Grallezar showed pointed teeth with a grin. "But we may not answer."

"North of Earth," Branna asked. "Does that correspond to Earth of Earth?"

"It does," Grallezar said. "Each direction hath its element, and each element its place."

Branna nodded, thinking this over.

Dallandra handed Valandario the horn. "Have you sounded it?"

"I haven't. Enj is most likely the only person who can blow the summoning. He belongs to the island by blood."

"True, but we should make sure it's not all sour or suchlike."

Val raised the horn to her lips, took a deep breath, and blew. The horn sang with one long note of the purest music, not loud, but so sweet that the four women smiled to hear it. Val started to speak, then realized that the horn was glowing brighter than the dweomer light above them. As the silver gleam swelled, the horn became longer, thinner, but at the same time weightless. It became a tangle of lines of light, wending around on themselves, until Valandario held a ball of blazing white light in her hands. All at once the sphere turned into a long ray of light and shot through the tent like an arrow. Dallandra yelped in surprise, and Branna made a futile grab in the direction of the ray of light just as it slid through the doorway and disappeared into the night outside. The four of them stared at each other until at last Valandario could speak.

"What have I done?" Val said with a little moan. "We'll never get the wretched island back now!"

"You've not done anything I wouldn't have done," Dallandra said, "so don't berate yourself. Didn't I tell you to try it out?"

"I suppose, but—"

"Besides," Grallezar put in, "why be you so sure that this does mean disaster? The horn may well be flown off to its true home. For all we know, this be part of the working."

"For all we know." Val made a sour face in her direction. "Well, I'll hope and pray that you're right."

"That's all we can do," Dallandra said. "But oddly enough, I *feel* right about this. Somewhat's on the move, Val. Don't despair just yet."

In the far-off land of Alban, a howl of wind woke Dougie in the middle of the night. He sat up in bed just as the wind slammed into the side of the house and made it shudder. A flash of lightning lit the room with a blue glow. Thunder roared directly overhead. With a yelp his brothers woke and sat up next to him. Dougie heard his mother scream, and his father's voice, loudly soothing, right through the wall.

"What in God's name?" Gavin said.

"Just a storm," Dougie said, "but a strong one."

For some while the wind howled around the steading. Now and again lightning split the sky and cast an eerie pattern of light through the shutters, banging hard at the loft window, on the opposite wall. Thunder followed, louder at first, then softer as the peak of the storm moved off to the north. Both Gavin and Ian fell asleep once the thunder slacked, but Dougie lay awake, worrying about Berwynna, out on an island with the wind kicking up big waves all around her.

With dawn the rain slacked, and the sky began to clear. When the family gathered around the table to eat breakfast and discuss the storm, Dougie gobbled down a bowl of porridge. He did his chores, then left the steading. Rather than argue about his destination, he told no one that he was going out to Haen Marn.

At the lake, the silver chain hung from its boulder on the shore, but from the chain dangled—nothing. One bent loop of metal marked where the silver horn usually hung. He swore aloud, then squatted down to examine the ground. Not there, either. He straightened up and glanced around, but no glint of silver lay among the scrubby bushes and new grass. Had someone stolen the thing? A cold ripple of fear ran down his back. What if he couldn't reach the island? What if he never saw Berwynna again?

Dougie cupped his hands around his mouth and called out a long halloo. Only the lapping of waves answered him. He tried again, louder. When he finally saw the boat heading out from the pier, his eyes filled with tears of relief. He shook his head hard and wiped them away with the edge of his plaid.

When the boat arrived, Lon greeted him with a bare wave of one hand. Dark pouches under his eyes and a bleary smile marked him as exhausted.

"Up all night, were you?" Dougie said.

Lon merely nodded and handed him the mallet for the gong. Dougie hit it as hard and as fast as he could. He'd never seen so many beasts in the lake; the water roiled and splashed as they rose to the surface, swung their heads this way and that, then dove again to disappear. *Somewhat's frightened them,* Dougie thought. *They're acting like netted fish.*

Berwynna was pacing back and forth at the end of the wooden pier. She looked pale, and her uncombed hair fell untidily around her shoulders. When he caught her hand and kissed it, she smiled, but her eyes showed traces of weeping.

"I'm so glad you're here," she said. "Something peculiar's happening."

"That storm was peculiar enough for me!"

"Beyond that. I can feel some baleful thing in the air. It's all around us."

"Oh, is it now?" Dougie glanced over his shoulder but saw nothing but the lake. "Did you know that someone's stolen the silver horn?"

"I didn't." Her eyes grew wide. "Come up to the manse. We'd best tell Mam that."

Angmar met them at the door of the manse and raised a gentle hand to keep them from entering. "Keep your voices down," she said. "Marnmara's studying the patterns on the walls and can't be disturbed."

Dougie glanced through the open door of the manse. At the far wall Marnmara was standing with Tirn, both of them facing the wall and waving their hands as they pointed to this mark or that. On a table behind them, Evandar's book lay open.

"Dougie," Angmar continued, "you'd best leave us straightaway. I'll tell the boatmen."

"What?" Berwynna clutched his arm with both hands. "Mam, why?"

Angmar gave her daughter a black look. "There's no time to argue," she said, "if Dougie wants to see his mother and clan ever again. The boat—"

"Wait," Dougie broke in. "I shan't stay if you'd rather not have me here, but let me tell you one quick thing. Your silver horn's been stolen. It's not chained to the rock anymore."

Angmar muttered something in a language he didn't understand. "Then it's too late," she said at last. "My heart aches for you, Dougie, truly it does."

"Mam!" Berwynna snapped. "What are you talking about?"

"We're going home," Angmar said, "and Dougie's going with us, whether he wants to go or not."

The light around them suddenly dimmed. Dougie shook his arm free of Berwynna's grasp and spun around to look at the lake. The sunny spring day had vanished. Like a silver bowl, fog arched over loch and island both, a strange swirling fog, touched with pale purples and blues. He saw the boatmen hauling the dragon boat up onto the shore and heard them yelling back and forth in near panic.

"I should go help them," Dougie said.

"It's too dangerous," Angmar said. "You don't truly belong to the island, and it can't protect you. Let's go to Avain's tower. We'll be safer there."

The square stone tower rose gray and menacing over the apple trees. Angmar hurried them inside to an oddly cold room, empty except for the rickety wooden stairs. Marnmara's cats, their ears laid back, their tails bushed, bounded up ahead of them.

Avain met them at the landing by her little chamber. She was abnormally tall, perhaps an inch taller than Dougie, and pudgy, with a big puffy face and a round head crowned with a tangled mass of blonde hair. She kept rising up on her toes and then falling back on her heels while she grinned and clapped her hands. She was repeating a single word over and over, not that Dougie understood it, "Lin, lin, lin."

"What may that mean?" Dougie asked Berwynna.

"Home, home, home," Berwynna said, then began to tremble.

Angmar ushered them into the chamber, where a wooden table stood by the single window. They sat down in the straw on the floor. With a cautious glance at Angmar, Dougie put his arm around Berwynna's shoulders and drew her close, but Angmar never noticed. She was staring at the window. When Dougie followed her glance, all he could see was the mist, swirling outside with a hundred pale colors.

Avain hummed a strange tuneless music under her breath as she sat down at her table and reached for a silver basin. A dribble of water slopped over its edge as she pulled it close. She stared into it for a long time, by Dougie's reckoning, and during that entire long time, nothing seemed to happen, nothing moved, except for the mist outside the window.

Carved deep into Haen Marn's wall, the sigils of the Kings of Aethyr glowed pale lavender. Nearby a peculiar set of marks that Laz had never seen before glimmered turquoise, though flecked with an unpleasant red orange.

"If I only knew what these sigils be—" Mara pointed to the flecked glow.

"It doesn't matter," Laz said. "There's truly naught that we can do, one way or the other. The island will go where it wills to go, and what we want or think is worth the fart of a two-copper pig, no more."

Still, she went on studying the symbols carved into the wall, her eyes narrow as if she could force meaning out of them. In his chair by the window old Otho turned toward her with a scowl.

"We're probably all dead already," he announced. "I can't see one cursed thing out this blasted window but an ugly fog. Hah! It's probably the fog of the Otherlands. I only ever wanted to die in Lin Serr, you know, but I'm not in the least surprised that I won't get to. Whole cursed life's been like that. Bound to have a bad end."

"Otho," Laz said wearily, "we're not dead. I don't know where we're going, but it's not the Otherlands."

"Indeed?" Otho glared at him from under fierce eyebrows. "What makes you so sure we're going anywhere, eh?"

"The way I came here. I know what it feels like to travel between worlds." Laz felt a line of cold sweat run down his back. *I may hate it,* he thought, *but I'll never forget it.*

Otho snorted in loud contempt. Mara laughed aloud, the high-pitched giggle of a terrified girl.

"Come sit down," Laz said to her. "There's naught else you can do but wait."

She hesitated, then followed him to the long table. They sat down on one of the benches, but, Laz noticed, they made sure that their backs were to the window. Otho leaned back in his chair, crossed his arms over his chest, and glared out at nothing. *Are we traveling on one of the Rivers of Time?* Laz wondered, *or are we going through a place where there's no time at all?* A second trickle of fear-sweat joined the first. He leaned back against the table edge, stretched his legs out in front of him, and did his best to appear at ease for Mara's sake.

Although he acted confident around others, much of the time Enj felt like a fool in his belief that some day Haen Marn would return. The entire dwarven community of Lin Serr kept telling him that he was a fool or perhaps even daft. *Maybe they're all right,* he would think, *maybe I'm eating empty hope for a cold dinner.* Yet he couldn't stop himself from hoping, couldn't keep himself away from the place where once the lake and its island had lain. Only one thing remained to mark its former location. On a particular riverbank—no one had ever named it, since only a handful of people knew it existed—stood a boulder of gray granite, roughly half-a-sphere and about four feet at its highest point. Just below that point was a red stain that looked like blood from a distance. Up close, however, it revealed itself to be the much-rusted remains of an iron ring bolted into the rock.

A good many times in the past forty years Enj had returned to that boulder, camped for a few days, and then moved on, heart-struck with disappointment. For this visit, however, he had Rori's news to give him fresh hope. On a fine spring day he hiked up through the budding trees and pale grass along the bank of the river, full and chattering with runoff from the mountain snows. As he came clear of the forest, he saw the boulder in its usual spot, but near the point something winked and gleamed in the bright sun. It shone like silver. He stopped for a moment and took a deep breath. *Don't get your hopes up too high,* he told himself. *There are other things it could be.*

But when he reached the boulder, he saw the silver horn, whole and gleaming, hanging from a bright silver chain, which hung in turn from a polished iron ring. He swung his pack down from his shoulders and took a few steps closer. He was afraid to touch the horn, he realized, lest it prove to be some kind of illusion. He looked upriver but saw only the water winding between the usual pair of low hills, covered with bright new grass. Apparently the Westfolk dweomer had managed to repair the horn but failed to bring back the island.

Oddly enough, it was his disappointment that gave him the courage to pick up the horn. The metal, cool to the touch, weighed like silver in his hand.

"It's solid enough, then," he said aloud.

Without really thinking, he raised it to his lips and blew. A long sweet note echoed off the hills and the silent valley, echoed oddly loudly, he realized, as if a thousand horns were singing out in answer. A mist began to rise from the river, a strange, opalescent mist—just a breath of it upon the water at first, then a few long tendrils reaching for the sky—then a sudden explosion of mist. With a roar, a wall of lavender fog rose up like a breaking wave. Silver lights shone within it as the fog poured up and out, spreading into the windless air, rising so high that it blotted out the sun.

Enj spun around, looking up and around him. The opalescent mist gleamed and shimmered in an enormous dome that covered the valley and the two hills. Suddenly the earth trembled, then shook hard. Enj fell to his knees and threw one arm around the boulder. The shaking stopped, the trembling died away, but slowly. He realized that he was still holding the silver horn.

Sound it!

He was never sure if the voice came from his own mind or out of the mist, but he raised the horn again and blew a long call. As the sound rushed out, the mist receded, winding itself up like a sheet and falling back into the river once again. Something—perhaps a tendril of mist—snatched the horn from his hand. The boulder disappeared, and he fell forward onto the grass. When he sat back up, the sun shone down on a changed valley and winked on the surface of a lake.

Enj staggered to his feet and shaded his eyes with one hand. Sure enough, out in the last of the mist sat the island with its long dock and its tower. He began to laugh, then sobbed with tears running down his face, laughed again and wept again, over and over, until he saw the dragon boat putting out from the dock and heading his way.

The dragon prow dipped and swayed as the boat crossed the loch, but near the shore the oarsmen began to back water. Enj saw Lon run to the bow. The boatman shaded his eyes with one hand whilst he peered at the shore.

"Enj!" he called out. "We're home, lads! It's Enj!"

Lon began weeping, but the rowers all cheered as they edged the boat closer in. Holding his pack above his head, Enj waded out. Lon took the pack from him, then helped him clamber aboard.

"Oh, well-met, lad!" Lon said, snuffling. "Well-met, indeed!"

"And the same to you!" Enj said. "Here, I'd best take a turn at that gong."

On the pier two women were waiting for the boat to dock. His mother Enj recognized immediately, a fair bit grayer than she'd been before, but her posture still was straight and strong. Before the boatmen had finished tying up the dragon boat, Enj leaped onto the pier and ran to her, laughing. She threw herself into his arms. They clung together, weeping and laughing in turns, until Angmar at last pulled away.

"This be one of your sisters," she said, sniffing back tears, "Berwynna, my younger twin."

The young woman came forward and smiled at him, a pretty lass, as he might have expected of Rhodry's daughter, with Rhodry's raven-dark hair, but with their mother's strength in her cornflower-blue eyes.

"And a well-met to you, then, Sister," Enj said. "It gladdens my heart to meet you at last."

"And mine to meet you." Berwynna dropped him a curtsy. "Oft-times Mam did speak of you, but I wondered if ever we would meet."

"Well, now we have." Enj glanced around. "I take it our other sister's up in the manse?"

"She is, and Mara's her name." Angmar slipped her arm through his and gave him a significant look. "Marnmara, that be."

The Lady of the Isle reborn, then! Enj wondered exactly how to greet a grandmother who was now your younger sister, then decided that questions of courtesy didn't truly matter on a day as happy as this one. Arm in arm, they walked up to the manse with Berwynna trailing after.

In the great hall the others waited for them—Mic, old Otho, Lonna, a lass so like Berwynna that Enj knew she must be his other sister, and two young men, red-haired Dougie, enormously tall, and tattooed Tirn with his scarred and malformed hands. As the introductions went round, Lonna and Mic both wept.

"Ye gods!" Otho snarled. "There's no need for everyone to carry on so! For all we know this wretched island's got some evil plan in mind."

"Ah, Otho!" Enj said. "I take it your sunny mood means you're glad to be home."

Otho, a frail whitebeard now, shook a feeble fist in his direction, then suddenly smiled. Lonna wiped her eyes on the hem of her apron, and Berwynna took her handkerchief out of her kirtle.

"Here, Uncle Mic," she said.

Mic snuffled, smiled at her, and wiped his eyes vigorously.

"Dougie, well met to you, too," Enj said.

Dougie gave him a blank look, then shrugged, holding up empty palms.

"He's deaf?" Enj murmured to Berwynna.

"No!" She laughed at him. "He doesn't speak Dwarvish, and he doesn't know much Deverrian, either, that's all. I'll translate for him."

"Tirn does speak Deverrian, though," Marnmara said, "and Dougie had best learn more of it, so I say we all use it this day."

"I agree, but first," Enj spoke in Dwarvish, "since the outlanders can't understand us, what's all this about 'uncle' Mic?"

"He's Mother's half brother," Berwynna said. "Didn't you know?"

Enj turned to Mic in some exasperation.

"I didn't want to tell you when I was here before," Mic said, "because Rhodry Maelwaedd was with us at the time, and it was none of his affair—"

"Hah!" Otho broke in. "I should think not, him a cursed elf and all!"

Everyone laughed, perhaps at the predictability of the insult, perhaps in general good feeling. At length everyone sat down at the long head table, and Lonna and Berwynna bustled off to bring tankards and flagons of ale. Enj sat at Angmar's right hand, and Marnmara took the seat to her left. The others sat randomly toward the far end, though Enj noticed Dougie keeping the seat next to him clear. While Berwynna poured ale for the men, Enj leaned close to his mother.

"I see the twins favor Rhodry Maelwaedd mightily," Enj said, too softly for the lasses to hear, "but they look too young to be his children."

"What? Of course they be his!" Angmar spoke normally. "How long think you that we've been gone in Alban?"

"More than forty years, Mam, getting on to fifty, truly."

"Ye gods!" Mic put in. "To us it seemed a bare seventeen years."

Enj shook his head to show his bafflement. He shouldn't be surprised by anything that happened on or to Haen Marn, he supposed.

"Time be like water," Marnmara leaned forward into the conversation. "Rivers flow at many different speeds."

This pronouncement struck Enj as more a riddle than an explanation. He had a long swallow of ale to help clear his mind. Haen Marn's good dark brew, and the sight of the great hall around him—he'd worry about the Rivers of Time some other day, he decided, and enjoy this one.

"It's been so long here, then," Angmar said suddenly. "Ai! I doubt me if my Rhodry still walks the earth."

"Um, well." Enj hesitated, then decided that blurting the news out would be best. "He does, Mam, but not as you remember him. He ran afoul of great dweomer, and it turned him into a dragon."

Angmar stared, her mouth half-open. Berwynna translated for Dougie, who made a strange gesture with one hand, describing what appeared to be a cross in midair in front of him. Marnmara, however, nodded as if she were merely thinking things over.

"Not the silver wyrm?" Tirn leaned forward as if to ensure that he'd heard a-right.

"The very one," Enj said. "Mam, my heart aches for you. He's been changed into a dragon, a real dragon, huge, wings, the lot. But there's hope. Some of the Westfolk dweomerworkers are trying to turn him back, but it seems to be a blasted hard job."

"Mayhap I can help them," Marnmara said. "After all, he be my father."

Angmar started to speak, then let out a sigh that carried half the woe in the world. She leaned her head against the back of her chair.

"Mam?" Enj said in Dwarvish. "Are you going to faint?"

Angmar shook her head no. Her eyes gazed far across the room and her lips moved briefly, as if in prayer. Marnmara got to her feet.

"Mam, Mam!" she said. "The shock's been too much for you, hasn't it? Here, Dougie, help me! Let's get her up to her chamber."

The Albanwr, a giant by Enj's standards, rose and joined her. He easily picked up the exhausted Angmar and carried her away up the stairs with her two daughters trailing along behind. The men left behind merely looked at one another for a long space of time; then Mic broke the spell by burying his nose in his tankard and drinking deep.

"Goes to show," Otho snarled. "This is what happens when you have dealings with a wretched elf. Turning into dragons! Hah!"

"Now, now," Enj said, "it's not somewhat that happens every day. He's the only man of the Westfolk I ever heard of who grew wings."

"That's exactly what I mean." Otho snorted again. "You never know what they'll do if they get some crazed thought in their minds."

Enj decided that arguing the point was hopeless. Fortunately, Tirn changed the subject.

"The silver wyrm hates me," Tirn remarked. "And I don't even know why. Are you saying that he's got Westfolk blood in his veins?"

"Cursed deep in them, apparently," Mic said. "With all that dragon covering them."

"True spoken." Tirn flashed him a grin. "But I'd best be gone ere he arrives here."

"Well, I don't know if or when he'll arrive," Enj said. "There's more trouble brewing with the Horsekin, you see, off to the east of Dwarveholt. He's sworn to help protect the border."

"Yet more war?" Tirn's grin disappeared.

"Mayhap. No one's sure if these raiders are a feint or a sign of worse to come."

"I see. I was hoping that the burning of Zakh Gral would put an end to it, but obviously I was being an optimistic fool. Enj, I have Gel da'Thae blood, but truly, I hope the Deverry men beat the Horsekin back." Tirn spoke quietly but firmly. "They represent the worst of my kind."

"So we've learned," Enj said. "Unfortunately."

In her usual brisk way, Marnmara took charge of her mother. She helped her lie down on her bed, then opened the windows of the bedchamber to let in fresh air and sunlight.

"I'll go get some herbs," Marnmara said. "Dougie, you may go. Wynni, stay here until I get back!"

"As if I'd leave!" Berwynna said.

Marnmara bustled out as if she hadn't heard her sister. Dougie gave Berwynna a comforting pat on the shoulder, then left the chamber. Berwynna sat down next to her mother and clasped Angmar's hand in both of hers. Angmar sighed and lay limply, her eyes half-closed.

"I've had many a hard slap in my life from the Fates," Angmar whispered in Dwarvish, "but this has to be the cruelest. I swear, Wynni, it would have been easier to hear that your father was dead than this."

"Well, maybe those dweomerworkers can turn him back." Berwynna did her best to sound optimistic. "After all, if magic made him a dragon, it should be able to unmake him. Shouldn't it?"

"I've no idea, none." Angmar let her eyes close, then opened them again. "My poor darlings! It must be just as hard on you."

"Not truly. We never knew him like you did. Don't vex your heart about us, Mam. You've got enough grief to bear as it is."

"My thanks."

"Besides, in a way it's rather splendid, thinking I have a dragon for a father. Do you think mayhap he was always a dragon and could just take human form? If that's so, then maybe he can change himself back and be with you again."

"Wynni!" Marnmara came striding into the chamber, her arms

full of sacks and supplies. "Don't prattle! You'll only upset her more."

"Oh, my loves!" Angmar said. "Please, not another of your squabbles!"

For her mother's sake, and hers alone, Berwynna held her tongue, even when Marnmara smirked at her—at least, she took her sister's smile as a smirk, not a conciliation. Still, her thoughts were her own, and she found herself thinking about the strange book that Dougie had brought to Haen Marn. She'd heard Tirn tell Mara that it seemed to have somewhat to do with dragons. *What if there's a spell in it?* She'd heard them mention dweomer, too.

"I'll brew you up a restorative," Marnmara said to Angmar.

"My thanks," Angmar said, "but I doubt me if aught will help. My time must be upon me. There's not much reason left to me to live, now that we're home, and I know that I'll never see your father again. At least you children will have your proper place and your proper destiny now."

"Don't talk like that, Mam, please?" Berwynna said. "Enj thought the Westfolk could help. Who are the Westfolk, anyway?"

"Ask Enj," Angmar said. "I'm so weary in my very soul, and there's somewhat important I needs must tell Marnmara. Help me sit up, Wynni."

Berwynna piled pillows between Angmar and the bedstead, then helped her mother lounge comfortably against them. At the hearth Marnmara was lighting a small fire. Once it caught, she placed an iron kettle of water next to the flames to heat.

"Mam?" Marnmara turned around to face the bed. "You're not about to die. I'd know it if you were, and you're not, so please don't talk about dying."

"I know your heart must ache, though," Berwynna said. "Mine would in your place."

Angmar smiled, but she looked only at Marnmara. "Come here, child, and listen."

With a backward glance at the kettle, Marnmara walked over.

"Now that we're home," Angmar began, "I shall tell you an important thing. There was no use in worrying you with it when we were so far away. I've told you many a time that you were born to be the Lady of this isle, though I doubt me if you know all of what it means. The Lady before you did bear no daughter to take her place when her time came upon her, only a son, and him I did marry. But our firstborn daughter was poor little Avain, and never could she take on such a task. Then my husband died. Your father found me, or perhaps the gods sent him. Either way, at last the isle had its trueborn Lady once again."

What about me? Berwynna thought. *I suppose I'm just here by chance or such, for all they care!*

"It were a grave thing if the isle should have no Lady," Angmar went on. "So one day you'll have to marry in your turn, that you may mother a daughter."

"But I don't want to!" Marnmara laid a hand over her mouth.

"That matters not," Angmar said. "You'll have to marry a man of the Mountain Folk, not merely any man. That's the rule of the isle, that the Lady must marry a Man of Earth and bear him children. Had I been the true Lady, I never could have taken your father to my bed, but I wasn't, and the times were desperate."

Marnmara had gone pale. She lowered the hand from her mouth, looked at her mother for a long moment, then got up with a toss of her head. She hurried back to the hearth and knelt down to add herbs to the water in the iron kettle. *We're home,* Berwynna thought, *so maybe I can marry Dougie now, since I obviously don't matter to the stupid island.* She was about to ask her mother when Marnmara left the hearth and rejoined them.

"I don't want to marry," Marnmara said. "Surely I should be able to adopt a girl child instead."

"You most certainly can't." Angmar sat up a little straighter. "Wynni, run along now. Go ask Enj your questions, because truly, you must have many of them."

Berwynna considered protesting, but her mother and sister were glaring at each other in a way she recognized all too well. *They'll argue the whole wretched afternoon,* she thought. With a sigh she left the chamber and went downstairs. After all, she reminded herself, she had a brother to get to know, an unexpected gift from the gods.

Fortunately Enj considered her a gift, as well. He was more than glad to answer her questions, explaining who the Westfolk were, and the Horsekin, recounting the story of how her father had been turned into a dragon in the far-off city of Cerr Cawnen in order to save his life after a traitorous woman had wounded him to the point of death. Tirn talked as well, telling her of the recent wars between his civilized folk and the wild Horsekin of the far north.

Berwynna did her best to divert some of this flood of information Dougie's way, translating when she could, explaining strange names when she couldn't. He listened, but his stunned eyes and slack mouth revealed a shock almost as great as her mother's. Finally he roused himself sufficiently to ask a question, which she translated for him.

"This sorcerer who turned my father into a dragon?" Berwynna asked Enj. "Was his name Evandar?"

"It was indeed," Enj said. "Fancy our Albanwr knowing that!"

At the news Dougie groaned and buried his face in both huge hands. "I might have known," he said to her. "Truly, I might have known."

Not long after Angmar and Marnmara came downstairs. Angmar looked much restored, but Berwynna was pleased to notice that Marnmara's usual composure had disappeared. Lady of the Isle or not, she kicked a chair out of her way as she passed it, yelled at her cats to get off the table where they were lounging, and strode out of the great hall without looking anyone's way. Tirn got up and followed her out with the cats trailing after. *What's this?* Berwynna thought. *Don't tell me she's got an admirer in that poor beggar of a man! Huh! Serve her right!*

Angmar sat down in her usual chair at the head of the table and smiled at everyone. "Do forgive me my fit," she said in Deverrian. "It were but the surprise."

"No doubt, Mam," Enj said. "I doubt me if anyone here holds it to your shame."

"My thanks. Well, tonight we shall have a feast," Angmar went on, "to celebrate our homecoming, like. Wynni, if you'd lend your aid to Lonna, there be that haunch of beef hanging in the kitchen hut that a farmer did give our Marnmara. It be the last Alban beef we shall taste, so let us roast it now." Her smile suddenly darkened, and she spoke to Dougie in his own language. "I do apologize again, lad, for not forestalling you in time. My heart aches for your mother."

"Mine, too," Dougie said. "No doubt she'll know what happened to me when she hears that the island's gone."

"It will be a bitter hearing." Angmar considered for a moment. "Maybe one of the Westfolk sorcerers can find a way for you to return home."

"Should I want to go." Dougie laid his hand over Berwynna's. "My mother has other sons and daughters."

"I know, but it be perilous here for you." Angmar hesitated, then shrugged. "Marnmara can perhaps explain it." She glanced Berwynna's way. "You'd best set that beef to roasting soon."

Berwynna choked back an angry reply and got up. She curtsied to her mother, then stalked out of the great hall.

Once Berwynna got the beef salted and roasting over the hearth fire in the great hall, the boatmen came in to turn the spit, spelling each other at regular intervals. Berwynna and Lonna went back to the kitchen hut. They made a salad of herbs and greens to go with the beef, then brought out the day's bread. Lonna had started the dough in Alban, and now they were baking it in the home country—the thought made Berwynna a bit dizzy as she considered it.

"Lonna," she said, "what do folk call this country?"

"The Roof of the World," the old woman answered. "We be high in the mountains, lass. Now, I know not who owns the land, like. No one, I'd say. But if anyone does, then it belongs to Dwarveholt and the city of Lin Serr."

"A city? Is it as big as Din Edin?"

"Bigger, no doubt. Oh, it be a fine place, all made of stone. Mayhap one day you'll see it." Lonna paused to wipe her hands on her apron. "Anything might happen now, since we be home."

Once the loaves were baking in the stone oven, Berwynna left Lonna to tend them and went back to the great hall, perfumed with the scent of roasting meat. At the table Enj was telling their mother some long complicated story about the city of Lin Serr. Tirn had come back inside and now sat beside Mic to listen, but Otho had fallen asleep in his cushioned chair. Berwynna sat down next to Dougie.

"Did my sister ever come back inside?" she said.

"She didn't," Dougie dropped his voice to a whisper. "Tirn came creeping back in not long after you left, and he looked like a whipped hound." He let his voice return to normal. "It wouldn't hurt your sister to give you some help with all that kitchen work."

"I've often had the same thought, strangely enough."

"Well, here, when it's time to serve, let me help. I don't need to sit here like a lump on a log, and me not understanding a word of what your brother's saying anyway."

"That would gladden my heart, and while we work, I can teach you a bit more about the language we speak."

"I'd best learn it." Dougie gave her a grin. "I'm going to be here for the rest of my life."

Berwynna smiled in return, but her mother's words hung over them like a sword. What if he did come to grief, now that they'd come into this strange country her mother called home? All through that evening, during her work in the kitchen and the feast that followed, she did her best to forget that question. Yet she was always aware of him, first helping her in the kitchen, then sitting close at dinner.

"Your mother's talking up a storm with your brother," Dougie said, then slipped one arm around her waist.

With his free hand he fed her tidbits from their trencher as if she'd been his wife, and when she took a choice bit of meat from his fingers, she would smile and at times, when her mother looked the other way, lick them. His smiles grew ever softer, ever warmer. Berwynna began to feel a languid sort of warmth herself, as if she'd downed a double tankard of the strongest ale ever brewed.

At the meal's end Enj announced that Berwynna had done enough hard work for the day. "You've shamed us all, Dougie," he said. "Come now, Mic, you and I can clean up the mess."

"I do love having a brother!" Berwynna called out. "My thanks!"

When the men began to clear the table, Angmar bade everyone a good night and went upstairs to bed. Berwynna and Dougie made a grateful escape to the cool night air outside. As soon as they were well away from the great hall, Dougie caught her by the shoulders and kissed her, a long lingering kiss.

"Let's find somewhere to sit down," she said. "You'll break your back, bending over like this."

"Ever the practical lass!" he said with a soft laugh. "Splendid idea!"

"I've got an even better one." Berwynna looked up at the manse and pointed to a window, glowing with candlelight. "That's Mam's chamber window."

As they watched, the light went out.

"She'll be asleep soon." Berwynna dropped her voice to a whisper. "If we're careful and quiet, we could go up the back stairs and go to your chamber."

"I like that one even better." He paused to take another kiss. "Quiet, it is!"

Laz woke in the middle of the night from dreams of sorcery so vivid that he wept, thinking of how much he'd lost. He sat up and wiped his moist eyes on the edge of his blanket. Dweomer lay thick all around him on the island, but he himself could do nothing—or so he thought, wrapped in self-pity. Yet something about the dream nagged at him, a brief image of a book, open to a page of Gel da'Thae script, his book, left behind with Sidro here in this familiar world. Perhaps his power lay waiting for him, too, now that he'd returned to his proper place.

You could at least try, he told himself, *not the raven, perhaps, something simpler, a divination, mayhap*. He got up, pawed through his heap of clothing with his mangled hands, and found the black crystal. In the darkness of his chamber, he could see nothing in the gem or elsewhere, for that matter. Without thinking he summoned the Wildfolk of Aethyr. Although snapping his fingers lay beyond him, he clapped his hands together. A silvery dweomer light bloomed in the air above his bed.

"Ye gods!" He wanted to throw back his head and howl with joy, but regard for the sleep of the house stopped him. He contented himself with grinning.

When he looked into the black stone, he saw only darkness, though here and there the dark seemed to be moving. Water, most likely, and if so, the white crystal still lay at the bottom of the lake. When he placed his scarred palms on either side of the crystal, he felt a quiver of force that might have signified some sort of link between the pair.

"There are too many beasts in this lake for anyone to try diving for your twin," Laz said aloud.

The crystal's emanation never changed. He set it aside, then considered his dweomer light, the visible sign that once again, he could work magic. He basked in its glow for some long while before he dismissed the Wildfolk and allowed the light to fade. By then he felt far too excited to sleep.

When he went to the window and looked up, he could see by the wheel of the stars that dawn lay close at hand. He dressed, then made his way downstairs and through the dark and silent great hall. Outside, the stars gave just enough light for him to pick his way down to the lakeshore. Slow waves lapped onto the graveled shore with a pleasant sound, and the fresh breeze smelled of spring and growing things. He breathed deeply and smiled, telling himself that yes, he was still a sorcerer.

Footsteps crunched on the path behind him. He spun around and saw a slight figure walking toward him. Cats darted around her.

"Mara?" he said.

"It be so," she said in her odd dialect of Deverrian. "You did rise early, Tirn."

"So did you."

She laughed and came to stand beside him. "Be it that you feel the difference in this world?" she said. "I do feel power flowing all around us."

"I do as well, most certainly. What about you? You told me that your dweomer might blossom here."

"It has." She sounded as exultant as he felt. "Already have I learned new things."

He smiled, waited, but she said nothing more, merely turned away to look out over the lake.

"I'd not pry into your secrets," Laz said finally.

"My apologies. I did but wonder if you knew how the two worlds differ."

"Do you remember what I told you about the etheric plane?"

"I do."

"Well, here the etheric flows freely into and out of the physical plane, while back in Alban, there was a rift between them, a chasm is probably the better word. If we can't draw upon the etheric, then we can't work dweomer."

"I do understand now. It gladdens my heart that we're back."

"Mine, too."

In the east a thin sliver of gray appeared, the herald of the sun. Seeing the light, knowing that it shone upon his homeland, filled Laz with such good cheer that he held out his arms to the silver dawn and chanted the first few words of an ancient Gel da'Thae prayer.

"Be that your native tongue?" Mara said.

"It is." He let his arms drop to his side. "Welcome, O light of truth that shines upon our land. That's how it begins."

"Lovely, that."

By then the sky had lightened enough for him to see her smiling at him. Perhaps it was the mention of truth, but Laz felt an odd sensation, something he'd never felt before. At last he deciphered it. He felt dishonorable, that he'd lie to someone who had healed him.

"There's somewhat I have to tell you," Laz began. "About my name. It's not truly Tirn, you see. That's a name I've used, but the name my mother gave me was Laz Moj. When your boatmen fished me out of the loch, I was frightened. I didn't want them to know I'm Gel da'Thae, because I thought they might throw me back again to drown."

"I do understand such a fear."

"My thanks, but truly, it weighs upon my heart that I deceived you."

"You have my thanks, as well, for that truth. I did wonder about your name, truly, because I did see somewhat of the liar about you."

Laz winced, and she laughed at him.

"Do let us go inside," she said. "There be a need on me to see how my mam does fare, and a need on you to tell the others the truth about your name."

Laz winced again at the thought of standing up at breakfast and admitting he'd lied—another new sensation, as he thought about it.

It had never bothered him before. *I've changed here,* he thought. *Thank all the gods I'll be leaving soon!*

As soon as the sun rose, Berwynna woke. She grabbed her clothing from the floor and crept out of Dougie's chamber before anyone could find her there. Once she'd gained the safety of her own chamber, she got into her bed. She only meant to rumple her blankets and pillow as if she'd slept there, but in the familiar comfort, after her tiring night, she fell asleep almost immediately.

When she woke again, bright sunlight filled the room. Her mother was standing at the foot of the bed.

"Hadn't you best get up?" Angmar said. "The sun's well on its way to noon."

Berwynna sat up and yawned. "My apologies," she said. "I suppose everyone's waiting for me to serve their breakfast."

"No, I did it."

"Oh, Mam! You shouldn't have had to do that. Why couldn't Mara take a turn?"

"Because she's the Lady of the Isle." Angmar spoke solemnly. "Never forget that, love. Your sister was born to be the Lady of the Isle."

And I suppose the rest of us are worthless, especially me, but Berwynna kept that thought to herself. Aloud she said, "Very well, Mam. I will."

"You missed the big announcement, too," Angmar went on. "I told you that I didn't trust Tirn. Well, it turns out that he was lying about his name. He admitted it at breakfast. His real name is Laz, he tells us now."

"Huh! Do you think that's the truth?"

"I don't know." Angmar smiled at her. "We'll have to wait and see."

Berwynna dressed, then went downstairs to the great hall. Angmar had saved her a bowl of porridge and a thick slice of bread and butter. Although the great hall was otherwise empty when Berwynna sat down to eat, Enj and Mic came strolling in not long after and joined her and Angmar at table.

"Ah, it's good to be home!" Enj said in Dwarvish.

"And it's truly good to see you here," Angmar said. "I've been vexing myself for many a long year now, wondering if you fared well."

"Well enough, I suppose. Soon I'll have to leave, though. I made Rori a promise on the night that the island disappeared, that I'd come find him and tell him if it should return when he was elsewhere."

"Was that before he became a dragon?" Berwynna put in.

"It was." Enj glanced at Angmar. "He was heartbroken, Mam, and truly, he still is. I was thinking of leaving on the morrow."

"What?" Angmar snapped. "How can you leave so soon? I've barely gotten a chance to talk with you."

"Well, Mam, I'm not rejoicing at leaving the isle, either," Enj said. "But I thought I should, for your sake."

"To find Rhodry for my sake, you mean?" Angmar leaned back in her chair and rested her head against it. Berwynna feared that her mother would weep, but Angmar merely sighed.

"Would you rather I stayed a while?" Enj asked.

"I would," Angmar said. "Who knows where the silver wyrm's flown to?"

Enj got up and stood beside her chair. He caught her hands in his with a gentle squeeze. "Mam, I'll stay till you give me leave to go."

"My thanks." Angmar spoke so softly that Berwynna had to lean forward to hear her. "It won't be long, I promise you. But some few days, mayhap."

Good! Berwynna thought. *That gives me time to plan my escape.* What if she were the one to find her father? What would her mother think of her then? The thought filled her with a secret delight.

"I'll be leaving with you," Mic said, "I've promised Uncle Otho that I'll take him home to Lin Serr. I've got kin in the city, too, that I'm longing to see. Ye gods, they must have given me up for dead years ago."

"Well, yes," Enj said. "You did vanish in the middle of a war, so it was an easy enough mistake to make."

"I can't argue," Mic said, "I just hope they'll be glad to see me again."

"Do you truly think they wouldn't?" Enj laughed at him.

"Um, perhaps I'm being a bit dense," Mic said. "I'll hire Dougie again to come with us, since the poor lad's stuck here. He was my bodyguard in Alban, when I went to trade. Uncle Otho taught me the jeweler's craft, you see."

"With what?"

"He always carries his tools, or did, I should say. They're mine now. Your mother had some silver coins, and we had those gems we'd brought as the price of your assuming Otho's debts, and that gave us our start."

"Very good, and very clever!" Enj nodded his approval. "So, we'll need a couple of boats. Do you think the island will part with its coracles?"

"You'll have to ask Marnmara about that," Angmar said. "I'm not sure where she is."

"I'll look for her, Mam." Berwynna rose and curtsied to her mother. "I need to get myself out to the kitchen, anyway. Lonna will have the next batch of bread ready for the oven by now."

"Please do, child, and my thanks."

Berwynna walked to the door and saw Marnmara come hurrying up the path. Berwynna stepped outside to speak with her.

"I gather Mam wants to see me," Marnmara said. "Well, doesn't she?"

"Uh, yes, but how did—"

"I had one of my special moments. They seem to come more often here." Marnmara smirked at her, then hurried past to go inside.

There were times when Berwynna wondered if she hated her sister, and this was one of them. She stuck out her tongue at Marnmara's retreating back, then stalked off to the kitchen hut to start her day's work.

Lonna had warmed to Dougie ever since he'd started helping them in the kitchen. Berwynna was shaping loaves when he came in to rake the embers out of the stone oven. Lonna mumbled something about well water and ambled outside to leave them alone.

"Dougie," Berwynna said. "I'm going to go with Enj when he leaves. I want to find my father."

"Then I'd best go with you, hadn't I?" Dougie glanced at her over his shoulder and smiled. "With the way the landscape flies around these days, I'm not letting you out of my sight."

"I was hoping you'd say that."

They shared a laugh. Berwynna slapped two loaves onto the big wooden paddle. He opened the door to let her slide them into the hot oven, then closed the door while she got two more loaves onto the paddle. Once they were in, he shut the door tight to keep in the heat. Since the oven would only hold four loaves, she punched down the rest of the dough. It would rise while waiting its turn.

They walked outside to the cooler air away from the hot stones. Berwynna wiped the sweat from her face.

"The thing is," she said, "we'll have to plan my escape. Uncle Mic wants you to come along, but I'll have to sneak away."

"I doubt if your mam would let you go." Dougie looked suddenly troubled. "Mayhap you should just stay here. I'd hate to add to Angmar's heartache—"

"Oh, and why would she miss me, except in the kitchen? It's Mara this and Mara that, never me, and I'm sick of it, Dougie! If I can find my father, maybe then Mam will think of me as somewhat more than a servant."

"Here, I'm sure she does just that already."

"I'm not." Berwynna felt tears gather in her throat and choked them down. "I'll wager she doesn't even realize I'm gone at first."

"Oh, come now! Of course she will. And how will she feel when she realizes you're gone? She won't even know where you are."

"Yes, she will. Avain will tell her."

"You're going to tell Avain before you go?"

"I'll make sure she knows where I am." Berwynna consoled herself with the thought that she wasn't precisely lying, since Avain would doubtless be able to see her and Enj both in the water of her silver scrying basin. "And she'll tell Mam everything."

Dougie raised a skeptical eyebrow, but she ignored his doubts.

When the bread had finished baking, Dougie stoked up the fire again. While the oven heated in readiness for the next four loaves, Berwynna went inside the manse to ask her mother about serving the leftover beef for dinner. Angmar and Enj were sitting together at a window on the far side of the great hall. Laz and Mara were studying the book together at the table. As she passed, Laz was just pointing out a word. Berwynna lingered to listen.

"It finally dawned on me," he was saying, "that this name, Eh-vay-an-dare-ree, must be Evandar, or Vandar, as my people call him. Dougie knows the name, and I heard him mention it."

"What does the 'ree' at the end mean?" Mara said.

"It means he did somewhat or other. An agentive, it's called. I wish I'd learned more of the Ancients' language."

"So do I." Mara suddenly turned round in her chair. "Wynni, don't eavesdrop! It's so rude."

"Here, here!" Laz said. "There's no harm in her listening. I think me this book concerns everyone on the island." He lowered his voice. "And someone off it, too, mayhap. One word I do know is that for 'dragon,' and another is 'dweomer,' and both are repeated all through the book. It may have somewhat to do with your father and how he got to be the way he is."

"Do you think it might tell how to turn him back?" Berwynna said.

"Hush!" Laz held up one hand. "Since I can't really read the cursed thing, I don't know that or anything else for certain. I don't want to give your mother false hopes. Understand?"

"Of course! I shan't say a word to her." Berwynna glanced toward the window, but her mother was safely engrossed in conversation with her long-lost son.

Over the next pair of days, Berwynna spent her time cooking flatbread, cutting and wrapping cheese, and smoking dried meat, provisions that were ostensibly for the men when they left. She included extra for herself. In among the packed gear and provisions, she secreted the things she'd need for the journey.

On a sunny morning, when the wind had dropped and the lake stretched out clear as glass around the island, the boatmen brought the coracles out and tied them to the pier. Berwynna and Dougie loaded them while Enj and Mic discussed the route ahead. As usual, Berwynna told Dougie what they were saying.

"We need to get to the river mouth," Enj said, pointing south. "The problem is the beasts in the lake."

"Lon gave me a spare gong," Mic said, "but he only has one."

"I can yell a battle cry." Dougie took a deep breath and let out a howl that made Berwynna's ears ring. "I'll follow you in the second boat safely enough."

"No doubt." Enj shook his head as if clearing the last of the war cry out of his ears. "On a hot day like this, they'll be sluggish anyway."

As Berwynna was leaving the manse with the last pack of supplies, she noticed that the apple trees, rather than being thick with blossoms, showed little buds and the beginnings of green leaves. She stood staring at them until she heard someone walking up the graveled path: Marnmara, followed by a pair of brindled cats.

"What's this?" Berwynna pointed at the blossoms. "I never knew that time could run backward."

"It can't." Mara glanced at the buds, then shook her head in amazement. "I suppose in some ways this is a different island, that's all."

"That's *all*, you say?"

"Wynni, if I knew more I'd tell you more! Haen Marn turns out to be a stranger place than we ever realized back in Alban."

"What? But you're the Lady of the Isle. Aren't you supposed to know every little thing about it?"

"Oh, don't be so nasty!"

Marnmara jutted her chin into the air and stalked into the manse. With a stamp of her foot, Berwynna turned and hurried toward the boathouse.

On the way she passed a little bench among the trees where Mara and Laz often sat. Apparently they'd been studying the book there, because it lay open on top of its oiled leather wrappings. *How odd of them to just leave it!* she thought. Normally Mara guarded it like a dragon with its hoard. Berwynna knew that she should take it back to the manse, but the coracles would be leaving, and she refused to get left behind just because Mara had been so careless. *It would serve her right if I just took it.* It seemed to her that she heard this thought as someone else's voice.

Berwynna glanced around—no sign of Laz or Mara. If that book did contain the spell to restore her father, and if she found him, and if the mysterious Westfolk could work the spell—she could imagine how happy her mother would be, how glad that she had two daughters, not merely one.

The impulse hit her too hard to resist. She put down the slab of flatbread she'd been carrying, then wrapped the book carefully in its coverings. When she put the other packet on top of it, no one could have seen the difference twixt the two. She trotted off to the pier, where the coracles were waiting.

With Mic and Otho as passengers, Enj shoved off first in the lead, larger coracle. The sound of the gong and their shouts drifted back across the water. Berwynna handed Dougie the last packet of food, then sat down on the edge of the pier. She leaned over and gave Dougie a kiss, as if saying farewell.

"The boatmen are all watching Enj," Dougie whispered. "Now!"

Berwynna slid off the pier. He caught her by the waist. Without a rock of the boat his strong arms lowered her into the coracle, then he grabbed the paddle and shoved off from the piling. Her heart was pounding, and she bent over low in the hopes of blending unseen with the bundles and blankets. She hid the book safely among the bedding. Yelling his war cry at the top of his lungs, Dougie began paddling fast, heading after Enj and Mic. No one called out in alarm. The sun was hot on her back, and bending over was beginning to make her muscles ache. Berwynna risked a cautious glance back at the island, disappearing fast across the lake.

Behind them something broke water, a narrow head, a long neck, a pair of black greedy little eyes. Berwynna sat up and screamed out a curse, kept screaming and cursing while Dougie yelled and howled at the top of his lungs. The gong in the first boat sounded louder—Enj had turned back to help drive the creature off. The beast hesitated, then turned slowly away. For a few yards it paddled on the surface, then dove with a swell of ripples that bobbed the coracle. Both boats swung round and headed for the river mouth as fast as their passengers could paddle. With a jerk and a pull the current caught them and swept them onto the river and safety.

"That was close!" Dougie called out.

"Too close, truly!" Berwynna said.

Ahead of them Mic looked back, then began yelling and pointing. Berwynna glanced back, saw nothing following them, and realized that Mic was pointing at her. With a laugh she waved to him.

Her adventure had begun, and with the river carrying them fast along, no one could send her back now.

"I've been thinking," Laz said. "Do you remember what I told you about the Wildfolk's true existence?"

"Of course." Mara gave him one of her small, secretive smiles. "That they be in truth but patterns of force on the inner planes."

"Exactly. Now, when the Wildfolk appear here, they have weight and definite form, they can hold items, they leave tracks when they run, and the like. To do this, they borrow substance from the world around them—dust, earth, leaves, whatever lies at hand. You've doubtless heard the songs that the common folk sing about them. That's why they always describe the Wildfolk as wearing clothes made of flower petals and the like."

She nodded, considering this.

"But notice how the apple trees went backward, as it were, with their blooming." Laz gestured at the branches of the tree under which they were sitting. "It should be impossible."

"That does puzzle me, too."

"So, this morning I thought, well, the time's not ripe here in this world for the trees to be blooming, so they've taken the form appropriate to their location. Which led me to another thought—what if Haen Marn shares the same nature as the Wildfolk?"

"I think I do understand that, in a way." Mara was frowning. "Laz, you be the scholar among us. What—"

"Perpend!" He grinned at her. "I'm suggesting that this island and everything on it, the manse, the trees, the boat, are physical manifestations of a pattern woven up on the astral plane. However, and here's a crucial point, it's an artificial creation, this island, not a natural part of life like the Wildfolk."

Marnmara gasped and looked away, her eyes wide as she seemed to see vast possibilities. "It were taking a powerful dweomer indeed," she said at last, "to build this island out of the hidden forces."

"Immensely powerful, but I wager someone did just that. Several someones, it would have to be, working over a long period of years." Laz paused for effect. "The Ancients, Mara. It would have to have been worked by the Ancients. Many of the peoples in Annwn have dweomer of a sort, but only the Ancients have—or I should say, had—dweomer of that magnitude."

"From what you and my mam have told me, I do see what you mean, but then, what about us? Those of us who do live on Haen Marn, I mean? Be we naught but force taking form?"

"Very unlikely, partly because I'm here, too. I traveled with the island, and the gods all know that I'm made of real meat." He held up his maimed right hand in illustration. "Besides, your mother had children in the usual way."

Marnmara smiled in relief and nodded.

"I suspect," Laz went on, "that real physical persons exist here the way we'd ride in a cart. We can climb in and out of a cart. It moves, we go along with it, but it's made of different stuff than we are."

"That does ring true to me."

"Good. On the other hand, I do wonder about some of the boatmen. Lon and his mother are most definitely actual Mountain Folk, and quite probably so is one of rowers, but the others seem to appear and disappear like Wildfolk. I think the one real rower is the pattern, like, for the others. I certainly can't tell them apart."

"No more can I. Laz, this all be—"

A voice began calling, loudly and insistently, old Lonna's voice, "Wynni! WYNNI! Where be you?" The voice came closer and closer, and eventually Lonna came walking through the apple trees to stop in front of the bench where they sat.

"Mara?" she said. "Where be your sister?"

"Oh, how would I know?" Mara said. "We were discussing somewhat of grave importance."

"Here now." Laz got up and smiled at Lonna. "I'll help you look, if you'd like." He glanced back at his sulky pupil. "Lonna's a bit elderly to go running all over the island."

Mara blushed. She forced out a smile and got up with a pleasant nod Lonna's way. "My apologies," she said. "Lonna, I'll be looking upstairs for you. Doubtless, Her Laziness has gone back to bed." She glanced at Laz. "I want to fetch the Ancients' book, too. I do get impressions from it, and mayhap it will add to our discussion."

While Mara went back to the manse, Laz searched the island,

but he found no trace of Berwynna. He returned to the great hall to see a worried-looking Angmar talking with Mara by the staircase while Lonna listened, hands on hips, and a scowl on her face.

"Laz!" Angmar called out. "Found you Wynni?"

"I didn't," Laz said. "I take it Mara didn't, either."

"I didn't." Mara sounded close to tears. "And the dragon book is gone."

"What?"

"I did lock it in the chest by my window, and it be not there now. I'll wager that wretched Wynni stole it!"

"Now, now," Angmar broke in. "More like you just mislaid it somewhere. What would Wynni be wanting with a book, and her not able to read? It be your sister's whereabouts that worry me, anyway, not some book."

"I do wager she knows value when she sees it." Mara started to say more, then glanced Laz's way and forced out a hypocritical smile. "But of course I do worry about her, as well. Avain may have the power to see her."

In an anxious pack they hurried outside to Avain's tower and trooped up the stairs along with a cloud of Mara's cats, who always seemed to know excitement when they saw it. Avain was sitting at the table by her window, her big puffy head bent over her silver basin of water. Two of the cats jumped onto the table and advanced upon the basin as if they were planning on having a drink from it. Avain raised a huge hand and shooed them away.

"Avain, my love," Angmar began.

"She be on the water, Mama," Avain said.

"Wynni, you mean?"

"Wynni be on the water with Dougie."

Although Angmar asked her many a question more, always the answer was the same, "Wynni be on the water with Dougie."

"Mama, no more asking!" Avain looked up from the basin with tears in her eyes. "Avain see no more."

"Well and good, then, my love." Angmar ran her hand through Avain's hair and smiled, soothing her. "My thanks for telling us what you did see."

"Avain," Mara said, and with her mooncalf sister, her voice was always gentle and kind. "Be it that I may ask you a question?"

"Not about Wynni."

"Not about Wynni. About a book, a big big book with a dragon on the cover."

"Dragon?" Avain grinned wide, exposing her oddly large teeth. "Avain see a dragon?"

"Be it that you can?"

Once again she bent her head to her scrying basin. This time, however, she shook her head in a no. The tears came back to her eyes.

"No dragon," she said, "no book, no blanket, no dragon."

Blanket? Laz thought. *Ah, she took the word "cover" that way!*

"Mama will be coming back with food for you in just a bit, my sweet," Angmar said. "Worry not, and my thanks."

Avain smiled, sunny again.

"Does it gladden your heart to be home?" Mara asked her.

"Home be good." Avain's smile grew broader. "Bad Alban. No dragons in Alban."

"A serious lack, no doubt," Laz said, "in any place."

Avain stuck her tongue out at him, a normal pink tongue, albeit huge. *What did I expect?* Laz thought. *A split like a snake's?* Just that, he realized, to match her strangely round eyes, green and lashless.

"Mara make bread," Avain said. "Wynni gone."

"I know not how to make bread," Mara said, smiling at her. "Lonna will make bread."

"You know, my sweet," Angmar said. "Though you be the Lady of the Isle, with your sister gone, it behooves you to help Lonna at her tasks. She be old, indeed, older no doubt than you ken or can imagine."

"It be so hot in the kitchen, and smoky." Mara turned toward the door and took a few steps. "I shan't work there."

"I did warn you, did I not?" Angmar followed her. "Never have you honored your sister's work enough. Now you shall see how much she did."

Mara said a few words in Dwarvish, then stalked off with Angmar right behind, talking in the same language. Laz heard them arguing all the way down the stairs. By the time he caught up with them outside, their argument had become heated.

Laz considered the swaying pale leaves of the apple trees. He might as well attempt to scry for the book, he decided, with a living focus like the leaves. Once again the thick etheric water veil surrounding the island defeated him. *When I leave,* he thought, *I'll be able to scry then.* The book, while interesting, lacked any real meaning for him, but these days Sidro was always in his thoughts.

In the warmth of an Alban spring day, the apple blossoms in Domnal Breich's steading hung heavy on the branches. Domnal himself was weeding his vegetable garden when Father Colm came puffing up to the front gate. The priest paused to mop his red face with the sleeve of his cassock, then called out a hallo. Domnal laid down his hoe and strolled over.

"Come in, Father." Domnal reached for the latch. "Cool yourself with some well water."

"I can't stop, but my thanks," Colm said. "I just came to bring you the news. Those witches and their flying island have disappeared. When my lord's shepherd was chasing down lost sheep after the storm, he saw that it was gone."

Domnal tried to speak, but his mouth had gone dry. Dimly he was aware of Jehan, walking out of the front door.

"I just wanted to make sure," Colm said, "that your lad was safe at home."

Jehan cried out, then covered her mouth with both hands.

"He's not." Domnal forced himself to speak calmly. "He never came home last night."

Colm crossed himself, then did it again for good measure. "I'll pray for him," the priest said. "I'd advise you to do the same."

Jehan began to weep, then turned and rushed for the house. Domnal heard the door slam hard.

"I will," Domnal said. "And my thanks for the news."

The priest murmured a blessing, made the sign of the cross over them both, then set off down the road, heading for Lord Douglas' dun. For a long time Domnal stood at the gate, clutching the wooden bar with both hands, watching until the priest disappeared.

"Evandar's doing," he said aloud. "I'd damn his soul, but it would be a waste of breath."

In his mind he could hear the words of an old song:

"The road to Heaven's a high road
The road to Hell runs low.
In between on no road at all
The Host drifts to and fro."

With a shudder he left the gate and went inside to comfort his weeping wife. He would have given up his prosperous steading and everything he owned to have his eldest lad back, but he knew in his heart that the giving would be futile. His worst fear had come to pass. His son was the price of Evandar's boons.

PART II

THE NORTHLANDS
SPRING, 1160

All matter be naught but a concatenation of force, even that which makes what we call our bodies, but in some matter the forms be more stable than in others, depending upon the proportions of the Five Elements in each.

—*The Secret Book of Cadwallon the Druid*

On a glorious spring afternoon, a pair of couriers arrived at the Red Wolf dun, bearing letters from Prince Daralanteriel. The letters told his honored vassal, Tieryn Cadryc, that he was making a progress through his lands along their eastern border.

"That's our western border." Lady Solla glanced up from the letter. "Or wait! We're inside the prince's rhan now, so I suppose we're on his eastern border ourselves."

"So we are." Cadryc paused for a sip of ale, as if he needed to wash this thought down for the digesting. "Um, do go on, my lady."

Solla cleared her throat and resumed reading. "We shall be stopping at Lord Samyc's dun for a brief visit before proceeding to yours. We hope and trust that you, your clan, and your vassals have survived the winter in good health. Yours in high regard, Prince Daralanteriel of the Westlands, heir to the Seven Cities and the Vale of Roses."

"Must have been a splendid place, his rhan," Cadryc said with a sigh, "before the accursed Horsekin burnt the lot. Well, one of these days maybe we'll see about getting it back for him, eh?"

"It's a pretty thought, Your Grace," Solla said. "Shall I write your answer now?"

"Let me think on it a bit, though I suppose I don't need to say much, eh?"

"Probably not." Solla rose with a curtsy. "Well and good, then, Your Grace. I'll be in the women's hall."

Yet another pair of speeded couriers arrived some days later, Deverry men, this time, with a letter from Prince Voran, inquiring politely if Tieryn Cadryc had heard anything of his overlord's plans. He had also sent along a sealed letter for Daralanteriel on the off chance that Cadryc would see him first. Unfortunately, Prince Dar's couriers had left by then, but at least Cadryc could tell the messengers that Prince Daralanteriel was riding north. Voran had sent the message from Pren Cludan, where he was visiting its tieryn on his way to Cengarn. On the morrow his messengers left with a letter from Cadryc to rejoin their prince.

It was some days later, when Gerran was sitting with the tieryn at the table of honor, that Cadryc brought up the subject of the prince's coming visit to Cengarn.

"Now, I've been thinking, Gerro," Cadryc said. "You'd best ride with our overlord when he heads north. You need to go to Cengarn yourself to ask about that inheritance. Ridvar never gave you a dowry, the mingy little bastard, so he's got no reason to withhold it."

"And what will Ridvar say when I turn up at his gates?" Gerran said. "Will he even let me in?"

"I owe him one last set of dues. It's the scot to settle my breaking free of his overlordship. If you're delivering it, he'll have to treat you honorably."

"True spoken. You know, Your Grace, an odd thing: I hate to leave Solla now that she's with child."

"Oh, it's best to let the womenfolk handle these things on their own. They know all about it, eh? We don't. Besides, my wife tells me that your lady won't be delivered for a fair many months yet."

Gerran was inclined to argue further, but he suspected that to do so would be unmanly in the extreme. Late that afternoon, when he and Solla got a chance to speak privately in their chamber, he asked her outright if she'd be distressed if he were to leave. She considered the question while she arranged a couple of pillows against the headboard of their bed. She kicked off her clogs, then climbed up and sat, leaning against the pillows and stretching her legs comfortably in front of her.

"I'd rather you were here," she said at last, "because I love you, but I'm a warrior's daughter as well as a warrior's wife. I know full well that the Horsekin are going to start raiding again, and we've to build the dun and gather the warband to stop them."

"So we do." He perched on the edge of the bed, facing her.

"Besides, you'll be happier in the saddle, riding out to settle important matters. This winter was awfully hard on you, shut up in the snows."

"It was a cursed sight easier than most winters, because of you, I mean."

"My thanks." She smiled again, briefly. "But you've had too much time to think."

"I have, truly. I suppose I should stop brooding about that battle."

"That's the reason I want you to be out and about. It's vexed you all winter, hasn't it?"

"It has. I never should have turned on that Horsekin with the broken leg. My father's killer—huh, he deserved what he got, but that other fellow? Ye gods, he couldn't even stand!" With a shake of his head, Gerran tried to dismiss the memory. "It doesn't seem to matter how many times I tell you the tale, either. The shame keeps coming back like a witch's curse."

"I honestly don't understand why. He would have killed you if he could have."

"But he couldn't. That's what makes all the difference." Gerran reached over to pat her hand. "Don't vex yourself about it, my love. I'll get over it. But you're right enough that I need somewhat to do."

"I hope Cadryc will let Mirryn go with you. He really should take a look at Lady Egriffa."

"Who?"

"One of Drwmigga's serving women. She's the second daughter of a tieryn, you see, and Galla thinks she might be a good match for Mirryn."

"Then he'll be going with us. Do you truly think that Cadryc can hold out if our Galla lays a siege?"

They shared a laugh.

Sure enough, that night at dinner Cadryc announced that when the time came, Mirryn and ten men of the warband would accompany Gerran on his ride north. Gerran would take his page, young Clae. Salamander volunteered to go as well.

"The spring is upon us, good tieryn," Salamander said. "I've eaten more than enough of your food, and you've heard enough of my tales and chatter, so I shall be on my way when our Gerro rides north."

Later that afternoon Gerran had a private word with Salamander. They met out by the stables, but the grooms were mucking out the stalls with Clae and Coryn to help them. Gerran had caught them persecuting young Ynedd again and decided they deserved the punishment. Salamander led the way down to the cleaner air near the dun wall.

"Much better!" Salamander pronounced. "I don't know which was worse, the stench or the swarming flies. I take it you have somewhat to ask me."

"Just that," Gerran said. "How far away is Prince Dar's alar?"

"Not very. They've reached Lord Samyc's. Which reminds me. Would it be a wrong thing for me to tell them about that secret road through the forest? It would save much needed time."

"I don't see why you shouldn't. Dar's the overlord for all our lands now, and so in some sense he owns that road."

"Ah, very good! I shall pass along the secret, then."

Gerran paused, struck by Salamander's remark. "Why much needed time?"

"Because the Wise One, Lady Dallandra, is vastly pregnant," Salamander said. "The sooner they get here, the better."

Mother's saddle or no, Dallandra was having a hard time staying on horseback during the day's march. Whenever their route ran uphill, she would cling shamelessly to the cantle with one hand and the pommel with the other and pray to whatever goddess came to mind first. Once they reached the tieryn's secret road, however, the traveling became a little easier. Around noon on their second day on the road, they came free of the forest. Dallandra saw the Red Wolf dun from a distance, its tower a dark mark just cutting into the horizon.

"There it is," she told Pir. "Probably some five miles away."

Pir smiled and nodded, but, as usual, said nothing.

As they plodded onward, Dallandra slowly became aware of an ache in her back. *It's this wretched sidesaddle,* she thought. In another mile, however, the pain became more insistent, then localized itself around the baby just as the dun came clearly into view. Still, that contraction passed easily; they went another mile more before the second. The third, however, followed on fast. *I've got to hold on,* Dalla told herself. *Almost there.* Pir abruptly raised his head and sniffed the air.

"You're in labor," he said.

"I am, but it's early yet. I—oh! curse it all!"

Her water broke, a sudden gush that soaked her leggings and the saddle both. The mare snorted, tossed her head, and might have bucked had Pir not laid a hand on her neck. She steadied down immediately.

"Sidro!" Pir bellowed. "Come quick!"

Calonderiel came galloping back with her. Up at the head of the line of march, Prince Dar called out something—Dallandra wasn't quite sure what—but she did see a single rider peel out of line and head at a gallop for the Red Wolf's gates.

"It's just started," Dalla gasped in Elvish. "I can make it to the dun."

So she did, but barely. As the royal procession straggled in through the dun gates, Dallandra saw Lady Galla on the steps of the broch, yelling orders at her servants. Calonderiel caught Dallandra as she slid down from her saddle, only half voluntarily.

"I can walk," Dallandra gritted her teeth as pain swept through her.

"No, you can't." Calonderiel picked her up and, swearing under his breath, carried her into the broch.

As far as Gerran could tell, every woman in the dun, except for the lowly servant lasses, rushed upstairs after Dallandra to help with the birth. Exalted Mother Grallezar followed more slowly, her arms full of saddlebags. While the rest of the Westfolk made camp outside the gates, Prince Daralanteriel joined Gerran and Cadryc at the honor table. Not long after, Calonderiel came down to sit with them as well.

"I've been told to leave her alone," Calonderiel said. "At least they don't mind me waiting down here. When Maelaber was being born, the women nearly chased me out of camp. I suppose I was a little bit unreasonable at the time, though."

"There's naught we can do, after all. I know it from bitter experience, lad," Cadryc gestured at a servant lass. "Mead for our guests!"

"Why bitter?" Calonderiel said.

"My elder son died before I could even fetch the midwife. Back in our old dun, that was." Cadryc glanced at Cal's suddenly pale face, then went on hastily. "Not that such will be happening to your child, mind. Your lady's got the best help in the world."

Calonderiel gulped his mead down before the lass finished pouring for the others. She refilled his goblet, curtsied, and hurried away to help serve Daralanteriel's warband, who were filing into the great hall a few at a time. Cadryc turned to his royal guest, sitting at his right hand.

"It gladdens my heart to see you, my prince," Cadryc said. "Among other things, I've got a letter for you from Prince Voran. He didn't know where else to send it." He rose from his chair and looked around, then bellowed at Clae, who was talking with Neb over by the servant's hearth. "Page! Neb, come over here, too, would you?"

Cadryc sent Clae off to find Prince Voran's letter. Neb waited to read it, standing behind and to one side of Prince Dar's chair. Neb had changed over the winter, Gerran noticed, grown taller, for one thing, though he was as skinny as ever. The biggest change proved harder to pin down. Something about his eyes caught Gerran's attention, a certain confidence, a new strength, and yet along with those qualities he displayed a surprising kind of world-weariness, as if his eyes had looked upon a measure of sad experience proper to a much older man.

When Clae returned with the message tube, Prince Dar broke

the seal, then handed the tube to his scribe. Neb shook out the parchment, glanced over the letter, then read it aloud in a voice that had deepened since last Gerran had heard it. On the far side of the hall, after a susurrus of shushing each other, the servants and warbands fell silent to listen. Tankard in hand, Salamander drifted over to lean against the nearby pillar.

"To his royal highness, Daralanteriel, prince of the Westlands and the Seven Cities of the Far West, I, Voran, prince of the Gold Wyvern, clan royal of Dun Deverry, send greetings. I have news of great import and am most desirous of speaking with you face-to-face in order to discuss its ramifications for our two kingdoms. The high king of all Deverry and Eldidd, Gwindyc the Third, has decided that under the threat of the savage Horsekin it behooves us to look to our northern and northwestern borders. You may not be aware of the eternal-seeming discord and feuding in our province of Cerrgonney—"

"You could say that twice," Cadryc muttered. "Eternal, indeed!"

Neb cleared his throat, then went on. "But such discord threatens the stability of the entire border. In order to promote a greater tranquillity within his lands, King Gwindyc has appointed me Justiciar of the Northern Border, in order to establish a continuing royal presence in Cerrgonney and incidentally in Arcodd—"

Calonderiel, Daralanteriel, and Cadryc all laughed, a sharp bark, a guffaw, and an outright whoop from the tieryn. Gerran and Neb exchanged a smile.

"Incidentally, is it?" Dar said. "Sorry, Neb, go on."

"As Your Highness wishes," Neb said, grinning. "And incidentally in Arcodd. Since the threat from our mutual savage enemies emanates from the west of the north, I wish to establish a residence in the northwest corner of the kingdom, where my court of law will be available to the lords of Cerrgonney but on neutral ground. I assure you that my presence there, with a warband of seventy-five riders and twenty-five royal archers, is in no way to be construed as any threat to your sovereignty along the western border. Rather, I hope to work hand in hand with you to ensure the safety of our two peoples. To this end, if we could confer at some spot you designate along our western border, I should be most grateful. I would suggest Cengarn would answer most admirably for this purpose—"

Another round of laughter interrupted the scribe. "Indeed," Dar said. "It'll answer that purpose and also the purpose of showing Ridvar who's the stallion in this herd. Neb, go on."

"That's the body of the letter, Your Highness," Neb said. "Though there's rather a lot of formal farewells and good wishes for your health and the like."

"We can skip all that now," Dar said. "Later I'll have you write an answer." He turned in his chair, gestured to Salamander, then spoke in Elvish. The gerthddyn answered in the same.

Gerran was just wondering what they'd said when Branna came down the stairs to the great hall. For a moment he didn't recognize her, because she was wearing Westfolk clothing—boots, leggings, and a tunic heavy with embroidery. She'd braided her hair in the Westfolk manner as well. Her voice, like Neb's, held a new authority.

"Banadar," she said, "you can go up now. You have a daughter."

The labor had gone as well as anything that painful could be expected to go, Dallandra supposed. This baby had come quicker than the previous one, if she could trust her memory, perhaps because her new daughter was a fair bit smaller than Loddlaen had been. At the moment Calonadario, a chubby little hairless thing with tightly furled ears and a bright red face, lay asleep in the crook of her father's arm, while Dallandra herself lay propped up with pillows on the bed in the dun's second-best chamber. Gnomes perched on the edge of the bed and stared, puzzled, at the baby. They were wondering where she'd come from, Dallandra supposed, since they never seemed to have offspring of their own.

"Well, what do you think of her?" Dallandra said.

"She's splendid, of course," Calonderiel said. "I intend to indulge her every whim, once she's old enough to have whims, anyway."

"Good. I'm so tired, but curiosity is eating me alive. What was in that letter?"

Calonderiel broke into a grin, and his eyes snapped with good humor as he told her about Voran's new post on the border. Exhausted though she was, Dallandra had to laugh when he'd finished.

"I wish I could have seen Ridvar's face when he heard the news." Dallandra paused for a long yawn. "Blast it all! I can't stay awake! Could you find Grallezar for—"

"I be right here." Grallezar opened the chamber door and hurried in. "Let me put her in her cradle."

Dalla fell asleep as soon as Grallezar took the baby, only to wake soon after to a repetitive chirping noise. At first she was puzzled—had a bird gotten into the chamber? Then she realized that Dari was crying. She sat up and pulled back the bed-curtain to peer out. The golden light of late afternoon fell through the unglazed window onto Sidro, who was sitting in the chair and murmuring to the baby.

"Here's your mam!" Sidro said. "Hush, hush, little one, I'll take you to her."

Dallandra settled the baby at her breast—the false milk had come down in profusion—while Sidro pulled back and tied the bed-curtains. Dari was a straightforward nurser, Dallandra was relieved to see, sucking the liquid down as fast as she could without dainty pauses or fussy fits, unlike Loddlaen. *Pray to every goddess I have enough milk this time!* Dallandra thought. *I owe it to this child to feed her well.*

"Exalted Mother Grallezar went down to the great hall for dinner," Sidro said. "So I was taking a turn at being nursemaid. She'll be back in but a little while."

"That's fine, and my thanks," Dallandra said. "Do we have rags for the baby's bottom?"

"We do, Wise One, all freshly washed, too. I'll fetch them."

"My thanks again! These things are so much easier out on the grass."

When Grallezar returned, carrying food for Dallandra from the dinner down in the great hall, Penna came with her. Since Cadryc's wife fed her servants decently, Penna had filled out some over the winter, becoming merely thin rather than far too thin. Her short brown hair gleamed like fur in the sunset light. She had a new dress, too, of clean pale linen with a touch of embroidery at the neckline.

"Well, Penna," Dallandra said, "do you remember me?"

"Of course, Lady Dallandra." Penna curtsied. "You saved my

brother's life. I came to tell you that he's all healed up now. And I wanted to give you my humble thanks again."

"You're most welcome."

By then Dari had fallen asleep. Grallezar took her and tucked her into the cradle beside the bed while Penna watched, smiling at the baby.

"Lady Dallandra?" Penna said suddenly. "You have dweomer, don't you?"

Dallandra hesitated, then saw no reason to lie to this strange creature, who seemed to have some sort of instinctive dweomer herself. "I do, truly."

"Then what are we?" Penna turned to look at her. "Me and Tarro, I mean. We're not Westfolk, and we're not just people, are we?"

Behind Penna's back, Grallezar opened her mouth in surprise, flashing a gleam of pointed teeth.

"You see that, then," Dallandra said to Penna. "I'd wondered. I'm afraid I don't know yet, but maybe you can help me find out."

"I will, and gladly. The folk in our old village—I didn't feel so different there. But I do here, and I wondered." Penna curtsied again, then began backing toward the door. "I should let you rest. I don't mean to be discourteous." She turned and fled the chamber, leaving the door open behind her.

With a shake of her head Grallezar shut the door, then came back to pull the chair up to the bedside. She sat down with a sigh.

"What a strange lass that one be!" Grallezar said. "Not human, indeed, I'd have to say. It gladdens my heart that she can see it, or she'd be in for a truly bad shock."

"Just so. I find myself thinking of Envoy Kov's staff—I told you about that, didn't I?"

"You did. And the missing element of water."

"The unfortunate thing is, Penna's terrified of going near rivers and other large bodies of water, according to Neb, anyway. So I don't really see how she can be somehow linked to it in the Elemental sense."

"Alas. A fine theory, slashed by a nasty fact." Grallezar grinned at her. "Well, no doubt we'll find the truth sooner or later."

"There are so many truths we need to find, and sooner rather than later. It makes me tired just thinking about them. I—"

Someone knocked, and Grallezar went to open the door. Valandario walked in, then stood hesitating a few steps into the chamber. *She knows Dari was Loddlaen once,* Dallandra thought. With the thought came rage. Much to her utter shock, Dallandra felt like growling at her fellow dweomerworker, wanted to shout at her to go away and stay away from that vulnerable infant lying in her cradle. Yet she knew full well that Val would never stoop to hurting any child.

"I thought I'd come pay my respects," Val said, her voice hesitant. "And see if you needed anything."

"I don't, my thanks."

"Come see the pretty little lass." Grallezar, who knew nothing of Val's murdered lover, spoke cheerfully. Her voice broke the spell motherhood had worked on Dalla's mind.

"Please do," Dallandra said. "I suppose she's pretty, anyway. She's still awfully red and squashed."

Valandario laughed, a normal soft chuckle, and walked over to the crib. As she stood looking down at the baby, Dari woke, yawned, and briefly opened her murky blue eyes. Val went tense and leaned a little closer. Dallandra felt that Val was looking through those eyes to the soul who inhabited this little body, so fragile and new. All at once Val smiled, but tears glistened in her eyes. Dari yawned again and fell back asleep.

"She's very pretty indeed," Val said, then spoke in Elvish. "And not at all the fellow of whom we spoke, not any longer. Dalla, I know that the core of the soul's the same, but by the Goddesses, she's not him."

"Yes, that's very true," Dalla said. "And this time, I'll make sure she doesn't suffer the way he did."

Grallezar was looking back and forth between them, her mouth a twist of annoyance at being shut out of their talk.

"I'm sorry," Val said to her in Deverrian. "I forget that Elvish is so hard to learn. I keep thinking that you know it."

"Not well enough, truly." Grallezar smiled again. "It be a complicated affair, your language. Not all of us have a hundred years or so to spend upon the learning of it."

They all shared a laugh. Dallandra would have explained, but the door opened again—Branna, come for a look at the baby, followed by Carra and her daughter, Elessi. They stayed but a little while to chat, then left, taking Val with them, when Galla, her daughter Adranna, and her granddaughter Trenni came up for a look. Galla brought a small clay pot of honey to keep the new mother's strength up, or so she said.

"I'll mix somewhat of that with boiled milk," Grallezar told her. "My thanks."

Galla handed Grallezar the pot, but she did it at arm's length, as if offering a tidbit to a dog who might bite. "Now, Dallandra," Galla went on, "I want you to know that you're welcome to stay here for your lying in. Travel could be dangerous."

"My humble thanks, my lady," Dallandra said. "But I'll be up and about soon."

"Is that wise?" Adranna put in.

"My folk heal differently from yours," Dallandra said. "If we lie in after childbirth, the blood pools and makes our legs swell."

At that, they stopped fussing. Dallandra got out of bed to demonstrate and walked back and forth across the chamber a few times. When they left, she sat up to nurse her daughter and then was glad enough to lie down again.

Once Dallandra's baby had arrived safely, the first person that Branna sought out in the dun was Midda, her old nurse, whom she found up in the chamber shared by Adranna's children. In a shaft of light from a window, Midda sat mending one of Trenni's dresses. When Branna walked in, Midda dropped her sewing and got up. She rushed to Branna's open arms.

"Oh, it's so good to see you safe!" Midda stepped back, her hands on Branna's shoulders, and surveyed her former charge. "You look well, but why are you wearing lad's clothing?"

"It's not lad's clothing. All the Westfolk women dress like this."

Midda snorted and pursed her lips.

"But how are you?" Branna said. "Adranna told me that she'd taken you as a nurse for the children."

"For the child, rather, Trenni that is. They'll be sending Matto off to be a page soon."

"Well, it's time for him to start his training, truly."

Branna looked around the chamber, pleasant, large, with a hearth of its own and three beds: two narrow for the children, one wider for Midda herself. Midda smiled as she pointed out the proper mantel over the hearth, where a red-and-blue pottery vase added a note of cheer.

"It's a nice position," Midda said. "I'm grateful to you and your cousin, I am. She told me you'd commended me to her before you left."

"I did, most strongly, and I'm glad she took me up on it. I'd best go now, but I'll see you again before we leave."

For her stay in her uncle's dun, Branna returned to wearing dresses. She spent long hours up in the women's hall, catching up on all the local gossip with Galla, Solla, and Adranna, who seemed to be taking her widowhood well. Branna's gray gnome wandered around the chamber, occasionally unrolling a skein of yarn when no one was looking. The dun cats bore the unjust blame for the resulting messes.

"It's been nearly a year since Honelg died," Adranna told her, "and truly, I've come to realize just how frightened of him I was. He never beat me, never so much as said that he might slap my face, but the threat hung in the air at times—just at times. It was the way he'd look at me and the children, all glowering and grim." She let her voice trail away to a whisper. "It happened more and more often toward the end."

"I never wanted you to marry him," Galla said. "I suppose I'm being awful, saying I told you so, but it's one of the few nasty arguments your father and I ever had."

"You were right." Adranna managed to smile. "But who else was there, way out here?"

The women were sitting near the window in their hall, Adranna and Galla in cushioned chairs, while Branna sat on a stool and turned the handle on the yarn spinner. The tieryn's own sheep had just been sheared, producing the first fleeces of the year. Solla was feeding the wheel long twists of carded wool, adjusting the tension to Branna's rhythm. Little Trenni wound the finished threads onto sticks. The skeins built up fast, thick bundles of yarn, spun in an afternoon, when they would have taken the women days to produce with drop spindles.

"I'll turn for a while if you'd like, Branna," Adranna said. "We should train one of the pages to do that, really."

"Ynedd would do a good job," Trenni put in, "but Gerro would throw an absolute fit."

Solla laughed in agreement. "He says we're ruining the lad," she said. "If you believe my husband, Ynedd will be fit for naught but mincing around the high king's court if we don't stop coddling him."

"Has Gerran ever been to Dun Deverry?" Branna let the wheel slow and stop, then stood to change places with Adranna.

"Of course not," Galla said, "none of us ever have. And we're even less likely to go now that we have a new overlord. I doubt me if anyone minces in Prince Dar's court."

Everyone looked to Branna, who smiled. "Of course they don't. Life's very different out on the grasslands." She smoothed her skirts under her and sat down in a cushioned chair. "It can get rather dangerous, truly."

"Do tell us more," Adranna said. "I just can't imagine it, wandering all over the country like that."

As the spinning went forward, Branna obliged with stories about her life during the winter past, the flash floods, the endless squabbles among the Westfolk, the sea fogs, lost horses, and the like. Yet she could never tell them about the real challenges and dangers she faced, studying dweomerlore and dealing with a Neb who had grown withdrawn and troubled as his own studies progressed.

That night at dinner, and later when they went up to their chamber, Neb seemed more his old self. By candlelight they lay in bed, face-to-face, and talked over the day. He'd spent time with his brother, he told her, and gone round and chatted with all his old friends in the dun.

"Lord Veddyn told me that Lady Solla's been helping him with the taxes," Neb said. "His memory's not what it once was, you know."

"True spoken. I remember how that used to worry Aunt Galla."

He nodded, started to speak, then suddenly turned away.

"Is somewhat wrong?" Branna said.

"Naught." Neb got out of bed, then strode over to the window. "It's chilly tonight. I think I'll close the shutters."

With them, he closed his heart, or so Branna thought of it. When he came back to bed, he'd arranged a masklike smile on his face. He blew out the candles, announced he was tired, and turned on his side with his back toward her. She lay awake for some while and tried to understand what had caused the change in him. *Mentioning memory?* she wondered. The subject seemed a slight one to have such a great effect, but it was the best answer she could come up with.

On the morrow, the silver dragon flew in, bringing Dallandra a good reason to leave her chamber. Although he landed out in the meadows behind the dun, Branna went down to tell him to come lair on the roof of the broch itself, a shorter distance for Dallandra to travel.

"There's no need to fuss," Dallandra said wearily. "I may be sore, but I didn't tear, and I can certainly climb up to the roof on my own."

"Oh, I assumed that," Branna said. "I'm not fussing, truly I'm not. You were just so tired by all the traveling."

"Now that, alas, is true." Dallandra had a sudden thought. "Would you go fetch Penna? If she's not afraid to come see the dragon, I'd like her to look at Rori's wound."

"I will. She's an odd lass, isn't she?"

"Very."

"Have you ever seen her wash?"

"Um, I haven't. Doesn't she?"

"Oh, all the time, Solla tells me. But she takes a little bit of water in a basin and washes only one small bit of herself, her hands, say, or one arm, or a foot. Then a little while later she'll get more water and wash another small bit. It takes her a couple of days to wash all of herself."

"How very odd indeed! Now, keep this to yourself, but I've come to the conclusion that she's as different from us as we are from the Horsekin."

"But she's not Horsekin?"

"Somewhat else entirely. When I feel stronger I'll have a good long talk with her. For now, I'll go see Rori."

Up on the roof there was barely room for the dragon and Dallandra both, but Penna did climb the ladder and stick her head out of the trapdoor. Dallandra leaned against the dragon's massive haunch and watched the lass study the wound on Rori's side.

"There's a hole in the blue shadow part," Penna pronounced at last. "Did someone cut a piece out of his side?"

"They didn't," Dallandra said. "It's just a stab wound in the flesh."

"Well, in the blue shadow it's a hole, like you'd scoop out of the dirt with a trowel, if you were going to plant a seedling."

"That's most interesting, and you have my thanks, Penna. I thought you might be able to see somewhat that I couldn't."

"It gladdens my heart to help." She dropped her voice to a whisper. "May I go now? I don't mean to be rude, but there's this smell about him."

"I stink, you mean," Rori said. "I know it, no need to mince words."

"My apologies anyway." Penna turned a little pale at the deep growl of his voice. She bobbed her head Dallandra's way to substitute for a curtsy, then climbed down the ladder and disappeared from view. Dallandra could hear her speaking with someone on the landing below—a male voice, Neb's, she realized. She could hear that Penna was telling him about the wound in the "blue shadow part," as she termed the etheric double. Their voices faded away down the stairs. *Someone else who'll need teaching,* Dallandra thought, a trifle wearily. *Well, all in good time.*

Rori crossed his front paws and looked at her expectantly.

"Thanks to Penna, we have somewhat of an explanation," Dallandra said. "No wonder I can't get that wretched cut to heal."

"So!" Rori said. "The wound *is* cursed after all."

"It's not, not in the usual sense." Dallandra sighed. It seemed that evil curses were the first thing everyone thought of whenever some bad thing needed explaining. "I'm not sure what exactly is wrong, but Raena didn't attach any evil spirits to you or invoke any nasty godlets, either. I suspect Yraen's silver dagger is what's to blame. That beastly spell on it drains etheric force, somehow, when one of the People touches it, if that makes sense to you."

"Is that what makes the blade glow?"

"It is. Eventually it would kill one of us, if we held it long enough, or so I think. I don't care to actually try it to see."

"I should think not." He turned his head to contemplate the pink stripe of wound. "Can you do anything to heal it?"

"I don't know, but I'm willing to try. The roof's not much of a place to do a working."

"And you shouldn't tire yourself." Rori fell silent, looking down over the dun wall to the green country beyond. "Dar and Cal are waiting for me down in the meadow. Branna told me that they want to discuss the Horsekin threat."

"I could go down later—"

"I've seen you work dweomer. It saps your strength, and you need to rest. At least now I know what's wrong. Let me go off and scout for Horsekin, and by the time I return, you'll be stronger."

"That might be best. I'll admit to being surprised that you'd offer to wait."

"Some dragons have good hearts." His voice rumbled in amusement. "Besides, I want to make sure the spell or whatever it is you'll do works."

Dallandra laughed with him. "Very well," she said. "I'll go down now, and you can go off to talk with Cal and Dar. May you not find any Horsekin anywhere nearby!"

"So we may hope," the dragon said. "You'd best go down that ladder before I fly."

Dallandra climbed down and watched from the safety of the landing as he flung himself into the air with a rush of wings.

The sun had almost set by the time that Calonderiel returned to their chamber. When he walked in, he gave her a bright, cheerful smile.

"What's wrong?" Dallandra said.

"Trying to hide things from you is a waste of time." Calonderiel sat down on the chair next to the bed. "Do you truly think you can turn Rori back into a man again?"

"I don't know yet. I won't until we find that wretched book. If Evandar didn't leave us some sort of guide, then no, I can't. I don't have the slightest idea of how to work such a powerful dweomer."

"Good."

"Good? What do you mean by that?"

"Hasn't it occurred to you that Rori's the best weapon we have against the Horsekin?"

Dallandra leaned back against the pillows with a sigh. "No, it hadn't."

"Not so much for the fighting itself," Calonderiel went on. "The Gel da'Thae aren't stupid. It won't be long before they have archers of their own. They'll learn to fight unhorsed, too. He won't have much effect on ranks of spearmen, once they get used to him. Oh, it sounds fearsome, the terrible dragon of the skies! The Horsekin don't fight in the sky."

"That's true."

"But the scouting!" Cal got up and paced over to the window. "By the Black Sun Herself, he can range so far and so fast! I know that dweomerfolk can give themselves wings, but how long and how far dare you fly?"

"Not very, not without a terrible risk. I've no desire to spend the rest of my life as a linnet."

"Just so." Cal leaned back against the windowsill. "Rori brought up the question of the dweomer spell."

"And?"

"He knows that it killed Evandar. He told me that he has no intention of allowing it to kill you."

"How very kind of him! Neither do I."

He smiled in genuine relief. "But if you don't even know what it entails—" he began.

"I can't tell you all will be well, no. That's not the real issue, anyway. Rori doesn't know if he wants to become a man again or not. He's searching for excuses."

"Oh." Cal considered this for several moments. "I hadn't thought of that."

"I thought maybe you hadn't."

He came back to the chair beside the bed and sat down again.

"Still," Cal said. "I don't want you working that dweomer if it's going to hurt you. I'll burn the cursed book myself if it comes to that."

"Since we don't know if the book still exists, or where it is if it does exist, or if we could find it even if we knew where, or what's in the thing, for that matter, I'd suggest you stop worrying about it."

Cal opened his mouth and shut it again. Through her east-facing window, Dallandra could see the sky darkening to a velvet blue. The chamber filled with shadow. With an irritable wave of her hand she sent a golden dweomer light spinning toward the opposite wall. It stuck and swelled, filling the chamber with a soft glow.

"It is really me you're worried about?" Dallandra said. "Or do you just not want to lose your scout?"

"What?" Cal went white around the mouth, a sure sign that he was furious. "It's you, of course. How could you think otherwise?"

"Well, you started this by talking about the Horsekin."

"I started this? Started what? A stupid squabble, I suppose you mean."

"No, I didn't mean that!" Dallandra stopped herself from snarling at him. "I'm very tired, you know."

"So am I. No, I mentioned scouting because I was looking for some reason to keep you from working that dweomer." Cal got up and perched on the edge of the bed. He reached over and caught her hand in both of his. "Forgive me? I'm just so cursed worried these days. There aren't enough of us, you know, to stop the Horsekin if they decide to come down and take the Melyn Valley."

She hadn't known. Dallandra felt as if her heart might freeze in her chest. She caught her breath with an audible sigh.

"We'll have to depend upon Ridvar and other Deverry lords," Cal went on. "That's why I'm glad we're meeting Prince Voran at Cengarn."

"I'm glad you are, too," Dallandra said. "I really should go to Cengarn with you."

Calonderiel opened his mouth to argue, but she continued before he could speak. "But I can't, I just can't. Cal, I feel like such a weakling, but I'm tired, and especially tired of riding sidesaddle. I still feel too sore to ride normally."

"I'm not in the least surprised." He smiled at her. "I want you to rest. If some sort of problem comes up, Ebañy will be with us. He can always consult with you."

"That's true, isn't it? I'll stop berating myself, then."

"Please do. There's going to be a mob riding with the prince, anyway." Cal frowned at the far wall. "Let's see, Dar will need a royal escort, which means me and fifty men, Mirryn, Gerran, and a few men from the Red Wolf. Then there's servants and horse handlers and, of course, Ebañy. I'll wager it all adds up to about a hundred people and some extra horses."

"It sounds like it. You know, Cadryc can't feed everyone you're leaving behind. He'll need the pasture grass for his own animals, too."

"Dar's already thought of that. He's leaving Cadryc some sheep to help feed the dun, and then Carra and Val are going to lead our people west. The herds and flocks need fresh grass, anyway. The prince and I will ride back here from Cengarn, get you and your women, and then join the others at Twenty Streams Rock." He got up to leave, then paused. "Oh, Neb's going to be going with us."

"Oh, is he? Tell him I want to talk with him, will you?"

"I will. I think he's in the great hall."

Neb must have been close by, because he came to her chamber not long after Calonderiel had left it. He bowed to Dallandra, smiled at the baby sleeping in her cradle, then sat down on the chair when she offered it to him.

"Neb," Dallandra said, "I hear you're going to Cengarn."

"I have to," Neb said. "Prince Voran's called me as a witness. I was present when the high priest insulted him."

"That's right, you were. I'd forgotten that."

Dallandra considered his expression: perfectly polite, a bland little smile, his eyes watching her attentively but not too closely. She wondered why she was sure he was hiding something.

"Are you looking forward to the trip?" she said.

"I am. Ridvar's chirurgeon has a book I particularly want to see again. I suppose I'll have time to read it while the malover's in progress."

"No doubt. These things always seem to drag on so. Is it a book of healing lore?"

"Of a sort." Neb frowned a little, considering. "It has a description of a plague that ravaged some of the towns down in Deverry proper during the Time of Troubles. It sounded much like the illness that killed my father." His voice caught, then steadied. "I want to read it again to make sure."

"Well and good, then. I take it you've been studying your herblore."

"I have. Is that all right?"

"Most certainly. The more healers in the world, the better."

"So I thought. I'm taking the herbs I've collected with me, unless you need them here. I want to memorize their properties. I'll take the book of herblore, too. Branni's not much interested in it."

"Well and good, then. I have plenty of herbs here. Ranadario's laid in a good supply for the alar. Now, do continue with your dweomerwork, too. If you have any questions about the exercises I set you, just ask Salamander."

"I will. They're fairly simple, after all."

Again Dallandra hesitated, then decided that he couldn't possibly be implying that only simple things lay within Salamander's reach. Yet after he said a polite farewell and walked away, the sight of his bland smile hung in her memory, an annoyance like dirt under a fingernail.

"We'll be leaving on the morrow," Gerran said. "I'll need to be up with the first light."

"Very well, my love," Solla said. "You can leave the shutters open so the dawn will wake us up."

"I'll try to leave without waking you."

"Don't be silly. I'll want to say farewell."

Gerran turned from the window of their bedchamber and smiled at her. In her linen shift, she was sitting on the edge of their bed, combing her hair. Through the thin pale cloth he could see the contours of her body. The baby was beginning to show, just a soft curve, these days, invisible when she was fully dressed, but a definite promise of a child to come.

"Tell me somewhat, Gerro," she said. "Dallandra's child made me wonder. If I give you a daughter, will you be disappointed?"

"What? Of course not! I'm just terrified that you'll die."

"I doubt that's going to happen." She smiled, but a tinge of fear colored her voice. "The women in my clan have never had that sort of trouble. I—" She paused, tilting her head to one side and considering him. "Are you truly frightened?"

"Of course."

"I've never seen anything frighten you before. Even the dragon—Sidro told us all how you saved her life."

"My life doesn't matter to me half as much as yours does." He sat down beside her. "As for the child, our rhan needs a son, truly, but there'll be plenty of time for that if we have a daughter first."

Tears welled in her eyes and spilled.

"Here, here, my love!" Gerran raised a gentle hand and wiped them from her cheeks. "I didn't mean to distress you."

"I'm not distressed." She snuffled back more tears. "What you said—it gladdens my heart."

"That's a cursed odd way of showing it."

"Is it? Truly, I suppose it is." She nestled against him. "Don't let it trouble you."

"Well and good, then." Gerran kissed her on the forehead. "Another thing, my love. I'll be asking your brother about that inheritance."

"Splendid!" Solla sat up again. "I've got a bit of parchment to give you. It's in my dower chest, the letter from my uncle, telling me he was leaving me some coin in his will. He died not long after, but I was only a lass, and so my brother—not Ridvar, but our older brother, Adamyr—took charge of the coin." Old grief touched her face. "It was just before he rode out for his last battle."

"And a sad thing that was." Gerran made his voice soft. "For the rhan as well as for you and your kin."

She nodded, then sighed before she spoke again. "But the coins must be in Cengarn still."

"I feel dishonorable, spending your coin on the dun."

"Why? It'll be my home, too."

"So it will, and my thanks. I'll take the letter with me, then."

Before he went to bed, Gerran found the letter and stowed it in his saddlebags, then put them by the door with his other gear. He woke with the dawn and dressed. He considered kissing his wife awake, but she looked so comfortable, nested in their blankets, that he decided to let her sleep. He gathered his gear and crept out of the chamber.

Mirryn and the riders from his warband had gathered in the great hall to bolt down a hasty breakfast. The prince, Mirryn told him, had already left to assemble his retinue down in the meadow. Gerran grabbed a chunk of bread from one of the baskets on the table and stood to eat it.

Over by the door, Branna and Neb sat on a bench and talked, their heads close together. Now and then Neb reached up to touch her cheek with gentle fingers. Finally he gave her a farewell kiss, rose, and strode out of the great hall. Branna got up more slowly, glanced around, then smiled at Gerran and came hurrying over.

"Gerro," Branna said, "Solla told me yesterday that she hoped you'd ask for her inheritance when you're in Cengarn."

"I'll be doing just that," Gerran said. "We need every coin we can get for that new dun."

"True spoken." Branna was looking away with a slight frown. "Solla probably told you this already, but she mentioned that Ridvar told her once that she didn't have any such inheritance due. She thought he was just teasing, because he laughed when he said it, but I wonder."

"She didn't mention that to me. Huh! I wonder if the little bastard just doesn't want to let go of the coin."

"That was my thought, too. Although—" She hesitated again. "Oh, I'm probably just going daft, but be careful what you say to Lord Oth about it."

"What?"

"Maybe it won't matter." Branna smiled brightly. "But Oth—oh, never mind!"

"But I do mind. What do you mean?"

"It's just one of my feelings. I'm a little daft, is all."

"Daft? Huh! Here, Prince Voran's been appointed justiciar. What if I take the matter to him?"

"That would be far better." For a moment she seemed to be about to say more, then turned and trotted away before he could call her back.

With so many men and horses, servants and carts, the ride to Cengarn took two days. Whenever the road came to a bend, Gerran would turn in the saddle to look back at the end of the line out of sheer habit. Not so long ago, keeping track of the supply carts would have been his responsibility, not Mirryn's. Salamander and Neb were also riding among the servants. At times Gerran noticed Neb riding with his head tipped back as he studied the perfectly clear and sunny sky. Finally, on the second day, with Cengarn not more than five miles away, Gerran's curiosity won its battle with his attempt to mind his own affairs. He dropped back in the line of march to ride next to the prince's scribe and the gerthddyn.

"What are you looking for?" Gerran asked Neb. "Another dragon?"

"It wouldn't surprise me to see one," Neb said, "but it's not that." He hesitated briefly. "I wouldn't worry about it, Gerro. Everything seems safe enough."

Gerran considered probing further, but Neb was looking straight ahead with the sour expression of a man who's got nothing more to say. Salamander rolled his eyes in mock disgust.

"He's looking for that raven," Salamander said, "the one I told you about last summer, the one who stole the crystal from me."

Neb slewed around in his saddle and started to speak, but Salamander held up one hand for silence.

"There is no use," Salamander went on, "in keeping secrets from a man who already knows them."

Neb returned to staring at the road ahead. Gerran made the gerthddyn a half-bow from the saddle, then turned his horse out of line and trotted up to take his position behind the prince.

"Oh for the love of all the gods," Salamander said, "there's also no use in sulking."

Neb glanced his way with a scowl, then replaced it with an expression that revealed no emotion whatsoever. Salamander waited, letting his roan gelding amble along on a slack rein. Around them the countryside burgeoned with spring grass in the meadows and sprouting grain in the fields. They passed white cows with rusty-red ears, grazing busily in a long meadow, while in the distance stood a farmhouse circled by a low packed-mud wall. The sound of barking dogs drifted out to the road.

"Well," Neb said suddenly. "I don't see why you'd tell Gerran about dweomer matters."

"Why not?" Salamander said. "Some of them he needs to know. When it comes to mazrakir, another pair of eyes on watch is always a good thing."

"I suppose so. Still, I don't see why he gets to know things I don't. You never told me that Laz Moj stole that crystal when he was in raven form."

"My apologies. I thought I had. There were a fair number of things on my mind, you know, what with the war and all just over. What counts after all is the theft, not how it happened. There's no need for you to resent—"

"Well, how do you think I feel?" Neb said with a snarl in his voice. "I only hear half of what goes on. Dalla dribbles out information like honey out of a spoon."

"That's part of being an apprentice."

"Oh, I suppose, but ye gods! Here I used to be the Master of the Aethyr, and now they don't even recognize me."

"They? What?" Salamander looked straight at him. "Have you been trying to contact the Kings of Aethyr?"

"I—" Neb turned scarlet. "Uh, I—"

"You have, haven't you? I can't believe that Dalla thinks you're ready to do so."

"And I suppose you're going to run right to her and tell her, you fool of a chattering elf!"

"Ah, alas, Nevyn used to refer to my younger self in just that unflattering manner. Here's somewhat Neb needs to know. I can still play the chattering fool when I need to, but I'm much less of a fool than I used to be. For one thing, I know a dangerous trick when I see one played."

Neb set his lips together tight. He slapped his reins on his horse's neck, turned out of line, and trotted back toward the rear. Salamander twisted in the saddle and watched until he saw Neb guide his horse safely into line behind the wagons. Salamander turned back and let his horse follow the riders ahead while he focused his mind on contacting Dallandra. When he reported his conversation with Neb, Dallandra's first response was to blame herself for not riding to Cengarn with them.

"Don't," Salamander told her. "You would have had to bring the baby, and how much attention could you have paid Neb anyway?"

"That's very true. Getting pregnant when I did was the worst thing that could have happened. Dari's going to take more and more of my time and attention."

"Oh, come now. It's not like you and the child are all alone in the world. You've got as many women around you as the queen herself!"

Dallandra's image grinned at him. "Very true," she said, "and a very bracing thought. I don't mean to wallow in self-pity. I just wonder if I should have asked you to take Neb on."

"He would never have listened to me. He remembers too much, though not, alas, enough."

"Judging from the way he insulted you, I'd have to agree. Of course the Kings of Aethyr won't recognize him! He hasn't developed the proper symbols in his aura, and he doesn't really know how to greet them, either. Wretched little colt!"

"Mayhap we should be glad he doesn't remember everything."

"Well, that's true. He might just leave his apprenticeship and try to strike off on his own."

Salamander felt a ripple of omen-warning run down his spine. "Just so," he said. "Wild and stubborn colts have a tendency to bolt. And then they get eaten by wolves."

"Another good thought." Dallandra pursed her lips in a sour scowl. "Do share it with Neb, if you'd not mind, and as soon as possible. Anything you can do to help him—I'll be grateful."

Late that afternoon Prince Daralanteriel and his escorts reached Cengarn. High on its rocky cliffs the gray city loomed above the green meadows below. The gwerbret's dun loomed over the city, with its dark towers that rose high from a forest of slate roofs and stone walls. The prince called a halt in the meadow at the south gate, then turned in the saddle to consult with his vassals.

"Gerran," he said, "I'd rather we all camped out here. Is that going to be acceptable to the gwerbret?"

"It won't be, Your Highness," Gerran said. "It'd be taken as an insult to his hospitality."

Dar muttered something in Elvish under his breath.

"Most of our men can raise tents, if you'd like," Gerran said. "But you and the banadar—and maybe Mirryn and me—we'll have to stay in the broch for courtesy's sake. Well, assuming his grace offers to put me and Mirro up. I'm sure Your Highness and the banadar will be welcome."

"If my vassals aren't welcome, then I'll be leaving suddenly."

"Your Highness?" Mirryn bowed from the saddle before he spoke. "I'd rather make a camp with my men out here if I can. It's because of the way the gwerbret insulted my father. I'll eat at his table tonight for the sake of peace, but cursed if I'll sleep under his roof."

"Very well. I'd feel the same, were I you." Dar looked over the warbands, assembled behind them. "Let's leave most of the men here now, and just take a minimal escort up with us. I remember how much trouble Oth had trying to cram all the wedding guests into that dun. Mirryn, bring your men, and the banadar and I will take twenty-five of ours. Gerran, well, I guess your page will have to do for an escort at the moment. Oh, and Neb had better come with us."

As they rode up to the gate at the base of the cliff, Gerran noticed Salamander tagging along uninvited after Neb. At the city gates, the guards raised a cry of "Prince Dar, Prince Dar!" and ushered them into the winding streets of the town. As the prince led his men up the long steep ride to the gwerbret's dun, the townsfolk turned out to greet this welcome novelty of a royal visit with shouts and cheers.

Despite Gerran's worries about the sort of reception he'd get in the dun itself, the gatekeeper welcomed him warmly along with the prince and his escort and Mirryn and his. As the men were dismounting in the ward, Lord Oth, the gray-bearded chamberlain, and Lord Blethry, the stout equerry, hurried out of the great hall to greet them, followed by a bevy of pages and grooms. Oth bowed low to Prince Daralanteriel, then to Mirryn and Gerran with one sweep of his arm that included them both.

"His grace Ridvar's listening to witnesses in his chamber of justice, Your Highness," Oth said to the prince. "A thousand apologies, but he couldn't come out to greet you."

"I quite understand," Dar said. "Is it an important affair?"

"One of the local farmers has accused a neighbor of stealing his chickens." Oth smiled briefly. "It may not sound like much of a trouble, but his grace has jurisdiction over every little thing that happens in his rhan."

"Just as I have in mine, so I quite understand."

"Then do come in, Your Highness, and partake of our hospitality," Oth continued. "Ah, here are the grooms to see to your horses. Lord Blethry, if you'll ensure that our guests get somewhat to drink, I'll sort out the matter of chambers."

"My lord?" Mirryn stepped forward. "I'll be making camp down in the meadow with my escort. I'm the captain of my father's warband now, and that's where my duty lies."

"Oh." Oth paused in surprise, then nodded. "Well and good, then, as you wish."

As Oth bustled away, dispensing orders to the flock of pages, Gerran found himself remembering Branna's strange remarks about this most punctilious of servitors. Once he would have dismissed them, but now that he knew about dweomer and the insights it gave those who could work it, he decided he'd best take the remarks seriously.

"Salamander? Mirryn?" he said. "Don't mention Solla's inheritance until Voran gets here."

Salamander's eyes widened. "Very well," the gerthddyn said, "but may I ask why?"

"When we get somewhere private."

The gerthddyn's eyes grew wider, and his nose twitched as if he smelled the secret.

As they walked into the great hall, the gwerbret's wife, Drwmigga, dressed in flowing blue, was just coming down the winding stone staircase. The flowered scarf of a married woman wrapped her raven-dark hair. Around her flocked her unmarried serving-women, each with their hair caught back in a simple clasp.

Mirryn elbowed Gerran in the ribs and whispered. "That blonde lass there in the green dress. I think that's Lady Egriffa."

"And she's the game your mother's marked out for your hunt?"

"The very one. Should I go speak to her right now?"

"Wait till dinner, I'd say, lest you appear too eager." Salamander broke into the conversation. "I see we have somewhat to celebrate. Drwmigga's with child."

"How can you tell?" Mirryn said.

"Dolt!" Gerran said. "Look at her kirtle. It's tied up high."

"Oh, I suppose you know everything, now that you've got a wife!" But Mirryn dutifully looked. "You're right, I suppose."

"Of course he's right," Salamander said. "She's not got a waist anymore, and it gladdens my heart to see it. Or not see it, I mean. Let's hope she's carrying a son for the rhan's sake."

Lord Blethry seated the prince, the banadar, and the two lords at the table of honor, which stood in front of the enormous dragon hearth. He gave Salamander a scowl when the gerthddyn sat down with them, then trotted off to assign tables on the riders' side of the hall to the men of the escorts. Lady Drwmigga and her women arranged themselves at the table next to the table of honor but engrossed themselves in conversation to give the men their privacy. Servant lasses appeared and brought mead in silver goblets.

"Where's Neb?" Salamander said abruptly.

Gerran looked over the warbands, just settling themselves among a flurry of servants. "Huh!" He stood up for a better view. "No sign of him."

Salamander cursed under his breath in Elvish and got up, grabbing his goblet. He downed a mouthful of mead, then carried the goblet with him when he hurried over to the other side of the hall. Gerran sat down again, but he turned in his chair to watch the gerthddyn, moving among the men and asking questions in between sips of mead. Finally Salamander handed his goblet to a servant and ran out of the great hall.

"What in the icy hells is that all about?" Calonderiel leaned across the table.

"He's looking for Neb," Gerran said.

"Oh." Cal shrugged the problem away. "Well, no doubt he'll find him."

Gerran thought of going after Salamander to help him search, then remembered that the gerthddyn doubtless had his own ways of finding someone.

A small procession was coming down the staircase. Two guards in tabards decorated with the golden sun blazon of Cengarn led the way, followed by Gwerbret Ridvar and a shaved-bald priest of Bel. Bringing up the rear were two roughly-dressed men, one of them sullen and scowling, the other triumphant, bearing a wicker cage full of squawking chickens.

"I take it that justice has been done," Prince Dar said, grinning.

"So it seems, Your Highness," Gerran said. "And the lwdd paid."

The guards ushered the farmers out, then more courteously escorted the priest. Ridvar paused at the door to bid the priest farewell. He'd grown taller over the winter, Gerran noticed, and his upper lip sported a dark shadow, the beginnings of a moustache. With a last word to the guards, Ridvar came over and bowed to Prince Dar.

"My apologies for not being here to greet you, Your Highness." He glanced around the table. "Banadar, it gladdens my heart to see you again. My lords, welcome to my hall."

Nicely put, Gerran thought. "My thanks, Your Grace," he said aloud. "I've come to bring you the last scot due from the Red Wolf."

"Then my thanks to you." Ridvar sat down at the head of the honor table. "You can give it to Lord Oth when he joins us." He turned to the prince. "Well, Your Highness, I hope you've fared well over the winter."

"I have indeed, Your Grace, and the same to you," Dar said. "But alas, I fear I'm the bringer of evil news. The Horsekin are pushing into the wilderness north of your borders. The silver wyrm spotted them and flew to tell me."

Ridvar went icy still for a moment, then swore. "I can't say I'm surprised," he said at last. "How far away are they?"

"A good distance, thank all the gods. I doubt me if they'll stay far away."

"I doubt it, too. It's a good thing, then, that Prince Voran's on his way. One of his men rode in this morning with the news that he and his retinue will be here on the morrow." Ridvar's voice turned sour. "Have you heard about his highness' new title and appointment?"

"I have," Dar said. "I don't know much about Cerrgonney affairs, but I gather the province is a troubled one."

"Well, *Cerrgonney* is, truly." Ridvar clamped his lips as if he were sucking back words. He cleared his throat. "Now, about these Horsekin. What precisely did the dragon see?"

Since Calonderiel had already given him the substance of the dragon's report, Gerran only half listened to their talk. That Neb had gone missing troubled him. Finally he murmured an excuse and left the table. He stopped at the riders' side of the great hall, found Daumyr, and asked him if Salamander had mentioned where he might have been going.

"Down to town, my lord," Daumyr said. "The scribe might have gone looking for inks and suchlike."

"That's a good guess," Gerran said. "Well, no doubt the gerthddyn can find him."

Daumyr raised a quizzical eyebrow, but Gerran walked away without saying more. He sat down at the table of honor again, but as the talk and the mead flowed, he drank but little, just on the off chance that Salamander might need him.

⦾

As soon as he left the dun behind, Salamander stopped in the shelter of a narrow alley and scried for Neb. He found him easily, standing in front of a shabby tavern. Salamander took off at a dead run and reached it just as Neb was bargaining with the tavernman, a stout fellow in a greasy leather apron, for the right to sleep in his hayloft.

"This won't be necessary," Salamander said briskly. "Just a slight misunderstanding."

Neb whirled around and glared at him.

"Now here." The tavernman set massive hands on his hips. "A bargain's a bargain."

Neb opened his mouth to agree, but Salamander got in first.

"Are you going to argue with the gwerbret, my good man?" Salamander said. "This lad is a witness in an upcoming proceeding in Ridvar's court." He turned to Neb and smiled. "I take it you didn't realize that you'd been offered shelter in the broch itself."

"Oh, well, then!" the tavernman took a hasty step back. "Never you mind, lad. You've got better quarters waiting for you than my loft."

Salamander laid a firm hand on Neb's arm. "Come along," he said, "I'll take you back." He switched to Elvish, sticking to the words Neb would know. "You made a vow. Dallandra said stay with us. You promised to do what she said."

"Oh, well and good, then!" Neb's voice hovered near a snarl. "Fine. Let's go."

As a precaution Salamander took the reins of Neb's horse and led it. The yellow gnome materialized, standing on the saddle. It bowed to Salamander with a gape-mouthed grin, as if saying thank you. *The gnome has more sense than the man!* Salamander thought with a certain sourness. Neb strode away, walking fast ahead of him toward the dun at the top of the hill, but soon the steepness of the street made him slow down. When Salamander caught up with him, he stopped walking altogether.

"We need to have a chat," Salamander said in Deverrian. "There's no market today, so let's go up to the commons."

On the grassy hilltop a few white cows with rusty-red ears stood grazing or lay down in the shade of a cluster of trees to rest and ruminate. A sleepy-looking lad with a dog and a long stick sat nearby and watched over the cows. Salamander made sure that they stopped where the lad couldn't overhear. He slacked the bit of Neb's horse to let it snack on the spring grass, then stood facing Neb, who looked steadily back with his mouth twisted in anger.

"Now then, let me guess," Salamander began. "You were going to lurk in that tavern overnight, and in the morning ride out on your own. I'll guess further. You want a different master in our craft and think you can find one."

"Oh, curse you!" Neb snapped.

"Ah, I see that I was perspicacious, sharp-eyed, and just plain correct. You know, every now and then an unruly colt will stray from its herd. It always ends up eaten by wolves. Dweomer has its own pack of wolves, you know. They'd welcome a smart lad like you, but you wouldn't care for what they'd do to you."

"I know that. I'm not stupid enough to link up with them."

"You might not recognize who they were at first, not until it was too late to get out."

Neb crossed his arms tightly over his chest.

"Be that as it may," Salamander continued, "there's this little matter of the gwerbretal malover. It's not just some tale I made up to impress that tavernman. If you run away before you give your evidence, his grace will send out messengers to his peers, branding you as a criminal. The branding could become a reality, not a mere metaphor, if they catch you."

Neb looked sharply away. "I didn't realize that."

"I thought perhaps you didn't. And what about Branna? You're a married man. Now, a fair many married men have decided they made a grave mistake, and thus have taken themselves away from their wife's bed and ken, but they've not sworn the vows you have."

Neb turned half-away and blushed scarlet. Salamander realized that he'd scored a sharper hit than he'd intended. He waited, but Neb said nothing. "As well as all that," Salamander went on, "wouldn't you miss her?"

"I'd get over it." Neb spoke so softly that it was hard to hear him. "I'm a man. Love is for women."

"Ah, so now you're the hardened and hardhearted warrior type, eh?" Salamander rolled his eyes heavenward.

"Oh, hold your tongue!" Neb raised his voice, but it shook with barely-suppressed tears. "Very well, I would miss her. A lot. That's why I didn't just leave the Westlands this spring."

"And are you still thinking of leaving now?"

"I'm not. I won't go anywhere. Let's go back to the gwerbret's blasted dun."

"Will you promise me you won't try to bolt again?"

Neb hesitated for so long that Salamander began to fear he'd lost him, but finally Neb nodded his agreement. "I promise," Neb said finally. "You're right about being a witness at the malover."

"You know, if things trouble you, you can always talk them out with me."

"My thanks." Neb looked down at the ground, then kicked a pebble so hard that it sailed for some yards across the cropped grass. "I'll think about what you've said."

From his seat at the honor table, Gerran kept a watch for Neb. He finally saw him when the scribe, his arms full of blankets and saddlebags, followed Salamander and Lord Oth into the great hall. Oth conferred with one of the pages and sent him and Neb both up the staircase, doubtless to find Neb a chamber. This time, Gerran noticed, Salamander sat down at one of the riders' tables rather than ranking himself among the lords. Oth hurried over to the table of honor to stand beside the gwerbret. Gerran rose and greeted him with a bow, which Oth returned.

"I hear you've brought coin from Tieryn Cadryc," Oth said.

"I have," Gerran said. "It's the last scot from the Red Wolf."

"Well and good, then. It will gladden my heart to see that matter tidied away."

Gerran had been carrying the money in a small pouch tucked inside his shirt. He took it out and handed it to Oth, who clasped it tight in one bony hand.

"No need to count it, I'm sure," Oth said.

With Branna's odd warning very much in his mind, it occurred to Gerran how easy it would be for a servitor to pocket one of the coins, then claim a mistake had been made in order to extort another from the person paying a debt.

"No need, but it would be best if you did," Gerran said, as blandly as possible. "Tieryn Cadryc asked me to make sure it got counted in front of his grace. He was afraid he might have made a mistake in the amount." Gerran glanced at the gwerbret, then at the prince. "He thinks highly of you both, Your Highness and Your Grace, and he wants this done right." He looked at Oth and smiled. "It would ache his heart if the prince and the gwerbret thought him miserly."

Ridvar and Daralanteriel nodded their agreement. Oth smiled, but his eyes had narrowed in some odd fit of feeling. He had trouble looking Gerran in the face and bowed again to cover his reluctance. *What's this?* Gerran thought. *Shame, mayhap? Fear? It's not, but rage!*

Oth opened the pouch and spread the coins out on the table. "All in order, my lords," he announced with a brittle sort of cheer. "I'll just take this up to the treasury."

Gerran sat down next to Mirryn and watched Oth scoop up the coins and transfer them back to the pouch. The old man bowed to the gwerbret, then hurried away.

Although he kept watch for the chamberlain, Gerran saw no sign of him all that afternoon. At dinner, Lord Oth did appear, but he headed up a table of servitors far from the table of honor. Salamander and Neb took places with the men of Mirryn's escort on the far side of the great hall. When the food was about to be served, Lady Drwmigga came to the honor table to sit at her lord's left hand, opposite Prince Dar. With her came the young blonde woman, whose name, Drwmigga announced, was Lady Egriffa.

"My lord Mirryn?" Drwmigga said. "If you'd not mind, may Egriffa share your trencher?"

"I'd be honored, my lady," Mirryn said.

Egriffa smiled and sat down next to him. She was a pleasant-looking lass, with pale hair, big blue eyes, and a small but full-lipped mouth. Unfortunately, she seemed to lack an intellect. Every time Mirryn spoke to her, she answered as briefly as possible, then giggled at some length. Now and then she would lay her fingertips upon her lips as if stuffing the giggle back in. Mirryn said less and less as the meal went on. When the ladies left the table and went up to their hall, Mirryn sighed in deep relief.

"You're not going to marry that, are you?" Gerran said.

"Pray to every god I don't." Mirryn grabbed his goblet of mead from the table and drank off a long swallow. "I don't care who her kin may be. I'm cursed glad now that I told Oth I'd camp with my men. This way I won't have to face her with my breakfast."

As soon as he decently could, Mirryn left the table with the excuse of making sure his men fared well. Gerran accompanied him out to the gates of the dun. Carrying a candle lantern, Salamander joined them. In a pool of dappled light they stood just out of the hearing of the night gatekeeper.

"What's all this with Neb?" Gerran said. "Or can you tell me?"

"I promised him I'd keep most of this in confidence," Salamander said. "Let's just say he's generally unhappy with his lack of progress in his apprenticeship."

"I still don't understand why he'd go off on his own."

"I think he may have been entertaining the idea of finding another master of his craft."

"Indeed?" Mirryn put in. "That's a serious thing, isn't it? The scribes' guild must have rules and suchlike against it."

"It most assuredly does," Salamander said. "I truly shouldn't tell you much more than that."

"We won't pry, don't worry," Gerran said. "Do you think he'll bolt again?"

"I doubt it. If he does, Clae's promised to come tell me. He'll be sharing a bed with his brother during this stay. Oth's put them in the broch itself, not in the servants' quarters out by the barracks, thanks to Neb being a witness against Govvin. Which reminds me, Gerro. Why did you ask me to hold my tongue around Oth?"

"Because Branna told me to stay on guard when it comes to him. I'll be bringing the matter of Solla's inheritance to Prince Voran, not to the gwerbret."

"I see. It's usually a good idea to listen when Branna delivers one of her pronouncements. They may sound daft, mad, or just plain confused, but they contain truths." Salamander yawned and shook his head. "Well, I'd best get off to bed, and doubtless you both want to do the same."

"I'll admit to being tired." Gerran glanced at Mirryn. "What about you?"

Mirryn hesitated, appeared to be thinking something through, then shrugged. "I'd best leave before the city guards shut the gates."

Mirryn strode off downhill to join the encampment outside the city walls, while Salamander headed off to the barracks. Gerran went back inside to drink with the prince and the gwerbret as courtesy demanded.

"So," Neb said. "It gladdens my heart that we'll get to spend a bit more time with each other while we're here."

"Mine, too," Clae said. "It was decent of Oth to let me stay in the broch with you." He glanced around the bedchamber. "It's so quiet here, though, not like the barracks."

"Think you'll be able to sleep without all that snoring?"

"Oh, no doubt." Clae grinned at him. "Being a page tires you out, what with my lord's horses to tend and all that."

They lay awake for some time that night, sharing a bed as they always had in their father's house. Clae talked about the things he'd done and learned during the winter; Neb told him details of how the Westfolk lived and avoided the subject of his own experiences. Soon enough Clae fell asleep, but tired though he was, Neb stayed awake with humiliation for a bitter companion.

The worst of it, he decided, was the way Salamander had guessed exactly what he was going to do—ride away from his master and his wife both and try to find another master of dweomer to take him on. He'd brought his supply of herbs along to sell in order to get the coin for his journey. Now, he supposed, he needn't have bothered, since that chattering fool had found him out.

Salamander's remark about colts eaten by wolves stung most of all. *I know all about dark dweomer,* Neb thought. *The last thing I'd ever do is join up with that lot of deformed scum!* He was sure that he knew a great deal more about many things than either Salamander or Dallandra gave him credit for. Over the winter he'd meditated upon the correct symbols to open the treasure-house of images. Hard work, but he'd remembered more and more of Nevyn's long life, the dweomer knowledge he'd had, the power he'd commanded, all of it out of Neb's reach but easily in sight.

Those cursed women! It was no wonder, he reflected, that Branna was learning so much so easily while he stumbled along behind. Dallandra and Grallezar, even Valandario, favored her shamelessly—

or so he believed. And then, of course, there were her dreams, filled with memories and lore. Although she denied it, Neb was convinced that Branna looked down on him because he'd had to work so hard to retrieve his own past life from the astral while her knowledge came effortlessly.

Round and round his mind went, rehearsing grievances. *Who am I?* he wondered. *Nevyn was the Master of the Aethyr—why can't I have the same position?* He knew full well that he'd have to work to regain such exalted powers, but somehow he'd not expected the work to take so long. Branna remembered Jill so clearly, and she seemed to him to be speeding through her apprenticeship whilst he dragged along behind. *It's not fair!*

Even his meditations upon Nevyn's life fell short, in Neb's opinion. He would try to recover some bit of dweomerlore only to feel his mind wandering off to other things, mostly images of herbs, blooming along roadways, or of sick children, drinking out of a cup as Nevyn held it for them. Memories of warriors, cut and bleeding, disrupted his attempts to call upon the Lords of the Wildlands as once Nevyn had done. Every now and then he considered stopping his study of the healer's craft. Maybe then those intrusive memories would die away. But every time he stopped, some question would nag at him until he took it up again.

The herbcraft would come in handy, he supposed, when he left the Westfolk. Eventually he'd make his escape. He would simply take Branna with him. He wasn't sure why he was so determined to leave, except that it annoyed him to see Branna so at home among these alien lives, while he struggled on behind, trying to learn Elvish as fast as she—

"Oh, stop it!" he whispered aloud. "You're being stupid!"

He heard the dun's watchmen calling out the mid-mark of the night before he finally fell asleep, only to dream of finding Brangwen's dead body on the river sand, sodden, wide-eyed but unseeing, her deathly-pale skin touched by the rising sun. In the dream he heard Rhegor's voice once again, saying, "You failed her, lad."

Neb woke covered in cold sweat to find the room bright with sunlight and Clae gone. He sat up and perched on the edge of the high bed to run his hands through his sweaty hair.

"You can't leave her," he said aloud. "A vow's a vow."

As he thought about Branna, it seemed to him that he could see her, standing in the women's hall in a pair of woad-blue dresses, her hair swept back in a flowered scarf. His thought formed without his willing it: *I love you, Branni.* Her thought floated back to him: *I love you, too, but you shouldn't be doing this working without Dalla's permission.* Neb jumped to his feet and growled, a sound so like a dog that it startled him. *Stupid wretched females!* His yellow gnome materialized, took one good look at him, then vanished again. In a foul mood Neb dressed, then went downstairs to find some breakfast, growling to himself all the way.

With no dreams that troubled him, Gerran slept till a few hours after dawn. He lay in bed, yawning, and was just considering getting up when someone knocked on his chamber door. Clae darted in without waiting to be asked.

"My lord?" Clae said. "There's a silver dagger down at the gates."

"Indeed?" Gerran said. "What—"

"The gatekeeper wasn't even going to let him in, but I told him to wait just outside for a while. We don't have anyone in our warband, and so I thought—"

"Right you are! I'll get dressed and go down. Tell him to keep waiting."

The silver dagger turned out to be a tall fellow with broad shoulders and the long arms of a swordsman. Under a thatch of dirty brown hair his face was hollow-cheeked and touched with a certain paleness about the mouth. He revealed no emotion whatsoever when Gerran allowed him inside the walls for a chat. His horse, a chestnut gelding, looked well cared for, with healthy legs and hooves. As the silver dagger knelt before him, Gerran had the odd feeling he'd seen him before, but he couldn't place where.

"What brings you out here to Arcodd?" Gerran said.

"Horsekin, my lord," the silver dagger said. "I heard about last summer's fighting and figured there might be a hire for me."

"You're right enough, but I can't pay you much beyond your keep."

"If we don't see any fighting, my keep will be pay enough. If we do, you can decide what I'm worth then."

"How long has it been since you've eaten?"

"A while." His pale mouth twitched in what might have been a smile. "I spent my last copper on oats for my mount. We ran out of those last night."

"Well, I might have a hire for you, I might not, but I can stand you a meal at least."

"My thanks, my lord." This time he did smile. "May I ask your lordship's name?"

"Gerran of the Gold Falcon. And you are?"

"Nicedd, my lord, from Pren Cludan, over in Cerrgonney." He scrambled up and busied himself with brushing the dirt off the knees of his brigga. "I'd beg you not to ask me why I left it."

"I don't go prying into silver daggers' personal affairs." Gerran glanced around and found Clae waiting nearby. "Take this lad down to the encampment," he said to the page, "and ask Lord Mirryn to feed him and his horse both and keep him in the warband. Who knows? We might have a hire for him eventually."

"Done, my lord." Clae turned to the silver dagger. "I'll ride behind you on the way down."

As they mounted up, Gerran noticed that the saddlebags at the saddle's pommel had once borne a leather blazon. Nicedd had taken off the patch, but its shadow remained, dark against the faded leather of the bags themselves, the outline of a wolf. He'd once ridden for some distant relation of Tieryn Cadryc's, then, a member of the ancient and conjoint clan of the Wolves, white and red.

Gerran returned to the great hall and the table of honor. As he was sitting down, Salamander trotted over to join him.

"Where's Prince Dar?" Gerran said.

"Off in the stables with our host the gwerbret," Salamander said. "I gather that discussing horses is somewhat of a ritual among the noble-born."

"It is, truly." Gerran glanced around. "What about our scribe?"

"He seemed much subdued this morning at breakfast. I think me he's thought better of the various follies that he stood on the brink of committing."

"Good. You know, I'd forgotten that Mirryn doesn't know about Neb's real craft."

"I had, too. Well, he assumed we were talking about a scribal guild, so all is well."

"Just so. Once Prince Voran gets himself here, Neb will have his testimony against Govvin to keep him busy. Has Ridvar summoned the priests yet, or do you know?"

"I generally know what there is to know." Salamander paused for a grin. "Because the dun's lasses generally have overheard it and then tell me. His grace has sent two summons. The first Govvin ignored. The second he answered, saying he might well come here to deliver his opinion on the matter, if the omens were favorable or some such thing. So we're waiting for him to arrive, or perhaps it might be more accurate to say that we're waiting to see if he arrives."

"It all boils down to waiting," Gerran said.

"True spoken. I take it that vexes you?"

"It does. If the old man doesn't get himself here soon, I say we ride out and fetch him, priest or not. He didn't strike me as particularly holy."

"Me, either, and indeed, fetching him is exactly what we might do, once Voran gets here." Salamander paused, glancing around the great hall. "Speaking of annoyances, have you seen Neb just now?"

"I have. He was going into one of the side brochs. When I hailed him, he said he wanted to talk with one of the chirurgeons."

"I hope he's not unwell. I'll go look for him." With a wave Salamander strode off.

Gerran watched him go, then accepted a bowl of porridge from a hovering servant lass. He reminded himself that even though he hated sitting around doing nothing, he had no choice in the matter.

Raddyn, the head chirurgeon of Dun Cengarn, was a stick-thin man with several day's growth of gray beard and narrow dark eyes. He lived in a chamber high up in one of the slender towers that nestled next to the main broch of Dun Cengarn. Apparently he was unmarried, because a narrow bed, a stool, a square table, and a vast amount of clutter made up its furnishings. Raddyn fished and rummaged among the heaps of dirty clothes, candle ends, and small bags of unrecognizable things until he found the leather-bound book, as long as Neb's forearm and reeking of mold.

"Here you go." Raddyn laid it down on the table, which wobbled under the weight.

"My thanks," Neb said. "I much appreciate this."

"What I don't understand is why a scribe wants to look at a book like this. It describes medicaments, not letters."

"I come from Trev Hael. That plague or somewhat like it is mentioned in here. I'm wondering if it explains how the thing spread so fast."

"Ah. Well, corrupted humors, as usual, would be my judgment."

"But how do they get from one person to another? I mean, I can understand if a person with an excess of watery humors becomes ill. But why should the person next door or the wife who's sharing his bed then become ill in turn?"

Raddyn shrugged with a look of profound regret. "If I knew that," he said, "I'd be serving down in the king's court, not moldering up here with our miserly gwerbret."

"One person's corrupted humors must corrupt the next one's. Somehow."

"No doubt. 'How' is indeed the question. You know, sometimes I wish I were but a scribe like you." Raddyn turned away and perched on the stool. "Ye gods, it drives me half mad sometimes, how little we know!"

He leaned over sideways, rummaged in the clutter a bit more, and pulled out a leather bottle. When he unstoppered it, Neb caught the smell of mead.

The scribe who'd copied the book of Bardekian lore had done a splendid job, writing in a clear large hand that could be read easily by candlelight. He'd left wide margins, too, which generations of chirurgeons had filled with notes about their successes or failures with the various herbs. One set of notes, concerning ulcerations of the stomach, struck Neb as oddly familiar, even though they weren't in Nevyn's hand. He turned back to the first page and found a list of men who'd owned the book, but none of the names jogged his memory.

Eventually Neb found the passage he'd seen before only to realize that it offered him no answers, merely a brief description of the effects of the plague. The marginal notes remarked only that no herbal remedies had proved efficacious. He shut the book with a sigh.

"My thanks," he said to Raddyn.

"Welcome," the chirurgeon said. "If you ever find out how these poisons spread, let me know, eh?"

"Oh, I will, rest assured."

Neb left the chamber and hurried down the stairs. He was just coming out into the ward when he saw Salamander, heading toward him. He was tempted to duck and run, then decided he was being foolish by avoiding the gerthddyn. *Besides, I do need to concentrate on my real work,* he told himself. *I've been wasting too much time worrying about herbcraft.* Yet something Raddyn had said—poisons, he called the plagues. He'd doubtless only been describing them in a fancy way, but what if, Neb thought to himself, what if there was some substance involved, something that acted like a poison? Caught by the idea, he nearly ran into Salamander, who stepped aside just in time.

"There you are!" Salamander said. "I was just wondering if you were ill or suchlike."

"If I were, I wouldn't go to Raddyn," Neb said. "I feel sorry for anyone who comes under his knife."

Salamander blinked at him.

"Any news from Dallandra?" Neb said. "About Haen Marn?"

"None," Salamander said. "The problem is that it's an island. Scrying it out will therefore be impossible. All we can do now is hope it returned, and if it didn't, then, well, we'll just have to wait and see."

Riding the river down to Lin Serr proved to be both more tedious and more dangerous than Berwynna had been expecting. During that first day, the river ran slowly between broad banks, thick with forests and ferns. In places the shallow water became nearly solid with purplish-green water reeds. The little coracles bobbed peacefully along at the river's whim. Dougie and Enj used their paddles mostly to steer clear of floating tree branches and other debris. The slow water allowed the spring crop of mosquitoes and blackflies to swarm around the boats. Berwynna took off her apron and flapped it to keep them away from her and Dougie both. By midafternoon, her arms ached.

Toward sunset Enj yelled over from his coracle that it was time to go ashore. When they saw a sandy beach at a bend in the river, Enj paddled hard across the current and headed for it. Dougie followed his lead, and the river reluctantly let the men run the coracles up onto the land. Dougie helped Berwynna out and grinned at her.

"My rosy-cheeked lass!" he said.

"That's sunburn," she snapped. "I'm also bug-bitten and damp."

Another difficulty came storming up to them in the person of Mic, who planted himself in front of Berwynna, set his hands on hips, and scowled.

"I know what you're going to say," Berwynna said in Dwarvish. "I never should have come along, Mother will worry, and I'll only be a burden and nuisance."

"I was going to say that you'll be putting yourself in danger," Mic said, "which is more to the point than calling you a nuisance. What in the name of Gonn's Hammer did you think you were doing?"

"Getting away from Haen Marn. Mara can clean the stinking fish and sweat over the bread oven from now on. I'm sick and tired of being her servant, thank you very much!"

"Ah." Mic suddenly grinned. "Well, good for you, lass! I have to admit that I'm glad to see you finally stand up for yourself."

"You are? I always knew you were my favorite uncle for a reason."

Mic laughed. "A true compliment," he said, "and you can't blame an uncle for worrying about his favorite niece."

"Well, that's true. But I also do want to find my father, and Enj is going to look for him."

"Reason enough, I suppose. But what about your mother?"

"Avain will see us in her basin. She'll keep an eye on all of us. Did you think she wouldn't?"

"No, you're right." Mic paused to study her face. "You'd best put some butter or lard on that sunburn. Did we bring any?"

"I did, and a good thing too."

Berwynna helped Enj unpack the food for their meal. While he carried it over, she hurriedly checked the precious dweomer book and found it safe and dry. Looking at it lying among the mundane supplies made her profoundly uneasy. *I shouldn't have stolen it,* she thought, *but it's too late to take it back now.*

Their dinner of flatbread and jerky did nothing to soothe Berwynna's aches and pains, nor did sleeping on hard ground. She reminded herself that she'd been determined to sneak away for this adventure and had, therefore, only herself to blame. If the travails of travel were proving ill for her, though, they were far harder on Otho. That morning she had to help the old man get free of his tangled blanket and sit up.

"Otho," she said, "can you truly do this?"

"Hah!" Otho snorted like an angry horse. "And what choice do I have now, eh? I was stupid enough to start the journey, and now I'll have to finish it. Here, lass, if you'll lend me your shoulder to lean upon, I think me I can stand up."

So he could, but barely. Mic hurried over and helped the old man walk to the privacy of a cluster of young saplings to relieve himself. By the time they returned, Otho seemed more his old self, grumbling and griping about the weather, the flies, the choice of campsite, and the food.

The day's travel started out much like the last, but by noon the river had narrowed. Instead of ferns and water reeds, big tan boulders lined the banks or sat sullenly on the river bottom itself. The water turned choppy. At times the boats swirled through white water that slammed the coracles back and forth between rocks and threatened to tip them with swift curls of waves. Fortunately, taking her sister over to the mainland had taught Berwynna to handle a paddle. It took both her and Dougie's efforts to keep the leather boat upright and untorn. When they finally beached for the evening's camp, she ached in every muscle and tendon.

So, apparently, did everyone else. Except for the occasional curse from Otho, no one spoke during their soggy meal of moldy bread and cheese, eaten around a small, smoky fire. After dinner, Berwynna had a moment alone with Enj. She tried her best to sound casual when she asked him how much farther they had to go.

"I'm ever so eager to see Lin Serr," she told him.

"Not too long now." Enj paused to think something through. "About two days and a half, and we'll reach the canyon wall. Then we'll have to climb up the cliff, and finally hike the rest of the way. So four days more, say."

Berwynna blinked back tears and smiled as brightly as she could. "That'll be splendid. I wonder how I'm going to get up the cliff in these dresses, though."

"Imph, well you might wonder. That lad of yours, too—does he always wrap himself in that blanket thing?"

"It's called a plaid, and he's wearing all the clothing he's got. He wasn't planning on leaving Alban, you know, when the island took us away."

"Of course not! Doltish of me! But as for you, Mic should have a spare pair of brigga in that overstuffed pack of his. Ye gods, did he bring everything he owns?"

"Most likely. I'll ask him about the brigga. They should fit me well enough."

Indeed, Mic did have a pair of brigga to give her, and a shirt as well. Wearing them made her feel as if she were no longer the Berwynna she'd always been. *I'm not just Mara's twin anymore.* The thought made her feel like dancing in joy. That night, wrapped in Dougie's arms, she decided that the ground made a soft enough bed.

With the rapids past, the river turned calm again, and the rest of the journey passed more easily. For the final day's run, Berwynna rode in the first boat with Enj, who surrendered the larger boat, and Mic and Otho, to Dougie and his longer arms and greater strength. Just as Enj had predicted, they reached the canyon when the sun had climbed almost to zenith. Its pale walls rose so steep and straight that Berwynna asked him if mortal hands had cut them out of the rock.

"They did, truly," Enj said. "But I'm not sure who the hands belonged to. The stone masters in Lin Serr say they had naught to do with it."

"Well, if it's linked to Haen Marn, I'm not surprised there's a mystery behind it."

"Neither am I." Enj smiled at her. "Now hang on, sister of mine! Dangerous water ahead!"

Inside the canyon the water at first ran fast though reasonably smooth. Berwynna had the leisure to look up from time to time at the pale limestone walls, glaring with light since the sun stood directly overhead. She thought she saw markings of some sort upon the walls, but she had to pay too much attention to her paddle to ask questions. As the space between the walls narrowed, the water ran faster and faster. The final cliff loomed over them by the time that Enj shouted the alarm.

"Dougie, bring her in!"

The two coracles spun out of the river to a shallow beachhead cut out of a cliff face. The men leaped out and hauled the little boats ashore. As Dougie helped Berwynna out, she looked up and saw a narrow set of stairs cut deep into the rock face in a serpentine pattern. Together with Mic, they unloaded both coracles and piled their gear on the strip of sand while Enj helped Otho sit down in the shade of the cliff.

"The river runs into the city, you see," Mic spoke in Alban for Dougie's sake. "I was hoping we could just ride in all the way." He turned to Enj and repeated the remark in Dwarvish.

"We can't risk getting sucked in where the river goes underground," Enj answered in the same. "The water comes up to the roof, as far as anyone knows, and we'd drown. There's a cataract deep inside the caverns where the river comes down to bedrock."

Mic translated, then added, "I didn't realize all that. It's a good thing Enj knows what he's doing."

"Oh, we could have guessed." Dougie pointed at the juncture of the river and the cliff. "Follow the bubbles, Mic."

Indeed, gleaming in the last of the noontide sun, a raft of bubbles was swirling in an unsteady vortex just where the river fell under the stone. With one last swirl it disappeared, and another clutch of bubbles formed in its place.

"Ah, truly." Mic rubbed his chin. "That's why I hired you as a bodyguard, Dougie. You've got better eyes for danger than I do."

Berwynna turned to Enj. "Do those stairs reach all the way up?"

"They do." Enj tilted his head back to look at the rim. "Now, the lads at Lin Serr did cut those, they told me. By Gonn himself, they're steep! I've only ever seen them from the top, so I had no idea. We'd better watch our step, eh?"

"You think they would have cut a railing while they were at it," Berwynna said.

"Oh, there are handholds now and then. Getting our gear up's going to be a job and a half, though. It's a cursed good thing we've got rope with us."

Berwynna spoke in Dwarvish. "It's Dougie I'm worried about."

"He does have big feet," Enj answered in the same. "And there's no Mountain blood in his veins. Well, I'll give him a quick lesson in climbing. And then there's Otho."

"Haul him up on ropes," Mic joined in. "Just like the gear."

Although Otho protested in a storm of foul curses, in the end carry him up they did. Despite Berwynna's fears, Dougie made the climb fast and safely. At the top, dressed only in his shirt and loin-wrap, he used the boat ropes and his plaid as a sling to haul up first the gear, then a sputtering, snarling Otho, with Mic panting along behind to keep the old man from swinging out and banging back against the rock.

Berwynna went next with Enj close behind her. Near the top, she paused to catch her breath on a flat landing beside a secure knob of rock cut for a handhold. She refused to look down and focused her gaze on the cliff face. Next to the cut knob she could see one of those mysterious markings she'd noticed earlier, but rather than a rune or some other symbol, it appeared to be the edge of some roundish flat thing embedded in the rock itself. It looked like the edge of a pottery plate but beveled like a coin. She had no idea what it might be and returned to climbing.

At the top Dougie was waiting to catch her hands and help her to safety. She walked well away from the edge of the cliff, then allowed herself to look down. The river looked only as wide as a riband, shiny between the cliffs. The sheer distance made her head swirl like the river vortex.

"All up!" Enj's good cheer steadied her down again. "Mic, here's what I suggest. I'll go on ahead while you all make camp here. There's a farm not far away where we can borrow a mule."

"How far?" Mic said.

"Oh, about half a day's walk. I'll be back on the morrow by noon, no doubt."

"How far is it to Lin Serr?" Berwynna said.

"Another half a day past the farm. Near, but too far to carry all our gear and Otho."

The elderly dwarf was sitting on a flattish boulder nearby. Berwynna knelt down next to him. His face had turned bright red, and he was sweating profusely.

"Otho?" she asked. "Are you well?"

"No, of course I'm not!" Otho snarled. "Hauling a man around with ropes doesn't fetch him much good, lass. I'm not a cursed fish."

"Would it have been better for you to climb? I don't think so."

When he scowled at her, she took the expression as a silent admission that she was right. Rather than say so, she fetched a water bottle and helped him drink.

They had come up onto a fairly flat stretch of tableland, a good many miles wide, she decided, since it ran from horizon to horizon. Nearby stood a copse of straggly second-growth pine trees. Enj took his pack and walking stick, then set off, heading south. The rest of them got Otho into the shade of the trees and set about making camp.

Yet, as it turned out, they had no need to camp. Enj had barely disappeared into the glare of the horizon when Berwynna noticed a cloud of dust at the same spot. Quickly it resolved itself into Enj, a pair of mules, and a squad of Mountain Folk, all coming their way. At first Berwynna thought that the men were carrying unusually long walking sticks, but when the sun glittered on the flat blades at the end of each handle, she realized that she was seeing war axes, the weapons her mother had so often mentioned in her tales of the homeland.

"Ye gods!" Mic said. "I wonder how they got here so fast?"

Enj announced the answer to that question as soon as he came close enough to shout. "Someone saw our boats on the river," he said. "So they sent guards to investigate."

"And welcome they are!" Mic stepped forward to greet the leader of the squad. "Pel! Ye gods, you're a grown man now!"

The man called Pel laughed aloud and came striding up to them. Instead of an ax, he carried a short-bladed sword. Judging from the way he used it to point at things while he called out orders, it marked him as the squad's officer. He was a solid-looking fellow, with dark hair and a messy dark beard straggling over his chin and neck.

"You've been gone a long time, Mic," Pel said, smiling. "I was just a sprout, not even thirty, when you up and disappeared on us." He turned to Berwynna and bowed. "Greetings, my lady. Enj tells us that you hail from Haen Marn."

"I do, indeed." Berwynna dropped him a curtsy in answer to his bow. "And this is my betrothed, Douglas of Alban."

Pel looked at Dougie—looked up at him, in fact, as if he were surveying a tree—and bowed to him as well.

"He doesn't speak the Mountain language," Berwynna went on, "but I've been teaching him some of the tongue that Deverry men speak."

"Well and good, then." Pel spoke in that language. "Welcome to Dwarveholt, Douglas."

"My thanks," Dougie said. "It glads—it gladdens my heart to meet you."

Pel in turn introduced the other men in the squad, but so quickly that Berwynna could remember none of their names. She contented herself with smiling as the men milled around, fussing over Otho, who spoke pleasantly to some of them.

"The old man actually looks happy," Dougie whispered to her. "The end of the world must be near or suchlike."

Berwynna stifled a laugh.

For the trip to Lin Serr, Berwynna and Otho shared one of the mules while the rest of the men walked. Just at sunset they reached the farm Enj had mentioned, a cluster of wooden buildings. A high stone wall separated it from its fields, just bursting with the green life of young grain.

"By the gods!" Mic said. "This place looks like a Deverry dun."

"There's a reason for that." Pel glanced at Berwynna and lowered his voice. "I'll tell you later. It's more than a bit grim."

Berwynna was about to protest that she didn't need sheltering from grim truths, but their hosts, a noisy troop of about twenty young men of the Mountain Folk, had flung open the gates and were inviting them in. When they heard that Berwynna came from Haen Marn, they all bowed to her and her alone.

"Come in, come in, my lady." The man who spoke seemed older than the rest. "Welcome to our humble house."

With its rough plank floor and whitewashed walls, their great hall may have been humble, but it seemed like luxury after the river trip. A big hearth graced one wall, and a plank table ran down the length of the room. On the wall opposite the hearth hung a row of double axes, gleaming in the sunset light that came in the windows.

As the evening went on, Berwynna realized that she was being treated like a great lady—*like Lord Douglas' wife back home,* she thought, since Dougie's grandmother was the only great lady she'd ever seen. They seated her at the head of the long plank table and served her meal first. She drank mead when the rest were given ale. When the mead made her yawn, several of the young men lit candle lanterns and showed her and Dougie to a chamber that, judging from the sock left lying on the floor by the door, had been hastily vacated by someone else. Another fellow brought up hot water for them to wash with, and he took away her dirty dresses to launder them.

"I'll be glad to have my dresses back," Berwynna told Dougie. "I didn't want to go to Lin Serr wearing Mic's spare brigga."

"It sounds too grand a place for that." Dougie scowled at his own filthy shirt. "I could use a bit of washing myself, but naught I could borrow here would fit me."

"You look like a stork among chickens, truly. I'll have to make you a second shirt if we can find some cloth somewhere."

On the morrow, when they set out for Lin Serr, once again Berwynna and Otho rode while everyone else walked. Although the road ran through peaceful-looking farmland, here and there beside it stood stone towers some forty feet high, each circled by a stone wall.

"Do people live in those?" Berwynna asked Enj, who was leading her mule.

"They do," Enj said. "They're easily defended in case the Horsekin come a-raiding."

"They look new."

"They are. The Horsekin didn't raid until about forty-some years ago."

Toward noon they came to a small grove of oak trees. Although some had reached full growth, and their green canopies nodded high in the light wind, a few were mere saplings of some six feet, while others of various heights stood in between. Their regular arrangement in a rough square made it clear that they'd been planted and coppiced over long years. In the open middle of the square grew brushy shrubs and short grass. Berwynna assumed that they were about to stop for a meal and a rest, but Enj had a surprise in store for her. He handed the lead rope of Berwynna's mule to Dougie, then knelt down among the shrubs. He picked up a flat-sided rock and pounded it sharply on the ground.

"What in God's name?" Dougie muttered. "Has he gone daft?"

"I don't know," Berwynna said. "But when he beat on the ground, it sounded hollow."

Sure enough, in but a few moments Enj stood up and stepped back. Berwynna heard a massive rumble, then a loud creaking, and slowly a square of ground slid sideways, bushes and all, to reveal a hole of some ten feet on a side.

"The entrance to the city," Enj called out. "Or one of them."

A long easy slope of stone ramp led down into dim light and shadow. Thanks to the descriptions Enj had given her of the city, Berwynna was expecting that the ramp would lead a long mysterious way down, but in about fifty yards it leveled out onto the floor of a huge, rough-hewn room that smelled of mules and dust. A squad of men armed with war axes stood around, at ease when Berwynna first glimpsed them, but suddenly one of them shouted. Axes at the ready, they advanced on Enj and Pel and began to all talk at once. Enj shouted back and joined the argument, which was so loud and disjointed that Berwynna couldn't follow it. She did clearly hear "red-haired giant" and "from Haen Marn."

"Ah," Mic said. "My people haven't changed any, I see. Our folk love to argue, Wynni."

"So I see, or maybe I should say, so I hear. What's the trouble, Uncle Mic?"

"Dougie. They don't want to allow him into the city because he's not one of the Mountain Folk."

"Well, if he can't go in, neither will I, and that's that."

"I'll go tell Enj that."

"Please do! What do they expect? That we're supposed to let him sleep outside by himself like a dog?"

"Well, no. They said something about a trading caravan camping outside the main gates. Apparently they think he'd be welcome there or suchlike. But do be patient! I'll talk with them and come up with something to change their minds."

Mic hurried off to join the shouting match. Dougie helped Berwynna down from her mule. She considered telling him about the argument, then decided it would be better to refrain from worrying him, since she had no intention of deserting him. While Dougie watched the argument, Berwynna took the chance to look in the mule pack where she'd hidden the dweomer book. Much to her relief, it lay safely nestled in her spare clothing.

Finally Mic returned triumphant.

"Very well, Lady Berwynna," Mic said in the Alban tongue, "you and your betrothed, the noble lord, Douglas of Alban, may enter the city together. You'll have a chamber called the envoy's quarters, set aside for visitors of the right sort."

"Lady and noble lord are we?" Berwynna laughed at him. "I take it you lied about us."

"Well, that you come from Haen Marn is as good as being a lady." Mic turned to Dougie. "Remember that your father is a rich and powerful man back in your home country."

"Of course he is," Dougie said, grinning. "Vast holdings of land and many cattle."

"That's it! Good lad! Now, we're waiting for someone to bring a carrying chair for Otho. See that tunnel over there? It leads to the entrance of the high city, where your chamber is." Mic paused to wipe away sudden tears, but he was smiling in delight. "And my father—that's your grandfather—will meet us there, too."

One of Envoy Kov's duties was setting up trade terms whenever caravans came to Lin Serr. A typical summer brought six or seven, thanks to the demand for Mountain-worked jewelry. The largest, however, always came from Cerr Cawnen, a city that had been founded by escaped bondfolk from Deverry some centuries earlier. The first caravan leader Kov could remember was a man named Verrarc, replaced upon his death by his apprentice, Jahdo. Recently Jahdo, too, had given up making the long hard trip from the east and turned the trading business over to his grandson, Aethel.

That morning Aethel had brought his caravan in to Lin Serr's open parkland behind its first walls. Twenty muleteers were busily setting up camp and unloading a long line of mules. The huge panniers appeared heavy but in truth weren't much of a burden for the animals, because Aethel had brought woolen goods, his usual items for trade. None of the Mountain Folk cared to raise sheep, not that they would have had much pasture for them if they had.

This trip, however, Aethel had brought something of more value as well, or so he told Kov as they stood at the foot of the zigzag stairs that led up to Lin Serr's doors. He was a stout young man, Aethel, a good six feet tall with a broad face, brightened by perennially ruddy cheeks, and narrow blue eyes under pale eyebrows that matched his pale hair. At the moment he was leaning like a shepherd on his long quarterstaff of heavy oak.

"You may or may not remember," Aethel said, "that our first traders brought opals and suchlike to Lin Serr."

"I don't remember," Kov said, "but I've heard of it. Fine stones they were, too. The vein petered out some years ago, didn't it?"

"It did just that. But another's been found. I did bring some good stones with me."

"Splendid! No doubt you'll have customers for those."

"We were thinking that mayhap one of your jewelers would be wanting to come back to Cerr Cawnen with me—to give us some advice, like, for the mining of them. We'd pay a good hire, of course."

"Now, I can't speak for anyone else, of course, but I wouldn't be surprised if someone found your offer tempting. I—What's all this?"

Kov turned around to look up at the landing at the cliff top. Someone was standing at the edge, waving his arms, and yelling, "Envoy Kov!" over and over.

"What is it?" Kov yelled back.

"Haen Marn! Haen Marn's come back, and some of them are here! Enj and his sister."

Kov's first thought was that he'd misheard. The fellow up top ran down the stairs to the first bend.

"From Haen Marn," he repeated. "Enj is here with his sister and a red-haired giant."

"Well, now," Aethel said, "that does sound interesting, I must say."

"So it does. If you'll forgive me, I'd best go up."

"We'll be here when you come down again." Aethel laughed at his own joke. "Now, my grandfather, he did tell me somewhat about Haen Marn. He'll be wanting to know what's happened with the place."

"I'll share the news when I return, fear not!"

Kov puffed up the stairs and met the messenger, who turned out to be his cousin Jorn. The Haen Marn party had been put up in the foreign envoy's quarters.

"Because of the giant," Jorn told him. "By Gonn's hairy cock, I've seen some tall Deverry men, but this one's the biggest yet! Anyway, Enj's sister wouldn't let us keep him outside, so we compromised."

"Good, good. I take it the island's found its way home, then."

"Enj will tell you all about it. He thinks Westfolk dweomer brought it back."

"I wouldn't be at all surprised if he's right."

Jorn stared at him in stunned disbelief. Kov smiled and continued up the stairs.

At the top of the cliff, they crossed the broad landing and walked through Lin Serr's steel-clad doors to the circular entrance hall. A small crowd had gathered on the mosaic floor. Enj and a couple of guards from the upper plateau hovered over a frail elderly man in a carrying chair. Nearby, a man named Mic that Kov faintly remembered from many years past stood with his arm around Vron. Vron, Kov remembered more clearly, a man always in mourning for his son, killed by Horsekin—or so everyone had believed. Now Vron was grinning as if his face would split from having that son restored to him.

The red-haired giant, wrapped in a plaid blanket, towered above them all, including the most beautiful girl Kov had ever seen, or so he thought her at that moment. She was tall for a Mountain Woman, just his own height, slender, with raven-dark hair, dark blue eyes, and high cheekbones. Much to Kov's annoyance, the red-haired giant was resting one huge hand on her shoulder in a proprietary gesture.

"There's Kov!" Enj called out. "Kov, this is my half sister Berwynna. Wynni, this is another cousin of ours."

"But a distant one," Kov said hastily. He wanted to avoid any chance of her thinking of him as too close a relative to marry or suchlike.

"I'm beginning to wonder," Berwynna said, "if we're related to everybody in Lin Serr."

"Not quite." Vron kept grinning at everyone and everything. "I hope my son here's been a decent uncle to you?"

"He has, most certainly, Grandfather."

Berwynna turned slightly to look up at her giant. She spoke quickly in a language that Kov didn't know, though its cadences sounded much like Deverrian to him. He could catch names here and there, though, and assumed that she was translating the conversation for him.

"Cousin Kov," she said in the Mountain tongue, "this is my betrothed, Lord Douglas of Alban."

"Ah." Betrothed? Kov decided that he disliked the man. "Please tell him how pleased I am to meet him, then. Um, and where's Alban?"

"A very long way away," Berwynna said. "It's rather hard to explain."

"I'll tell you later," Enj said. "Mic, no doubt you'll want to go down to the deep city to see your mother."

"I certainly do!" Mic was grinning almost as hard as Vron. "This is a grand day indeed! Here, Wynni, come with us, although—" He hesitated, then turned to Douglas and spoke in the same strange language that Berwynna had used earlier.

Douglas glowered and spit out a few words in answer. Berwynna joined in, and for a few moments the three of them argued. Finally Douglas shrugged and wiped the scowl off his face.

"Wynni won't go without him," Mic said to Kov, "and really, I do understand why. It's not like my mother's her grandmother, after all."

Berwynna stood on tiptoe to reach up and kiss Douglas on his dirty cheek. Kov managed a thin smile at this display of loyalty.

"Kov," Enj said, "would you get Otho settled in a guest chamber?" He gestured at the elderly man in the chair, who had dozed off. "He's not very well."

As much as Kov had been hoping to speak with Berwynna, he had too much respect for the aged to refuse. "Of course," he said, "and then I'd best get back to Aethel's caravan." He glanced at Vron. "Cerr Cawnen's very interested in hiring someone from your jewelers' guild. You might want to go talk with him before he leaves."

"I'll do that," Vron said, "after I help you get Otho settled in our compound."

Vron squatted down by the carrying chair to speak to his aged brother. Kov lingered, watching as Berwynna followed Enj across the entrance hall to take a look at the envoy's quarters. She moved so gracefully—*entrancing*! Kov thought. Someone cleared his throat entirely too loudly. Kov glanced up to see Douglas the Giant, arms crossed across his broad chest, glaring at him.

"Dougie?" Mic stepped forward and spoke in Deverrian. "Go join Berwynna. Go take a look at your chamber."

"Good," Dougie said in broken Deverrian. "I need wash, too."

Kov turned away fast and from then on, concentrated on the tasks he had in hand.

Berwynna had never seen a room as heavily decorated as the foreign envoy's quarters. The pierced carvings on the wooden shutters, folded back on either side of the one large window, shamed the moldy tapestries she'd noticed during her one visit to Dougie's grandfather's dun back in Alban, when Marnmara and her herbs had been called to treat a fever. The tall steel panels, set at intervals along the walls, far outshone anything else in that lordship's possession. She spent a long time studying the engraved pictures upon them: hunting scenes and battles set off by borders of delicate patterns.

"This is a lovely chamber," Berwynna said. "These pictures are beautiful."

"So they are," Dougie said. "But it's better because you're staying with me."

"Well, it annoys me that everyone treats you like some kind of large dog."

"Not half as much as it annoys me." But he grinned at her.

"Wynni, please tell him I'm truly sorry," Enj said. "It's just the way that the Mountain Folk are. It has naught to do with him personally."

Berwynna translated, and Dougie smiled Enj's way to show that he understood. Berwynna continued her slow circuit of the room. The bed would be just wide enough, she decided, for the two of them. It certainly looked comfortable with its finely woven blue blankets. On top of a carved chest lay a strange stone object in the shape of a tube tightly wound into a spiral. At first she thought it was a carving of a snail, though oddly flat and as big as both her hands laid side by side.

"Enj," Berwynna said, "what is that?"

"I'm not sure," Enj said. "The miners find them embedded in sea-rock when they're splitting slates and then clean them up for trinkets."

"I wondered because I saw part of one sticking out of the cliff. I thought maybe it was some sort of rune or magical mark."

"Alas, naught so interesting," Enj said, smiling. "The cliff's made of sea-rock, so I'm not surprised you saw one there. Now, would you tell Dougie that there's not a bathing tub in all of Lin Serr that'll fit him. If he'd like, we can go down to the parkland for a swim. I could use a wash myself."

Berwynna translated back and forth.

"That would do splendidly." Dougie told her. "But will you mind my going?"

"Not at all. Mic promised that someone would bring me hot

water up here." She returned to speaking Dwarvish. "But one last question, brother of mine. Where are all the women?"

"Down in the deep city," Enj said with a furtive glance Dougie's way. "I'll explain some other time."

Dougie's eyes narrowed; apparently he suspected that once again, he was being excluded. Berwynna patted him on the arm.

"There, there, my love," she said in the Alban language, which Enj, of course, couldn't understand. "I'll tell you whatever they tell me, and they won't have to know a thing about it."

After they found a chamber for Otho near Vron's own, Kov and Vron arranged for an elaborate dinner to be served in Berwynna and Dougie's chamber. Kov shamelessly invited himself, and Otho insisted on joining them, but Vron bowed out.

"I'll let you get acquainted with them all," Vron said. "I want to go bargain with that caravan leader. I want to get some of those opals before they're all sold."

"Do that," Kov said. "They've found a new vein of the fire opals, by the way. The city wants our help to mine it properly."

Vron's eyes gleamed, and he smiled. "Do they?" he said. "It's too long a trip for me, but my son's back now. I'm off to have a bit of a chat with Aethel. And then I'll see what Mic thinks about it."

For the dinner Kov put on his best shirt and took his envoy's staff along, too, simply because it looked impressive, carved as it was with ancient runes. Servant boys brought extra chairs to the envoy's quarters and set up a table; other boys loaded the table with food and flagons of ale so dark and strong that it was almost black. Fried bats, roasted root vegetables both red and white, served with butter, and brown loaves of warm bread—the cooks had outdone themselves, and everyone ate with little conversation till the platters shone, free of the last drip of gravy.

"Well, here we are," Enj said at last. "You've finally seen your home country, Wynni, and a bit of its city."

"It's truly splendid," Berwynna said. "I never knew places like this existed." She turned to Dougie. "Is it more splendid than Din Edin?"

"A thousand times better," Dougie said, "and it doesn't stink."

When she translated the exchange, everyone laughed. Mic saluted him with his stoup of brown liquor.

"Tell me somewhat, Brother," Berwynna went on. "Where's the kingdom of Deverry from here? I'm wondering where my father might be."

"Deverry's due south," Enj said, "but we're not far from the lands of the Westfolk. He could be in either place."

Otho made a rude noise. "Cursed Westfolk!" he announced. "Rori was half an elf before he turned into a blasted dragon, you know. Never did trust him. Goes to show what they're like, getting turned into dragons."

"Why don't you like the Westfolk?" Berwynna asked.

Otho snorted for an answer.

"Don't get him started." Enj rolled his eyes skyward. "Which reminds me, Otho, my lad, the silver dragon told me a fascinating little tale. There are more Mountain Folk down in Deverry itself, not far from a place called Cwm Pecl. Have you ever heard of them?"

"I haven't," Otho said. "They must have come from the eastern cities."

"Not according to the dragon," Enj said. "He told me they looked much like our folk here."

"Nonsense! All the Lin Rej refugees came here, those that lived, anyway." Otho glanced at Berwynna. "Cursed elves wouldn't shelter them when they begged for help."

"And a good thing, too," Kov put in. "They were at the gates of Tanbalapalim, you see. The Horsekin captured the city soon after and slaughtered everyone in it."

Otho made a growling sound deep in his throat.

"An excellent point, Envoy," Enj said, grinning. "If you ask me, this pack of Mountain Folk down in Deverry? They must be those Lost Ones, Otho, the same group you've been carrying on about for the last five hundred years or so."

Otho's mouth dropped open, and he sputtered with a drool of brown liquor. Berwynna grabbed a napkin and handed it to the old man, who wiped his beard with great dignity.

"Can't trust a thing an elf tells you," Otho said feebly.

"He's not an elf but a dragon." Mic joined in. "Go on, Enj. This is interesting."

"Not much more to tell, alas. He swears that there's a colony of our people in the hills near this Cwm Pecl place, and that the women there walk about in the sunlight just like the men, the way they did in Lin Rej all those years past."

"Wormshit and maggot slime!" Otho's color had turned a bright pink, a dangerous shade. "I don't believe a word of it!"

"Otho, please!" Kov said. "There's a lady present."

The silence hung awkwardly over the table. Otho busied himself with wiping an imaginary speck off his beard.

"Uncle Mic, can you tell me," Berwynna said at last, "just how deep does Lin Serr go? It looks absolutely huge from what I've seen."

Good lass! Kov thought.

"A mile or more," Mic said, "and down near the lowest level you can feel the heat of the earth's fires. That's what keeps us warm in the winter, in fact."

As the conversation continued on safe subjects, Otho's color slowly returned to normal. Long before the meal was over, the old man had fallen asleep, nodding over his plate.

When the time came for everyone to leave, a pair of Mountain Folk appeared with the carrying chair to take Otho to his chamber. Mic and Kov went with them. Servant lads hurried in to clear away the remains of the food. When they left, Berwynna shut the door behind them with a grateful sigh.

"Tired?" Dougie said. "I am, and confused as well."

"So am I." Berwynna managed a smile. "The city's overwhelming, and the way the people live—I still don't understand it all."

"Particularly your clan." Dougie frowned at the wall. "Now, Mic is your mother's brother. Right?"

"A half brother. His father is my mother's father, and my grandfather."

"But his mother, she's not your grandmother?"

"She's not. My mother's mother is dead."

"So your grandfather had two wives? One after the other, I assume."

"Well, I wouldn't call them wives, not like back in Alban. And I think it was more or less at the same time."

Dougie sat down on the edge of the bed with a sigh. "Heathen, then, these people," he said. "The poor women!"

"Heathen, truly, but don't waste your sympathy on the women. They choose the men they want, Enj told me." Berwynna grinned at him. "Like I chose you."

"Then there's somewhat to be said for being heathen." Dougie returned the smile. "Not that we could be telling Father Colm that, if ever we return to Alban."

Berwynna took off her outer dress and placed it folded onto the chest by the window. She perched on the sill with her back to the long drop down and began to comb her hair. The crowded events of the day were finally settling in her mind, at least enough for her to begin to think them through.

"You know, I'm worried about Otho," Berwynna said. "He's not well."

"He hasn't been well in three years, lass," Dougie said. "But truly, I didn't like the look of him tonight either."

"Mic's mother is somewhat of a healer, and Mic told me she'd look in on Otho tonight. I hope she's as good with her herbs as Mara is."

"Or good enough, anyway. Your sister's a fair marvel, and I doubt me if anyone can match her."

"True spoken." For the first time it occurred to Berwynna to wonder if she missed her sister. *Mayhap,* she thought, *but I don't miss waiting upon her hand and foot!*

The morning justified their foreboding. With the rising sun someone knocked hard on the door. Dougie got out of bed, wrapped his plaid around him for modesty, and opened the door. Berwynna sat up just as a grave-faced Mic walked into the chamber.

"I've got ill news indeed," Mic said. "I'm afraid Otho's gone to the ancestors."

Berwynna's eyes filled with tears, and she found that she couldn't speak.

"That's a shame," Dougie said. "How did it happen?"

"In his sleep." Mic flung himself into a chair. "I suppose that it's the best way to go, if you're going. We found him in his bed this morning. His heart must have given out, or so my mother thinks."

Berwynna wiped her tears away on the edge of a blanket. "He always told me," she said, "that he wanted to die back here in Dwarveholt. At least he got his wish."

"So he did, and he'll be laid to rest here, too. My mother will preside." Mic turned to Dougie. "Wynni can go to the funeral, but it's going to be down in the deep city, so I'm afraid they won't let you come with her. I'm truly sorry, Dougie."

"Don't trouble your heart over it." Dougie paused for a yawn. "Funerals are a grim duty, and I shan't mind missing one."

"Well and good, then," Mic said. "Wynni, I'll stand outside while you get dressed. We bury our dead quickly, and so they're waiting for us."

Once she'd dressed, Berwynna joined Mic out in the circular entrance hall. He led her across to the mouth of one of the tunnels, where Vron was standing, carrying a big basket of what looked at first glance like cabbage.

"For the light." Vron hefted the basket. "It's a kind of fungus."

"I see," Berwynna said. "I'm so sorry you've lost your brother. I shall miss him."

"You may be the only soul in Lin Serr who does," Vron said, but his wry smile took any sting out of the words.

As soon as they left the dim sunlight in the entrance hall, Berwynna noticed that the fungus in the basket glowed with a pale blue light, just enough to light their way through a short tunnel with polished stone walls. At the head of a flight of stairs, Vron paused.

"It's a long way down," he said. "I hope you've got strong legs."

"The way down won't bother me," Berwynna said. "The way up may be another thing."

"Well, we'll see. If naught else, Mic and I can carry you."

They went down, and down, narrow stair after narrow stair, set steeply into the rock. The blue gleam from the basket of light reached only a short way into the darkness, a cold silent dark that grew deeper and colder with every flight of stone steps down. It was the only light Berwynna saw, even when they reached a landing. From these resting places side tunnels curved away into shadow.

She could just make out doors set into their walls, but she never saw anyone go in or come out of them. After some five flights of stairs she stopped counting. The entire world seemed to have funneled into Lin Serr, and its only direction was down.

At last the stairs led to a small open space and a broad corridor, running off to their right. The walls here, glowing blue, rippled with light. As they walked past, the glow brightened, then faded, only to brighten again. Berwynna could make out some sort of algae or mold, growing like fur across the worked stone. Ahead of them she saw stronger light, fungal blue laced with yellow candlelight, coming from a wide room.

Inside, a procession had assembled: six men carrying a bier, covered with a heavily embroidered coverlet, a small group of mourners standing behind, Envoy Kov among them, and at its head a woman. Set into niches on the wall, candles glowed.

"That woman is my mother," Mic whispered. "Her name's Miccala. You'll walk with her in front."

Vron handed her the basket of fungus. Mic patted her on the shoulder, then turned and walked away with his father to take their places behind the bier. Watching Mic leave her side made Berwynna shiver with fear, even though she felt like a fool for doing so. Miccala came forward and smiled at her. She was a pleasant-looking woman, somewhat stout, with a streak of gray in her brown hair and a strong jaw. She wore a long dress of pale gray, clasped at the waist by a belt set with irregular chunks of onyx.

"Welcome to the Halls of the Dead." She had a soft voice, tinged at the moment with sadness. "I'm sorry we couldn't meet at a happier time."

"So am I," Berwynna said. "What would you like me to do?"

"Just carry that basket of light and follow me. The ceremony's a simple one, but it requires at least two women."

The Halls of the Dead. The name made Berwynna shiver once again, but she decided that she had no reason to let the fear show. She held the glowing basket high and steadily as she followed Miccala. The funeral procession fell in behind them as they made their way down one last short stairway to level ground and a level path. Above them she saw the rough stone of a crudely cut tunnel.

"We go to the Hall of Bone," Miccala called out.

The men behind them sang one low note, almost a growl in the echoing chamber.

As they turned onto the path, distantly Berwynna heard a murmur that at first she mistook for chanting. As they came closer, she realized that she was hearing the river, plunging down over its cataract somewhere far ahead. The cold air became damp, as clammy with silence as with water. Miccala called out, a long high note that hovered on the edge of song, and led the procession into a vast cavern. On the far side, several hundred yards away, the river ran, blue with phosphorescence.

By its light Berwynna could see a stone forest. Misshapen cones of rock rose from the floor and strove to touch their twins hanging from the ceiling. Pale tan and white, they glittered with the water that dripped through the limestone. In and among them stood round platforms where the cones had been cut away about three feet from the ground. On each platform lay a skeleton, curled like a baby in the womb. From above, the lime-tinged water dripped, relentless.

"They shall become part of the mountain forever," Miccala said. "Soon enough the soft flesh rots away, leaving the hard bones. Slowly the stone covers the bones. They meld with the rock, become rock. Such is the destiny of our folk."

"I see," Berwynna whispered. "Born of the mountains, and to the mountains we'll come in the end."

"Just so." Miccala smiled at her. "You learn fast, child."

The men carried the bier to one of the platforms and laid it down on the ground nearby. Miccala pulled back the coverlet to reveal Otho's naked body, lying on its side, his limbs curled and his hands tucked under his cheek. He looked so peaceful, with all his bitterness and complaints stilled at last, that Berwynna felt her grief lighten. Two of the men picked him up and laid him onto the platform. Miccala carefully rearranged his body to fit.

"Sleep well," Miccala said. "You are home forever now."

Everyone raised their arms into the air and stood for a long moment, praying, perhaps, to the gods whose names Berwynna had yet to learn.

"We shall remember our kinsman until we join him here," Miccala said. "For now we shall leave him in peace." Yet she laid a light hand on Berwynna's arm to keep her at her side.

The men picked up the bier and trooped out. Mic lingered, caught Berwynna's attention, and murmured, "We'll wait outside." He hurried off after his father.

"I have something to show you," Miccala said. "If you'd not mind."

"Not at all," Berwynna said. "This is fascinating."

Miccala took the basket of light and led the way into the approximate center of the cavern. As they passed the various platforms, Berwynna noticed skeletons, some covered with a thin film of translucent rock, others, more recently placed, merely spotted here and there. It would take a long time, she supposed, for the dripping sea-rock to do its work. Miccala stopped at a pair of very different platforms, rectangular and cut out of ordinary stone.

Each on its own platform, two skeletons lay full-length on their backs, their ghostly hands crossed over their chests. The travertine had completely covered them to a depth of perhaps an inch, making it difficult to pick out details. In the blue light from the mosses and the river, they seemed to be encased in smoke turned solid.

"Those aren't Mountain Folk," Berwynna said.

"No, they aren't," Miccala said. "Some say they're of the race known as the Children of Air, the ones that Deverry men call the Westfolk. Others say that they're Deverry men. I don't know which is correct."

"They must have been here a very long time."

"Well over a thousand years. The founders discovered them when our people first came to Lin Serr." Miccala held up her basket and moved it this way and that to make the light fall upon the rib cage of one of the skeletons. "When I was a child, you could still see a gold bird with spread wings lying under the blanket of rock. It must have been some sort of ornament around the person's neck. I can't make it out now, though. I was a child a very long time ago." She lowered the basket with a sigh. "Let us return to the land of the living."

At the entranceway they paused to put out the candles. Mic and Vron accompanied Berwynna the entire way up, but Miccala left them, turning down one of the side tunnels after they'd passed several landings. By the time they climbed the long stairways back up to the entrance hall, Berwynna was panting for breath, and her legs seemed to have turned to mud under her. Fortunately, Dougie was waiting by the inlaid maze. He picked her up and carried her down the corridor to their chamber.

After Otho's funeral, Kov invited Mic and Enj to his quarters to partake of what he called a "restorative," a golden liquor less potent than the dark brown stuff he'd served the night before. In his small reception chamber stood a stone bench with a wooden back and a welter of cushions for guests. After he set out the bottle and stoups, he himself took the only chair. In the dim bluish light from baskets of fungi, the liquor shone green. They toasted each other with the stoups, and each had a long sip.

"I'll be leaving soon," Enj spoke first. "I promised Rori that I'd go find him if the island returned, you see. Little Berwynna's bound and determined to go with me, too. He's her father, after all." He paused, thinking. "Well, he fathered her when he was still a man. I don't suppose his being a dragon now would change that."

"Legally he'd still have paternity," Kov said. "In my opinion, anyway. I suppose we could ask Garin if you'd like to make sure of that."

"No, no, your opinion's good enough for me. You've studied the laws. I haven't." Enj swirled the liquor in his stoup. "I wish my sister had stayed safely at home, but she didn't, and so here we are. I'd best start searching, but ye gods, he could be anywhere!"

Mic leaned forward in his chair. "Enj, I've been thinking. I know your heart longs to return to Haen Marn. I'm minded to go west with Aethel's caravan to see about those veins of opal-bearing rock. From what he told me, the city of Cerr Cawnen's offering a nice bit of money for an assessment. I can keep an eye out for Rori easily enough. Why don't I take on your vow? If we find him, I'll tell him about the island's return, just like you promised."

Enj nearly wept. He roughly wiped his eyes on his sleeve before he spoke. "A thousand thanks," Enj said. "I'll be in your debt for that."

"And doubtless someday I'll call that debt in." Mic grinned at him. "But we'll worry about it then."

"Going with the caravan's a wise decision," Kov said. "You and Berwynna will be safer that way. The Northlands are wild and rough, worse even than down in Deverry."

"Have you ever traveled across them?" Mic said.

"No, I've never had reason to." Kov hesitated, shocked at the wild idea that was forming, seemingly of its own will, in his mind. "But you know, I wouldn't mind having a chat with the silver wyrm myself. Enj, that story you told about the other Mountain Folk to the south—it's been nagging at me ever since. I consulted Garin about it, and we both wonder if they're indeed the Lost Ones from the old city. If Rori can give me some idea of where he saw them, I just might gather a few good men and go down into Deverry to search for them."

"It would be worth doing, all right," Mic said.

Enj nodded his agreement and had another sip of liquor. *Besides,* Kov thought, *there's Berwynna.* She had her giant, who'd be traveling with her, but what if she tired of that Roundear lout?

"Of course," Kov went on, "my going depends on Garin's permission. He's my master in my craft."

Enj accompanied Kov when he went to see Garin, the head envoy. Over the winter, his beard had gone completely gray, and he'd taken to spending the vast majority of his time in his quarters. They found him sitting at a writing table littered with parchments, plates bearing scraps of food, and ancient maps, which he was consulting by the light of two thick candles. He put his pen down and listened while Kov explained his idea. Much to Kov's relief, his master in the guild approved.

"I'll be interested to hear what the dragon can tell you." Garin tapped a finger on the map spread out in front of him. "Besides, we know next to nothing about the country between us and Cerr Cawnen. Oh, the traders have told us a fair bit about monsters in the rivers and suchlike." He rolled his eyes. "But what we need, with those maggot-born Horsekin riding around up there, is solid information. Can they feed their horses on the way to Lin Serr? What's the rock like? Can we build traps and tunnels? That sort of information, not fancy tales."

"Just so," Kov said. "I should take something to write upon and take notes."

"Good idea." Garin turned to Enj. "Will you carry letters back to Haen Marn for me?"

"Gladly," Enj said. "In return, may I borrow one of your mules? It can haul the empty coracles upriver, and I'll get him back to you eventually."

"Yes, certainly. You see, I can't go to Haen Marn myself, even though I should go welcome your kin home. I'm going to be consulting with a representative of the Deverrian high king about establishing a formal border between Dwarveholt and his highness' territory."

"It's about time," Enj put in. "I'm surprised there hasn't been trouble between us already. An unmarked border's a dangerous border."

"So they always say," Kov said. "I suppose we can thank the Horsekin threat for the lack of trouble. This is no time for allies to start bickering among themselves."

"Just so." Garin sighed and looked away. "I hate traveling, these days, but Voran specifically asked for me, so I can't get out of it. We'll meet in Gwingedd."

"Voran himself?" Enj said. "I would have thought a herald would—"

"This matter is too grave to leave to the heralds," Garin interrupted him. "Voran's been newly appointed Justiciar of the Northern Border."

"Um, what?" Enj said. "What does that mean?"

"Anything he wants it to, I wager." Garin smiled, as sly as a bargaining merchant. "Whatever power he can gather, whatever teeth he can put into the new law."

"I see," Kov said. "Then knowing Voran, I'd say it's going to amount to a very important position indeed."

Not just the Mountain Folk, but everyone in Dun Cengarn, and especially its gwerbret, had been wondering about this new post of justiciar as well. While they waited, Prince Daralanteriel had been inquiring about the exact meaning of the term, but neither Lord Oth nor the priests of Bel in Cengarn's own temple could give him much information.

"It's a new post that the high king's invented," Dar told his curious vassals at an impromptu council. "Cerrgonney has no gwerbretion, you see, so it needs some sort of legal officer. Voran will be able to try criminals and adjudicate feuds and disputes, just like a gwerbret, but his post won't pass from father to son. The king wants someone who owes fealty directly to him rather than drawing his power from a holding of land."

"But is it just for Cerrgonney, Your Highness?" Gerran said. "I thought the title was Justiciar of the Northern Border."

"It is indeed." Dar paused for a sly grin. "And Ridvar's very aware that Arcodd stretches along the northern border for a good long way."

"What's east of Cerrgonney?" Mirryn asked.

Everyone turned to look at Salamander, who shrugged. "Not much," the gerthddyn said. "Mountains, mostly. I've always assumed that Mountain Folk lived in them, but you know, now that you mention it, I'm not sure if they do or not."

No one else knew, either. They were all sitting in the warm sunlight down in the meadow below Cengarn's grim cliffs. The Westfolk had raised their tents and made a proper camp along the river's edge among the scattered trees. On the other side of the ford, their horses grazed at tether.

"From what I hear about Cerrgonney," Dar continued, "Voran will have more than enough trouble to occupy him without worrying about the eastern hills."

"Or about us," Calonderiel said. "Which gladdens my heart. As long as their own territories keep them busy, the cursed Roundears won't be trying to take ours." He glanced at Gerran and Mirryn. "No offense meant to our allies, of course."

"Of course." Dar rolled his eyes. "Your son has turned out to be a fine herald. He must have gotten his tact from his mother."

"Actually, Rhodda didn't have any, either." Cal grinned at the prince. "The lad grew up listening to us fight, and I think that's what made him decide to be a peaceable man."

"Well, once Voran gets here, Maelaber's going to have plenty of official work to do," Dar went on. "And I hope Voran gets here soon. We don't have a lot of grain left, and the first harvest won't come in for some weeks yet."

Fortunately, Voran arrived in the middle of the next afternoon, accompanied by a retinue of officials and servants and a warband of seventy-five riders. They had brought supplies with them from Dun Deverry, a good thing, as Lord Oth remarked, considering how many of them there were. Except for an honor guard of ten, the warband camped out in the meadows with the Westfolk archers, but the officials had to be accommodated in the dun itself.

The two princes and the gwerbret seated themselves at the honor table while the servitors sorted out the arrangements. At Dar's invitation, Gerran and Calonderiel joined them there. Ridvar played the perfect host, inquiring after his royal guest's health, apologizing for his primitive dun, so different from the splendor of Dun Deverry, adding a few direct compliments to the prince. Voran smiled and replied in kind, but once a servant had brought mead in the dun's best silver goblets, he turned the talk to more serious matters.

"I very much appreciate your hospitality, Your Grace," Voran said. "Besides my lawsuit, I need to discuss a small matter with you, so it can be settled before I go back to Cerrgonney. I'll be negotiating with Envoy Garin of the Mountain Folk. About Lord Honelg's old dun—is it ready to be settled upon whomever their council's chosen to man it?"

"It is, Your Highness," Ridvar said. "I left a fortguard there over the winter to repair and maintain the place. Lord Blethry had my scribe draw up the necessary documents, which you can take with you, if you'd be so kind, to deliver them to the envoy."

"Splendid!" Voran saluted him with his goblet. "My hearty thanks! That'll give us a fixed point where we can start drawing the border."

"Which reminds me. Lin Serr's envoy sent letters for you here, Your Highness," Ridvar said. "Do you have a scribe with you?"

"I do, my thanks. I have a letter for you as well, this one from the high priest in Dun Deverry, official seal and all. It authorizes you to take action against Govvin."

"Good. Then we're on firm legal ground in this matter."

Gerran had his own legal matter on his mind, but he hesitated to bring it up so soon after Voran's arrival. After that evening's formal dinner in the great hall, he sought out Salamander and asked his advice.

"Well, you want to do it soon," Salamander said. "Before Govvin arrives for the gwerbret's malover, because that will take precedence, of course. On the other hand, you don't want to push yourself forward too strongly."

"I just hope that Ridvar isn't insulted or suchlike because I'm taking the matter to the justiciar instead of him."

"He won't be, because you're no longer a vassal of his vassal. That's another thing justiciars are good for, truly, to preside over matters between folk who owe loyalty to different overlords, or in our case, to an entirely different royal line."

"I see. So it all comes down to how to approach Voran."

"Just so." Salamander thought for a moment. "I know! I'll write a note asking him when he as justiciar can hear your question. I'll get some ink and pabrus from Neb."

"Ink and what?"

"Pabrus. It's a writing material made of water reeds. The Westfolk in Mandra make it as trade goods, and it's much cheaper than parchments and vellum."

Salamander wrote the note standing at the servants' hearth, and Clae delivered it to Voran's scribe, who was lingering at table with Lords Oth and Blethry. The scribe in turn read it silently, then left his seat and rushed over to Salamander. Gerran could see them talking, heads together. The scribe kept waving the pabrus in the air as if he thought it a great marvel, as indeed he did, according to Clae.

"It's peculiar stuff, my lord," Clae told Gerran. "It's thin and crackly. Neb told me that it takes ink really well."

"Well, the scribes would know, I suppose," Gerran said. "I just hope he doesn't forget to tell the prince about my question."

Apparently the scribe did remember the message. After the morrow's breakfast, Prince Voran summoned Gerran to the table of honor. Salamander, who seemed to have appointed himself Gerran's second in the matter, tagged along. They both knelt beside the prince's chair.

"My scribe tells me that you have a matter to lay before me, Lord

Gerran," Voran said. "The gwerbret has given me leave to use his chamber of justice, where indeed he's waiting for us."

"My humble thanks, Your Highness," Gerran said. "May I call Lord Oth as a witness to this matter?"

"Indeed you may." Voran turned in his chair and summoned a waiting page. "Have Oth and my scribe join us in the chamber of justice." He rose and beckoned to Gerran and Salamander. "Come along, then."

The chamber of justice, a half-round of a stone room, sat high up in the main broch on the east side. A flood of sunlight from its high slit windows fell across the polished table, where Ridvar was sitting to the right of its center. The gold ceremonial sword of the rhan hung on the wall under the sun banner of Cengarn rather than lying in front of the gwerbret, who would merely advise, not preside, since Gerran had appealed directly to the new justiciar. At the door two tabarded guards stood lounging against the wall, though they did straighten up and then bow when the prince walked in.

Voran took the central chair behind the table. Gerran and Salamander knelt in front of it. When Oth and the scribe appeared, they sat at either end. A servant lass followed them in with a tray full of tankards of ale. She placed it on the table, curtsied, and hurried out. Ridvar helped himself to a tankard.

"Now, then," Voran said. "What is this matter, Lord Gerran of the Gold Falcon?"

"It's a question of an inheritance, Your Highness," Gerran said. "My wife tells me that an uncle of hers left her a hundred silver pieces when he died, but she never got it. The coin came to Dun Cengarn—she's sure of that—but her share was never disbursed."

Ridvar snickered and glanced at Oth with a grin, as if at a shared joke. "That old matter," Ridvar murmured. "Ye gods, you think she'd give it up."

"May I speak, Your Highness?" Oth said.

"That's why you're here, Lord Oth," Voran said.

"There never was any inheritance." Oth gave Gerran a pitying sort of look. "She seems to think there was, but I've tried very hard to explain to her that she was left nothing. Women do have trouble understanding these things."

Gerran opened his mouth, but Voran raised a hand to silence him.

"I don't understand, Lord Oth," the justiciar said. "Why would she claim she was due coin, then?"

"No doubt Lady Solla made up a little tale, Your Highness, to increase her chances of a good marriage."

Gerran rose. He slammed both hands palm down upon the table so hard that the tankards clanked and spilled on their tray.

"Lord Oth," he said, "are you calling my wife a liar?"

Dimly Gerran was aware of Salamander, rising from his seat to stand beside him, but he kept his gaze fixed on Oth's face, suddenly pale, his eyes as wide and rolling as a spooked horse's. Voran leaned back in his chair and crossed his arms over his chest. Gerran took his silence as permission to speak again.

"Are you?" Gerran went on. "If so, we'll have this out between us in the combat ground."

"It's his right to challenge a man who insults his wife," Voran remarked casually, as if speaking to the empty air.

Big drops of sweat broke out on Oth's face and slid down his wrinkled cheeks. Salamander laid a warning hand on Gerran's arm.

"Very well," Oth whispered. "Your wife speaks the truth. I—I—" He began to sob, but still he stared with wet eyes at Gerran like a rabbit staring at a weasel.

"Gerro, kneel!" Salamander tugged at Gerran's arm. "You can't kill a man of thrice your years. Be calm and hand over that letter." He bowed to the justiciar. "Your Highness, we have written proof."

Gerran let out his breath with a puff and knelt. Oth wept silently, his nose running like a child's. When Salamander knelt beside him, Gerran reached into his shirt, brought out the letter, and handed it to Voran's scribe, who looked it over with some surprise.

"Read it," Voran said. "Or as much as pertains."

"As you wish, Your Highness." The scribe cleared his throat, then read. "My beloved and dutiful niece, I am leaving you a hundred silver pieces. When our clan turned against me, you spoke out in my favor, and I want you to know that I remember your kindness well and warmly. Put it aside for your dowry, dear Solla. Your brothers will receive some of my wealth as well. Do not mourn for me, though I am dying slowly—" The scribe paused. "The rest, Your Highness, though touching, seems a private matter."

"No doubt," Voran said. "Gwerbret Ridvar, if I may ask, did you receive an inheritance from this uncle?"

"I most certainly did. He was my mother's brother, and he became somewhat of a merchant, which is why the clan disowned him." Ridvar turned to Oth. "Ye gods, pull yourself together, man!"

The scribe handed an ink-stained rag to the councillor, who wiped his face and blew his nose. Oth slumped in his seat and crushed the rag into a soggy lump with one hand.

"Very well, Lord Oth," Voran said. "What happened to Lady Solla's inheritance?"

Oth slumped down a little farther and spoke to the table. "I purloined it," he whispered. "I was so heavily in debt. The gambling, and the cursed Mountain Folk—they threatened to go to the gwerbret—his grace's brother, that was—I had to pay up, and I had to pay them within the fortnight."

"What?" It was Ridvar's turn for anger. "You told me my sister was lying because she'd not gotten anything. You told me she was jealous, and—"

Voran held up one hand and cut him off. "Let's let Oth finish, Your Grace, if you'd not mind."

With a gulp for breath Oth rose from his chair. Gerran was expecting the old man to kneel, but he remained standing. With an angry grunt, he threw the damp rag hard onto the table.

"My thanks, Justiciar," Oth began. "It gladdens my heart that someone's willing to let me speak. No doubt I'll be turned out of the dun with my hand cut off and end up a maimed beggar on the roads, but I'll have my say first." He paused, gulping for breath. "Ye gods, do you realize, does anyone realize, what my life's been like? Although I'm noble-born, I come from a land-poor clan, so I was reduced to bowing and scraping to one great lord or another to earn my meat and mead. And the worst of all was this arrogant child, this wretched lad who's run me ragged for years." He spun around and glared at Ridvar. "You little swine! It's been my lot to hurry this way and that at your beck, smoothing over your lapses of courtesy, placating the men you've angered with mincing flatteries, and never getting a word of thanks, much less any sort of decent reward. My one pleasure was the dice, and then they betrayed me."

Ridvar gaped at him. No one in the chamber moved or spoke or even gasped in surprise. *We're as stunned as cows at slaughter,* Gerran thought.

"I meant to repay it," Oth went on, "but how could I, with only a coin thrown my way now and again as if I were some beggar at the gates? You never offered me the slightest bit of praise or profit, Your Grace, no matter how many times your judgment failed the dun and the rhan, and I had to work like a madman to repair the lapse."

Still Ridvar did nothing but stare.

"Besides—" Oth's voice caught in his throat. He wept again, swaying from side to side as he sobbed.

"Sit down." Voran rose from his chair. "Sit down, for the love of the gods!"

Oth crumpled into the chair behind him and went on weeping. Ridvar's mouth still hung open. Gerran felt like screaming at the gwerbret to shut it and look away. Instead he turned to Voran.

"Your Highness," Gerran said. "If I didn't need that coin to build my dun, I'd wipe out this debt here and now."

"The thought becomes you, Lord Gerran." Voran sat down again. "But the defense of the border's a grave matter. Gwerbret Ridvar, your sworn servitor has stolen the monies, and it falls to you to make restitution if Oth cannot."

Ridvar did shut his mouth at that. Automatically he turned toward Oth as if to ask his advice, remembered the circumstances, and flushed red, his eyes darting this way and that.

"A hundred silver pieces is a large sum," Voran went on, "but I trust that you can repay it with due speed. After all, you just received some money from Tieryn Cadryc."

"I don't see why I should—" Ridvar began, then caught himself. "As the justiciar rules, then. What about Oth?"

"By rights I should order one of his hands cut off, as he himself just stated," Voran said.

"Your Highness?" Salamander got to his feet. "Will you forgive me if I ask for mercy for this man? Do you remember the matter of the various Alshandra worshipers in the dun, and how Oth moved His Grace to mercy then?"

"I do at that." Voran hesitated, thinking. "Indeed. I'm minded to sentence him to exile only, if Your Grace will agree."

Oth turned to Salamander and mouthed a silent thanks. Ridvar, however, was looking at Oth with murderous eyes. Oth drew himself up and glared back at him.

"He's done much good in your service," Voran went on. "Surely you can find it in your heart to—"

"Oh, very well!" Ridvar snarled. "Exile it is! But I suggest most humbly, Your Highness, that we search his chamber before he goes. Who knows how many stolen coins might go with him if we don't?"

"Well and good, then." Voran shrugged. "A thief, after all, usually steals more than once." He fixed Oth with a steady stare. "I've had doubts about you, my man. During the wedding last summer, I overheard a thing or two, but naught enough to bring to his grace."

Oth made a sound halfway between a moan and a curse, but he rose to bow to the prince with perfect courtesy. He turned toward the gwerbret without a bow. "Let us go now, Your Grace," Oth said. "So I may leave your dun as soon as I possibly can."

"Done, then." Voran stood up. "I declare this court adjourned."

Ridvar joined him. "Guards! Come with us."

Gerran and Salamander stayed where they were as the others trooped out of the chamber of justice. Gerran heard the gwerbret snarling at someone, a lass' flustered voice apologizing, and the sounds of a crowd of people rushing out of the way.

"Eavesdroppers, I'll wager," Salamander whispered. "Lots of them."

Gerran nodded. They waited unspeaking until the footsteps died away, then left. They walked down the stairs in dead silence to find a whispering, buzzing crowd waiting at the bottom. Apparently the news had reached the great hall. Gerran was in no mood to gloat or explain. He shoved his way through the pack of gossips and strode outside with Salamander behind him.

"Gerro, wait!" Mirryn caught up with him. "Is it true? Did Oth really snatch your wife's inheritance?"

"He did," Gerran said.

"Hah! I always though he was too honorable to live."

"A little compassion wouldn't hurt," Salamander put in. "Oth's had a hard life of it, dealing with Ridvar."

Mirryn blushed and looked away.

"Well, by the black hairy arse of the Lord of Hell," Gerran said. "Branna was right again."

"Just so." Salamander let out his breath in a puff. "She sees things, that lass, that the rest of us miss."

"You know, there's somewhat—" Mirryn began, then stopped speaking and dropped to a kneel.

Gerran and Salamander joined him on the cobbles as Prince Daralanteriel came out of the dun.

"Oh, get up!" Dar snapped. "Here, is it true about Oth, that the gwerbret's exiled him?"

"It is, Your Highness." Gerran followed the order and rose, dusting the bits of straw and dirt from his brigga. "But the justiciar stopped him from having one of the old man's hands cut off."

Dar made a sour face at the thought of the maiming. "What's going to happen to him now?"

"I've got no idea. He's got a clan to go to somewhere, if they'll take him in."

Dar frowned down at the cobbles. Eventually he said, "I'm half minded to give him a place with us. There's not much to steal out on the grass, and no doubt he's learned where thieving gets a man. He did keep Ridvar from committing some grievous errors, after all." He looked up. "Gerran, would you object?"

"It's not my place to object, Your Highness," Gerran said. "But truly, it's not the theft so much that aches my heart, but the way he turned Ridvar against his sister."

"Doubtless he did that to cover up the crime," Salamander said.

"True, but—" Gerran ran out of words, torn between pity and rage.

"Dar?" Salamander went on. "I'd advise you one thing, however. Wait until you find out how much the old man's stolen. If his only fault was Solla's inheritance, then take him in. But I have my doubts."

"I'll go consult with the justiciar, then," Dar said. "My thanks, Wise One."

It was the first time Gerran had ever heard anyone refer to Salamander by that title, and it shocked him, even though he'd known for nearly a year that Salamander had dweomer. When the prince hurried back inside the broch, Gerran considered Salamander, slender and dapper in his fine wool brigga and heavily embroidered shirt. His tricks and tales made it too easy to think of him as nothing more than what he pretended to be, a chattering fop. Salamander smiled blandly back.

"Who do you think's going to be Ridvar's chamberlain?" Mirryn said.

A gaggle of servants passing by stopped to listen.

"I don't know," Gerran said. "Blethry can take over some of Oth's duties, but I doubt me if he can do them all and still manage his own."

"My lord?" A serving lass curtsied to Gerran. "True spoken, and now the bard's announced that he's leaving as well. He says it aches his heart to see Oth treated so shabbily. Though I say that the old swine never should have taken Lady Solla's coin that way."

The other servants all nodded their agreement. A footman murmured, "Cursed right!"

"Lady Solla was ever so kind and fair to us when she was here, my lord," the lass continued.

"Not like now." The footman murmured the words, as if perhaps he was addressing them to no one, but Gerran had no doubt that he was supposed to overhear.

"Is your lady well, my lord?" A second servant lass spoke up. "We all do hope so, if I'm not getting above myself to ask."

"She is," Gerran said. "I'll tell her you asked after her, if you'd like."

"We would, my lord." The lass smiled at him, then glanced at the broch. "The prince is coming!"

The servants all hurried away as Daralanteriel came striding out of the broch. The prince joined Gerran and the others with a shake of his head and a shrug.

"Did they find more evidence of thieving?" Mirryn asked.

"None that would stand in malover," Dar said. "But naught that would clear him, either. Still, I did offer the man my shelter."

"Let me guess," Salamander broke in. "Oth refused your offer."

"You've guessed right." Dar looked utterly puzzled. "He drew himself up and thanked me, but he said he'd rather starve on the road than take another great lord's charity. I've no idea what he's going to do now."

"I do." Salamander turned and broke into a run, heading for the stables.

"What?" Dar spun around and started to hail him.

"Let him go, Your Highness," Gerran said. "I think I know what he means."

Gerran waited with Mirryn and the prince to see how the matter would play out. The sun had climbed high into the sky before Oth, escorted by two Cengarn heralds, came out of the broch. Though he must have been aware that Gerran was standing off to one side, Oth looked straight ahead as if determined not to see him. The bright sun picked out every wrinkle on Oth's thin face and showed up the exhaustion in his pouchy eyes. Out in the ward pages and grooms waited with the one horse allowed an exile.

Salamander came hurrying up, leading his own horse, saddled and bridled. When Oth mounted up, Salamander did the same. No one in the crowd spoke or jeered as Oth rode out of the gates. Salamander followed a decent distance behind. Gerran wondered if Oth realized that the gerthddyn was trailing after him, but if he did, Oth gave no sign. Once both of them were out of sight, the crowd dispersed, wandering off to the varied business of their day. Mirryn and Gerran went back into the great hall together.

"I don't understand," Mirryn said. "What in all the icy hells is Salamander going to do?"

"Talk Oth out of killing himself, most likely," Gerran said.

Mirryn opened his mouth and shut it again.

"Let's see if one of those servant lasses will pour us some of his grace's mead," Gerran went on. "I want somewhat to drink."

It was close to sunset before Salamander returned. Gerran saw him walk into the great hall and got up to go meet him. Since the two princes and the gwerbret were all sitting at the table of honor, Salamander never could have seated himself there.

"Well?" Gerran.

"I think I succeeded." Salamander's voice rasped on the edge of hoarseness. "I talked myself breathless, and in the end Oth agreed that life was a pleasant thing and worth keeping. Since I couldn't ride with him all the way to Trev Hael, I don't know if he'll change his mind or not."

"Trev Hael?"

"His brother holds a lordship near the city. Oth also agreed that said brother will shelter him. Humiliating, truly, but better than the shadowy Otherlands. I gave the old man some coin for his journey, by the way."

"Generous of you."

Salamander shrugged. "I earn it with a mouthful of lies and a handful of cheap tricks, so why should I hoard it?"

"True spoken. You'd best get yourself somewhat to drink. It sounds like you're about to lose your voice."

"And that would be a great pity, though some might term it a blessing. I shall do so."

All that evening and the next morning as well, gossip in Dun Cengarn gushed like a river in spate concerning Lord Oth's sudden disgrace. Salamander, who could become not invisible but unnoticeable when he wanted to, wandered through the dun to eavesdrop. The majority of the servants regretted the lord's departure. Though most agreed that he had made off with more than one lord's coin, Oth apparently had never stooped to stealing from his inferiors.

The gossip grew even louder when the bard made good his threat. He packed up his goods, his wife, and his children, and headed back east to look for a better position closer to the heart of the kingdom. Bets went round that he'd turn up at Oth's brother's dun. Wondering why, Salamander asked outright questions of some of the servants who knew him.

"The chamberlain and the bard, they each turned a blind eye, like," the cook told him, "to what the other was up to." She hefted a cleaver and glared at Salamander over the blade. "Now don't you go telling his grace any of this, like."

"I've forgotten every word you told me already," Salamander said, grinning. "My thanks."

As the day wore on, Gwerbret Ridvar looked angry and baffled by turns; Lord Blethry began to look exhausted. Prince Voran wandered around the dun and asked discreet questions of its inhabitants, from Blethry down to the widow who tended the gwerbretal hogs. Salamander doubted that they'd told the prince as much as they'd told the gerthddyn. Eventually he went to look for Gerran and found him avoiding everyone who might make sharp remarks.

"Ye gods," Gerran said. "I didn't realize how much trouble Oth's leaving would bring."

"No more did the gwerbret," Salamander said.

"I've gotten a fair number of ugly looks today. I wonder if the pages are going to poison my meat."

"I doubt it, though they might be slow in bringing it to you. Still, you did the right thing, Gerro. Don't let it trouble your heart. Voran's here to keep an eye on the upheaval, a most fortuitous happenstance indeed."

"Well, true spoken. With the Horsekin on the prowl up north, Cengarn's vital to the whole blasted kingdom. He can't let it tear itself apart."

"Lest the kingdom be blasted, indeed."

They were leaning against a wall near the stables, idly watching Clae curry Gerran's horse. Grooms trotted back and forth, watering the mounts of the various warbands, bringing them to the long stone troughs two at a time. It was one of life's little pleasures, Salamander reflected, to lounge in the warm sun and watch other men work.

"Any news of Oth himself?" Gerran said abruptly.

"And why do you think I'd have some?"

"Oh, spare me the horseshit." Gerran gave him a sour look. "Wise One."

Salamander laughed, then answered. "He's joined up with a merchant caravan heading toward Trev Hael. The suicidal fever's broken, and I think he's out of danger now."

"Good. He had his cursed gall, insulting my wife and stealing from her, but he didn't deserve a madman's death."

"My thought exactly, and you've got the coin, which is what matters. With that many silver pieces you'll be able to hire a master stonemason to oversee the building."

"Just so. I'll doubtless use the same man Cadryc did. I want to get started, curse it all!"

"Who's going to supply the labor?"

"Ah, horseshit, I don't know!" Gerran sighed and looked away. "Life was a lot simpler when I was just the captain of Cadryc's warband."

"No doubt. But there might be more immigrants arriving from the Southern Isles, come autumn."

"Good idea. My thanks."

"We've got plenty of other troubles on our hands for now, for that matter. No doubt you'll be well occupied this summer."

"True spoken. Here, can you find out where Govvin is? I'm as sick as I can be of waiting around for that stinking, arrogant priest."

"I spied upon him yesterday morn, and lo, he and his men were praying in their temple. I can't believe he's staying away, frankly. To refuse a direct summons to a gwerbretal malover goes beyond arrogance to rash stupidity."

When Clae finished with Gerran's horse, Gerran led him back to the stable himself. Clae took his brushes over to Salamander's roan, tethered nearby, and began currying it down. Salamander was considering going back inside when a young page with Cengarn's blazon on his dirty shirt came skipping up to them.

"Gerthddyn?" he said. "Lord Blethry wants to talk to you. He's just over there." He pointed to the end of the stable row, where, hands on hips, Blethry was standing in the shade of the stable wall.

"I'm on my way," Salamander said, "though it looks as if he wants to scold, berate, and castigate me."

The equerry, however, had something quite different in mind. "It's about that scribe of Prince Dar's," Blethry said when Salamander joined him. "Is he daft?"

"At moments I can think of him no other way. What's he done now?"

"Well, late last night it was, and I couldn't sleep, what with worrying about everything." Blethry paused to scowl in the general direction of Gerran, who was just coming out of the stable. "So I got up and left the broch for a bit of air. I came down here to take a look at one of the mares who's due to foal, and as I was leaving the stables again, I looked up. Right on the roof of the main broch there's

Neb, standing with his arms in the air and not a stitch of clothing on, far as I could see by the moon's light."

Salamander groaned inwardly.

"So I hurried inside to speak to him about it," Blethry went on, "but he'd already left the roof. What if our lady Drwmigga had seen him, eh?"

I'm sure she's seen a naked man before, Salamander thought, *considering she's pregnant.* Aloud he said, "True spoken. I'll speak to Neb about it."

"Good. He seems to be a friend of yours and all, which is why I'm bringing the matter to you." Blethry hesitated. "But what was he doing up there?"

"Praying to the Star Gods, most likely." Salamander pulled a useful lie out of the air. "Now that he's a servitor of the Westfolk prince, he's adopted their gods."

Blethry slapped his forehead with the flat of his hand. "I should've thought of that," he said. "I've heard the Westfolk calling on them, now that you mention it. Worms and slimes, I'm just so tired today."

"No doubt, and you have my profound sympathy."

"My thanks. Here, gerthddyn, how about giving us a tale in the great hall after dinner tonight? It'll take everyone's mind off things, like."

"I'll do just that, and I'll make it a good one."

Gerran had wandered off, and Clae had finished with Salamander's horse. Salamander hailed the lad as he was coming out of the stable.

"A question for you," Salamander said. "Did your brother leave your chamber last night?"

"He did," Clae said. "I woke up just as he was coming back in. He told me he'd gone down to the privies, because he'd eaten somewhat that disagreed with him, and he didn't want to stink the chamber up by using the pot."

"Ah, I see."

"It didn't seem worth bothering you about right then, but I'm truly afraid he's ill. It would gladden my heart if you'd go look in on him. He didn't eat any breakfast this morning, and he looked sort of pale."

As he walked away, Salamander scried for Neb and saw him lying on his bed in his chamber. Salamander hurried up the stairs in a crowd of anxious Wildfolk. He found the door unlocked and walked in without knocking. The yellow gnome darted in ahead of him and jumped onto the bed, where Neb was lying with his hands tucked under his head. He wore only a loin-wrap, and his seminakedness revealed how thin he'd become. Every rib showed, his clavicle stuck out, and his thighs were nearly as narrow as his calves.

"Clae asked me to see how you fared," Salamander said. "Did you truly eat spoiled food last night?"

Neb sat up, swung his legs over the edge of the bed, and turned away without answering. The gnome waved tiny fists at his unresponding back.

"Considering that Lord Blethry spotted you up on the roof," Salamander went on, "I don't believe your little tale."

Neb winced and began studying the floor.

"You do look half starved, however. Let me guess. You're fasting in hopes of making your astral visions more vivid."

Neb never answered. Salamander walked over to the window, which Neb was facing, and sat on the wide sill.

"It's a bad idea, fasting at your stage of the apprenticeship."

"Oh, and how would you know?" Neb's voice hovered just above a growl. "I don't see what's wrong with it."

"That's the crux of the trouble. You don't."

"Nevyn used to do it."

"He did no such thing, and besides, you're not Nevyn."

Neb looked at him with murderous eyes, then returned to studying the floor.

"You're forgetting that if you remembered me from your time as Nevyn, then I must, conversely and all that, remember him. He was not the fasting sort, especially when good dark ale and a roast swan were on the table."

Neb sat up a little straighter.

"Let us consider this." Salamander went on, "You say I can't know that what you're doing is wrong. But I can because I did somewhat similar in the folly of my youth, and you, as Nevyn, told me to stop it. Had I listened to him, I would have been spared years of madness, and the family I loved so dearly would have been spared the pain I caused them. I lost them because I refused to listen to the old man." Salamander heard his voice choke on that remembered grief. "Now, if you wish to spend a long day listening to all of my errors, I'll tell them in detail. But the one and only thing you really need to know is that now you're going down the same path."

"What path is that?" Neb spoke softly.

"Refusing to listen to the masters of your guild, sure you know better than they what's harmful and what's safe."

Neb looked up again. "I do have memories, you know," he said, "of lore."

"But what, pray tell, is memory? The memories of our own childhoods are unreliable enough. How can you expect to remember what happened to you two hundred years ago, when you wore a different being?"

"I've been working on the astral—"

"Ah, building a dun at the water's edge, where the waves slide in to undermine it. Surely Dalla's told you how unreliable those images are, how slippery, shifting, melting, merging—"

"Oh, hold your cursed tongue!" At that moment his expression did resemble Nevyn's, not that Salamander would have told him so. "I've been testing the images with sigils."

"Has Dalla taught you those, or are you remembering them?"

"Remembering them."

"Are you sure you're remembering them correctly?"

Neb opened his mouth, then shut it again.

"You're not, are you?" Salamander said. "Why are you so determined to recover those memories, anyway? You don't need to learn the lore that way. You've got good teachers."

"It's all taking so long."

"Ah, I see that you've fallen into an opposite error from one of mine. When I was a lad, I thought that my teacher was rushing along like the winter winds. I felt so burdened that I kept running away. Val didn't much care for my wandering ways, as you might guess, but did I listen to her? Hah!"

"Valandario was your teacher?"

"She was. But here's somewhat you may not remember. When I

was a tiny child, Nevyn's the one who told her that some day I'd be her pupil."

If they'd been playing with swords, Salamander thought, he would have just scored a touch. Neb looked at him wide-eyed, his lips a little parted.

"I didn't realize," Neb said at length, "that you were taught by a woman, too."

"Is that what's troubling your heart? All those women around you?"

For a long moment Neb hesitated, then spoke in a flood of words. "It's just that they tell Branna things they don't tell me, and Branna's so far ahead. She remembers things in her cursed dreams. I've never had dreams like that, so I thought I'd—" He suddenly blushed scarlet.

"Aha!" Salamander said. "I think me we're reached the heart of the matter. So you thought you'd produce visions instead of dreams?"

Still scarlet, Neb nodded his agreement.

"Branna's dreams, alas, are not always true. Did you realize that?"

Slowly Neb's color returned to normal. He shook his head.

"I didn't think you did," Salamander went on. "I can't reveal any secrets about her, being as I don't know any, but here's somewhat I can tell you. When we were at the Red Wolf dun, Branna came to me to ask me about a dream. She'd always dreamt that she could fly as a falcon. This is quite true. Jill could do that. But our Branna dreamt about flying over Bardek during her first trip to the islands. Since I happened to be with her at the time, I know perfectly well that dream was false. Jill hadn't learned how to fly then."

"So Branna doesn't always get true lore in those dreams?"

"I'd say that she's gotten very little lore, only memories of using the lore that Jill learned the same way we all do, the long slow painful way. Years of study, Neb, years of study—even I, wild lad that I was in my youth, have put in years of study. It's the studying that builds the skills."

"Dalla told me the same thing, but I—well, uh, oh never mind."

"Nah nah nah, you won't wiggle off my hook that easily."

"Oh, very well! I thought I knew better. I thought if I could only remember enough to be Nevyn again, I'd have all the skill I needed."

"Alas, such is not the case. Dweomer operates through the person you are in each life. You have to build its precepts into the flesh and blood and aura you have in each life. Memories of Nevyn would be just that: memories. You can remember, perhaps, a fine meal you had years ago. Will it nourish you now?"

Neb shook his head in a no, then looked away. Salamander could see tears in his eyes but made no comment.

"Let's think," Salamander said instead. "For example, consider our Gerran and his desire to build the Falcons a fine dun on the border, a noble aim that all approve. He now has the coin, he has an idea of the dun he wants, he has the charter from his overlord to build it—but is it finished, therefore?"

"And the coin represents my talent, and the idea my memories, and Dalla's my overlord?" Neb smiled, a bare twitch of his lips, but a smile.

"Just that. It's going to take the workmen a couple of years to build the Falcon dun. It will take you, alas, a fair bit longer to become a master of your craft, just as it took all of us years and years. It took Nevyn years, for that matter."

Neb nodded, thoughtfully this time, his eyes narrow as he considered. *That's one fever broken,* Salamander thought, *but I'll wager that others lie ahead.* Aloud he said, "Dalla gave me permission to work with you—if you wanted."

"She told me that, too."

The silence hung between them, as palpable as the dust motes dancing in the sun through the window. Salamander forced himself to stay silent and wait. The yellow gnome stuffed one fist into its mouth in sheer anxiety.

At last Neb took a deep breath. "Will you help me. Ebañy?"

"I most assuredly will. And I appreciate how much the asking has just cost you."

Neb smiled, then stood up. "I'd better get dressed. I didn't mean to make Clae worry. It was the only excuse I could think of, when he woke up."

"Well and good, then. By the by, if Lord Blethry asks you what you were doing on the roof, tell him that you were worshiping the Star Gods. It was the only excuse I could think of, when he asked me."

They shared a laugh. *Ye gods,* Salamander thought, *I have an apprentice of sorts—for the nonce, anyway. I must be getting old.* The yellow gnome skipped around the chamber in joy.

The door to the chamber banged open, and Clae came trotting in. When he saw Neb sitting up, he smiled.

"I'm feeling much better, truly," Neb said. "No need for you to worry."

"That gladdens my heart," Clae said, "and it's a good thing, too, because Prince Dar needs you. He's going to have some sort of meeting with Voran and Ridvar, and he wants you to write things down."

"I'll get dressed, then." Neb stood up and grabbed his shirt from the end of the bed. "Where is the prince?"

"He says to meet him up in the chamber of justice."

"Very well. Run and tell him that I'm on my way."

Everyone in the dun, of course, wanted to know what the princes were saying to each other, but since the servants had been caught eavesdropping on the malover concerning Lord Oth's theft, they were afraid to listen at the door again. Gerran and Salamander waited in the great hall with the crowd. At last, when the sun hovered low in the western sky, Prince Daralanteriel came down the stone staircase. Gerran and Salamander hurried over to meet him at the foot.

"Where's Neb?" Salamander said, glancing around.

"Writing up his notes," Dar said. "Here, you two, come down to the meadow with me. We discussed a good many other things, and I'd like your opinion and Cal's, too."

Since a prince couldn't be seen walking through the streets like an ordinary man, Clae and two of the dun's pages rushed to the stables to saddle horses. While Gerran and Salamander waited with Dar, standing out in the ward, Dar told them some of what had transpired in council.

"Ridvar's furious with the way Govvin's ignoring him. He's decided to drag him out of his wretched temple if he won't come voluntarily, so he's sending his captain and some twenty-five men to fetch him."

"And if Govvin won't come out?" Salamander said. "Will they lay siege to the place? Twenty-five men doesn't seem like enough."

"Voran's taking twenty from his warband and going with them. After all, the prince has that letter from the high priest in Dun Deverry to deliver. Besides, his men are getting restless, camping in the meadow with naught to do."

"That should be enough men to make Govvin think about things." Gerran joined in. "If naught else, they can hold his blasted white cows hostage."

Daralanteriel and Salamander both laughed.

"I'm minded to offer to send some archers along," Dar went on. "Voran and I swore a pact of mutual aid in time of war this afternoon. This isn't a war, but it'd be a good gesture, I think, to offer aid. Here, Gerran, as my vassal, will you command the men if I send them? I want Cal to stay with me. The silver dragon's been off scouting for Horsekin up in the Northlands, and he might meet us here. Cal has to hear his report if he does."

"Of course, Your Highness," Gerran said. "May I take Mirryn and the Red Wolf men with me? Mirryn needs to get used to leading the warband."

"By all means. This will be a good opportunity for him to do just that. After all, nothing much is going to happen." Dar suddenly grinned. "And take your silver dagger. Cal tells me he's been beating everyone in camp at dice. I don't want my warband impoverished."

"I'll do that, Your Highness." Gerran turned to Salamander and quirked an eyebrow.

"Oh, I shan't be coming with you," Salamander said. "I've got to play shepherd to our sheepish Neb."

"What? Has he gotten himself into trouble again?"

"Of a sort." Salamander smiled vaguely, then continued. "Besides, the lad's an important witness against Govvin. We can't have him riding all over the countryside."

On the morrow, the warbands assembled in Cengarn's ward. Gerran watched as Mirryn gave orders to the Red Wolf men about their line of march. The men certainly obeyed him, but in their own time. That and the easy way they sat in their saddles made Gerran wonder if they respected their captain as much as they liked him. He doubted it. When Gerran walked down the line, they sat up straight and brought their horses to the ready with a slight tug on the reins. He glanced over his shoulder and saw Mirryn watching with an utterly impassive face—but watching.

The first night out, the expedition camped at the edge of Ridvar's demesne, about halfway to the temple. Gerran and Mirryn set up their tents near the Red Wolf's warband, but they ate with Prince Voran and his captain, Caenvyr, who turned out to be nobleborn, the younger son of a younger son of the Rams of Hendyr. Now that they were away from the gwerbretal dun, Voran assumed a bluff and hearty air, as if he were merely minor nobility like the rest of them, but Gerran had no doubt that any insult would be remembered and payment demanded, should anyone there be foolish enough to offer one.

Mirryn, Gerran noticed, seemed lost in some sort of unpleasant thought. He said nothing except in answer to direct questions, few of which came his way. When they were walking back to their tent, Gerran asked him what was troubling him.

"Oh, it's naught," Mirryn said. "I guess."

"Out with it!"

Mirryn stopped walking, and Gerran joined him. A few campfires still burned, casting an uncertain light here and there through the camp. All around them the men were spreading out their blankets for the night. The camp stank of smoke and sweat and horses, such a familiar smell that Gerran found it soothing.

"Well," Mirryn said, "it's about Branna and the daft things she says sometimes. Last summer, when you all were riding off to Zakh Gral, I was furious at being left behind."

"I remember that, truly."

"On the day the army left, she twitted me about it." Mirryn hesitated. "When she warned you about Oth, it came true, and so that made me wonder."

"What are you getting at? Did she give you some sort of warning?"

"Just that. In this truly peculiar voice she told me that I needed to stay in the dun for some reason, Wyrd, most likely. Then she said that at the turning of the next year toward spring my time of war would come. I don't know why, but I got the impression that she was surprised, or I was going to be surprised. Well, here it is, early in the spring. And my mind keeps reminding me of her words. Do you think it might mean somewhat?"

"I'd wager high it does. Surprised, huh? I don't see any harm in sending a few scouts ahead of us, but we'd best wait till dawn. We'd best tell the prince, too. In the dark the Horsekin have the advantage with those noses of theirs."

"Horsekin?"

Gerran smiled, just briefly. "Who else would give us trouble? The silver dragon saw an army far to the north. This could be an advance force."

"Good point." Mirryn's expression turned grim. "Dawn it is for those scouts."

Gerran woke at the first light of a clear, dry day. He found Nicedd the silver dagger and a Red Wolf man whose wits he trusted and woke them to give them his orders. Once they were on their way, he went to Prince Voran's tent. Voran had already risen and was standing outside, watching his servant rummage through a sack of provisions. Gerran told him that he'd sent off scouts, though he left out any mention of dweomer omens.

"Good thinking, my lord," Voran said. "You never know what might happen up here on the border."

"So I thought, Your Highness," Gerran said. "We'll see what news the scouts bring back, if any."

The scouts left on foot just as the rest of the men were beginning to roll out of their blankets and pull on their boots. The entire camp was awake and eating their breakfast rations when the scouts came running back.

"We didn't have to go far, my lord," Nicedd said. "Maybe a mile. We found tracks and rubbish and a couple of latrine ditches, all fresh, and hoofprints, too big for an ordinary horse. I'd say that Horsekin raiders aren't far ahead of us on the road."

"Well and good, then," Voran said. "When we ride, we ride

armed and ready for trouble." He turned to Caenvyr. "Make sure everyone hears the orders."

With the scouts trailing after him, Gerran hurried back to his own part of the camp. While the Red Wolf men and the Westfolk archers gobbled the last of their breakfast, Gerran mentioned to a man here and there that it was Lord Mirryn who'd originally thought of sending out scouts. The news would spread quickly enough. Clae had already laid out his lord's chain mail and helm. Gerran put them on, then ate a chunk of bread standing up while Clae saddled and bridled his horse. Mirryn joined him, his own breakfast in hand.

"With luck," Gerran remarked, "we'll catch the bastards on the road."

"Good," Mirryn said.

"Now look, you're a good man with your sword, but I'll warn you somewhat. In battle things happen a cursed lot faster than they do on the tourney ground. Don't overreach yourself, foster brother. Make sure you stay with your men. Plenty of fighting will come your way. Don't worry about that."

"Oh, I've no doubt of it!"

"You look troubled."

"I'm not. I was just thinking that tonight my life is going to be completely different—one way or the other. It's an odd thought to have with your breakfast."

When the army rode out, the Westfolk archers rode at the head of the line of march with their curved hunting bows at the ready and a full quiver of arrows at each man's hip. Once they spotted the enemy, they would peel off and attack the Horsekin from the flanks. Prince Voran's men rode behind them and the Dun Cengarn men after them, with the Red Wolf bringing up the rear guard.

"Ye gods," Mirryn said, "the dust!"

With seventy horsemen on a dirt road, the dust rose up in a high plume, a clear signal to any enemies ahead of them.

"True spoken," Gerran said. "We can blasted well forget about catching the bastards by surprise. Here, Mirro, I've got to ride forward and take charge of my archers. If there's a scrap, good luck."

"And the same to you." Mirryn gave him a grin. "Lots of it."

Gerran trotted his horse up the line and pulled in next to Vantalaber, the leader of the archers' squad. As a sign of his position, Van wore a bird's wing sewn to one side of his helm, which was mostly leather though reinforced with brass strips over the crown and around the base. Van grinned at him with the exact same expression as Mirryn and patted the bow laid across his cantle.

"We'll aim for the horses first," Van said.

"Good. If you can bring down a few in front, they'll have to make a messy charge."

About a mile on, the road entered a forest, a thick stand of old growth maple, larch, and scattered pine. Here and there branches overhung the road and scattered the dust cloud, but in a couple of miles more the road broke free of the cover. Dust rose again as the warbands followed the road into a wide meadow.

To either side stretched open farmland. A mile or so off to the left a plume of smoke rose, the sign of a burning farmstead, no doubt. Ahead of the oncoming Deverry force, armed and ready Horsekin sat on their heavy horses in two-deep ranks, formed into a rough crescent. Thirty raiders, maybe forty—Gerran had no time to count. He reached down and pulled a javelin from the sheath under his right leg. With a silver horn in hand, Prince Voran urged his horse up to the front rank.

"Now!" Voran shouted at the top of his lungs, then raised the horn and blew.

The archers peeled off, five on each side. The prince's men threw their javelins in a hail of deadly steel, then drew swords on the follow through. The Horsekin shouted and flung up shields to deflect them. One javelin found its mark; a Horsekin in the second rank slumped in the saddle, then fell over his mount's neck, but the raiders in the front rank held their position until the arrows began flying. With a whistle and hiss, death struck from the side. Horses screamed and reared; two fell to their knees, dying. The Horsekin in the rear rank screamed war cries and pressed forward; those in the front had no choice but to charge. In an answering roar of war cries, Voran's men charged to meet them.

Gerran found himself caught in the front rank of the charge. Through the choking dust he spotted a Horsekin toward the edge of the enemy formation who was wearing the red tabard of the

Keepers of Discipline. In dead silence, Gerran rode straight for him. A Westfolk arrow hissed by him and grazed the Keeper's bay horse. A red stripe opened on the horse's flank as it neighed and reared, pawing the air. When it came down, Gerran was there to meet its rider.

The Keeper swung down with his falcata. Gerran twisted away, ended up low in the saddle, then struck up from below. He caught the Keeper full in the face, just under the nasal bar of his helm. With a scream the Keeper tumbled backward just as another arrow struck his mount full in the neck. The horse went down, and Gerran spurred his own mount past them into the thick of the fighting.

So thick, in fact, that he found himself unable to face off with another Horsekin rider—the prince's force outnumbered them at least two to one. The Westfolk archers had done their work to broaden the odds further. The remaining Horsekin were trying to turn and flee; the arrows kept coming, and Deverry riders were pushing hard into the center of what had been the Horsekin formation. Over the melee a brass horn sang out as somewhere a Horsekin officer signaled retreat.

Gerran pulled free of the hopeless mob and turned his horse. The Red Wolf men, trapped as they had been in the rear rank, were just joining the fighting, or trying to. Gerran allowed himself a grin at the thought of how frustrated Mirryn must be, then rose in the stirrups and looked for his archers, spread dangerously around the edge of the field. He began riding after them, yelling for them to join ranks and return to safety. A few heard him and turned their horses just as a Horsekin squad broke free of the mob and headed straight for Gerran, caught isolated on the edge of the battle.

You rash dolt! Gerran had just time to think it before the squad mobbed him, four riders, swinging hard with falcatas, pressing in two at a time. No time to think of attack—Gerran had shield and sword and parried with both. He swayed and ducked as his horse danced and kicked, but one of the Horsekin had managed to edge round to the rear. A hard blow caught Gerran on the back of his left shoulder. He nearly dropped the shield but clutched the handhold with all his arm's failing strength and saved it.

All at once a Horsekin yelled, another screamed; the horse directly in front of his went down, an arrow in its throat. Gerran heard shouting, "Red Wolf! Red Wolf!" Swinging a blooded blade, Mirryn burst into the scrap from the side. A Horsekin went down. Daumyr spitted another in the back. The last raider tried to turn his horse and run, but a Westfolk arrow struck his horse full in the chest. Mirryn finished off the rider as the Horsekin fought to jump free of his falling mount.

Panting for breath, Gerran lowered his shield and saw only Deverry riders and Westfolk archers on the field. Prince Voran's silver horn was singing the order to hold and stand. Mirryn pulled his horse up beside Gerran.

"My thanks," Gerran gasped it out.

"You had the luck," Mirryn said. "Daumyr spotted you off on the edge."

With his drawn sword Gerran saluted Daumyr, who shoved his helm back and grinned with sweat running down his face. Vantalaber guided his horse up to join them with his bow slung over one shoulder.

"I've collected all our men, Gerro," Van said. "All accounted for. It gladdens my heart to see you alive."

"I got careless," Gerran said. "I nearly paid for it, too."

"It happens." Van shrugged the comment away. "The prince's captain tells me that a couple of Horsekin got clean away. He says it's too dangerous to go after them, because they're probably going to rejoin a larger force somewhere."

"Most likely," Gerran said. "This lot didn't have a baggage train, not so much as a pack mule with them. They can't be riding on their own."

Prince Voran had reached the same conclusion. By then, the sun had climbed to zenith. The prince and Gerran discussed the situation while Mirryn and the two captains, Voran's and Ridvar's, sat on their horses with them and listened. With the immediate danger past, Gerran could allow himself to feel the pain in his shoulder, burning like fire from the falcata blow. Still, since no one had mentioned seeing any blood seeping through his mail, he forced his mind away from it.

"Good thing you thought of those scouts," Voran said in an oddly mild tone of voice. "Now, we've got two men dead and a couple of wounded." He turned in the saddle and spoke to his captain.

"Caenvyr, make sure that any wounded Horsekin are disposed of. Then pick ten men for a guard to wait with our own wounded till the wagons catch up. It shouldn't be long now. We'll bury our dead in the oak trees near the holy temple."

"Your Highness." Caenvyr bowed from the saddle, then rode off.

Voran turned to Ridvar's captain. "Your lord needs to know what's happened here. Send messengers, but four of them, just in case any of the swine are hiding along the forest road. Bring them to me before they leave, so I can tell them the message."

"Done, then, Your Highness." The captain jogged off to follow orders.

"Now, as for us," Voran returned his attention to the two lords. "Let's gather our men and push on. I'm beginning to wonder if there's a good reason why Govvin hasn't answered that summons from the gwerbret."

"So am I, Your Highness," Gerran said. "The temple's defensible if the main body of raiders come back for us."

"Good thought, yet once again. Very well. Let's ride."

The temple complex stood at the top of a low hill. From the outside, it looked like a typical Deverry dun, with a high stone wall, crenellated, circling a tall broch tower. In the ward, or so Gerran had been told, the priests had built a round temple of Bel out of the sacred oak wood. When they rode up to the base of the hill, he could see that the gates to the dun hung open, smashed half off their hinges. The warm spring wind brought down the unmistakable stink of rotting blood and flesh.

"By all the gods!" Prince Voran whispered. He started to say more, then merely shook his head in disbelief.

The men behind him began to curse and mutter among themselves. Gerran rose in his stirrups and looked through the gates. He could see what appeared to be irregular tree trunks. standing in the ward.

"It looks like they've taken the temple apart, Your Highness," Gerran said. "Whoever they were."

"And then they left again," the prince said. "No man's going to live in that stink. Dead priests, I assume."

The prince had assumed correctly, but none of them could have guessed what lay ahead. Most of the prince's men dismounted and armed, then followed the prince and Gerran while the Cengarn men and the Red Wolf guarded the horses. Cautiously, three abreast, they walked up the hill, then stopped, stunned, at the gates. Ravens rose from a feast, shrieking in annoyance at being disturbed.

Mercifully, all of the priests had already died. Each one of them had been stripped, bound, and then impaled on a long Horsekin spear, inserted in the anus and shoved all the way through to the back of the neck and out again. Their faces, twisted in agony, showed that they'd been still alive during the impalement. A few must have lived for some while, judging from their pain-twisted faces and the way they'd bitten through their own lips. Twelve priests in all, plus four servants, made up the thicket of death.

Gerran heard men behind him turning out of line to vomit off to the side of the gates. Prince Voran himself had gone dead-white, and drops of sweat beaded his face.

"Your Highness," Gerran said. "Is the high priest one of these men?"

"He's not." Voran swallowed heavily. "Let's look in the temple. He might have taken refuge at the altar." He turned and called out to his men. "Get these poor bastards down! We'll bury them properly out in the oak grove."

The prince allowed Gerran to take the lead. They skirted the impalements and walked around the circular temple to reach the west-facing door. It, too, hung smashed from its hinges. Inside, a few shafts of sunlight streamed from the tiny windows up near the roof, plenty of light to see the remains of the statue of Bel, lying ax-hacked and scattered around the floor. On the stone altar Govvin lay stripped and gutted. The Horsekin had cut him open a few inches at a time and placed his internal organs in tidy lines on either side of him, bladder, guts, kidneys, stomach, and lungs, everything but the heart, which was missing. Ants crawled thick over the corpse and the altar, black with old blood.

"Just what I was expecting," Gerran said.

The prince dropped to his knees and vomited like a commoner. Gerran turned his back to give him some privacy, but Voran recovered himself quickly. Together, they walked outside to watch as the men lowered the spears and removed the pitiful corpses. Most stuck and had to be pulled free. Gerran couldn't begrudge the men the black jests they voiced to make the job bearable. "Like pulling pork off a spit" was the most common one.

By the time they'd finished, the wagons of the baggage train were creaking to a stop at the foot of the hill. Some of the men hurried off to fetch shovels. The prince watched them go, then turned to Gerran.

"I'd say that everyone's been dead about three days," Voran said.

"I agree, Your Highness," Gerran said. "We're going to find more carnage along the road to the north of here, I expect. I wonder how many more raiders there are?"

"I wonder where they are, too. What about Honelg's old dun? The gwerbret left a fortguard there."

"So he did, Your Highness. Let's hope they're standing a siege."

"Or standing at all?" Voran's voice turned grim. "Let's hope, indeed."

"Here comes Caenvyr. Looks like he's found somewhat."

The prince's captain came hurrying up, then bowed to the prince. He handed Gerran a bit of wood that had been cut and smoothed with an ax from the look of the marks left behind by the blade. It also carried two crude symbols carved with a dagger point: a drawing of a piggish creature and then a letter.

"I don't know letters," Gerran said. "Do you?"

"Just enough to know that's an A," Caenvyr said. "As in apred, perhaps?"

"Truly, that drawing looks like a boar to me, too," Gerran said. "What does this mean?"

"I have no idea, my lord." Caenvyr held out both hands palm upward. "I was hoping that you or his highness knew. I found it nailed up on the temple wall, so it must mean somewhat."

Murmuring apologies, bowing to the prince, Nicedd joined Gerran. "I heard the captain mention Boars, my lord." He looked at the scratched marks on the wood. "It's them, all right!" Nicedd turned away and spat on the ground. "I might have known, my lord! They're just the sort to murder a lot of helpless priests."

"Here, what's this?" Voran said. "Now look, silver dagger, Clan Apred was wiped out during the Cerrgonney Wars, or so I was told."

"If Your Highness says so, then." Nicedd ducked his head in an excuse for a bow.

"None of that!" Voran snapped. "If you know differently, tell me."

"Well and good then, Your Highness. I come from up north in Cerrgonney. Those bastards of Boars live just over the border, between us and Dwarveholt. They've got a couple of duns up there, and they raided us whenever they could."

Voran's jaw dropped in surprise. He recovered himself with a quick nod. "Some of them must have escaped my ancestor's justice, then," Voran said. "And so you recognize their mark?"

"I do, Your Highness. I've always been told that they worship that Horsekin goddess, Al-what's-it."

"Alshandra," Gerran said softly. "Well now, this is all starting to make sense."

"True spoken, my lord," Nicedd continued. "She's their excuse for raiding. The lord I used to ride for caught one once and got some information out of him before he hanged him."

"Why haven't I heard about this?" Voran said.

"Well, um, Your Highness." Nicedd began studying the ground. "I couldn't say for certain, but Cerrgonney lords like to keep their troubles to themselves, if you take my meaning."

"I'm afraid I do, but as justiciar, I'll have to look into this further." He waved the wooden plaque in Gerran's general direction. "Why would the raiders go out of their way to tell us who they are? It seems foolhardy."

"Good question, Your Highness." Gerran had been wondering the same thing. "They may have been leaving that bit of wood for the Horsekin, not for us, to show they'd done their part of a bargain. Or maybe they had a prisoner who wanted someone to know where she'd gone. I'm assuming it was a woman."

"It might have been a castrated lad. If it was a woman, why would they have brought her along on a raid? She couldn't have been taken captive here. The priests of Bel don't allow so much as a mare or a hen inside their compounds." Voran handed the plaque to Caenvyr. "Keep that in a safe place, Captain." He turned back to Gerran. "Be that as it may, let's get the dead buried. Then we'll send out scouts."

The scouts came back with grim news indeed. They'd gone a few miles north toward the Black Arrow's old dun and on the way found a farm.

"Burnt to the ground, Your Highness," the scout said, "and we didn't find any corpses."

The prince swore under his breath.

"We found a lot of hoofprints, too, Your Highness," the scout went on. "Some were fresh, heading north. I'll wager they were the scum who fled from us. But there were old prints, too, and a lot of horse droppings. Everything was pretty confused, but the tracks mostly pointed north."

"It was hard to tell how many riders there were," the second scout joined in. "Though I'd say there were a cursed lot more than we faced today, Your Highness."

"Well and good, then," Voran said. "Go rejoin your units, men." He turned to Gerran. "Let's see, we sent out messengers in mid-morning. They should ride straight through to Cengarn. Let's hope the night watch lets them in."

"It will, Your Highness," Gerran said, "since they're riding in your name."

"Most likely, indeed. How long do you think it will take Ridvar to reach us with more men?"

Gerran had been unaware that the prince had asked for reinforcements, but he was pleased to hear it. "Another day and a half, Your Highness," he said. "They can't risk tiring their horses with maybe a battle waiting at the end of the ride."

"True spoken. I'm thinking of making our night's camp in the temple. As you remarked, it's defensible, even without its gates. We can pull the supply wagons into the opening to block it."

"Good idea, Your Highness. I can't see the Horsekin dismounting to attack the compound. That's assuming they don't have spearmen with them, of course."

"Of course." Voran allowed himself a thin smile. "But I think it's a safe assumption. It's a long way to walk from their country to ours."

"That's one of the things that's going to save us, Your Highness. In the long run, I mean."

Voran winced. "True enough. One more thing. I want your honest opinion, Gerran. No agreeing with the prince just because he's the prince. I'm thinking of staying in our fortified camp on the morrow to let those reinforcements reach us. Will we be safer, or is it a death trap?"

"Well, Your Highness, since we don't know how many Horsekin are waiting up the road, riding out could be a death trap, too." Gerran glanced back at the stone walls. "I spotted a couple of wells inside the temple grounds. There's plenty of water, and we've got supplies left. I'd say we camp and hope Ridvar gets himself here fast."

"Done, then." He turned to a waiting servant. "Go find Caenvyr."

Gerran kept his darker thoughts to himself. They were assuming that the messengers would reach Cengarn safely. What if they'd been ambushed on the road somehow? It wasn't likely, since they'd headed south and the fleeing Horsekin north, but it was possible if another squad of raiders were prowling the roads. *It's in the laps of the gods,* he reminded himself. *And we'll know soon enough.*

Once everyone had set up camp inside the temple walls, and the carters had pulled the supply carts across the broken gates, Gerran had the leisure to attend to his injury. With Clae's help, he removed his mail and pulled off his sweat-soaked shirt and the padding underneath.

"There's ever so much blood on them, my lord," Clae said.

"Hold them up, and let me see."

A fresh bloodstain the size of a soup bowl soaked the padding. The blood had oozed through onto his shirt, as well, to make a smaller stain.

"Is the wound still bleeding?" Gerran said.

"It's not," Clae said. "It looks like a peach or suchlike when it's really ripe and the skin splits."

"Not a deep cut, you mean."

"Just that. But you've got a bruise the size of my hands put together."

"What color is it?"

"Red, mostly, and purple."

Gerran raised his left arm over his head. The shoulder throbbed and a line of fire ran down his back, but the pain was bearable. "I must be in one piece still," Gerran said. "Well and good, then. Hand me my shirt."

"Here it is, my lord. Shouldn't you see a chirurgeon?"

"The prince didn't bring one along. Everyone thought we were just delivering a summons."

Once he'd dressed, Gerran went looking for Mirryn. He found the Red Wolf men back by the stables where the priests had kept their riding horses—stolen by the Horsekin, along with the temple's herd of white cows and every other scrap of food in the complex. The men of the warband were tending their own horses while Mirryn stood and watched. This time no one slacked off; every man jumped to when his captain spoke to him; now and then someone glanced Mirryn's way with admiring eyes. When Gerran joined him, Mirryn turned to him with a grin.

"What was that you were telling me before the scrap?" Mirryn said. "About not getting separated from my men?"

"I knew you wouldn't let that slip by," Gerran said.

"Of course not. But still, I'm cursed glad we got there in time."

"Not half as glad as I am." Gerran considered congratulating Mirryn on his first battle, then decided that if he did, he'd be reminding everyone that it had been the first. "Here, Caenvyr's going to set a night watch. Don't let him take my silver dagger for it, will you? Nicedd did the morning's scouting. That's enough extra duty."

"Done, then. He can have his night's sleep." Mirryn looked away. "If any of us can sleep well, that is. Think the Horsekin will try a night attack?"

"I don't. But why take chances?"

Just as the sun was setting, Gerran and Vantalaber climbed up the rickety catwalks to the top of the walls. Since the compound had once been a lord's dun, merlons topped the walls, good cover for archers, as Van remarked.

"How many arrows do your men have?" Gerran said.

"A quiver each of unused ones. We retrieved as many as we could from the field, as well. The shafts are mostly broken, but the points are sound, and we carry feathers with us for the fletching. That hacked-up statue inside the temple itself? How will you

Deverry men take it if we whittle some of the bits down for shafts?"

"We won't care one way or the other." Gerran started to shrug, regretted it, and winced with a choice couple of oaths for the pain in his shoulder. "I doubt if Bel will, either. They say he's a warrior himself."

"Splendid! It's good oak. I hate to waste it. Those shit-sucking Meradan cut the statue up pretty thoroughly. Kind of them to spare us the hard work."

They shared a laugh.

"Now, when night falls," Van continued, "tell whoever's setting the watch to make sure that there's a couple of Westfolk on guard at all times. We see a fair bit better at night than your folk do."

"True spoken. I'll make sure the prince's captain knows it."

"Too bad we don't have one of the Wise Ones with us."

Gerran himself had been wishing that Salamander had come with them. Had he been there, he could have perhaps used his mysterious craft to see what the Horsekin were up to.

"I'm beginning to understand," Gerran said, "why the Westfolk honor their Wise Ones so much."

"They're going to make all the difference out on the grass. The Horsekin won't be surprising us, not with them on watch."

With a cheerful wave Vantalaber climbed back down to rejoin his squad. Gerran lingered, staring off to the west, where the last spread of sunset flamed in the darkening sky. He was tired, he realized, with his shoulder aching like fire in the bone, and his mind wandering, but he couldn't shake the odd feeling that once before he'd been in a situation like this, penned up by an unexpected enemy, waiting for help that might or might not arrive in time. Yet he couldn't remember such an incident, no matter how carefully he searched his memories of war.

"My lord?" It was Clae's voice, calling from below. "My lord, I've brought a lantern."

Gerran turned around and saw the lad standing at the foot of the ladder in a little pool of candlelight. "I'll come down," Gerran called back. "Sure enough, it's getting dark."

Yet before he climbed down, he paused to look off to the south, where Voran's messengers were riding hard for Cengarn. *May they get there safely!* He could only hope that Great Bel had heard his thought.

Gerran's shoulder hurt so badly that he slept little that night. Without the weight of his mail pressing upon it, the bruised flesh had swelled and turned sensitive to every movement. He woke before dawn, squirmed in his blankets in a futile attempt to get comfortable, then admitted defeat and got up. He pulled on his boots—he'd slept in his clothes—then picked his way through the sleeping warbands and climbed up to the catwalks at the top of the outer wall. He made his way round to the area just beside the broken gates and found Prince Voran there ahead of him. In the east a pale arc of silver announced the rising sun.

"Ye gods, Lord Gerran," Voran said, smiling, "don't you ever sleep?"

"Oh, now and then, Your Highness. Did somewhat wake you?"

"Just my thoughts." With a sigh Voran turned and leaned back against a merlon. "You know, Gerran, you strike me as a man who doesn't repeat what other men tell him."

"I do my best not to, Your Highness."

"Do you know why I was appointed justiciar?"

"Most likely because you were the best man for the honor."

"My thanks, not that I'd call it an honor. I suppose the king knew that I could do whatever the post demands. But in truth, it's a sort of exile, not that anyone ever mentioned that word."

"What?" Gerran was startled enough to forget the courtesies of rank. "I can't imagine you doing some shameful thing."

"My thanks again. I certainly did naught that shames me in my own eyes. Perhaps the opposite." Voran rubbed his chin with one hand while he considered the problem. "I apparently made a great many enemies at court, and here I didn't even realize it, just by refusing to ignore certain things and by speaking openly of other things. Every granary has its rats, as the old saying has it. The granaries in Dun Deverry are huge, and rats abound."

"Rats of the same kind as Lord Oth?"

"Indeed, though they'd scorn a prize as small as a handful of coins from a woman's dowry. There are mice as well, the kind that wait under the table in the hopes of falling scraps. They don't have the guts to leap up and steal. They just flatter and beg instead."

"Ye gods!" Gerran struggled to find words. "He sent you away to please a pack of courtiers? That's vile."

"I had a few thoughts that way myself. The kingdom's changing. In my better moments it gladdens my heart that I'm out of Dun Deverry." Voran glanced up at the sky. "Dawn's here. I'd best go down."

With a nod the prince began making his careful way along the catwalks. Gerran watched him as he climbed down the ladder to the ward. *Sent away by the high king!* Gerran thought, *I'm cursed glad now I swore to Prince Dar*. In the rising light Voran strode around the side of the temple, calling to his men to wake. Gerran lingered till the sun had come clear of the horizon, then went down to join his own squad.

Even with the priests buried, the smell of their evil deaths seemed to hang in the air inside the walls. As the morning wore on, the men spoke but little. Vantalaber and his archers, joined by Deverry men, kept a constant watch from the top of the walls. Near noon they finally spotted a cloud of dust coming down the road toward the temple.

"Coming from the south," Vantalaber reported. "It's too soon for anyone to reach us from Cengarn, Your Highness, so the cursed Horsekin must have circled round for some reason."

"Unless it's a second group of raiders entirely," Voran said. "Gerran, have your men and Mirryn's arm and man the walls. I doubt if these bastards have scaling ladders, but you never know, and we'd best be ready to push them back if they do. Caenvyr, put ten of our best right behind those wagons to guard the gates. Ridvar's men should wait mounted just behind them."

Gerran followed orders and for good measure told Mirryn to have his men saddle and ready their horses, just in case of a sally. He rejoined the Westfolk archers on the walls. In the hot sun the men stood between the merlons to catch what shade there was. Gerran arranged his small force with the archers closest to the gates. All the while, the plume of dust grew closer and closer. Vantalaber suddenly broke out laughing, and in a few moments the other archers joined him.

"The rose, the rose!" Van called out. "It's Prince Dar's banner, and I see Cengarn's sun right behind ours."

"It might be a trick," Gerran snapped.

"Don't be a dolt," Van said, grinning. "I can tell Westfolk from Horsekin."

As the dust resolved itself into men and horses, Gerran's human sight confirmed what the elven eyes had seen: Prince Daralanteriel himself, riding with Ridvar and Calonderiel. When the news spread through the compound, the men cheered in a long wave of sound that lapped at the walls and rose above them to greet the relieving force.

As the reinforcements rode up the hill, Voran, with his mounted escort behind him, rode down to meet them. Gerran mounted up and followed until he saw Salamander turning his horse out of line. Gerran waited until the gerthddyn rode up to him.

"How by all the hells did you get here so quickly?" Gerran said. "The messengers can't have reached Cengarn till sunset."

"We left yesterday and met them on the road, that's how," Salamander said. "Thanks to the ghastly tedium of sitting around and watching over a fractious Neb, I scried for you at regular intervals. Thus I saw the battle."

"I'm cursed glad you did. Do you know where the Horsekin are now?"

"I do, and it's not good news. They're north of here, besieging Honelg's dun." Salamander cocked his head to one side and looked away with curiously unfocused eyes. "Aha!" he said eventually. "Allow me to amend that. Only half of them are besieging the dun. The others are on their way here. Let me just go tell Dar. I suspect that you'd best get your men ready to ride."

"They already are. And a blasted good thing, too."

As soon as Salamander told the princes and the gwerbret what he'd seen, they gave their men orders to arm and draw up in battle order at the foot of the temple hill. Salamander left the military matters to those who understood them and rode into the temple compound. As he dismounted, Clae came running to meet him.

"Will you stable my horse for me?" Salamander said.

"Gladly," Clae said. "But I need your help. Lord Gerran's hurt, but he's going to try to fight anyway. He can barely lift his shield 'cause he got hit on the shoulder yesterday. Can you make him keep away from the battle?"

"I can't, not being one of the gods, but fortunately, we've got someone who's almost as good as a god. Here, I'll take care of my own horse. You run and find Prince Dar. Tell him that I sent you, then tattle upon our noble lord. I'll take whatever blame may be. You've got time before the Horsekin get here."

Clae grinned and bowed to him, then ran off through the gates and out. Salamander led his horse free of the confusion and tied him in the shade near the stables. In his scrying of the day before, he'd picked up traces of what had happened to the priests. With a sigh of deep reluctance, he went inside the desecrated temple.

He could tell by the etheric feel of the place that he was too late to help the murdered men find rest. The temple was so curiously free of the etheric traces of so many horrible deaths that he could hope that they'd already found it on their own. Perhaps their belief in their god had led them to the white river, or perhaps they'd chanced upon it as their souls fled from the scene of their bodies' deaths. A glance at the bloodstained altar, where black ants still crawled, made him shudder. He hurried outside, grateful for the sunlight.

Armed men and horses filled the ward around the temple walls, men shouting, running back and forth, horses neighing and rearing, servants yelling at each other as they packed up the supply wagons. He could never have scried in such chaos. He climbed the ladder up to the catwalks, then walked around the top of the wall to a spot opposite the gates. He sat down, cross-legged for balance, with his back against a merlon, and let himself slip into trance.

His body of light, an enveloping silver flame, appeared at his call. He transferred his consciousness over to it and let himself drift upward in the silvery-blue etheric light. All around the temple compound the mist-streaked light quivered and shimmered with the growing force of the spring. The new grass, the leafing trees, the clover and wildflowers: all glistened red with their surging vegetable auras. Seeing clearly through so much bristling life proved difficult, but from his high vantage point he could discern a distant plume of dust—dead black against the blue etheric glow—coming down the road from the north.

Salamander glanced behind him and made sure that the silver cord that fastened his body of light to his physical body appeared thick and strong, pulsing with each slow beat of his heart. He thought himself toward the plume of dust and drifted away from the temple.

When he passed over a field of sprouting winter wheat, the reddish-brown auras of the burgeoning plant life swirled and seemed to bubble. Ahead lay a red mass of another sort, the color of blood, surging and leaping above Alshandra's army. From the etheric, he could plainly see individuals through the bloodshot glow of their auras—a man who seemed to be a commander, riding at their head, the ranks of soldiers, falcatas in hand, and the heavy horses, their horizontal equine auras shot through with the greenish-gray of fear.

Behind them rode someone so surprising that Salamander instinctively flew up higher to avoid her gaze—a priestess, her aura a pure pale blue, riding a white mule led by a child on a pony. She had her head tipped back and her arms raised high. *Working dweomer?* he thought. *Couldn't be!* Still, she was staring so intently upward that at first he assumed she was seeing his body of light. Then he thought to look behind him.

Towering above him in the light-shot etheric sky floated the image of Alshandra that he'd created to ease Rocca's death. He recognized it by the details—the elven longbow he'd given her, the braiding of the long blonde hair, the sigil upon her quiver. Salamander realized that while he'd sent the image toward the white river to lead Rocca there, he'd never seen it actually cross, which would have destroyed it. Down below, the priestess smiled and stretched her arms out farther. Her mouth moved as she began to chant. The army riding before her roared in answer, their howl strangely distorted and echoing in his etheric consciousness but still recognizable:

"Hai! Hai! Hai!"

Oh, you really botched it, Ebañy, old lad! Whether or not the warriors could see the Alshandra image, their priestess could, and they believed what she told them. The image floated to a position high enough above the marching ranks of cavalry to remain stable despite the magnetic effluent of their massed steel weaponry. Yet it stayed close enough to feed off their auras. Salamander saw slender tendrils of raw energy rising like lines of smoke to wrap themselves around the image's booted feet. Alshandra's simulacrum fattened, strengthened, until to his etheric consciousness it looked solid, clear in every detail. The priestess chanted again, and once again came the cry, "Hai! Hai! Hai!"

Salamander turned his attention back in the direction of the temple and saw the confused mass of auras in front that marked the presence of the Deverry army. Calculating the precise distance between the two forces lay beyond his state of consciousness, but a good stretch of ground remained between them. He waited, hovering above in the road, as the Horsekin rode closer and closer, and the priestess chanted, waving her arms, invoking the image that she believed to be divine. At last the Horsekin force rounded a bend in the road and saw the waiting warbands. Different kinds of cries rose—shock, sudden fear, confusion. Salamander realized that they'd been expecting to find a much smaller warband ranged against them.

Let's make it worse! Salamander called upon the Light and saw raw power like silver sheets of lightning appear around him. From within his silver flame he invoked the pentagram, that sigil of all things natural and true, by drawing it with sweeps of his right arm. Each motion left a solid-seeming trail of blue light behind it. Silver light flowed in to strengthen it until it hovered, as huge and bright as a second sun in the sky.

At each point and in the center Salamander drew and placed the sigils of the Elements. He called upon the Light once more, then gathered his will. As the light flowed into his etheric form, he felt it throb with power. He rose to a position right behind the pentagram and laid etheric hands, shaped like flames, upon it. With a last call to the Light, he thrust it forward straight onto the image of Alshandra.

Begone! I banish you in the name of the Light! He seemed to hear his own voice echoing through the etheric like a tidal wave of sound. The image froze, then shattered, bursting into a thousand slivers like a glass bowl dropped from high onto a stone floor. He heard the priestess' answering scream of pure terror, looked down to see her swaying in the saddle, lowering her arms as she screamed again and again.

She nearly fell, but clutched at the mule's mane just in time to right herself. The child leading the mule nearly tumbled off as the pony reared in terror. The army paused in the road, their auras shrinking, turning greenish-gray, billowing again blood-red. The shards of the image were scattering, melting, falling in the etheric like transparent rain.

Another sound drifted up to Salamander: the shouts and war cries of the waiting Deverry and Westfolk men, the pounding of hooves on the road as the Horsekin charged. Salamander realized that he was utterly drained. He turned and followed the silver cord back to his body waiting on the walls of the temple compound. He hovered over the slumped form, then sank down, heard a rushy click, and felt sudden pain. He was back, aching in every muscle, panting as if he'd run a long, long way.

"I'd hardly call a bruise a wound, Your Highness!" Gerran said.

"I would when it's that serious a bruise," Prince Daralanteriel said. "Clae tells me it bled a fair amount."

Gerran scowled at the page, who was studying the ground at his feet. "The skin just split or suchlike," Gerran said. "It's not like a proper cut."

"Well, Ridvar brought a chirurgeon with him. After this scrap you're going to have him look at it." Dar leaned over his horse's neck to speak to the lad. "Clae, my thanks. You've done your master a service today. Now get back into the temple compound where you'll be safe."

Clae bowed and ran back uphill to disappear into the gates.

"No taking it out on the lad later," Dar said.

"I'd not stoop to such a thing, Your Highness," Gerran said, "but truly, I'm—"

"*Truly,* you're staying back here with me as part of my escort. Here comes Calonderiel."

Faced with a direct order, Gerran could do nothing but obey. They were both mounted, waiting to ride down closer to the battlefield. On a golden gelding, his hunting bow slung across his back, Calonderiel trotted up to join them. He held his reins in one hand and, in the other, a silver horn.

"The archers are in position," Cal said. "Here, Gerran, your silver dagger told me you'd been wounded and shouldn't fight."

"Not wounded," Gerran snapped. "Merely bruised."

"But not fit to lift a shield," Dar said firmly. "He's staying with me."

"Good," Cal said. "Here, if the Horsekin break through our lines, you'll both be fighting anyway."

With a wave of the silver horn, Calonderiel turned his horse and trotted back downhill to rejoin his men.

The two princes and the gwerbret had disposed their men, all mounted, across the road and the field beside it in a typical Deverry formation. Massed at the center of a crescent-shaped line were the best swordsmen from every warband, armed with javelins as well as their blades. The rest of the riders spread out to either side. At both of the splayed ends of the crescent rode mounted archers. Up on the flanks of the hill a small squad of unhorsed longbowmen stood on either side of the gates, in readiness to guard a retreat into the temple compound should one prove necessary. The two princes, the gwerbret, and a small escort sat on horseback about halfway up the temple hill and several hundred yards away from the actual battle lines.

The plume of dust announcing the Horsekin army was coming closer, a little faster, then abruptly paused. Daralanteriel rose in his stirrups to survey it, then sat back with a pleased little grunt.

"We outnumber the hairy bastards," Dar said. "And somewhat seems to be troubling them as well."

"Not troubled enough, Your Highness," Gerran said. "Here they come."

To the sound of brass horns, the oncoming Horsekin charged down the road in a sprawling, disorganized formation. Deverry javelins and Westfolk arrows arched into the air, fell whistling among them. Riders screamed, horses reared, neighing, pawing the air, then fell. Horsekin pitched over their mounts' necks and tumbled to die among the dying horses as the arrows came again and again, a deadly slither through the air.

Gerran had never before witnessed a battle from the viewpoint of the commanders. From this distance, he felt detached enough from the rage-frenzy of fighting to feel as if he'd never seen a battle at all. The glory had evaporated like summer mist on hot stone. Watching men die while he faced no risk himself sickened him. Yet he couldn't turn away, transfixed as if by a javelin at the sight.

The sound of Calonderiel's horn floated over the shrieks and the battle cries. The archers fell back. The remaining Horsekin desperately tried to form some sort of line, but the mounted swordsmen charged, bursting in a thunder of hoofs and war cries into the midst of the enemy. Swords flashed, the dust rose high, and the battle became nothing more than slaughter. Two and three at a time the Deverry men and Westfolk mobbed the raiders and cut them down like cattle. A few Horsekin managed to pull out of the mob and try to flee. Westfolk arrows killed them before they'd gone twenty yards.

Gerran glanced around and saw Voran and Ridvar sitting as calmly on their mounts as if they were at table, their faces utterly expressionless. Prince Daralanteriel, however, looked sick at heart. When he noticed Gerran watching him, he shrugged.

"It's daft," Dar said, "all of this, them and their cursed goddess. She doesn't exist, and yet they're dying for her sake."

"True spoken," Gerran said. "Daft is a good word for it, Your Highness. The cursed thing is, some of our men are dying because of it, too."

Slowly the mob thinned as more and more Deverry men pulled back. Slowly the shouting and the screams died away. In a vast litter, spread across the road and meadow, the dying men and their dying horses lay on blood-soaked ground. Other horses, some wounded, some merely terrified, stood quivering in the midst of the carnage or wandered back and forth at the edge, as if they were trying to understand what had happened.

Yelling orders, Calonderiel and the two Deverry captains rode forward. The Westfolk began to round up the living horses. Most of the Deverry men dismounted and began to search for wounded men. They slit the throats of any Horsekin still alive. The Deverry and Westfolk casualties, what few there were, they carried up the hill to the temple compound where Ridvar's chirurgeons waited. Most of the men were looting as they worked, but Gerran's silver dagger found a greater prize than a few foreign coins or bits of jewelry.

Nicedd rode up leading a white mule and its rider—a woman, Gerran realized, dressed in a long leather tunic bunched up over a pair of leather leggings. The painted bow and arrow emblem of Alshandra the Huntress decorated the front of the tunic. She rode slumped over, her hands clutching the pommel of her saddle.

"Is she wounded?" Dar said.

"I don't know, Your Highness," Nicedd said. "I don't speak a word of her ugly language. I saw her just sitting there at the edge of the field, and when I rode up, she didn't even try to get away."

The woman raised her head and looked at them, a young woman, barely more than a lass, with dark eyes under angled, bushy brows. Across her face lay blue-and-green tattoos. Daralanteriel urged his horse up close to hers so he could face her.

"Are you hurt?" he said. "Bleeding? Hurt?"

She seemed to be about to speak, then suddenly lurched forward over the mule's neck and snatched the dagger from Daralanteriel's belt. Gerran shouted and spurred his horse forward, thinking she was going to attack the prince, but she turned the dagger to her own throat. Dar grabbed at her arm, but before he could stop her, she plunged the blade hard into the big vein at one side of her neck. The wound spurted and whistled—she'd cut into her windpipe, too. Without a cry or moan she fell forward, her eyes turning skyward, and rolled over the neck of her mount. The mule began to bray, then panicked, rearing and kicking.

Gerran dismounted fast, but by the time Nicedd managed to get the blood-streaked mule under control, the lass was dead.

"Daft," Gerran whispered. "Ah, horseshit and a pile of it!"

Gerran took the prince's dagger from her flaccid fingers. The hilt sported carved roses, blooming red now with her blood. Gerran wiped the blade off on the side of his brigga, then handed the prince the dagger. He mounted up again just as Salamander came riding out of the temple compound. When the gerthddyn joined the clot of men around Prince Dar, Gerran noticed that his face had gone pale with exhaustion, and under his eyes livid bruises throbbed.

"Ye gods!" Gerran said. "Are you wounded?"

"Merely tired." Salamander's voice rasped in his throat. "I've been fighting after my own fashion." He leaned forward in the saddle and stared at the dead woman lying on the ground. "Ye gods, who killed the priestess?"

"Is that what she was? She slit her own throat."

"Ai! There was a child with her."

"The little lass?" Nicedd urged his horse up to them. "She was dead, slain by an arrow, when I got there, and her little pony, too." He shook his head hard. "It ached my heart, a lass that young! Why would they bring a child to a battle?"

"They expected an easy victory, the bastard-born scum," Gerran said.

"It's more than that." Salamander's voice rasped again. "They thought their goddess would protect them."

"Well, she didn't," Nicedd said. Suddenly he laughed, the choked laugh of a man who's refusing to weep. "The arse-ugly demon-get fools!"

All afternoon the work continued on the field of battle. The Deverry men dug a trench and slung the dead Horsekin into it, but they put the priestess and the little lass into a proper grave some ways apart. The Westfolk tended what wounded horses they judged they could save and put the rest out of their misery. After they scavenged the horse gear, they left the dead mounts for the ravens and foxes. While the men worked, the commanders held a council back in the temple compound. When they met for dinner at Gerran's tent, Gerran told Salamander, his page, and his silver dagger about their decisions.

"As far as we know, none of the Horsekin escaped to get back to the contingent holding the siege," Gerran said. "Which means no one's going to tell them the evil news. It's close to twenty miles from here to the dun, so the besiegers won't be expecting their men to ride back tonight."

"Good," Nicedd said. "Then we've got a chance to fall on them before they realize who we are."

"Just that. Voran's going to mount some of his men on the horses we saved, put them at the head of the line of march, just to fool them for a little while longer." Gerran glanced at Salamander, who was staring slack-mouthed into the distance. "Are you well?"

"Um?" Salamander forced out a grin. "In perfect health, my thanks, just making sure that indeed, no Horsekin are riding from here to Honelg's old dun." He took a bite of flatbread and spoke with his mouth full. "They're not."

Nicedd made the sign of warding against witchcraft with his left hand.

"If naught else," Gerran went on, "we can drive them off and rescue their prisoners. They've doubtless rounded up the farm women around here for slaves."

"Doubtless," Salamander said. "The fate of one woman in particular aches my heart. She and her man used to hold the farm just north of here. She was captured by the cursed Horsekin once, then rescued, and now they've probably got her again."

"Well, if the gods are willing, we'll rescue her again," Gerran said. "Here, Nicedd, when you were helping bury the dead, did you see any of those Boarsmen you spoke of?"

"I did, my lord, and I meant to tell you, too." Nicedd paused to wipe his mouth on his sleeve. "Three of them, and I know they were Boars because they had their blasted pig tattooed right here." He pointed to his right cheek. "Must have hurt, that. And speaking of hurt, my lord, how's the shoulder?"

"It's just a bruise." Gerran spoke through gritted teeth.

"In a most vulnerable spot." Salamander waved a piece of cheese in his direction. "Do you truly want to fight without a shield?"

Gerran bit into his flatbread.

"Ignore me all you want." Salamander was grinning at him. "But Dar told me to ensure that you went to one of the chirurgeons tonight. So hurry up and eat."

The chirurgeons had set up their gear and supplies on the tailgates of several wagons in front of the temple. By lantern light a stick-thin fellow that Gerran recognized from Dun Cengarn examined his bruised shoulder. Raddyn grunted to himself, then shrugged and poked at the bruise with a finger.

"That hurt?" he asked.

"A bit," Gerran said through gritted teeth.

"No doubt. It doesn't look good, but it's too shallow for me to stitch. Wear your padding tonight when you try to sleep. If it's still bad on the morrow, come to me in the daylight when I can see better."

"I'll do that, and my thanks for the advice on the padding. I wish I'd thought of that last night."

With Salamander's help, Gerran put his shirt back on. They left the chirurgeon to tend to the badly wounded and walked back through the camp.

"Told you it was just a bruise," Gerran said.

"That is not precisely what the fellow apprised you of, not that I have much faith in him," Salamander said. "I'll wager Prince Dar keeps you out of the fight on the morrow, too."

After another near-sleepless night, Gerran woke early. When he stood up, the shoulder ached, but even more, it itched. He reached over the shoulder with his good arm and got his hand under his shirt and padding, but his fingers couldn't quite reach the bruise. The entire area felt hot to the touch. He managed to scratch around the edges, although he cursed himself for doing so as soon as he took his hand away. Dried blood caked under his fingernails, and fresh blood stained his fingertips, streaking his dirty hands. Worst of all, the itch resumed, twice as strong. *I'm as bad as that blasted dragon,* he thought. *I'd best leave it alone.*

Much to Gerran's annoyance, Salamander proved right about the prince's orders. When the army broke camp, Daralanteriel put Gerran in charge of the baggage train. Along with the provision carts, Gerran would command the servants, the wounded, and an escort of fifteen swordsmen and five archers. Gerran disposed the escort along the line, then took up his position just in front of the first wagon with his page and his silver dagger. When the main body rode out, the baggage train creaked along behind them. After a mile or so, the fighting men ahead had ridden out of sight.

"It won't be so dusty now," Clae announced. "That'll make the ride better, won't it, my lord?"

Gerran didn't bother replying.

"Is somewhat wrong, my lord?" Clae said.

"He's sulking, lad," Nicedd said with a grin. "Well, begging your pardon and all, my lord."

Gerran thought of a few choice insults, then decided that it was beneath his dignity to voice them.

Here and there stood coppices or a straggle of second-growth woodland, but mostly the road ran through fields of sprouting winter wheat and meadows fenced with stone walls, although they passed not a single cow or sheep. No doubt the Horsekin had taken the lot. Since no one remained to harvest the grain, the local deer would have a good spring feed. In a couple of miles, Gerran's slow procession passed the burnt ruins of a farmhouse and barn. A man with pale hair was searching through them, poking here and there with a long stick into the blackened wood and ashes, while his roan horse waited, tied up to a nearby sapling.

"Salamander!" Gerran yelled. "What in all the hells are you doing?"

Salamander tossed the stick away and started for his horse. Gerran halted the baggage train while the gerthddyn mounted up and trotted over.

"Looking for someone," Salamander said, "to see if he needed burying. He's been pretty much burnt, though, and a lad died with him. All I found were scorched bones."

"That's a sad thing, then. Friend of yours?"

"Not truly. He's the husband of that woman I told you about, the one who was taken by the Horsekin once before. Seeing if he needed burying just seemed a decent thing to do." Salamander sighed and looked away, his face pale, his eyes narrowed against the bright sunlight. "What's going to be interesting, Gerran my lad, is the fate of the other farms and the village along the way. The folk there all worshiped Alshandra."

"Interesting, indeed. Let's go."

The next farm they passed, some miles along, stood unburnt though deserted. Salamander rode over and searched it while the baggage train plodded on. He caught up with them again in a mile.

"Not a soul there," he said. "Either they took their livestock and fled to the woods, or they've gone along with the Horsekin army."

"As slaves?" Gerran said.

"Or as compatriots."

"Huh. If so, they've got a surprise coming their way."

"And a very unpleasant one, at that."

The village Salamander had mentioned turned out to be a straggle of houses roughly arranged around a well. Silence lay upon it like fog—not so much as the bark of a dog or the cluck of a chicken greeted them when the baggage train pulled up in the road beside the village. Salamander dismounted and walked over to the well. When he called out a greeting, only silence answered him. He strode over to the nearest house and peered in, then turned away with a shrug.

"It's been stripped," Salamander called out. "No furniture, naught."

"You'd best get back here," Gerran called back. "We need to get moving."

Salamander trotted back and mounted up, urging his horse up close to Gerran's.

"Stranger and stranger," Salamander said. "These were the people whom the ill-fated Lord Oth saved from being drawn and hanged last summer, the Alshandra worshipers among the servants in the dun. So I'd wager they went along willingly."

"I'd agree with that. Well, if the princes have won the battle, we'll find out soon enough."

Gerran used this particular pause to change the positions of the escorts. He set five of them to ride rearguard, then called the rest up to ride just behind him. He sent Salamander and Clae back to ride in the middle of the line, the safest position, but kept Nicedd up to ride beside him.

"Some of the Horsekin might flee the battle and head south," Gerran told his men. "Ride ready to fight."

Along this particular stretch of road there was some chance of an ambush or attempt at one. Beyond the plowed fields of the last farm stood woodland, open and brushy from years of harvesting deadfall and the like, but providing some cover still. The terrain slowly rose, too, toward the northern hills just visible on the horizon. When his men unlaced their shields from the left side of their saddle peaks, Gerran tried to do the same. Reaching down made his shoulder ache, a throbbing pain that reached a little way down his back. Worse than the pain, he suddenly realized that something was gravely wrong with the wound. He'd been cut before in battle, but never before had a wound—and such a shallow one at that—felt as if it were spreading, increasing its severity with every day that passed. He got the shield free, but when he settled its weight on his left arm, the shoulder above stopped aching and flashed with honest pain. He felt the blood drain from his face, leaving it as cold as winter.

"My lord?" Nicedd. "You truly are hurt."

"Ah, horseshit!" Gerran said. "I guess I am."

"If we do see some stragglers, please, my lord, pull back and let the rest of us take care of them, like."

"Depends on how many of them there are." Yet Gerran felt his stomach turn over from the pain of straightening up again.

"Well and good, then," Nicedd said cheerfully. "But if you get killed, who's going to pay me my hire?"

At that Gerran could laugh, and Nicedd grinned at him.

In the event, no fleeing Horsekin came their way. They realized why when they at last reached the dun that had once been Lord Honelg's. Made of dry stone patched randomly with mortar, the circular walls sat on top of a low artificial hill inside elaborate defenses. Ditches and earthworks wound around the hill and channeled would-be attackers into a narrow path to the gates. Apparently these defenses had served Gwerbret Ridvar's fortguard well. At the base of the hill, blocking the road, lay an elaborate siege camp of tents guarded by another set of ditches and earthworks.

The tents, however, were burning when Gerran and his charges rode up. Greasy smoke plumed the air, and he could smell a horrible stink of burning cloth, hair, and flesh. The horses, particularly the cart horses, began to pull at their bits and dance in fear. Gerran halted the baggage train some hundreds of yards away from the smoldering flames. Salamander rode up to join him.

"The gates of the dun are open," Salamander said, "but no one's inside. I'd say the fortguard sallied when the battle went our way."

"Here!" Nicedd snapped. "How can you know that?"

"Don't ask," Gerran said, grinning, "but take my word for it, he can."

Nicedd again made the fist to ward off witchcraft.

"Where are the princes and the gwerbret?" Gerran asked Salamander.

"Around the other side of the hill." Salamander rose in his stirrups to survey the smoldering camp in a more normal way. "Ah, here come some of our men now."

Guiding nervous horses, Vantalaber and Calonderiel rode around the edge of the camp. Calonderiel hailed Gerran with a wave, then trotted his horse over with Vantalaber following.

"All the sport's over, alas," Cal said. "We killed most of them. Unfortunately, some squads broke through our line and headed north. Probably thirty men in all, as far as I could tell. They'd rallied around a banner with their wretched goddess' bow and arrows on it. We tried to take it from them, but that's when they bolted."

"Is anyone following?" Gerran said.

"They're not. Dar was worried that they might lead our men into a trap. There's got to be a larger force off to the north somewhere."

"What about their prisoners?" Salamander leaned forward in his saddle. "The ones they took for slaves, I mean."

"We saved as many as we could." Cal made a sour face. "When they realized they were beaten, they started killing the women."

"What?" Salamander sat back, and he looked utterly stunned. "Alshandra worshipers, killing helpless women?"

Calonderiel shrugged. "All I know is what I saw."

Salamander turned his horse out of line and trotted off, heading around the smoldering ruins.

"It was a cursed horrible thing to see, truly," Calonderiel said. "No wonder he's troubled. Here, Gerro, let's get these wagons around to our camp. The chirurgeons need supplies."

"We took losses?" Gerran said.

"The Deverry men did. None of them are Westfolk or our vassals. We've got wounded, though."

Gerran turned the baggage train over to Calonderiel and went looking for Mirryn with Nicedd and Clae trailing after him. He found his foster brother eventually on the far side of the dun. Although the smoke hung thick in the air, some of the Red Wolf men were already setting up camp. Still in his mail, Mirryn was talking with Daumyr, who had a shallow cut down one side of his face.

When Gerran started to dismount to join them, he briefly rested his left hand on his pommel. The pain in his shoulder flared up without warning, so badly that he swore aloud.

"You're truly hurt," Mirryn said. "And don't tell me it's just a bruise."

"A bad bruise, then," Gerran said. "Damo, what happened to you?"

"Just a scratch, my lord," Daumyr said. "Close as I can tell, his blade bounced off the nasal of my helmet. Him being the Horsekin I was killing, I mean. The hairy bastards! Did you hear about the women?"

"I did, and it aches my heart."

"Our captain here," Daumyr went on with a grin Mirryn's way, "distinguished himself on the field again. Prince Dar his very self commended him."

"Oh, now here!" Mirryn stared at the ground. "It was but a small thing."

"Oh, was it? I'll want to hear about that tonight." Gerran paused, looking around. "There's Salamander. I need to have a word with him."

Salamander had seen him. The gerthddyn waved, then waited for him to catch up.

"That woman you spoke of," Gerran said, "did you find her?"

"I did, and alive, with her baby and daughters with her." Salamander looked vastly relieved. "Mirryn saved her life, actually. One of the Horsekin was about to kill her, but Mirryn charged up behind him and cut his head half off his shoulders. Canna's dress is dappled with his blood, as is the baby, in fact, a grim decoration for the pair of them. I've high-handedly promised her a place serving in your new dun. I hope you don't mind."

Gerran smiled, just because the gesture was so like Salamander. "Not in the least," he said. "I'll take her back to my wife when we return to the Red Wolf dun."

"My humble thanks." Salamander was studying his face. "Gerran, the shoulder's bad, isn't it? You could sit down somewhere."

"Sitting only makes things worse, because then I'll have to get up again." Gerran tried swinging his arm, slowly and gingerly. Pain stopped him. "I wouldn't mind some help taking this mail off, though. The weight of it's beginning to vex me. The cursed bruise feels swollen or suchlike, and the mail rubs a bit."

"A bit!" Salamander rolled his eyes heavenward. "Clae, get over here! Your lord needs you. Wait for me here, Gerro. I'm going to go to the Westfolk camp. I'll wager my old friend Danalaurel's brought mead with him, and a good long drink of that will do you good."

With the mail off, and the mead drunk, the throbbing sensation receded, though again, it never entirely went away. Pain or no, Gerran still felt that he'd done too little that day to justify his presence among men who'd fought two battles that he'd missed. When some of the servants asked for a guard to accompany them to a nearby coppice, just off to the west, to look for firewood, he took Nicedd along and went with them.

By then the sun hung low on the horizon, and the long shadows of the trees lay across the weed-choked field. Some distance to the north, mist rose from the river that once had watered fertile land, and that would again, no doubt, once the Mountain Folk took possession of the dun. The three menservants were chattering among themselves, and Gerran was thinking of very little, when Nicedd suddenly spoke.

"Hold!" he said. "There's someone in those trees."

Gerran shaded his eyes with his hand. "So there is." He turned to the servants. "Wait here."

Gerran drew his sword and stubbornly took the lead as he and Nicedd strode the remainder of the way across to the coppice. Their prey, such as he was, made no effort to escape but lay still among the second-growth saplings. At first Gerran thought he was dead, but when they approached him, the Horsekin sat up with a groan. Though he wore a mail hauberk, he lacked a falcata. He used his left hand to hold his right arm tight across his chest, because his right hand hung useless, covered with dried blood and, judging from the angles of his fingers, broken in more than one place.

"Disarmed with a good stroke, it looks like," Nicedd said.

"It does," Gerran said. "Nicedd, take a good look around. There might be another man hiding in here." He turned back to the enemy. "As for you, get up!"

The Horsekin managed to rise to a kneel, swayed, and slumped back to sit on his heels. He used his good hand to pull off his helmet, revealing a brush of short dark hair, slick with sweat. Gerran knew enough about the Horsekin by then to realize that the length of his hair meant he was young, just barely a warrior, most like. The boy crouched, his gaze on Gerran's drawn sword, his head tipped back, his eyes defiant, as he waited for the death stroke. The memory of the Horsekin warrior with the broken leg rose in Gerran's mind and with it the old shame, like a taste of bile.

"Oh, horseshit and a pile of it!" Gerran lowered his sword. "You're my prisoner."

The Horsekin lad blinked, uncomprehending.

"Prisoner," Gerran repeated. "Not kill you. Prisoner."

"Ah! Slave." Understanding dawned in his eyes. "Your slave now."

"Not a slave, just a prisoner of war. A hostage."

Again the uncomprehending stare. Gerran remembered the negotiations at Zakh Gral, and their early failure. The Horsekin didn't take prisoners of war or hostages, nor did they want theirs back in return.

"Do you want to live?" Gerran said. "Or should I kill you quickly? Your choice."

The Horsekin looked at his right hand, so badly broken in so many places, as if it belonged to someone else. The pain must have been winning the battle against the shock, Gerran figured, because the lad's eyes filled with tears. He cradled the bleeding wrist with his good hand.

"Live or die?" Gerran said again.

The tears spilled and ran down, leaving trails in the dust and blood that allowed streaks of blue and red tattoos to show through.

"Live," the lad whispered. "Your slave now."

"Good," Gerran said. "What's your name?"

"Sharak."

"Come with me, Sharak. The chirurgeon will bind that hand for you."

Nicedd returned with the report that the woods were clear of enemies. Gerran told him to guard the menservants as they gathered fuel, then returned to camp, leading his prisoner. Although Raddyn the chirurgeon seemed surprised at Gerran's request, he did agree to bind the lad's hand for him.

"He'll have information we need," Gerran said. "Like how big the army was that his squad come from."

"True spoken," Raddyn said, then beckoned to Sharak. "All right, you! Hold out that paw!"

Sharak stared at him. The chirurgeon demonstrated by holding out his own hand, then pointed a finger at the Horsekin. The boy nodded docilely and followed the order. Gerran was just wondering if he should tie his prisoner up at night or suchlike when Salamander wandered over to join him.

"Nicedd told me you'd taken a prisoner," Salamander said.

"That's him." Gerran jerked a thumb in Sharak's direction. "You know somewhat about the Horsekin. He's surrendered, but can we trust him? A Deverry man would know how to act when he was taken hostage, but what about the Horsekin? Do they understand honor?"

"About this, they do. If he thinks he's your slave, he'll be obedient. After all, they'd kill him if we sent him back."

Sharak suddenly yelped in pain. Once again tears rolled down his dirty face. Raddyn was binding the wrist tight with wet linen.

"It's not going to heal straight no matter what I do," Raddyn remarked to Gerran. "And the fingers are hopeless. I've bound and splinted each one, but all he can do is keep them still and pray to his cursed goddess that they heal. When the linen dries, it'll tighten. When we get back to Cengarn, I should be able to do a bit more for the wrist."

Salamander turned to Sharak and spoke to him in the Horsekin tongue, eking out his small knowledge of the language with gestures. The boy nodded, then wiped his face on the sleeve of his good arm.

"Interesting," Salamander said. "He knows some Deverrian."

"A few words here and there," Gerran said. "Like he'd just started learning it or suchlike."

"In preparation for an invasion, I wonder?" Salamander raised both eyebrows high. "Or to handle slaves at least. Not a good omen, Gerro."

"Ye gods!" Gerran felt suddenly cold. "I'd not thought of that."

"Thinking isn't your duty in life, though 'tis mine. Later, with your permission, I'll want to question this lad."

"Permission granted, of course."

Raddyn made a sling out of a square of linen, settled the arm in, and tied the ends behind Sharak's neck.

"He's a brave lad," Raddyn said to Gerran. "Most men would have screamed all the way through. One yelp—not bad, not bad." He fixed Gerran with a grim look. "And now what about you, my lord? Let's look at that shoulder."

Salamander insisted, the chirurgeon swore at him, and Gerran reluctantly agreed. Taking off his padding and shirt set the shoulder throbbing, even with Salamander to help him. Raddyn looked, poked, and grunted. He turned around, surveyed the various objects on the wagon bed, and picked up a pottery stoup.

"This might sting a bit, but I've got to get some of the old blood off." He slopped some of the liquid in the stoup onto the wound. "It's mead."

Fire exploded in Gerran's shoulder, or so it seemed to him. For a moment he could barely breathe.

"I don't like the way it's swelling," Raddyn said. "Sleep on your stomach tonight. Huh, maybe I should have stitched it after all."

"A bit late now!" Salamander snapped. "Perhaps you should take a bit more care with uncommon wounds like this?"

"Listen, you, I've got dying men here to tend." Raddyn set filthy hands on his hips. "I don't have the patience to listen to insults from the likes of you."

Salamander started to speak, then merely shrugged. The chirurgeon turned on his heel and stalked off among the wagons.

"Let's go," Gerran said. "I'll put on the shirt once we're away from here."

Sharak followed them meekly as they walked off. Since he himself would have been running off into the dark to escape, Gerran began to think of the lad as contemptible, but he reminded himself that the Horsekin saw such things differently. Besides, considering that Sharak was injured, exhausted, and no doubt hungry, his lack of the will to escape made sense.

At a decent distance from the chirurgeon's wagon, they stopped, and Gerran knelt to let Salamander get the shirt on over his head. Getting his left arm into the sleeve took an effort of will.

"I have my doubts about that chirurgeon," Salamander said, "deep and serious doubts."

"Why?" Gerran stood up with the shirt on at last.

"You know, that's a good question. He certainly seemed to do a decent job on your prisoner here." Salamander nodded in Sharak's direction. "It's because of Neb's low opinion of him, I suppose."

"Neb? How would a scribe know the difference twixt one chirurgeon or another?"

Salamander hesitated, then shrugged. "Another good question. Let's get back to your tent. I'm hungry enough to eat a wolf, pelt and all."

Gerran led his prisoner—he refused to think of him as a slave—back to the campfire Clae had built near his tent. Nicedd sat cross-legged at some distance from the fire. A red-haired woman in a gray dress dappled rust-brown with dried blood sat nearby, nursing a baby, while a young daughter watched with hopeless eyes. An older lass, red-haired like her mother, knelt behind her and stared at the ground. The number of Gerran's dependents had just grown considerably, he realized, thanks to Salamander, who, he supposed, was a dependent of his as well, at least for the duration of this campaign.

"Clae?" Gerran said. "Have the woman and her children been fed?"

"Not yet, my lord," Clae said. "But I got rations for them and the prisoner, too."

The woman looked up at him, then away. She must have been pretty once, Gerran realized, with her long red hair and green eyes, but now gray streaked the hair, she was missing half her teeth, her face was so thin that her bones looked sharp under her skin, and her despair hung around her like some foul perfume.

"My thanks, my lord," she whispered. "For your protection."

"You're welcome." Gerran made this banal remark only because he could think of nothing else.

"We'll ride back to his wife soon," Salamander said, "and she'll have a place for you and your children." He glanced at Gerran. "Her name's Canna."

"Ah. Well and good, then." Gerran pointed at Sharak. "Does looking at him trouble you?"

"It doesn't," Canna said. "No more than aught else."

Still, with gestures Gerran made Sharak sit farther away. The Horsekin took a place next to Nicedd, who patted his silver dagger in a meaningful way and glared at the lad.

"No trouble out of you," Nicedd said with a growl in his voice. "Or else."

Sharak flinched, then lowered his head in a gesture of submission.

"Here, Clae," Gerran said, "bring out those rations, will you?"

They all made a drab meal of flatbread, salt beef, and cheese around the small campfire. All around them the normal life of a military camp rippled like water—men coming and going, some exulting over their victory, some mourning dead friends, some swearing in pain, others laughing over their ration of ale. In the Falcon's tiny sector, no one spoke, not even Salamander, until they'd finished eating. Canna's baby fussed and whined, even when she laid her own food aside to nurse him.

"Do you have any milk?" Salamander asked.

"Precious little, my lord." Her voice had all the life of dead leaves rustling on an autumn branch. "Truly, I'm not surprised."

"Me, either, but I'm not a lord. I've got a clean rag if you want to make a sop for him to have some water."

"I would, and my thanks."

Salamander got up, rummaged in his saddlebags, which Clae had laid nearby, and brought out a rag and a cup. He sent Clae off to fill the cup with fresh water and handed Canna the rag as he sat back down. Gerran was honestly surprised that the gerthddyn would know so much about women's matters. The surprise reminded him of a painfully unanswered question.

"Tell me somewhat, Canna," Gerran said, "if you can. Why were the bastard scum killing their women prisoners?"

"So we couldn't be saved, my lord. They taunted us, like, saying that they were going to show you all that coming after us would do no good. We could be slaves or we could be dead, but they wouldn't let us be rescued."

Salamander swore under his breath, while Nicedd did the same, but loudly.

"So," Gerran said. "They want to raid and not have us chase after, do they? Wanting and having are two different things, or so I always heard."

Clae came trotting back with the cup of water. He sat and held it for Canna, so she could dip the sop into the water and allow the baby to suck enough to calm his thirst. Salamander, who'd finished eating by then, got up and went to kneel in front of Sharak. The Horsekin lad shrank back and raised his good arm as if to parry a blow.

"Before you start," Gerran said to Salamander, "can you please tell him that he doesn't have to act like a dog? He thinks he's a slave. I don't."

"I'll try," Salamander said, "but I suspect you'll have to wait till Grallezar or Pir can do the translating for that. I only know some basic words. It's going to be a very peculiar idea for his Horsekin mind to understand."

For some while Salamander and Sharak talked back and forth in a jumbled mix of Deverrian and the Horsekin language. Gerran soon gave up trying to follow the conversation. Once they'd finished, Salamander gave him the gist of it.

"It's as I thought," the gerthddyn said. "The priestesses firmly believe that Alshandra's still alive. They tell that to the faithful, who, I assume, believe them even though no one but the holy ladies can see her. She appeared to them in the sky now and then and gave them instructions to pass on to the common believers."

"Huh! Like those messages Great Bel sends to the priests, I'll wager, the ones that always say what the priests want to hear."

"You'd win that wager handily, no doubt."

"What does he think about the way they're threatening to kill the women they take?"

Salamander spoke briefly to Sharak, whose eyes filled with tears. He murmured a few words.

"It sickened him," Salamander said. "That's why he ran from the battle."

"Was he ordered to kill some of them?"

Again Salamander spoke to the lad. Sharak nodded his head in miserable agreement and murmured a few more words.

"That's why he ran," Salamander repeated. "The Keeper giving the orders followed and got one good cut on him. That's who broke his hand."

"Ah. Tell him he's a good man."

Salamander did so. Sharak tried to smile, then merely stared at the ground.

"I suspect that a good many of the loyal Alshandrites would be furious at the idea of killing the helpless," Salamander said to Gerran, "but I'm as certain as snow in winter that the rakzanir don't give a fistful of horseshit if they are or not."

"No doubt. What about the rest of the army?"

"The only Horsekin numbers I know are those from one to six and for some reason, fourteen, so I have no idea of how big it is. Huge, according to him, and very far off to the north. He told me they marched for weeks to get here. This was a scouting force, mostly, though they had orders to burn and raid where they could."

"I see. Well, when we get back to the Red Wolf dun, Lady Grallezar should be able to get more out of him."

"True spoken. I cannot imagine anyone refusing to answer Grallezar when she's in a questioning mood, as it were."

"No more can I. Very well, I'm going to go tell Prince Dar what we know." Gerran turned to Clae. "Let Canna and her children have my tent when she wants to sleep."

When Gerran started to get up, his head swam from the sudden pain in his shoulder. He shifted his weight to the other side, got to a kneel, then allowed Salamander to help him up the rest of the way.

"I'll just come with you," Salamander said. "I want to talk with the prince myself."

By then, those men who weren't on watch had rolled themselves up in their blankets and gone to sleep. Campfires were burning themselves out, casting a glow like sunset among deep shadows. On the ground by the supply wagons rescued women sat huddled together, weeping or silently rocking back and forth like terrified children. Most had infants clinging to them.

"Canna had a younger son," Salamander said abruptly. "Besides the one whose burnt bones I found, that is."

"And?" Gerran said. "I assume he's dead."

"He is. They tried to geld him, but the chirurgeon did a ghastly bad job of it. The lad's balls hadn't come down yet, of course, since he was so young. When the chirurgeon tried to get at them to cut them, he pierced the lad's guts. A long loop was hanging out, Canna told me, and of course he bled horribly. The chirurgeon swore and stamped, but there was naught he could do. He was going to slit the lad's throat, but the priestess insisted that Canna be allowed to hold him till he died."

Gerran briefly felt like vomiting. "I can't even think of an oath foul enough for that," he said instead.

"Me, either. I'm truly grateful that you'll take her in."

Gerran made a noncommittal noise. He was beginning to realize, he felt, what lordship truly meant, but not in a way that he could put into words.

Prince Dar and Calonderiel listened carefully to what little Gerran and Salamander had learned from Sharak. A little, as Dar remarked, was better than naught.

"Just so," Salamander said. "Cal, I have a question for you. There must have been two lots of Deverry people in the camp. The slave women we know about. But there had to be others, ones that worshiped Alshandra, and they doubtless came willingly when the Horsekin appeared. Some of them would be branded on their face from last summer's arrests."

"That's odd," Cal said. "I've no idea what happened to them. Dar, did anyone report to you?"

"No one," Dar said. "Some of the Deverry men might know."

"I'll ask around," Salamander said. "For now, though, I think I'd best escort Gerran here back to his camp. Gerro, you look like you're going to fall over."

"It's just a—" Gerran said. "Well, mayhap it's not just a bruise. Ye gods, that chirurgeon! I swear he made it hurt worse."

"I didn't like the look of him myself," Salamander said. "Well, we'll be heading back to Cengarn on the morrow."

On the morrow morning Gwerbret Ridvar reprovisioned the fortguard and left twenty more men to reinforce it as well. The rest of the warbands assembled out in the road, while the two princes and the gwerbret stood beside their horses and conferred. Gerran and Mirryn led their horses up to the princes, while their men trailed after them out of habit. Gerran noticed that Canna, the baby, and her younger daughter were riding Salamander's horse, while Salamander walked, leading it.

When Gerran started to kneel, the Deverry prince waved him up.

"A question, Lord Gerran?" Voran said.

"Just that, Your Highness," Gerran said. "I'm still wondering if we should chase the Horsekin right now, while they're at hand. They've fled north, but I'll wager they leave a trail we can follow."

"And I still counsel against it," Prince Daralanteriel said. "Who knows if your prisoner told us the whole truth? For that matter, who knows how well he and Salamander understood each other? It's likely there's a second scout force holed up somewhere near at hand. This lot was a long way from home to be traveling on their own."

"Now that's true spoken, Your Highness," Gerran said. "But what if they're heading for the Boar dun? They can be reprovisioned there at the very least."

"That's a very good point, Falcon," Voran put in.

"The decision's the gwerbret's to make, of course." Dar made a show of addressing this comment to Gerran alone. "It's his rhan, after all."

Ridvar attempted to smile at this belated recognition, but the expression looked more like a dog's snarl.

"Oh, I agree with the prince," Ridvar said. "The bastards have burnt what there was to burn out here. I'd best return to Cengarn and tell my vassals to ready themselves for raids. Some of their duns are nearly as isolated as this one."

"A sound move, Your Grace," Voran joined the conversation. "Now, when we get back, and our horses have rested, I've got to leave for Cerrgonney. The dwarven envoy's supposed to meet me in Gwingedd by the longest day. And then there's this matter of the Boars. I'm Justiciar of the Northern Border now."

"Your Highness?" Ridvar said. "If you'll take the advice of a lowly gwerbret, you'll move fast against them. If that squad that broke through our lines does go back to the Boar dun, they'll be bringing the news back that we know who they are."

"You're quite right. I want to move against them before the end of this summer." Voran hesitated so long that Gerran wondered if he was thinking of responding to Ridvar's "lowly gwerbret" comment. If so, the prince thought better of it. "My duty's plain," Voran continued. "I'm charged with bringing peace to the province. Wish me luck."

"No doubt you'll need it," Ridvar said, and this smile was genuine.

"No doubt. One last thing, Lord Gerran." Voran glanced around, then pointed to Nicedd. "When I leave Cengarn, may I hire your silver dagger away from you? I want his evidence when I confront the tieryn of Pren Cludan about these Boar raids."

Nicedd went white about the mouth and dropped to one knee before the prince.

"What's wrong?" Gerran said to him.

"Begging your pardon and all, my lord, Your Grace, and Your Highnesses," Nicedd's voice became unsteady. "But if I go back to Pren Cludan, they'll hang me."

"Oh." Voran blinked several times. "Well and good, then, you stay with Lord Gerran. I'll make up some tale for your former lord's ears while I'm on the way."

"My humble thanks, Your Highness." Nicedd's voice became stronger. "I'll praise your name always for this mercy."

"I'm tempted to ask you why you're riding the long road," Voran said, "but I'll spare you that, too. You may leave us."

With a sigh of profound relief, Nicedd rose and hurried back to his waiting horse.

"Well and good, lads!" Voran turned to the warbands. "Let's get back on the road."

As he mounted up, Gerran was thinking about the Horsekin raiders who'd fled the battle, no doubt to bring information to the commanders of the larger force. He could practically taste the danger they presented. Still, he had no right to argue with a gwerbret and a prince over a decision, whether or not he was one of their vassals. Besides, he reminded himself, there's naught out there but wilderness, anyway, off to the north and west.

From their posts high up on Dun Cengarn's walls, the men left behind on fortguard kept a watch on the roads north of the town. As soon as they saw the returning army, they blew their silver horns to announce it in a strident music that echoed around the ward. Inside the main broch, Lady Drwmigga came rushing downstairs to the great hall and began giving the orders to her servants that formerly Lord Oth would have handled. Her servingwomen followed, chattering about their tasks, flitting back and forth in their bright dresses like a flock of birds. Lord Blethry, the fortguard commander, ran outside to prepare the stable hands and pages for the coming influx of horsemen. Neb followed more slowly to look for a place to stand and wait out of everyone's way. He wanted to greet his brother and, much to his surprise, Salamander as well.

The ward had turned into a roughly organized mob of servants that allowed scant room for a man to wait. Neb climbed the ladder up to the catwalks on the main wall and gained a good place for a view. Far below him, the army was walking their horses through the town gates. In the warmth of the late afternoon sun, most of the riders let their horses amble up the main street, but some of the men, most likely local lads who knew the town well, broke out of line and followed a separate route through the back alleys. Behind everyone else creaked the supply wagons. The entire scene made Neb think of water flowing uphill, a fancy that made him smile.

He leaned on folded arms onto the top of the wall between two crenels and enjoyed the touch of sunlight on his back. Ever since he'd followed Salamander's orders to stop his astral scrying and eat more food, normal life had returned to him, filled with small pleasures. His dweomerwork was progressing better and faster as well. At moments he felt like a fool or worse for dismissing Salamander for so long. Perhaps the gerthddyn had been a chattering dolt back when Nevyn knew him, but Nevyn had been dead for sixty years or so now.

And I'm alive now, he thought. He now knew who he was, Nerrobrantos, scribe to Prince Daralanteriel of the Westlands, husband to Lady Branna—not Nevyn nor Galrion, either. He had assumed that "what I am" meant "Master of the Aethyr" once again. Now he knew he'd been mistaken. His true wyrd lay with the dweomer, certainly, but perhaps with something else as well. He simply didn't know what that something might be. Yet at the same time, he felt that the answer should be obvious, that in fact it lay close to hand.

The army began filing through the gates into the ward. Leading the way in a thicket of banners were the two princes and the gwerbret, and directly behind them, the banadar and the two noble lords. Gerran was holding both of his reins in his right hand. He'd tucked his left hand into his belt, as if the arm needed support. His posture, too, struck Neb as odd, not warrior straight, but slumped toward the right, again to favor his left side. Wounded! Neb turned away fast and grabbed the ladder, then climbed down as quickly as he could. Making his way through the packed and swarming ward took him some while.

When Neb reached them, Gerran had just dismounted while an anxious Mirryn watched. The effort of twisting his body free of the horse's back had turned Gerran's face pale. Clae came running and caught his lord's elbow to steady him. Slowly the color returned to his skin, and he managed to stand without aid.

"What happened?" Neb said.

"It's just a bruise," Gerran said, but his voice sounded as weak as a small child's.

"It's not!" Mirryn snapped. "Neb, he got hit hard on the shoulder from behind. It's a shallow cut, a split, like, from the blow, but somewhat went wrong with it."

"Indeed?" Neb let his eyes go out of focus and considered Gerran's aura, its usual sullen red, shot here and there with gold, but shrunken. At its strongest it extended barely a foot beyond his flesh, with one exception. Over the left shoulder the aura streamed out in a fetid greenish-gray plume that was drawing energy and life out of his body.

"I see," Neb said. "It's gone septic."

"How can you tell?" Mirryn said.

"Can't you smell it?" Neb found a quick excuse. "I know you're all filthy from the campaign, but that stink of rot's unmistakable."

"Ye gods!" Mirryn said. "Should I get the chirurgeon?"

"Raddyn? Not on your life! Get our Falcon upstairs to his chamber!" The crack of command in his own voice caught Neb by surprise. "Clae, get him to lie down on his stomach. Don't try to pull that shirt off! Cut it off! Then fetch me a kettle of water, a big one."

Much to Neb's further surprise, they followed the orders, even Gerran. While Gerran's silver dagger helped his hire up the stairs, Neb hurried to his own chamber and grabbed his saddlebags, which contained his precious supply of herbs. They would meet a better wyrd now than financing a lad's folly. He hurried on to Gerran's chamber.

With an anxious Nicedd hovering nearby, Gerran lay facedown on the mattress, his shirt off. Old blood and dirt crusted over the healing tear in his skin, a line of scabs inside a livid bruise.

"I can smell it now, too," Nicedd remarked. "Septic it is!"

"I've got to get that clean," Neb said. "I hope Clae hurries with that water. Here, go get me some mead, will you? Gerro, my apologies, but we've got to burn away the corrupted humors. The mead will do that."

Gerran made a grunting sound that might have been an answer.

"I'm on my way." Nicedd trotted out of the chamber.

Near the bed stood a brazier, filled with charcoal left over from the winter's cold. Neb summoned the Wildfolk of Fire and lit the coals. It was glowing nicely by the time an out-of-breath Clae returned with the full kettle. Neb set it among the coals to heat.

"Did you run all the way?" Neb said to his brother.

Clae nodded wordlessly.

"You may not want to watch this," Neb said, glancing around. "Get me that basin from the washstand, will you?"

Clae followed orders, then stepped back against the wall. Neb rummaged in his saddlebags, found the prunella and healall leaves, and put a big handful of each into the washbasin. He needed one more botanical—what was it—comfrey root, and he had not even a scrap of that. *I can find some on the morrow*, he told himself, *it grows all over pastureland.*

He slopped a good portion of hot water on top of the herbs he'd selected and put the basin on the floor to let the mixture steep. Among his scribal tools he found a clean rag, which he dipped into the heating water in the kettle. When he applied it to the abscess, the rag ran red with old blood, streaked with the dark brown of ordinary dirt. Neb was still washing Gerran's wound clean when Nicedd returned with a flagon of mead.

"I didn't know how much you'd need," the silver dagger said. "So I got a lot."

"Good," Neb said. "He may need to drink the rest when I'm done." He glanced at Nicedd's pale face. "You might need some yourself. Put that down! I'll need you to hold your lord steady."

Gerran's shoulder looked even nastier once Neb could see it clearly. Not only did the split in the skin ooze pus, but a thin web of red lines spread outward from the bruise. Neb had a bad moment of wondering if he were too late, but the red corruption stretched only an inch or two beyond the blue-and-purple edges of the bruise. *No use in giving up,* he told himself. He got out his penknife, then considered his own hands, more than a little dirty. He washed them and the knife blade both in the remaining hot water.

"Gerro," Neb said, "can you put your hands over your head? Stretch out, like."

"I can," Gerran said. "It's not that bad."

Neb decided against telling him the truth, that actually it was worse than he knew. Gerran slid down a little on the mattress to give himself room, then raised his arms over his head. Without being asked, Nicedd sat down next to him and caught his lord's wrists. *He's seen this before,* Neb thought.

"Hold on," Neb said. "This is going to hurt."

He grasped the penknife twixt thumb and forefinger as if he were cutting parchments against a straightedge, focused on the suppurating stripe running down the half-healed wound, and slashed the abscess open. Gerran let out a noise that almost amounted to a cry, then sucked his breath in sharply. Greenish matter welled in the wound and oozed in a trickle of blood.

"Get me more water," Neb said to Clae. "Just take the kettle from the coals and don't look at this. Use Gerran's old shirt for a rag! The handle's hot."

Neb soaked his rag in the herbed water in the basin and wiped away as much of the pus as he could. When he pressed around the edges of the bruise, more green-gray matter welled up and with it, black flecks of dirt. Neb kept cleaning the rag and wiping until at last he'd exposed raw flesh and naught else. Gerran never made a sound, nor did he move. Nicedd sat stone-still, holding down his lord's hands should Gerran's will fail.

The door opened with a fling and a bounce. Clae trotted in with the kettle in one hand and a wad of clean rags in the other.

"Lady Egriffa said you'd need these," Clae said.

"I do, indeed."

Neb took the rags gratefully. He should have remembered to bring more, he supposed. Clae nestled the bottom of the kettle into the coals, then returned to his place by the wall.

Neb never quite knew how long he worked on the wound, washing it, wiping the blood away, until at last it looked clean, and the only smell of contagion came from the rags on the floor. By the time he finished, however, the sky was beginning to darken with sunset. Neb stepped back a few feet and considered his patient's aura. The ugly gray plume had disappeared, but the envelope of etheric light had shrunk a little further, clinging around Gerran's body like a wet shirt. The pain had done that, Neb supposed. At least, he hoped it was only the pain. Neb tossed the rag he'd been using onto the floor, then picked up the flagon of mead.

"This is going to hurt worse," he said, "so brace yourself, but I've got to destroy the corrupted humors."

Nicedd tightened his grip on Gerran's wrists. Neb took a deep breath and slopped mead directly from the flagon onto the wound. Gerran gasped aloud and bowed his back as if he'd been flogged. Nicedd held on grimly and forced him back down again. Mercifully, with the second splash of the burning liquid, Gerran fainted. Neb kept splashing and wiping until at last the bleeding from his slash had eased up. He dipped a finger in the mead and tested the bruise. The swelling had gone down considerably, but for all he knew, more contagion lurked under the edges of the skin.

The room had grown too dark for him to see clearly. Without thinking, exhausted as he was, he called upon the Wildfolk of Aethyr, who clustered around his left hand in a cool silver light. Nicedd swore under his breath, and Clae yelped aloud.

"Hold your tongues!" Neb snapped. "I've got to see."

In the pool of dweomer light the wound looked as good as traumatized flesh could look after such treatment. A different light bloomed behind him, the yellow flickering of massed candles. Neb's shadow fell across Gerran's back. Neb tossed the ball of dweomer glow into the air, where it disappeared. When he glanced over his shoulder, he saw Salamander standing just inside the door and holding a four-candle candelabrum in each hand.

"I purloined these from a storeroom," Salamander said. "I thought you'd need light."

"I do, and my thanks," Neb said. "Nicedd, you can let go now. The worst's over."

Nicedd released Gerran's wrists, then stood up, stretching his back. He was staring at Neb with an expression halfway between fear and awe. Salamander glanced around, put one candelabrum on the washstand where the basin had stood, and the other on a carved chest that stood in the curve of the stone wall. Clae opened his mouth as if to ask about the mysterious light; Neb silenced him with a scowl, then ignored them all.

In the basin only a handful of spent herbs remained. He threw those onto the heap of filthy rags on the floor.

"Once the wound's rested," he said to Nicedd, "I'll bandage that, but I want it to dry."

"Well and good, then, my lord," Nicedd said. "Will he heal?"

"If the gods are willing." Neb picked up the rags and crammed them all into the kettle of simmering water. The coals had mostly turned to ash in the brazier. "Clae, when this cools, you can take it away, but wash it out well before you give it back to the cook. Those rags should be thrown away, too. Make sure they end up on the dung heap."

"I will," Clae said. "Do you think the wound was poisoned?"

"Not by poison on a blade, if that's what you mean. If dirt's a poison, then that's what it was, all right."

By that time Gerran had woken. When he tried to turn over, Neb pushed him down again. "Lie still," he said. "The worst is over, I hope anyway."

"So do I." Gerran's voice trembled. He took a deep breath and let it out with a sigh.

"Ye gods, Neb!" Salamander stepped forward. "I never knew that you were a chirurgeon as well as a scribe."

Neither did I. The thought struck him so hard that Neb couldn't speak.

"My thanks," Gerran whispered.

"Welcome, I'm sure." Neb found his voice again. "It must hurt like a cold wind from the hells."

Gerran mumbled something that might have been, "It does do that."

"Just rest." Neb patted his patient's good shoulder. "Get as comfortable as you can, Gerro. You'll be staying here for some days, by the way. You can't ride until the wound heals, or you'll open it up, and we'll have to start all over."

"Whatever you say," Gerran whispered, but the words were clear enough to understand.

Neb turned away and saw Salamander smiling at him with an ironic twist of his mouth. The sight woke Neb up—he could think of it no other way, that he'd been asleep, and now he was awake. *Close at hand?* he thought. *My wyrd's been sitting here right in my hands all this time.*

"That tunic, Neb," Salamander said. "I suggest you might want to change it."

Neb looked down at his front and found the linen streaked with blood and pus.

"So I do. Nicedd, don't let him get up just yet. The pair of you can finish the mead in that flagon. When I come back, you can go get your dinner."

"My thanks, my lord," Nicedd said. "I'll bring you back some, too."

"I'm not a lord."

"But I thought—" Nicedd stared at him, utterly confused. "Doesn't the king—ah, horseshit! I don't know what I'm saying."

Neb recognized him. He'd forgotten the lad's name, but he did remember that he'd known him once. Nicedd had been a silver dagger, then, too, somewhere in their mutual past.

"You're worn out, is why," Neb said briskly. "It doesn't matter what you call me, I'll be back in a bit."

Neb left his saddlebags with his supplies in the chamber, then left to change his shirt. Salamander followed him upstairs. He didn't speak until Neb had shut the door to give them privacy.

"How did you know the wound had gone septic?" Salamander

said. "When we were still down in the ward, I mean. It must have been obvious once you got that filthy shirt off."

"Do you remember when the dragon came to the Red Wolf dun?" Neb said. "Well, Penna saw some wrong thing in his etheric double. I happened to be nearby, and she told me about it. Then later I realized that if an injury showed up on the etheric, it must leave some sort of trace in the aura. There were a couple of people at the dun who had some small hurt—a cut finger and the like—but I couldn't see anything in their auras. So I discarded my idea until today, when Gerran rode in. I know now that a small hurt leaves no mark. His injury was serious enough to show. You could see the trouble plain as sunlight."

"You could. I couldn't."

"Truly?"

"Truly. I thought of that myself, but the aura revealed no secrets to me, even though I could see the aura itself, of course."

In sheer excitement Neb turned away and strode over to the window. Down below, servants were hurrying across the ward, carrying lanterns against the gathering night. He could smell roasting meat and woodsmoke from the cookhouse, comforting everyday smells and sights that calmed him. *You knew what Clae's wyrd was the moment that Gerran said he'd train him. Why wouldn't you know this?* Salamander joined him at the window.

"Ebañy, I realized somewhat today, somewhat truly important."

"So I thought. Could it be that you're meant to be a healer?"

"Just that. It has to be my wyrd, if I can see things that a dweomermaster like you can't."

Salamander started to speak, then looked away, so moved that Neb briefly feared he might weep.

"What?" Neb said.

"In an odd sort of way," Salamander said with a choke in his voice. "Nevyn finally approved of me, that's what. A mad thought, of no importance, truly."

"Oh, don't drivel! Of course it's important."

Salamander wiped his eyes on his sleeve, then grinned with his usual ease. "At times you do revert to Nevyn-hood, don't you?"

They shared a laugh, and the moment was over, but Neb realized it had been as important for him as it was for Salamander.

"There's only one thing against this idea," Neb said. "I don't want to give up my dweomer studies."

"Why would you have to? The question, my dear friend, is what you're going to do with the dweomer you know, not whether or not you know dweomer. You've just demonstrated that the two can go together quite nicely." Salamander grinned at him. "Let the rest of us chattering fools look for omens and the like."

"Here, I owe you an apology for calling you that."

"Oh, don't vex yourself over it. I've provoked many a nastier comment from others in my life."

They shared another laugh. Laughing made Neb realize that for the first time in months, he felt not merely happy but free.

Neb wasn't the only person in the dun who was thinking in terms of apologies. At sunset, the dun assembled for a victory dinner in the great hall. Salamander had just taken a seat next to Lord Blethry when a page trotted over to him.

"Gerthddyn," the lad said, "Gwerbret Ridvar wants to talk with you."

"Indeed?" Salamander got up and glanced over at the table of honor, empty at the moment. "Where is he?"

"Upstairs in his chambers," the page said. "I'll take you there."

Blethry quirked an eyebrow and shrugged, making it clear that he had no idea why the summons had arrived. Salamander set down his goblet and followed the page.

Gwerbret Ridvar's private quarters lay on the third floor of the main broch, just above the women's hall. He received Salamander in an outer chamber, a generous wedge of a room hung with tapestries on the wicker walls that divided it from the bedchamber beyond. Ridvar sat in a cushioned chair in front of the hearth, where a cluster of candles glimmered instead of a fire. In the soft dim lighting his face looked so smooth that it was hard to think of him as anything but a handsome child. Salamander bowed and knelt in front of him on a soft Bardek carpet.

"My wife tells me you can read and write," Ridvar said. "What I want to know is how well you can keep a secret."

"Very well when I have to, Your Grace," Salamander said. "The tales I tell in the marketplace are all completely untrue, after all. The truths I tend to keep to myself."

Ridvar smiled, but briefly. "My wife also thinks I shouldn't worry about keeping this secret. I want you to write a message to my sister, Lady Solla, apologizing for the way I treated her in the past."

"A very noble desire, Your Grace."

"Mayhap." Ridvar shrugged the flattery away. "Oth was a grand one for little lies, you see. When a coin disappeared or suchlike, he always had me thinking that Solla might have taken it. That's why I didn't give her a dowry. I thought she'd already gathered one on her own." He moved uneasily in his chair. "Somehow or other, I just don't want to have my own scribe write that letter. He can't keep secrets, not when he's among the servants, at least."

Salamander made a sympathetic-sounding noise.

"And," Ridvar went on, "I wanted to invite her to come here and tend her husband if she wished, as my guest of course. I understand that he's not supposed to ride for some while."

"Just that, Your Grace. The chirurgeon was adamant."

Much to Salamander's relief, Ridvar merely nodded rather than asking who the chirurgeon in question might be.

"I'll gladly write your message, Your Grace," Salamander continued. "It will be an honor to serve you."

"Very well." Ridvar stood up. "On the morrow, I'll leave the table after the morning meal. Follow me up here, and bring what you need."

"I shall, Your Grace." Salamander rose and bowed low. "My honor."

You arrogant cub! Salamander thought as he was leaving. *Not a word of thanks to someone who's not even one of your retainers!* He felt a pang of sympathy for Oth. Yet, on the other hand, he reflected, at least Ridvar was willing to apologize to his sister, while Oth had caused her much unnecessary misery in his attempts to cover up his crimes. Salamander could assume that Lady Drwmigga's urging lay behind the gwerbret's currently generous impulse, but many a noble lord had ignored his wife's pleas on behalf of those he'd wronged.

Salamander had just started down the staircase when he saw Neb, waiting at the foot. His quasi-apprentice hurried halfway up to join him.

"A question for you," Neb said. "I want to tell Branna what I realized, about my wyrd, I mean. Sometimes I can—" He paused to look around him but no one stood close enough to overhear. "Sometimes I can reach her, if you know what I mean. Would it be all right if I tried? I wanted to get your permission first."

He's saved! was Salamander's first thought, and the second, *We've won.* Aloud he said, "You have it, but only with Branna. She's your wife, and you're deeply linked to boot, and so I doubt if talking with her in this manner would cause either of you any strain or possible trouble. No one else, mind!"

"I understand, and my thanks."

Neb turned and rushed up the stairs, taking them two at a time. Salamander smiled at his retreating back, then more slowly went on down.

Since Clae would be one of the many pages serving the feast in the great hall, Neb had their chamber to himself. He climbed onto the bed, drew the bedcurtains for further privacy, and sat cross-legged in the middle of the lumpy mattress. When he thought of Branna, he saw her, perched on the windowsill of the chamber they'd shared in her uncle's dun. Dressed only in her thin shift, she was combing out her long blonde hair by candlelight. His longing for her became a physical ache.

"Neb?" she thought to him. "What are you doing?"

"It's all right," he thought back. "Salamander gave me permission to contact you this way. Branni, Branni, I love you so much!"

"I love you, too. I wish you were here."

"We'll be together again soon. But I've got somewhat to tell you straightaway. I've found my wyrd. The dweomer and healing—that's what I want to study. They go together somehow, I'm sure of it. I was rowing down the wrong river before, but I've found the right one now."

Her joy rose up like the light from the candle. It seemed to him that he could see it, a bright glow around her like a vast golden cloud, rising to cover her.

"I—" he began. "Oh, curse it all!" he said aloud. "That broke the stupid link!"

Try though he did, he never managed to reestablish the link between them. He still had a very long way to go in his studies, he realized, and a burden of work ahead of him, no matter how clearly he saw the end result.

For now his work lay with Gerran. When Neb returned to the lord's chamber, he found Nicedd waiting patiently.

"Go eat," Neb said.

"My thanks," Nicedd said. "My appetite's returned, finally. That was a grim bit of work you did. Gives a man's stomach a turn, like."

Neb laughed, and Nicedd made an attempt at a smile before he hurried out. Gerran lay asleep on his stomach, his head pillowed on his folded arms. The wound still looked clean, Neb was relieved to see. The fringe of red lines around the bruise had mostly disappeared. He was considering how to bandage it when Clae returned, carrying bread and beef in a wooden bowl.

"I told Nicedd I'd bring you dinner," Clae said.

His brother's voice was tinged with fear, Neb realized, and his eyes looked up at him warily.

"Is somewhat wrong?" Neb said.

"Uh, Neb? That light around your hand—"

"What light? You mean when Salamander came in with all these candles?"

Clae hesitated, puzzled.

"You had a long hard ride home," Neb went on, "you must be truly tired."

"I am. And I was ever so worried about my lord." Clae thought this through for a long moment. "You know, I think I was seeing things that weren't there."

"I wouldn't be surprised. It's naught to be ashamed of. Here, when I've done eating, I'm going to bandage up the wound. You and Gerran both will feel better once I'm done."

On the morrow Salamander did as the gwerbret asked and brought pabrus and ink up to his private chamber. What Ridvar dictated was curt, though to the point. Since Ridvar couldn't read, Salamander took the liberty of expanding the message into something more well-bred though not flowery. Ridvar put it into a silver tube, sealed it with wax and his signet ring, then handed it back to his temporary scribe.

"See that this gets sent straightaway," Ridvar said. "Give it to my captain, and he'll pick the messengers."

"As you wish, Your Grace, but if I may make a suggestion, Lord Mirryn and his men are leaving later in the day—"

"Splendid!" Ridvar broke in. "That will save my men the journey."

Salamander was just gathering up his supplies when Lady Drwmigga appeared in the doorway of the bedchamber. He bowed to her, and she favored him with a smile.

"Our thanks," she said, then shot her husband a glance.

"Indeed," Ridvar said. "Our thanks."

Salamander reminded himself to tell Branna that while Drwmigga did have her bovine qualities, she at least knew how to prod her husband into courtesy, which boded as well for the future of the rhan as did her obvious fertility.

When he came downstairs, Salamander saw Daralanteriel sitting at the honor table with Voran, Mirryn, and Calonderiel. Salamander stopped to mention that Ridvar wanted to send for Gerran's wife, though he left out any mention of the apology. Mirryn readily agreed to take the message back to the Red Wolf dun.

"I'll send a letter to Dalla at the same time," Dar said. "She and her women can come with Solla. Here, Mirryn, take Vantalaber and five archers with you, will you? They can escort the women back and spare you the journey."

"My thanks, Your Highness, " Mirryn said. "I'll do just that."

Dar turned to Salamander. "Ah, I see you've got pens and the like with you."

"I don't need to write a letter," Salamander said in Elvish. "I can just tell her."

"True," Dar answered in the same, "but it's for the sake of appearances, or do you want everyone in the Red Wolf dun wondering why Dalla's leaving?"

"Right enough." Salamander sat down with a sigh. "I'll write it out now."

Once he'd handed the messages over to Mirryn, Salamander went looking for Neb. He found him up in Gerran's chamber with something of a crowd. In the curve of the wall near the window, Canna and her children sat on some worn, thin cushions placed on a tattered bit of carpet. The younger daughter looked up when Salamander came in and smiled at him. She was too young, Salamander supposed, to understand the full import of what had happened to her family. The elder lass stared straight out at nothing. Canna herself seemed too exhausted to notice his arrival. The baby slept in his mother's arms, so soundly that Salamander assumed Canna or another woman in the dun had been able to nurse him at last.

Nicedd, Clae, and the Horsekin prisoner Sharak were all sitting on the floor at the foot of the narrow bed while Gerran perched on a high stool. Neb was examining the raw wound. On the bed nearby lay clean bandages, folded from rags, while at his feet lay filthy ones. Although Salamander knew nothing of the healer's craft, he did notice that no smell of contagion hung in the air.

"How fares our Falcon's wing?" Salamander said. "You look a good bit better this morn, Gerro."

"I feel better," Gerran said. "Now that I've survived what Neb did to me."

"I'll admit that it was a bit rough," Neb said. "But it looks to me like the mead washed out the corrupted humors. That was the most important thing."

"I don't understand what you mean by that," Gerran said.

"Have you ever watched someone make cheese?" Neb said. "You fill a bowl with fresh sweet milk, then stir in some rennet. In a few hours, the whole bowl is sour and curdled. Well, the dirt in your wound turned some of your blood into a substance much like rennet. If the curdling had spread—"

"Never mind," Gerran said. "I understand now. No need for the details."

"Very well. Now I'm going to bandage it up again. Do your best not to move that arm. Clae, you're going to have to cut up your lordship's meat for him, help him dress, and the like."

Clae nodded his agreement. Gerran muttered something foul under his breath.

"The cursed bandages itch," Gerran said, more loudly. "And I don't need my meat cut up like a child's."

"You'll have to endure it," Neb said with a snap in his voice. "Do you want to be able to parry with a shield again?"

Gerran made a sour face and nodded a yes.

"If that wound doesn't heal quickly and cleanly," Neb went on, "it'll leave a huge scar, and that scar will pull every time you lift somewhat heavy on the arm, like a shield."

"Oh, well and good, then."

"Clae will have help soon," Salamander joined in. "His grace has sent a message off to your wife, Gerran, inviting her here to take care of you."

"Oh, ye gods!" Gerran snapped. "I don't want her riding—"

"Gerro," Neb interrupted, "she's a tough northern lass, and she's not even that far gone with child."

Gerran's expression turned even more sour.

"The perfect wife for a tough northern lord," Salamander said. "She can always borrow that mother's saddle Dalla was using. Dalla and the rest will be coming with her, and then, alas, my Falcon, we'll be leaving you and heading west." He glanced Neb's way. "With Govvin butchered on his own altar, Voran's lawsuit has become rather more than superfluous, as the justiciar himself remarked this very morn."

"They won't be needing me as a witness, then," Neb said. "I'll teach Solla how to deal with this injury when she gets here, and then I'll return to the prince's camp."

As another consequence of the end of the lawsuit, Daralanteriel decided to remove all his people from the gwerbret's dun with the exception of Gerran and his pack of dependents. Since he wanted Gerran to save his wife's recovered inheritance for the building of the Falcon dun, Dar gave Lord Blethry a horse—a silver-gray gelding—in fee to feed his vassal and his vassal's people for as long as necessary. He also handed Nicedd some coins for his part in the battle. The silver dagger professed such fulsome gratitude that Salamander could assume Dar had given him far too much.

"What did you just hand over?" Salamander said in Elvish.

"Just some coins I had from the trading last autumn," Dar said. "A couple of silver ones and a bunch of coppers."

"Dar, you're going to have to learn about money and the handling of money."

"Ai! I suppose you're right. Another blasted thing to worry about!"

Before they left the dun, Salamander had one last detail to attend to. He wanted their Gel da'Thae allies to question Sharak, but as Gerran's prisoner, the lad would stay with him. Salamander had some coin of his own. He told Gerran what he had in mind, then made a great show of buying Sharak from him. Neb had already reset the boy's wrist and hand with proper wooden splints.

"I'll teach you some marketplace tricks," Salamander told Sharak in a mix of Deverrian and Horsekin, "once that all heals."

Sharak nodded and stared at the floor without speaking. Salamander doubted if the lad had really understood much, but since Sharak followed him out to the ward readily enough, he must have recognized Salamander as his new owner. When the pages and grooms brought out their horses, Salamander had Sharak mount up behind him. In a disorganized procession Dar led his men through Cengarn to the camp in the meadow below the town. Dar waved Salamander up to ride beside him.

"Pir came with us," Dar said. "Shall we have him talk to the prisoner?"

"I'd rather not put any more strain on Pir's loyalty to you," Salamander said. "It's been hard on him, this business of helping us in our war on his fellow Gel da'Thae. Besides, when Grallezar gets here, she'll know all the right questions. She understands the way they structure their armies and the like."

"Very well, then. We'll wait."

Besides Pir, of course, there were other Gel da'Thae men with the alar. When Salamander asked them, they took charge of Sharak, who was just about the same age as Vek, but he noticed, as the day wore on, that they gave him brusque orders and made him wait to eat until everyone else had finished. In their eyes, too, he was a slave.

Some hours after noon, Prince Voran, with all his men and his retinue, joined the alar down in the meadow. Salamander escorted the prince to Dar's tent.

"We'll be leaving on the morrow," Voran told Dar. "I can't say that I'm eager to get back to Cerrgonney, but duty is duty. I decided that we'd eaten enough of Ridvar's provisions. He'll need to bring his warband up to full strength, and his vassals will need to do the same, with the Horsekin raiding along the border."

"Just so," Dar said. "I wonder how many raiding parties they sent out? Huh, those men that broke through our lines—they'll have an interesting tale to tell their officers if they manage to rejoin the main force. I hope hearing it makes them shit into their boots."

Voran laughed and nodded. "Me, too. Now, if Lady Grallezar can get more information out of that Horsekin prisoner, I'd very much appreciate your sharing it with me."

"Of course. You'll be in—"

"Gwingedd. It's the westernmost town in Cerrgonney, but still a long ride from your border. Well, I'll be returning to Cengarn in late summer. If the news isn't urgent, it can wait till then."

News, however, arrived that very evening. Just as the sun was touching the western horizon, the silver wyrm flew in. Downriver from the camp and its nervous horses, the dragon met with the princes, Voran's captain Caenvyr, and Calonderiel for a council of war. Salamander tagged along on the pretense of acting as a scribe, since Neb was staying in the dun to tend Gerran's wound.

The dragon lay in the soft grass with his hind legs tucked under him and his forepaws neatly folded at his chest. In the silky twilight he seemed to glimmer, like a full moon, perhaps, shining among the green. The men stood around his enormous head, though Voran kept well back, more than glad, apparently, to let Daralanteriel speak for both of them.

"Rori, it's a good thing we agreed to meet here," Dar said. "We won't be returning to the Red Wolf dun."

"Very well," Rori said. "Where will you be heading next?"

"West to Twenty Streams Rock, and then perhaps north up to

the edge of the tablelands, depending on the grazing. Then maybe west again, assuming it's safe to do so."

"With luck it will be. I saw an army, all right. They're Horsekin, not Gel da'Thae, so they must have come down from the far north."

"I take it they're heading south."

"They are. I followed them for some days, keeping out of their sight. Here's the interesting thing. They had about five hundred horsemen, some spearmen, some archers—a sizable amount of men, truly—but the baggage train was far larger than they'd need for themselves. Riding with it were a lot of important-looking men who weren't armed, and then straggling behind were a troop of chained slaves."

Voran came closer with an acknowledging nod the dragon's way. "What I don't understand is what they hope to gain. Aren't the Northlands mostly wilderness, except for the Gel da'Thae towns and the like?"

"For now they are," Rori said. "Wilderness can be turned into farmland quick enough. We destroyed Zakh Gral, so now they'll have to start all over, if they want a fortress near the Westlands. No doubt they thought we'd never know if they built one out there."

"Of course!" Voran said. "The slaves—they're there to do the heavy work of building walls."

Dar cursed under his breath.

"This lot may not be building the fortress itself," Rori continued. "It doesn't seem like they have enough men for that, truly."

"They could be setting up a base camp for a push farther south," Voran said. "If they're going to build a new fortress, they'll have to move a lot of men and materials south to the site." He paused for a moment, thinking. "Then those raiders we just thwarted were most likely sent as a feint, a move to keep us watching the border and not farther north."

"An excellent point, Your Highness." The dragon inclined his massive head in Voran's direction. "Now, I intend to find out what they're doing, but I won't leave you unguarded. Arzosah will be joining you in a few days to keep a watch as you travel. I'll rest here tonight, then fly north again."

"My sincere thanks. We need to know what the wretched scum are up to, because I have an ally in the northwest." Dar glanced at Calonderiel. "One we need to warn at the very least."

"True spoken," Calonderiel said. "Cerr Cawnen."

"We'll be leaving on the morrow," Mic said. "I've made all the arrangements with Aethel."

"Splendid!" Berwynna said. "If Cerr Cawnen's as interesting as Lin Serr, I can hardly wait to see it."

PART III

THE NORTHLANDS
SUMMER, 1160

Each element of the four—Fire, Air, Water, and Earth—has its particular virtues and its vices. Thus the Mountain Folk are steadfast yet grasping, the Westfolk clever yet cold to those unlike them. Only in the Children of Aethyr do all the elements mix. This means that while our race can serve the Light to a greater degree than most, we also have the greatest propensity of all for furthering the Darkness.

—*The Secret Book of Cadwallon the Druid*

LORD MIRRYN LED HIS MEN back from Cengarn on a day washed with summer rain. Dallandra was sitting in the women's hall, watching Solla and Adranna spinning wool with Branna's device, when she heard the gatekeeper's horn, a joyous blast of notes. Solla let go of the spinner's handle and jumped up to rush to the window. She laid both hands on the sill and looked out, then turned back, her face pale and her eyes wide.

"Mirro and the men are in the ward," she said, "but not my lord, and Daumyr's got a cut on his face."

Dallandra got to her feet and hurried over to catch Solla's hand. Solla was trembling, and she looked up at Dallandra with the eyes of a frightened child.

"Let's go down," Dallandra said. "There will be messages, but I'm sure as I can be that Gerran's safe and well."

Since Salamander had already told her the news, Dallandra had solid grounds for that certainty, not that she could tell Solla. Hand in hand they hurried down the stairs and reached the great hall just as Mirryn came striding in. He paused halfway to the table of honor and bowed to the two women.

"Gerro's safe in Cengarn, Solla," Mirryn called out. "He's injured, truly, but it's not much as long as he doesn't ride and suchlike."

Solla smiled and laid her free hand over her heart as if bidding it to be still. The color in her cheeks slowly returned to a normal pink from pale. She squeezed Dallandra's hand, then let it go with a whispered, "My thanks."

"What's all this, lad?" At the table of honor Cadryc got to his feet. "Trouble?"

"There was, Your Grace." Mirryn reached inside his shirt and brought out two silver message tubes. "Horsekin raiders on the border." Mirryn allowed himself a brief smile. "They've been dealt with."

The Red Wolf men, followed by six Westfolk archers, were filing into the hall. Daumyr, who indeed had a long scabbing cut on one cheek, bowed to the tieryn. "Begging Your Grace's pardon and all for interrupting," Daumyr said, "but you should know that our captain acquitted himself cursed well on the field. Prince Dar commended him."

Cadryc grinned, beaming like the smile in the full moon. "That's my lad!" He glanced around and saw a servant lass. "Mead all round, lass! Bring it fast!"

The lass scurried off to do his bidding. Mirryn handed Solla the messages. "The one with your brother's seal is for you alone," Mirryn said. "Interesting things happened in Dun Cengarn."

Since Dallandra already knew everything in those messages and more, she left the tieryn's household to their celebration and went back upstairs to her chamber. Judging by the ache in her breasts, she judged that Dari was due for a feeding. Sure enough, she came in to see Sidro carrying a squalling baby as she walked back and forth, singing in a vain effort to distract Dari from her hunger.

"Here's your mama, little one," Sidro said. "Just in time."

Dallandra sat down in the chair by the window, pulled up her tunic, and took the baby, who fastened herself onto the nearest nipple with no need for coaxing.

"Like a leech," Dalla said. "Malamala's little leech."

Dari took no notice. Dallandra leaned back and watched the gray mist falling softly outside the window. Nursing her daughter filled her with a great tenderness toward the smelly little bundle, yet she wondered if she could honestly call it love. *When she's older,* Dalla thought, *she'll be more interesting then.*

"Nasty weather to be riding in," Sidro remarked.

"I hope it clears by tomorrow." Dallandra craned her neck and considered the pale gray clouds. "It probably will, but I don't much care. I want to get on the road."

"You must miss the banadar dreadful like."

Dallandra sighed and considered what to say. "Him, too," she said at last. "But more to the point, I'm needed up there, and so are all of us, you, me, Grallezar, Branna, and, of course, Solla, for Gerran's sake."

"I see." Sidro thought this all over carefully. "You know, Wise One, it's all been so much to my good, knowing you and Valandario. Before I did play with the dweomer like a toy, but now I see that it be a duty for those who have it, beyond what they might want in life."

"Very well put. Tell me, do you still long for Laz?"

"I know not if I do or not. The more days I do spend with Pir, the more I think he should be my first man, mayhap my only man, but truly, often before did I think to break free of Laz, and never could I do it." Sidro raised both hands palm up, then shrugged. "If never I do see him again, my heart will ache, but Pir's will be gladdened, and so I ken not if I wish Laz back or not."

"Your hands, they be mostly healed," Marnmara said. "It no longer be needful to pull the scars apart."

"I cannot tell you how much it gladdens my heart to hear that," Laz said.

They were sitting in Haen Marn's great hall at a table under a window. Sunlight streamed in and glinted off the surface of the bowl of herbed water in which Laz's hands were soaking. He lifted out his right hand and considered the scars while the water dripped away. They were soft, pink, and whole without the painful cracks between them. The left hand also looked as healthy as it would ever be. When Marnmara handed him a rag, he dried his hands, then laid them on the table for her inspection.

"Truly," she said, "there be naught more for me to do. Mayhap you'll master the fingers better as time goes on."

"I'll hope so. I suppose I'd best be on my way."

She smiled at the hesitation in his voice. "It were best," she said. "Your wyrd lies not here."

When Angmar came downstairs for the evening meal, Laz told her that he'd be leaving on the morrow morning. She considered him sadly, then nodded her approval.

"My lady?" Laz said. "Has Avain seen Berwynna in her basin?"

"She has," Angmar said. "Surrounded by stone, Avain said, so I think me Mic and Enj did take her down to Lin Serr." For a brief moment she smiled. "Avain did see Enj. He be coming home, at least."

The smile faded, and Angmar walked on past without another word. She sat down at the head of the table in her usual place, then leaned back, staring out across the great hall. Marnmara took Laz to one side and whispered.

"Her heart be so torn with fear for my wretched sister," Mara said, "that she does think of naught else."

"It's a sad thing." Laz dropped his voice as well. "I suppose Wynni loves her Dougie too much to let him go off without her."

Marnmara's eyes grew wide, and she stared at him, as puzzled as if he'd spoken in some foreign tongue. "Here," she said finally, "be that why she did run away? Because of Dougie?"

"I'm assuming so. Surely you knew she'd been creeping into his chamber at night."

"Never did such a thing occur to me! The little slut!"

"Here, that's a vicious thing to say! Why do you hate your sister so?"

"I don't hate her." Mara scowled at the floor. "It be just that Mam does favor her over me. Huh! Look at the small reward Wynni did give her for it, too."

"What? When did she ever favor Wynni?"

"Always does she talk of the work Wynni does for us all."

"Oh? Well, I've heard her speak more of the Lady of the Isle than the lass who helps in the kitchen."

"It be so unfair! I ken how grand it does sound, that I be the lady of this isle. Mam does go on and on about it, how I be the lady, and so I must do this, and I must do that, and truly, at times I do wonder if she ever does see me, just me."

"Ah, I think I'm beginning to understand. But she loves Wynni just because Wynni is Wynni."

"True spoken." She paused, looking up at him with wide eyes. "I be frightened, Laz. I must marry, Mam tells me, some man of the Mountain Folk, and I want not to marry or have aught to do with such things. All Wynni needs must do is live her life as she chooses, and it be not fair!"

"I see. You envy her."

Mara nodded.

"I'll tell you somewhat. I'll wager that Wynni thinks your mam loves you more, and that, in truth, Angmar loves you both the same."

Tears filled Mara's eyes. With an irritable shake of her sleeve she brushed them away. Moments like this one forced Laz to remember just how young she was, no matter how powerful her dweomers were or would become. "I think me," he said, "that when you meet a man who pleases you, what you want and don't want will change."

She looked up, shocked, then smoothed her face into an unreadably bland expression. "Mayhap. Mam does say the same. I'll think on it."

In the morning, Marnmara walked with him down to the pier. The dragon boat stood ready, bobbing in the slack waves of the lake. Some distance from it, out of earshot of the boatmen, Mara stopped Laz for a few last words.

"I slept not much, this past night," Marnmara said, "for there be much to brood about. The nature of this isle does much concern me, but you, too, were in my thoughts."

"For that I'll thank you," Laz said.

"You'd best wait for gratitude till you hear what I did see." She paused for a smile. "You did teach me many things it were needful for me to know, Laz, and for that my heart be grateful. So I did scry upon your wyrd. You stand in the middle of a dangerous road, and which way you might go, I cannot say. I will tell you, though, that one way leads to great evil, for I think me you did much evil in lives past. Go that way, and great evil will befall you in return. The other way leads to the saving of you. There be more than one way to pay the debts you owe."

Laz found himself shocked speechless.

"It be your choice, which way you turn on the road. For your sake I do hope you choose the correct way."

"So do I." Laz suddenly found himself laughing, a high nervous giggle. "So do I." He choked the noise back with an effort of will. "Can you tell me more about—"

"I can't. It be not given for me to know. My thanks again for your teaching."

Marnmara smiled again, patted him on the arm, then turned and walked back to the manse. As Laz watched her go, he found himself wanting to run after her and beg her to let him stay in safety on the island. Yet his old life lay close at hand, his men, his sorcery, and above all, Sidro. With a sigh, he picked up his meager bundle of belongings and headed for the pier.

The boatmen rowed him across without comment, but when they reached the shallows, Lon stopped him as he was about to go over the side.

"You sure you'll fare well here?" Lon said.

"I hope so," Laz said, grinning. "I always have before."

"Well and good, then. Here's luck to you!"

Laz jumped down into the shallows. When Lon handed down the bundle, Laz caught it twixt his lower arms and his chest. He distrusted his stumps of hands when it came to carrying something heavy, but he safely splashed across and gained the shore. By the time he turned to look back, the dragon boat had put out into deep water. The clanging of the gong echoed around the valley, then slowly faded away as the boat disappeared into the rising mist.

Laz had a moment of wondering if the island itself would disappear into that mist and never be seen again. If it did, would he regret it? A little, he decided, perhaps he'd regret it a little, for Marnmara's sake.

Clutching his bundle, he walked away from the lake and clambered partway up the side of a low hill to the shelter of three gnarled trees, bent low by a perpetual wind. He set the bundle under them, then sat down in the long grass. From his perch he could see that the island still stood in the middle of the lake. Perhaps one day he'd return—a pretty idea, he decided, but at the moment, what he needed to do was leave it behind.

"I'm home," he said aloud. "Well, in a manner of speaking. It can't be more than a few hundred miles away."

Now that he was free of Haen Marn's water veil, he could scry again. As an experiment he brought out the black crystal and looked into it. He realized immediately that he was seeing through it to its white twin: in a greenish murk of lake water a dead log lay directly in the crystal's narrow field of vision. Beyond it some large thing swam, indistinguishable in the clouded light.

"One of those beasts, no doubt," Laz said to the crystal. "Well, your twin came with us, but it's still well and truly lost. I can't imagine anyone being willing to dive down and fetch it out."

With a shudder at the thought of the lake beasts and their toothy mouths, he put the black crystal back in his sack. To scry for persons, especially those whom he knew well, the long grass waving in the wind would serve as an adequate focus.

The first person in his thoughts was Sidro. Her image came to him straightaway, standing outside a painted Westfolk tent and talking with Exalted Mother Grallezar. Both women looked excited and happy, laughing as they exchanged some sort of jest. Sidro must have left the forest on her own, he assumed, and sheltered among the Ancients with Grallezar and her refugees. As he watched, two blurry shapes, which he assumed belonged to Ancients, began to take the tent down. When he pulled back to see more of the area around Sidro, he realized that she was part of a small group who apparently had camped by a road.

What of the rest of his men? When he sent his mind out to Pir, he saw him walking through a herd of Westfolk horses in a very different encampment. Vek? He was in the same camp as Pir, spreading wet clothing to dry on tall grass. He scried out Faharn next, but rather than living among the Ancients, he and the remaining men had made a camp in open country—somewhere. Laz couldn't recognize the place, an undistinguished stretch of grass, a stream that wound through boulders and straggly trees, and in the distance, some hills. It could have been anywhere in the Northlands. As he scried through the camp, Laz recognized nine of the men. The rest appeared only as the blurry aura-shapes of persons he'd never seen in the flesh.

Interesting, Laz thought. *Faharn always envied Pir's horse mage abilities. I wonder if that's why they separated?*

The strength of his scrying images gave him hope that he could still perform the one dweomer he truly craved: flight. He got up and stripped off his clothes, a clumsy job with so few fingers left to him. Just in case he managed to transform, he packed the clothes away in the sack and tied it shut as securely as he could with his maimed hands. He hopped up onto one of the rocks and stood naked. In the warm sunlight he breathed deeply, steadily.

When he pictured the raven in his mind, the form came to him, as strong and clear as ever. He imagined it standing outside of himself, prepared himself for an effort of will, and found himself inside the raven form before he could even say aloud the formulaic names. With a caw of triumph he hopped up and down and flapped his wings.

When he spread his wings, however, the feeling of triumph vanished. Dweomer had created his wing tips from his hands, and like his hands, the tips of his wings showed damage. What would those missing feathers do to his control? The raven existed, but could he fly? Only one way to find out—with a defiant caw Laz leaped into the air.

Flapping hard, he gained height, found a rising thermal, and soared. *Success!* At least at first—when he tried to land, the missing feathers blunted his wings and spoiled their perfect camber. He tumbled in the air, squawked, fluttered, and finally managed to glide back to the rock with some of his dignity intact. *Not so easy,* he thought, *I'll need a fair bit of practice.* The next challenge would be carrying his sack of belongings. He hopped up onto it and sank his talons into the cloth, then chanced to glance at Haen Marn.

In the raven form Laz saw with etheric sight, not his normal vision. The island had disappeared into an enormous swirl of silvery blue energy that swept the lake up like a waterspout. At first, in fact, Laz thought he was seeing a real waterspout, then remembered that no wind blew in the cloudless sky. Inside the throbbing mass he could just discern slender lines of light like gold wires. They swung back and forth, twisted around each other only to uncurl, glimmered and darkened only to brighten again while the silver-blue energy-mist swirled around them.

As he watched, this tremendous play of dweomer force suddenly coalesced into images of the island, its lake, and its manse, a clear and vivid view. Another moment, and the images vanished. The play of lights began again—only to produce another image, slightly different, and then another, all of them laced with silver and gold.

For a long time he stared, fascinated, at the true form of Haen Marn.

Finally he wrenched his gaze away. He had his own affairs to attend to. Although he was tempted to fly straight to Sidro, he decided that it would be best to join up with Faharn first rather than go charging into the midst of an Ancients' camp. Faharn could tell him what had happened to everyone over the winter and explain why the outlaw band had split into two. Although he had no idea of Faharn's precise location, once he created an astral tunnel that would lead him to the mother roads, he could build an image of Faharn and use it as a focus. The road itself would find him as rapidly and surely as a hunting dog finds prey.

This close to the astral vortex that was Haen Marn, however, working any dweomer more complex than the raven transformation would be profoundly dangerous. The tunnel working—Laz's own discovery—was dangerous enough on its own. He would have to get some miles away, he decided, before risking it. Once again he got a secure grip on his sack, then rose, flapping hard, and headed straight west. As he flew, he was thinking of Sidro.

The misty rain had cleared, leaving the roads too damp for dust but not wet enough for mud. Dallandra, her women, her squad of archers, and Penna, driving a pony cart with their possessions and supplies, had a pleasant journey to Cengarn in the bright warm weather. On the second day, as they were riding through meadowlands only a few miles from the city, their escort received some unexpected reinforcements. Vantalaber, riding in the lead, suddenly raised his arm and pointed at the sky.

"Dragons!" he said. "Look!"

Dallandra glanced up to see two dragons circling high above them: Rori and Arzosah, she assumed. They dropped lower, allowing her to see them more clearly. While one of them was indubitably Arzosah, the other, a smaller wyrm, had wings as dark a green as a pine tree in winter, and its body shone a glimmery gold.

"Arzosah!" Dallandra called out. "Land over in the meadow, and I'll come join you."

The black dragon dipped her head to acknowledge the call, then lowered a wing and turned toward the meadow. The smaller wyrm followed. By the time that Dallandra had dismounted and walked over to meet them, they were both stretched out, nose to tail, basking. Some fifty yards' worth of scales glittered in the sun. Arzosah got up and waddled over to greet Dallandra. The smaller dragon lifted her head, but at a word from Arzosah she stayed where she was.

"That's my daughter, Medea," Arzosah said in Elvish. "That's her false-name, of course—a fancy of her late father, my former mate. He named her after a famous Greggyn woman that he admired."

"That's nice." Dallandra had never heard of Medea, famous or not. "She's very beautiful."

"Of course she is." Arzosah rumbled softly, her equivalent of a smile. "My second hatchling, she was, and I must admit that she turned out well. I decided to bring her along when Rori asked me to come guard you. Four wings shelter more eggs from the rain than two, as they always say. Rori's gone off to scout the Horsekin again, which is why he didn't come himself."

"Is that why you're here?" Dallandra said. "I'm sincerely grateful. These days you never know what might happen."

"Too true, alas. You're welcome. We'll stay with your alar after you all leave Cengarn. I want to keep an eye on Prince Dar. Now, if we run into trouble, I can summon my older daughter as well. Mezzalina, my elder mate called her for a false name. For the nonce, I've left her in the lair to care for my young son." Arzosah paused, then rumbled loudly and long. "The look on your face, Dalla! Absolutely bursting with curiosity! I know you're wondering who the father of that son may be."

"Well, I can't deny it."

"I think me you can guess the answer." Arzosah lifted a wing, then folded it close to her body.

Dallandra found herself utterly speechless. *Why am I surprised?*

she thought. *It's the dweomer of the thing, I suppose.* She had somehow assumed that two species so completely different could never—*but he is a dragon now,* she reminded herself. Arzosah was watching her with one huge eye half-closed, as if she were smiling to herself.

"You're embarrassed, aren't you?" Arzosah said. "I don't understand why. We've both had more than one mate."

Dallandra had to admit that the dragon was right—it wasn't the hatchling itself that was troubling her, but its getting.

"Is your lair nearby?" Dallandra managed to speak at last.

"No," Arzosah said. "It's off to the west in a fire mountain, in fact. By the way, I've been meaning to tell you, I destroyed that wretched bone whistle. I dropped it into a little pool of steaming rockblood down on the floor of the cavern. It burned with a puff of nasty smelling smoke."

"You're lairing inside a living fire mountain? I thought that you'd choose a dead one."

"What good would that be in the snows? But it's only a sleeping mountain. We'll be able to tell if it's beginning to wake. It takes a mountain a long time to wake. It groans, it shudders, and slowly its fires rise." The dragon rumbled again. "Unless, of course, it gets a bit of help from dragonish dweomer."

Dallandra shuddered at the thought. Arzosah raised her head and looked over Dallandra's shoulder to the meadow beyond.

"Who's that?" the dragon asked.

Dallandra turned to see Sidro trotting across the meadow toward them. "Sidro, a friend of mine," Dalla said. "She looks awfully excited about something. Here, she only knows a little Eluish, so if you could lower yourself to speak the language of men—"

The dragon heaved a massive, vinegar-scented sigh, but she did comply. "Here, Sidro," Arzosah called out in Deverrian. "I won't eat you. You may come closer."

With a hesitant smile, Sidro joined them. "Dalla, my apologies, but I did have the strangest feeling just now. Laz is back, I be sure of it in my heart, back and thinking of me. I did feel the touch of his mind on mine."

"Oh, did you now?" Dallandra said. "You're certain?"

"I am, and deep in my very soul. I thought I'd best tell you straightaway."

"And I'm glad you did. I wonder if this means that Haen Marn's back?"

The dragon growled under her breath. "Haen Marn? Is that where that slimy little sorcerer was, off in Alban with Haen Marn?"

"What? Alban? Where's that?" Dallandra felt like growling herself. "Are you telling me that you knew where Haen Marn was?"

"Um, well, not precisely." Arzosah's normally huge voice had dwindled to a hatchling's chirp.

"You knew!" Dallandra snarled. "You knew, and you didn't tell anyone!"

"No one asked me." Arzosah curled a paw and studied her claws. "Besides, I didn't *precisely* know. I was guessing, and as much as it pains me to admit it, I might have been wrong."

"You weaselly wyrm!"

"I truly wasn't sure." Arzosah spoke quickly, as if trying to change the subject. "I hoped it wasn't there. It's an awful place, Alban. I wouldn't wish it upon anyone, not even Haen Marn."

"You must have been in this Alban country, then."

"I have, and an even nastier country called Lloegr. Alban's a few miles north of it. Them and their wretched Lord Yaysoo! I never want to see either place again. Don't you try to order me to go there, either, because it would mean my death."

"I have no intention of ordering you to do anything of the sort if the island really is back, so you'd better hope it is." Dallandra's curiosity fought with her anger, then won. "Yaysoo? Is he their king or suchlike?"

"No, their god. He's a sheep. The Lamb of God, they call him, so I assume his father's a sacred ram. Yaysoo's mother was a human woman called Miriam, and the ram got her with child somehow or other. It's a very complicated story, and I only heard bits of it. The high priest carries a shepherd's crook, probably to summon Yaysoo with." Arzosah paused for a snort. "They weren't particularly sheeplike themselves, those worshipers, persecuting poor innocent dragons, chasing us with spears and trying to kill us for no particular reason."

"No particular reason, hmm?"

"Well, perhaps a few small ones." Arzosah flattened her ears like an angry cat. "Now, once I figured out that these people worshiped sheep, I tried to parley with them. I was quite willing to never kill a sheep again. There's not much meat on them, anyway, for a dragon, and that nasty wool gets stuck in your teeth. Unfortunately, the only language we had in common was the Rhwman tongue, and they spoke it very badly. I'm not sure they understood what I was offering. They started throwing stones at me, and the high priest actually hit me on the nose with his stupid crook."

"What did you do?"

"I ate him, of course. What would you have done in my situation?"

"I certainly wouldn't have eaten the high priest."

"Probably not." Arzosah considered this for a moment. "He was awfully tough. But after that, the persecutions only got worse. So we dragons left the sheep to Yaysoo and came here."

"Let me see if I understand you." Dallandra made herself speak calmly. "You can travel back and forth between these two worlds, ours and the sheep people's. That's why you think Haen Marn may have been able to do the same."

"I could once. Not now. Evandar's dead, and his lands destroyed, and I wouldn't care to get lost in what remains, thank you very much."

"Well, to be honest, no more would I. So you knew about Evandar's lands back then, did you?"

"We knew Evandar. He and his people used to go back and forth twixt here and Lloegr, probably to cause as much trouble as possible in both worlds. I will say one good thing about that nasty little clot of ectoplasm. When he realized that we dragons were in danger, he offered to bring us to a new home. Little did I know that he'd someday trick me out of my true name! How like him!"

Dallandra had heard her complain about Evandar so often that she saw no need to defend him, especially with more pressing matters in hand.

"But surely Rori told you we were trying to find Haen Marn," Dalla said. "You might have told him. Why didn't you?"

Arzosah squirmed, slapping her tail this way and that so viciously that cut grass sprayed up around it. Sidro took a few cautious steps back.

"Why?" Dallandra repeated. "Tell me!"

"Because of Angmar, of course. Do you think I don't know that she's my rival for Rori's heart?" Arzosah's tail arched up over her back, and she rose on her forefeet.

Sidro screamed. Arzosah flopped back, then swung her head around to look at her.

"Oh, do stop making that noise!" Arzosah returned to speaking with Dallandra. "I'm tempted to eat Angmar and put an end to her."

Dallandra drew herself up to full height. "Arzosah Sothy Lorez oh Haz!" She intoned the name with dweomer power behind every syllable. "By the power of your true name, I forbid you to do any such thing. I forbid you from bringing the least harm to Angmar, to her kin, to those who befriend her, to her island. I forbid you from threatening, frightening, or harassing them in any manner."

Arzosah whined like a kicked dog. Her head drooped almost to her paws. "So be it," Arzosah said. "I hate it, but I shall obey."

"Good!" Dallandra paused to gather her breath and her wits. "Besides, as things stand now, she's hardly a rival at all. What would she want with a dragon for a husband? She's what? A bare hundredth of Rori's size, and that's just to begin with. How would she feed him? Where would he lair on her island?"

"Oh." Arzosah turned her head and clacked her jaws. Her tail twitched, but only at the tip. If ever a dragon could be embarrassed, it seemed she was. "Humph, here I've been vexing myself for naught."

Dallandra had been on the point of admitting that she might not be able to learn the proper dweomers to transform Rori back again, and that even if she did, she might not be able to work them. Just in time she realized that Rori had been keeping a secret of his own.

"Now listen," Dallandra said instead, "I thought you agreed with me that turning Rhodry into a dragon should never have happened."

"Of course I do. But the blunder's been made, and now that you're healing that ghastly wound, and he's sane again, why would I want Rori gone?"

What's she going to say? Dalla thought, *if we do manage to turn Rhodry back again?* Worse yet, what would Arzosah do? Dallandra vividly remembered the last time Arzosah thought she'd lost Rhodry, when she'd threatened to waken a sleeping fire mountain and destroy an entire town. Arzosah looked away, her ears still flat and sullen, but she tucked her tail around her haunches in a mannerly gesture. *I'll have to forbid her to do every nasty thing I can think of,* Dalla thought. *And phrase everything exactly right, too.*

"Well and good, then," Dallandra said. "We'd best get on the road. Sidro, you and I can talk more while we ride. If Laz is back, I hope he still has that crystal."

"He should have two of them," Sidro said, "the white as well as the black."

"I'd forgotten about the white one," Dalla said. "Arzosah, my thanks for your aid and protection, but remember what I said about Haen Marn."

"I have no choice but to remember." The dragon hissed, but only briefly. "That wretched Evandar!"

When they reached the Westfolk camp in the meadow below Cengarn, the journey ended for Dallandra and most of her traveling companions, including the dragons, but Branna accompanied Solla and little Penna up to the dun itself. As they rode through the streets of the town, everyone who saw them called out their best wishes to Lady Solla; the men bowed, the women curtsied. The town remembered her many acts of charity. At the gates of the dun, the guards greeted her as if she'd been the queen herself. They bowed low, they yelled for pages, they helped her dismount and murmured compliments the while. Branna only wished that Drwmigga could see and hear them.

Though Drwmigga stayed elsewhere, Ridvar himself did come striding out of the main broch tower. For a long moment he and Solla stood face-to-face, considering each other.

"You look well, Brother," Solla said at last.

"So do you, Sister." Ridvar took a deep breath. "It gladdens my heart that you're here. We never had a feast to celebrate your marriage. Once your lord's recovered, I shall give one in your honor."

Solla smiled, nearly wept, snuffled back the tears, and smiled again. "I'd like that," she said in a steady voice. "My thanks."

Ridvar managed to smile, then turned to a waiting page. "Help Lady Solla's maidservant bring up her things," the gwerbret said. "Blethry will tell you what chamber to put them in. Come in, Solla, come in. I'll take you up to your lord."

Branna followed as they went in arm in arm. She was assuming that she'd find Neb in the same place as Gerran. Indeed, when Ridvar opened the door of an upstairs chamber for Solla, Neb came hurrying out. He'd put back some of the weight he'd lost, and he was grinning at her with the life back in his eyes. Branna rushed to his open arms.

For the rest of that day, they talked but little. In the evening, however, after a meal that a page brought up to their chamber, they sat half-dressed on the bed and discussed Neb's decision by candlelight.

"It truly started with the plague in Trev Hael," Neb said, "not that I could see it then. It's the questions, Branni. I have so many! How does an illness spread so fast? I've read all the usual things about humors and corruptions and the like, but none of them ring true. Where did the cursed illness come from, anyway? Townsfolk began falling ill a few days after the big summer market fair, so some visitor might have brought somewhat, the seeds of the illness, or a poison—I don't know. I thought mayhap the cause was bad air, but it was a lovely summer, that year, and the air was sweet."

"If you could find out," Branna said, "it would be a grand thing. Do you remember Salamander telling us that our dweomer was the hope of the border?"

"I do, truly. That's one reason I was flogging myself to be as powerful as I could."

"If you could find the root of pestilence, wouldn't that be powerful, too? I mean, what finally stopped the Horsekin, back when they destroyed the Westfolk cities, was the plague. What if they used a plague against us?"

"True spoken." Neb looked away, his eyes wide with remembered horror. "We'd better have shields in store against that kind of weapon. I doubt me if this particular bout came from them. How could it? But it was brutal enough as it was."

"Oh, it was that, sure enough, judging from everything you've told me. It's no wonder you want to study healing."

"And so I do." Neb was silent for a moment, looking away, his face slack with old grief. "Well," he said briskly. "I know my wyrd, and truly, it's such a relief, as if I've been ill myself. I envied you so much, you know, since you always knew yours."

"What?" Branna wondered whether to laugh or snarl at him. "What makes you think that?"

"Well, didn't you?"

"I didn't."

"But you'd gotten so far ahead of me."

"Here, what is this? Did you think we were running a race or suchlike?"

He had the decency to blush.

"All I know, my dearest darling," Branna said with some asperity, "is that I've set my feet on the dweomer road. I have no idea where it's leading me."

"Um, well, my apologies."

Neb got out of bed and began clearing away the remains of their meal like a page. *You should be embarrassed,* Branna thought. Still, as she considered the past few months, she realized that she might have shared her doubts with him. *Both of us were putting on a good show for the other,* she thought. *Just like a pair of gerthddynion!*

Branna saw the actual gerthddyn in the dun later that evening, when she went with Neb to visit Gerran. While Neb discussed his patient with Solla, Branna sat on the windowsill, the only available seat in the crowded room, and watched the candle smoke drift past her and out to the warm night. They had been there some time when Salamander nudged the door open with his foot and walked in with an armload of Westfolk tunics, old ones, judging from the faded embroideries.

"What are you going to do with those?" Branna asked him in Elvish.

"Give them to Canna and her children." Salamander nodded at the huddle of womenfolk sitting on the floor. "They can't go on wearing those bloodstained clothes. She can cut these down for dresses and the like."

"I'd wondered about that, the poor woman!"

Salamander handed over the clothing, spoke briefly with Canna, then gestured to Branna and left. She followed him out to the corridor, dark except for the wedge of candlelight through the open door.

"I take it that you and Neb have talked?" Salamander said in Deverrian.

"We have, truly. His decision seems like a sound one to me. But you know what's odd? Now that he's not trying to be Nevyn, he's a lot more like my memories of Nevyn."

"No doubt! Have you ever tried to squeeze a handful of water?"

"Of course not. It'll run right through your fingers—oh! That's your point, isn't it?"

"It is. The more Neb forced the issue, the more he failed."

"Well, I think he sees that now. I hope so."

"Good." Salamander reached into his shirt and pulled out a silver message tube. "I need to go give this to the gwerbret. Just as I suspected, Grallezar extracted a great deal of information out of Gerran's prisoner by sheer force of character alone. None of it is happy news, nor does it give me great hope for a peaceful future." He tapped the palm of his other hand with the tip of the tube. "Nasty, in short. Roving companies of Horsekin warriors are traveling throughout the Northlands, gathering information, making raids along our border, all to some greater and foul purpose, which he doesn't understand, alas. Sharak was only a young recruit. No one told him much, of course, and that's the pity."

"True spoken." Branna felt as if a cold wind had swept down the dark corridor. She shuddered and cast the feeling off. "But no one lives up in the Northlands, do they? I always heard that it was wilderness and little more."

"So did I, but if naught else, there's Dwarveholt, and various merchants from various towns do go to trade with Lin Serr." Salamander heaved a deep sigh and contemplated the message tube. "Anyway, since your husband's become Gerran's personal chirurgeon, I've been pressed into Dar's service as scribe and messenger both." He made her a bow. "And so, as much as it pains me to do honest work for my living, I must take my leave of you and go find Ridvar."

After Grallezar finished questioning Sharak, she asked Sidro to take him to Dallandra. While they stood beside Grallezar's tent to talk, the exhausted boy knelt between them on the ground. In the flickering light from a campfire, his eyes were unreadable pools of shadow.

"He told me that young Neb rewrapped his wrist and fingers," Grallezar said in their own language. "I don't know anything about the healer's craft, so I'd like her to make sure he did it correctly. I need to go consult with the prince."

"Very well, I'll be glad to take him," Sidro said. "Sharak, come with me."

He stood up, but he kept his gaze fixed on the ground.

"You look familiar," Sidro said. "Do I know you?"

"I'm from Taenbalapan." He spoke so softly that she could barely hear him. "I saw you in the temple there, Holy One."

"I do remember. Your mother was very poor and came to us for charity. Is that why you enlisted so young? So she could draw your salary?"

He nodded. "I'm the second son. It was the First Son's duty to stay with Mother and my sisters."

"Well, she'll have your death boon now," Grallezar said. "No one's going to know you're still alive."

His mouth twitched in the beginning of a smile, but he continued studying the ground at his feet. Would his mother mourn him, the expendable extra son? Sidro wondered. No doubt the coin would ease any grief she felt.

"You're not really a slave, you know," Sidro said. "You can look at me. No one keeps slaves among the Ancients."

He did look up then, his eyes wide with surprise.

"You could even go back, if you wanted," Sidro went on.

"I don't want to." He clenched his good hand into a fist. "They've betrayed our goddess, killing women like that."

"*Your* goddess!" Grallezar snapped. "She never was mine. But that doesn't matter now. Go along with Sidro, boy. I want to make sure that broken wrist's going to heal."

When Sidro walked off, Sharak followed her obediently, some three steps behind. It was going to take him a while to understand that he truly was a free man still. Later she'd make it plain to him that she no longer served Alshandra, Sidro decided. At the moment he appeared too dazed from all that had happened to him to understand subtleties.

They found Dallandra, who immediately agreed to look over Sharak's injuries.

"Come over to this fire here," Dalla said to the boy. "So I can see better."

He stared bewildered until Sidro translated, then smiled. He turned to Sidro and bent one knee as a sign of his lower status. "Thank you, Holy One," he said softly. "It's so good of you to help such as me."

"You're very welcome," Sidro said. "I'll wait here in case the healer needs to tell you something."

He knelt before her, then leaned forward and kissed the toe of her boot. With a bob of his head, he rose and followed Dallandra to the fire.

Sidro felt her eyes fill with tears, just a few and briefly. The boy's obvious respect had touched her, a respect she'd not received in a long while. With Laz so much on her mind, she found herself remembering how he'd seduced her away from her sacred vows. She'd come to believe that he'd been right to do so, come to see that Alshandra was no true goddess at all, but his utter contempt for a devotion she'd cherished more than life itself hurt her still. What had he said? Something like, "I thought you'd throw that asinine vow off like a cloak."

Had it been so asinine, to hope for something so grand, so much larger than herself, so much more wonderful than the handful of names and half-understood rituals offered by the old gods? That night she felt her loss of faith as keenly, as painfully, as she'd felt the loss of her first child. Either of them might have given her life a meaning that it had lacked, her, a mere slave-born half-citizen.

I have the dweomer now, she reminded herself. She might have another child as well, of course. She hoped for such every day, now that she had a man who wanted a child. She remembered telling Laz that their son had died of fever. He'd looked at her with such blank eyes, hesitated so long, and then finally said, "I'm so sorry." That was all. "I'm so sorry." For her, perhaps. For himself, he was relieved. *He didn't even bother to deny it.*

Why would I want him back? The thought hung in her mind like a sudden moonrise, casting strange shadows rather than clear light.

On the morning that Aethel's caravan left Lin Serr, Berwynna and Dougie went down the long flights of stairs to the parkland below the main entrance to the city. While the sun climbed higher in the sky, a crowd of men and pack animals milled around, seemingly aimlessly at first. The mules brayed, the men swore, and Aethel trotted back and forth, sorting them out into a decent order. Mic took the chance to remind Berwynna that Cerr Cawnen lay a long journey away—about a month, depending upon the weather.

"Now, once we get there," Mic said, "I'll look over this job of theirs. If I like it, I'll stay, but you should go back to Lin Serr with the last trading run. I'll arrange things with Aethel. Your grandfather will make sure that you and Dougie get safely back to Haen Marn."

"If you say so, Uncle Mic," Berwynna said. "By then, I'll doubtless be ever so glad to see Mam again, especially if we find my da. Everything's been so splendid so far. Even ordinary things are marvels to me after being shut up on that wretched little island."

One of those mundane marvels was the caravan itself. Berwynna had never seen so many mules gathered in one place, to say naught of the sixteen muleteers, tall men, all of them, and on the beefy side. Among them, Dougie seemed neither tall nor short, but his red hair did mark him as someone different. Most of the Cerr Cawnen men had yellow hair and pale blue or gray eyes, far different from the men of Alban that she'd seen, and names that to her sounded either strange or oddly plain, such as Whaw, Hound, Fraed, and Richt, Aethel's journeyman and his second-in-command.

"Why would anyone name their son Hound?" Berwynna asked Mic.

"Most likely it's an old name in their family." Mic dropped his voice and glanced around to make sure they couldn't be overheard. "A long time ago all of the Cerr Cawnen ancestors were slaves, Wynni. They escaped from their Deverry masters and headed west. It was the masters who gave them names like Hound and Ash. Now, remember, bringing up the subject of slave-ancestors is very discourteous, so don't."

"Oh, don't let it worry you. I can see that."

Since some of the mules would be carrying empty panniers home—Aethel had traded bulky woolens for fine metalwork, including a good many pieces of jewelry—Berwynna, Kov, and Mic would ride to Cerr Cawnen. Dougie, however, would walk alongside Berwynna's mule. Since Richt had given him a pair of stout boots and some brigga as well, he made no complaint when he led the mule that would be Berwynna's over to her.

"You look so different in those brigga," Berwynna said, grinning. "Now we're dressed alike, and no one's going to ask me why you're wrapped in a blanket."

"Huh, and them with their gall!" But he was smiling at her. "The plaid will do well enough for a cloak if it rains."

"You're sure you don't mind walking?"

"You're not much of a rider, lass. I can keep an eye on this mule this way. They're crafty, mules, a fair bit smarter than horses, and he won't be obeying someone who doesn't know how to handle him."

The mule snorted as if agreeing. When it tried to toss its head, Dougie's broad hand on its halter kept it still.

Mic wandered away to speak with Kov, who was nervously considering his own mule nearby. They were a contrasting pair, Mic stout and clean-shaven, with hair as black as soot, and Kov lean, a handsome man for one of the Mountain Folk, with his chiseled features and neatly trimmed brown beard. They were, however, also arguing about something—*what a surprise!* Berwynna thought. The Mountain Folk side of her clan had some traits that she could have done without, though she certainly had benefited from their generosity to inhabitants of Haen Marn.

Among other things, Vron had given Berwynna a pair of saddlebags for the journey. Before she mounted up, she opened them as surreptitiously as she could to make sure that the precious dweomer book was safe, tucked into its oiled wrappings. Dougie, however, noticed it immediately.

"What's that?" Dougie said. "Not that blasted book I dug up, is it?"

"Um, well, it is." Berwynna began lacing the bag back up before Mic noticed as well. "When I was going down to the pier, back home, you know? I saw it just lying on a bench, so I took it. I know I shouldn't have. Please don't berate me!"

"Well, it's here now, sure enough." Dougie rubbed his chin with one hand while he considered the problem. "We'll take it when we go back for the winter. There's naught we can do about it now."

Thinking that she could return the book relieved some of Berwynna's guilty feelings about having taken it in the first place. Whenever she thought about it, she was surprised all over again that she'd found it left out in the open. It was so unlike Mara to be careless with the few things she owned.

At last the caravan got itself assembled in the correct riding order, and all the farewells had been said. With a whoop and a yell, Aethel led his men and mules out of the massive stone gates of Lin Serr.

For the first few days, they followed a well-worn road through the hills east of the mountain city. It wound through forests, mostly pine mixed with aspens and maples, though now and then they did pass a farm worked by men of the Mountain Folk. Judging from the sun's position at its setting, Berwynna realized that despite the road's many turnings, they were heading northwest rather than straight west.

"This road does go away from Deverry, bain't?" she asked Richt.

"It does," he said. "The farther from them we do stay the better. There be bandits along the border. That be why we carry staves." He glanced at Dougie. "I hope you be good with that sword of yours, lad."

By then Dougie had learned enough of the Mountain dialect to answer on his own. "There be some who did tell me I am," Dougie said. "We should be hoping you get not the chance to judge for yourself."

Richt laughed and nodded his agreement. They were sitting together that evening on one side of a small campfire. On the other, Mic and Aethel were discussing opals while Kov merely listened. Richt picked up a thin stick of firewood and drew a rough map in the dirt between him and Berwynna.

"This curve here," Richt pointed to a half circle, "be the mountains. Down below here this line be the border twixt Dwarveholt and Deverry. Another reason to travel the northern route be the river." He drew a vertical line westward of the half circle. "It's so cursed broad that never would we get across on our own, but some folk who live there did build a bridge. For a toll, they do let us cross. Then we head south again, but not too far south, not on your life, nowhere near the Slavers' Country."

"This land north," Dougie said, "be it hilly or flat?"

"Flat, mostly, and forested. Not many do live there, though the land, it does look rich enough. Now, the far north, it be a strange place, a barren place, much rock and little soil. The gods did take a shovel and scrape it bare, I think me, some long while ago. Here and there along the streams, there be grass and suchlike, but not much land a man could farm. I heard tell that there be ghosts up there." Richt leaned forward and quirked a conspiratorial eyebrow. "And another thing. Once we do reach the flat lands, ride not off on your own, fair lady. There be dragons there."

"I do know that," Berwynna said. "One of them be my father. The silver wyrm."

Richt stared openmouthed, then glanced at Kov, who'd turned to listen to Richt's tale.

"He is," Kov said in his perfect Deverrian, "though the tale is far more complicated than you might think."

Richt looked back and forth between them. Berwynna smiled brightly and waited. Finally Richt muttered an excuse, got up, and left. It took all her self-control to keep from laughing at his retreating back.

The silver wyrm was, at that moment, lairing far to the west of the caravan. When he left Cengarn, Rori flew straight north to the spot where he'd earlier seen the Horsekin army. By then they'd moved on, but they left tracks and litter behind them, a trail that angled eastward. Rori eventually found them setting up an elaborate camp. He stayed high enough overhead to prevent them seeing more than a birdlike shape, white against the sun, if indeed they noticed him at all.

The spot they'd chosen, a low rise of hill that overlooked a shallow valley to the south of it, made a good choice for a fortress, but it lay too far north to offer any sort of threat to the Westlands. Since the Horsekin had marked out the site of its future walls by clearing away the grass and shrubby ground cover, Rori could estimate its size—too small to garrison any sizable number of troops. As a staging ground, however, to store provisions and provide support for an army on the march, it would do quite well.

The question then became: where was that army and when would it march? When he woke that morning, he decided that he'd best go take a look at the heart of Horsekin territory, just to see if troops were gathering or if more of the savage Horsekin from the far north were moving south to join their brethren. He could fly there and back in but a few days, a journey that would take men on horseback months.

Rori got up from the rocky ledge where he'd been sleeping and stretched. The wound on his side itched, as it continually did. He desperately want to scratch it, but fear of making it worse stopped him. It had nearly poisoned him to death, back when it was black and crusted, oozing a continual slime of blood and pus. *If only I had hands,* he thought, as he did every time the wound forced itself into his consciousness. Perhaps then he could find some relief, carry with him that willow bark Dallandra had used to soothe the itching for a little while, brew it up himself. All he had now were paws, four huge clawed paws, too clumsy for delicate acts like lighting a fire or peeling bark from a tree.

By turning his head at the right angle he could see the pink stripe on his belly. Before Dallandra had pointed out that he was making it worse, he'd licked it in a futile attempt to keep it clean—licked it like a dog, he reminded himself, not a man. Now he could do nothing to it or for it. He'd come to hate it more than he'd ever hated an enemy. Perhaps it *was* an enemy, a constant reminder of his lack of hands, of his lack of the ability to do all those little human things he'd always taken for granted.

With a growl he launched himself into the air. When he flew, hands became irrelevant. It was the one thing he could do to ease his soul as well as the wound.

During the day, when the caravan was making its slow way west, Envoy Kov had taken to riding at the head of the line with Aethel. This position spared him the sight of Berwynna and Dougie laughing together or talking in the intimate way that only young lovers have. More to the point, it allowed him to question Aethel thoroughly about the countryside through which they were riding. Kov was always mindful of his commission from Garin and the envoys' guild, to learn everything he could about the mysterious, exotic west.

After an eightnight of riding, they left the mountains for a stand of low hills, curving away to the north of them just as Richt's rough map had shown. The rocklands, however, still lay some distance away, or so Aethel told Kov. Directly ahead lay rolling country, grasslands, mostly, crisscrossed by the watershed streams for the Dwrvawr, as he unimaginatively named the central river: the Big Water.

"Now, mark this well," Aethel said. "The rivers hereabout, they be dangerous. Some kind of monster does live in the water. Shallow streams be safe, mind, but any that run over four feet deep or so—go not down to the banks, even."

"Monster?" Kov said. "What kind of monster?"

"I know not, exactly. Never have I seen one clearly, like, myself, though I did see some swimming when I were a good distance away. The local folk do warn us in no uncertain terms. Some furry thing, they do say, very fast and sleek, with huge fangs. It'll pull you under and drown you, then eat you for supper without even the courtesy of spoon and salt."

"I'll be careful, then." Kov was thinking of Garin, rolling his eyes at the thought of monsters. *Beavers, perhaps? Coupled with superstition? Flood waves, brown with mud?* Kov could think of a number of explanations, but he reminded himself to keep an open mind. He was here to learn, not to assume he knew.

The land had flattened out by the time they reached the Dwrvawr. The river lay in a grassy valley, no more than a dip in the land worn away by the placid water. Thick stands of purplish-green reeds grew along the banks, though the water ran fast out in the middle of its channel. A scatter of huge old willow trees grew along its banks. When Kov looked north, he saw what appeared to be fields of some sort of grain, growing tall but still green this time of year. Otherwise grass burgeoned, marred only by a dirt road that led up to the bridge, a ramshackle affair of rough-cut timbers held together with rope and wood pegs on top of wood pilings that slanted at various angles. It reminded Kov more of the skeleton of some long-dead animal than a proper bridge.

"We're going to cross on that?" Kov said to Aethel.

"The only ford be a full day's ride out of our way, and besides, there be those monsters, so cross it we will." Aethel gave him a good-natured smile. "Fear not, Envoy! Never has it dumped us into the water yet."

There's always a first time for everything, Kov thought. Aloud he said, "Well and good, then."

A few yards from each end of the bridge stood a small narrow building like a crate turned on end, made of wattle and daub and roofed in moldy-looking thatch. A tall man like Dougie would barely be able to stand upright in one of them, Kov figured, and only one of him would fit. He assumed that they existed only to provide shelter for the men who collected the bridge tolls. Sure enough, as the caravan drew closer, a short though stocky fellow stepped out of the booth and raised one arm in a signal to halt.

Aethel called out to his mules and men. In a dusty swirl the caravan halted while Aethel dismounted and strolled over to meet the toll taker. Richt signaled to Kov and his party to join the leader on the ground.

"We'll have to lead the stock across a few at a time," Richt said.

Clutching his rune-marked staff, Kov dismounted. The tollman wore not proper clothes, but a strange loose tabardlike garment, two long pieces of brown cloth sewn together at the sides up as far as his chest, then precariously fastened at the shoulders with ornamental pins in the shape of fish. Should he wish, he could have opened one pin then shrugged to send the garment to the ground. He had a narrow face that peered out of a thick white beard and a shock of white hair. For a moustache he had only white plumes at each corner of his upper lip.

Out here in the middle of wild country, coin meant nothing. Aethel opened his saddlebags and brought out a small, thin-beaded knife blade, a packet of steel fishhooks in oiled cloth, and two small glass balls that Kov took for net floats. The tollman fingered each in turn, held the objects up to his nose and sniffed them, then handed back the blade and the net floats. With a sweep of his arm he indicated that the bridge was theirs to cross.

With the toll paid, the men began to lead the mules across, five at a time—safely, despite Kov's fears. Kov followed, clutching his staff in one hand and his mule's halter rope in the other.

On the far side, two white cows grazed, watched over by a naked boy child carrying a long stick. He watched the caravan cross while he scratched his dirty stomach, but he never called out in greeting or alarm. Some hundreds of yards beyond him and his cows stood a huddle of thatched huts, maybe twenty in all, arranged around a stone pillar. Villagers came hurrying out as the last few mules crossed the bridge, and they all struck Kov as being as strange as the toll taker.

None of the villagers came close to the Cerr Cawnen men in height, but they were ordinary-sized men and women, taller than Kov's own Mountain Folk by a fair bit. They looked oddly similar to one another, with their short brown hair, dark eyes, and bushy eyebrows, though their faces showed differences—a sharp nose here, a pronounced lack of chin there, and the like. They all, men and women both, wore the strange tabardlike garment. The little children, however, ran around naked. *Inbreeding*, Kov thought, *I'll wager it's common among these isolated villages.*

"Will we be stopping here to trade?" Kov asked Aethel.

"We will, but not for long. They lack much in the way of goods to bargain with. Dried fish, though—it be handy to have on a long journey."

Kov noticed that some of the villagers carried big baskets of just that commodity. They walked up slowly, gravely, without a smile or a greeting among them. Even the naked children looked solemn; they stood a little way behind their elders and stared at these foreigners while they sucked a dirty finger or scratched themselves. A slightly older girl stood behind one small boy and hunted lice in his hair while he watched the muleteers. Now and then she brought her fingers to her mouth as if she were eating the small game she'd caught.

While Richt led the majority of the mules and muleteers a couple of hundred yards on, mostly to get them out of the way, Aethel and a few of his men unloaded one pair of panniers and laid simple goods out on a blanket—knife blades, needles, net floats, and a few bits of copper jewelry, roughly worked by apprentices in the jewelers' guild back in Lin Serr.

"I wondered why he wanted those." Mic strolled over to inspect the trade goods. "They're cheap work."

"Good enough to trade for dried fish, I gather," Kov said.

"Just." Mic grinned at him. "Barely."

While the haggling went on, Kov decided to have a look at the village. Since it lacked any sort of wall, he assumed that no one would mind him wandering around. Certainly no one stopped him as he walked among them. Some of the huts sat only a few feet from the riverbank, which made him wonder all over again if those reputed monsters were real. A few doors stood open, and when he glanced inside, he realized that these people led poor lives indeed. A stone hearth, a few blankets, some baskets, a spear or primitive bow leaning against a wall—these appeared to be the sum total of their goods.

What truly interested him, however, was not the huts but the stone pillar. It stood some fifteen feet high, a roughly shaped log of granite weathered into a uniform gray, a totally unprepossessing thing except for one detail. Deeply-carved runes, as big as a man's head, graced each side. Kov stared, fascinated, then raised his staff to compare. Sure enough, two of the runes on the pillar matched the pair on his staff that Dallandra had been unable to decipher. He walked all the way round the stone, studying the runes, six in all.

Behind him something hissed like a large cat. He spun around to find a woman, her gray hair streaked with white, her face a fine web of wrinkles, standing with her hands on her hips and glaring at him with narrowed eyes.

"Er, excuse me," Kov said. "Could you perhaps be so kind as to tell me what these runes mean?"

She continued to stare.

"Um, these runes." Kov pointed to the marks on the stone. "What be they? You tell me?"

"I will not." She turned and strode away.

Kov watched her as she joined the crowd around Aethel and his blanket of goods. *Not a friendly sort of crone,* he thought. Some of the men in the crowd turned to look back at him. He decided that he'd best leave the village before someone else took offense.

Just beyond the huts, on the far side of the village from the trading, stood a pair of ramshackle structures much like the tollbooth. Kov walked on through and headed for them, but as he did so, he became aware of the ground under his feet. Like all Mountain Folk, he'd been trained since childhood to stay alert for fissures and possible sinkholes in their underground world. He could tell now that he was walking over a tunnel from the sudden slight sponginess of the ground.

Aha! Kov thought. *Those peculiar cratelike things must protect entrances.* He took a few steps to one side, then walked back, did the same on the other side. As he walked he thumped the butt of his staff against the ground. He could trace out a wide tunnel, well reinforced, and leading straight for the booth ahead. As Kov watched, a naked little boy came out of the booth. He paused, stuck a finger in his mouth, considered Kov for a moment, then ran off into the village.

Beyond the booth stood another stone pillar, sitting between two willows on the riverbank. Kov trotted over to it. Sure enough, it, too, held runes, but in this case, only two, the same two that were carved on his staff.

"Water!" he murmured aloud. "They must mean water, and that's the fifth element. I must tell Lady Dallandra—"

Something grabbed his ankles from behind. Kov yelped, twisted around and struck out with his staff, but the water was roiling with creatures—creatures with brown fur. Clawed paws grabbed and yanked. He started to scream, but he hit the water hard enough to knock the wind out of him. His staff jumped from his hand and floated away.

"Hold your breath!" a voice hissed in his ear. "We be going down!"

Kov gasped and got a deep gulp of air just as whatever it was pulled him under. He flailed his arms, tried to kick, but a second pair of claws caught his wrists. Together, the two creatures pulled him fast along through water laced with streams of bubbles. His lungs ached until he was sure they would explode from the pressure of his hoarded air. Just ahead, the water turned black. He thought he was fainting, but the creatures dragged him into a dark tunnel on dry land and, mercifully, into air. Kov emptied his lungs of the fetid air and gasped for breath, panting. His chest ached as badly as if he'd been beaten.

He heard footsteps slapping along the tunnel and sat up, wishing he still had his staff. A pale blue light grew around him and cast his shadow on the dirt wall. When he twisted around to look, he saw a village man coming with two baskets of glowing blue fungus. His baggy brown garment stuck to his body, soaked with water. Kov turned back, expecting to see that his captors were villagers, too.

Instead, he saw a creature, a brown-furred creature, sleek and wet, about five-and-a-half feet tall, with bright black eyes in its intelligent though hairy face. Its arms—or forelegs—ended in clawed paws. As he watched, it shook itself in a shower of water drops, great silver drops that sprayed from its fur as it spun in a circle, around and around, the drops shimmering like flecks of light, cloaking the spinner, then fading away.

A man stood in the creature's place, a naked man with normal skin, short brown hair, slicked back, and a human face, distinguished by plumed eyebrows and tufts of brown hair at the corners of his mouth. He bent down and picked up a length of cloth from the ground, then tied it round his waist.

"Dwrgi," Kov said, and his voice sounded as feeble as the ancient crone's. "Otters. You. Shapechangers." He stopped himself before his speech degenerated into babble.

The fellow smiled, exposing strong white teeth, prominent in front.

"Clever dwarf," he remarked. "You know too much, you do."

"Just so," the other Dwrgi said. "I be sorry, Mountain Man, but we cannot let you leave. Ever."

Kov scrambled to his feet. "Then I shall face my death with dignity."

"What?" the first Dwrgi said. "Never would we kill you! That be a nasty thing, bain't?"

"What do you think we be?" said the second. "Monsters?"

And they both laughed.

Berwynna was watching Aethel trade net floats for dried fish when she heard a woman start screaming. Everyone in the crowd around the trader spun around to look back at the village. An elderly woman came hurrying toward them, waving her arms in the air, and screaming out a single word: "Gartak, gartak!" Swearing under their breaths the village men ran, racing toward the village, yelling orders back and forth. Berwynna and Dougie followed more slowly. Some of the men ducked into huts and came right out again carrying long spears. Metal points winked in the sun as they ran down to the riverbank.

"What's all this?" Mic, panting a little from the exertion, caught up with Berwynna. "Where's Kov?"

"I ken not," Berwynna said. "I've not seen him since we did cross the river."

"No more have I," Dougie said.

In the village the womenfolk ran back and forth, collecting children, lining them up, counting them, then shepherding them inside the various huts.

"I fear me that gartak means monster," Mic said. "The last I saw Kov, he was walking toward the village."

Berwynna's stomach clenched. When Aethel, who'd stayed behind to pack up his goods, joined them, the first question he voiced was, "Where be the envoy?"

"He didn't go with your men?" Mic said.

"Not that I do ken." Aethel winced and shook his head. "I do hope and pray that he went not near the river."

In the village the spearmen were returning, walking with their heads down, talking softly among themselves. One of them looked up, saw Aethel, and came trotting over. He carried Kov's staff, sleek and gleaming with water.

"We find this floating," the man said. "Yours?"

"It be not mine," Aethel said. "It does belong to Kov, the man of the Mountain Folk." He pointed to Mic. "Like this man, but not this man."

"Ai!" The fellow handed Mic the staff. "Gartak come. We find this. Your Kov, no see."

Mic stared at the staff in his hands as if he doubted its reality. He kept turning it round and round like an axle in his fingers.

"Let's search," Aethel said. "Mayhap Kov did run away, drop his staff."

"We search," the villager said. He turned and called out in his own language to the spearmen, who stood huddled around the stone pillar.

The search went on for a miserable hour or two while Berwynna sat on a pack saddle in the hot sun near the mules. Every time she saw someone approaching, her hope flared, and she'd get up, only to sit down again when the news came that they'd found nothing. Finally Aethel himself came back, followed by Mic, Dougie, and the muleteers who'd been helping them cover the ground around the village.

"It be no use," Aethel said. "Kov, he be dead. I understand it not! Why did he go down to the water? I did warn him. A fine caravan master I be, losing a man to a beast in the river!"

"Here, here," Berwynna said, "it be not your fault."

Aethel saw a small stone on the ground and kicked it so hard that it skipped some twenty feet. Mic walked up next, still clutching Kov's staff. His eyes filled with tears, and with a sob he let them run. Berwynna threw her arms around him and held him while he wept for their cousin. Although she'd not known Kov well, she felt like weeping herself, but even more she felt terrified. For the first time she realized just how dangerous this journey—her marvelous adventure—could become. Dougie, she noticed, was oddly silent, staring at the distant village in something like anger.

Later, after the caravan had moved on to make its grim night's camp beside a forest road, Berwynna asked him why he seemed more angry than sad. They spoke in the Alban language to keep their talk to themselves.

"This is so horrible!" Berwynna said. "Poor Kov, dead! It's just—just—horrible to think of him being eaten by some ugly thing."

"It is that," Dougie said. "But this whole affair smells of dead fish, if you ask me."

"What do you mean?"

"Did I ever tell you about the silkies, when we were back home in Alban? Men on land, but they change to seals in the water?"

"You did. Here, do you think these people are silkies?"

"Or somewhat like." Dougie frowned in thought. "We're miles and miles from any seashore, far as we know. But I saw Kov wander away, and I saw two men follow him. All at once they slipped into the river, and then we heard the crone screeching and carrying on. Gartak? Monsters, is it? They may be that. Mayhap they murder the odd traveler or two, for their coins, like, and mayhap they eat them as well."

"We should tell Aethel."

"Will he believe us? Dare he believe us? He needs their bridge. Your people back in Lin Serr, that's who we'll be telling when we get back there."

"We'll have to come this way again because of that bridge."

"When we do, not a word about this, lass. Just squeeze out a tear or two for poor Kov, eaten by gartak. If they think we suspect somewhat, we could be next."

"Very well, then, not a word."

That night Berwynna dreamt of Kov, laughing and talking during the dinner party back in Lin Serr. She woke to find the stars still out in the crisp dark sky and Dougie snoring beside her. She sat up without waking him and looked over the sleeping camp. One small fire still burned, and beside it sat Mic, Kov's staff cradled in his arms. She wanted to go to her uncle and say something comforting and wise, yet could think of nothing but a futile "It saddens my heart, too." Finally she lay back down and watched the stars, wondering if Kov's soul wandered among them, until she slept again.

His captors had shoved Kov into a small, damp underground room with only a basket of glowing fungi for company and a stout wooden door, barred from the outside, to keep him in. From the smell of the place, previous captives had relieved themselves in the dirt beside one wall. He sat with his back to the opposite wall and wondered if he were going to be allowed to starve to death or perhaps die of thirst. At least, as a man of the Mountain Folk, he was used to being underground in dim light. A Deverry man would have gone mad, he supposed, shut up in a place not much larger than a grave.

After what seemed to him to be most of the day, he heard footsteps approaching with the slap of bare feet on damp ground. Someone lifted the bar and shoved open the door to reveal a cluster of Dwrgi faces, all of them in humanoid form, peering in at him. A young female, dressed in the same odd tabardlike garment as the males, held up another basket of light and looked him over. He crossed his arms over his chest and stared back.

Finally she spoke, at some length, in a language he'd not heard before but which reminded him of the chattering of squirrels and excited ferrets. One of the men stepped forward and pointed at Kov.

"You get up," he said. "We go some place better."

"It could hardly be worse," Kov said.

Everyone laughed, and the female grinned in approval.

"They stop looking for you," the spokesman went on. "Your friends go away now."

Kov did his best to reveal not a trace of feeling. "I suppose they think I'm dead," he said.

"They do. Come with us."

When Kov stepped out of the room, the pack surrounded him. They half-led, half-shoved him through a wide tunnel that twisted, turned, branched off, doubled back, split, re-formed, and twisted some more. The vast majority of people would have been hopelessly lost, but thanks to a childhood spent in Lin Serr, Kov could memorize the entire route. For its last fifty feet or so, the tunnel sloped uphill, ending in a wooden door, reinforced with strips of iron. Along its bottom edge yellow light shone. Kov assumed that they were about to come out into the open air, about half a mile, by his reckoning, from the village.

The door swung back to reveal a blaze of light, but not sunlight. Candles gleamed inside a long narrow chamber. On every wall, in every corner, ornaments glittered and multiplied the light. Gold, most of it: pieces of jewelry, small statues, masks, caskets, coins all gleamed with gold, heaped up on the floor as high as Kov's waist, piled on shelves set into the walls. In among the gold Kov saw precious stones, rubies being the most common. Painted pottery jars, vases, and bowls all overflowed with more gold and gems. As his captors marched him past, Kov got brief glimpses of the ceramics, all of them beautifully decorated with animals and birds painted in realistic colors. The painted masks displayed faces that had to be Horsekin, the same pale skin, manes of black hair, and tattoos.

At the far end of the room, in a plain wooden chair, sat a Dwrgi woman dressed in a long, baggy garment that glittered with golden ornaments, a solid covering of abstract oval shapes, overlapping like fish scales. Beside her chair, in a basket roughly woven of reeds, sat an array of pyramidal crystals, some white, some black, all about six inches high and of a shape to fit comfortably on a man's palm. Despite the nearly overwhelming glitter of so much gold, they struck Kov as important, imposing, even. *Dweomer,* he thought. *I'll wager there's something sorcerous about them.*

As they approached the woman, his captors bowed. Two of the men shoved Kov to his knees at the foot of her chair. For a Dwrgi, her gray hair hung long, reaching to her shoulders in thick curls. Her plumed eyebrows, also gray, had been combed straight up into fan shapes.

"So, you're the captive?" she said to him in surprisingly good Deverrian. "Your name?"

"Kov of Lin Serr."

"Ah, the fabled city! I'm sorry, Kov, but we can't allow anyone to find out about us. They'd hunt us like animals and steal what we've gathered." She inclined her head toward the treasure heaps of gold behind him. "The Evil Ones hide the sun's blood among the dead. We bring it back to the land of the living."

"You'll forgive me," Kov said, "for not knowing how to address you. Priestess and holy one? Queen of great majesty?"

"She who gathers." The woman smiled briefly. "You may call me lady. You'll never learn my name."

"Very well, then, my lady. Who are these Evil Ones? The Horsekin?"

"That's the name that Deverry men have given them."

"I can assure you that I wouldn't tell them so much as the color of the sky. They're the bitter enemies of my people."

"Oh, I know that. I also know that your people love the sun's blood more than anything else in the world."

Kov tried to imagine talking his kinfolk out of looting this chamber. He failed. "How do you know so much about us?" he said.

"I lived with a Deverry clan as a slave for too many years." Her voice turned flat and hard. "They called themselves Boars, and they were all pigs in a sty, sure enough. I can promise you that you'll be better treated than I was."

"Except I can never leave."

"Except for that. And you won't find refuge in a river, like I did." She smiled again. "I suppose they thought I'd drowned. They saw me throw myself in, you see, but no woman ever climbed out again."

"You swam away."

"Of course. Now." She leaned back and tented her fingertips while she considered him. "I use the word slave because I don't know another for a worker who may not leave. But I have work for you that I think me you'll come to love. This chamber holds the gatherings of many a year. Long before I was born my folk gathered. I have daughters who will gather after me. Tell me, Kov, what do you think of our little treasures?"

"They're beautiful and wondrous. I've never seen anything like this chamber."

"Does it fill you with the lust for sun's blood?"

"I could never deny it."

"This is only one of several such chambers in our city. And you're in a city, Kov. It stretches far beyond the ugly little village by the bridge. We build those villages to fool everyone into thinking we're naught but poor savages."

"They do their work quite well."

Lady smiled and leaned back in her chair. "But look at the disarray," she went on. "It aches my heart, as the men of Deverry say, to see the disorder. You're a man of the Mountain Folk. You know the value of these things. You shall bring order into the gatherings."

"Sort them, you mean?"

"Just that, and tell a scribe their worth, piece by piece. I see you as an honored servant, not a slave. You shall have a nice chamber and all the fish you can eat."

"Fish? Only fish?"

"And porridge. We do cook porridge."

"How splendid!"

"I doubt me if you'd like our other foods—worms, leeches, and the like."

Kov felt his face turn cold—no doubt he'd paled.

"I thought not," Lady said. "Well, we'll see if our food gatherers can find fruits and suchlike in the summers for you. Your task will take years, more years than I have left, no doubt, and you and my granddaughters shall finish it. The Mountain Folk live long lives, or so I hear."

"Did your men kidnap me just because I come from the mountains?"

"They did not. They took you because you were measuring out our streets and chambers."

One of the men spoke briefly in their language.

"That, too," Lady said. "And because you were puzzling out the runes in the village. We keep our secrets no matter what the cost."

The cost to others, Kov thought. Aloud, he said, "Has it ever occurred to you to put a fence around your village, then, so strangers can't wander into it?"

Lady stared at him in a wonderment that was nearly comical. "It hasn't," she said at last. "But we shall do so. I believe the gods have sent you to us, Kov."

Kov's first impulse was to assume she was lying about the fence. No doubt they needed an excuse to grab and enslave the occasional traveler. Yet she was looking at him with such a sincere admiration that he doubted his own assumption. None of these people had ever thought to sort their treasures, either, not even to put like with like the way any dwarven child would have done.

"Now that you're here," she continued, "we needed to find important work for you, somewhat much grander than digging tunnels. It's our good fortune that you come from Lin Serr."

"*Your* good fortune, no doubt."

"But not yours?" She laughed, a low chuckle that reminded Kov of ferret sounds. "If you have kin at home, my heart regrets your captivity for their sake. As for your sake, if what I've heard about the Mountain Folk is true, soon our gatherings will become your kin and your love and your life. I think me that in time, you'll be happy here."

She's probably right, Kov thought, *and that's the worst thing of all.* Already he could feel a longing in his fingers to touch the gold, to run his hands through it, to pick up handfuls of it and squeeze it in tight fists. He'd grown up listening to every adult he knew talk about metals and jewels, whether precious gold or cold iron, the rare diamonds or the more common opals and turquoises. He'd learned the lust from them, he supposed, for the treasures of the earth. Lady was smiling at him as if she could read his thoughts.

"I was told," she said, "that the Mountain Folk have a name for gold, what we call the blood of the sun. Is it a secret name?"

"It's not. 'Dwe-gar-dway, the perfection of Earth of Earth.' "

"A lovely name, and I shall remember it. Now, while we prepare the binding ceremony, you'll sleep up in the village. Once it's done, you'll see more of the city."

"Binding ceremony? What do you mean, binding ceremony?"

"Oh, it's naught that will cause you pain, unless cutting a lock of your hair will cause such, which I doubt." Lady smiled in a way that was almost kindly. "Don't let it trouble your heart." She leaned forward in her chair and spoke in her own language.

The Dwrgi pack surrounded Kov again and led him away. The audience had ended. They left the Chamber of Gold through a different door to a different tunnel, which once again twisted, doubled back, and in general became part of a maze. This route, however, did lead up to the ground above and back to the shabby village. Kov's captors led him out into a starry night perfumed with the smell of fish grilling over a wood fire. In the glowing light of the fire he saw the crone who'd first spotted him. She was hunkering down and poking the coals with a stick.

"Food," one of the males said to Kov. "For you, and this hut. We chain your leg."

"Very well."

Kov stopped walking and stood head down, slump-shouldered, as if he were weighed down with defeat. As soon as they stepped a little away, he bolted forward at a dead run. He managed to get some twenty yards before they fell upon him, wrestled him down, and shackled his left leg to a long iron chain.

"Bad slave." One of the men was grinning at him. "Now you eat and not run no more."

Since they fastened the other end of the long chain to a ring in the stone pillar in the center of the village, Kov decided that he might as well sit down and eat. For the time being he could run no more, most certainly, but he had every intention of finding a way to do so, and as soon as possible. He could only pray that he could escape before this mysterious binding ceremony.

Someone handed him a plate of grilled fish fillets, accompanied by a ladleful of porridge, and a thin split of wood to use as a spoon. While he ate, he looked downriver, where he could see the dark bridge looming over the starlight-speckled water like the shadow of some huge monster indeed.

Kov spent a restless night in the hut with only the crone for a guard. The shackle, however, served better than a whole squad of axemen to keep him where he was. Whenever he heard the crone snoring, he would sit up and test the iron band for weaknesses. If he'd had a decent set of dwarven tools, he might have managed to pick the crude lock, but with only a splinter of wood for a weapon, he never managed to defeat it. On each try, the sound of the chain clanking would wake the crone; she would swear at him in a mix of several languages and then sit up, ready to shout an alarm, until he lay down and pretended to sleep.

Eventually he did nod off, only to wake suddenly at dawn to a crowd of villagers just outside his door. They were chanting a loud repetition of six syllables, one of which sounded like a click of the tongue. The crone rose from her blankets and nudged him with a foot in his ribs.

"Up, Mountain Man," she said. "Ceremony is now."

Kov let fly with a few choice oaths of his own. He crossed his arms over his chest and lay where he was. *They can just come and fetch me,* he thought. The crone kicked him again, then stuck her head out of the door and yelled, most likely for help, since three burly fellows arrived and stomped into the hut. They grabbed Kov, peeled the blanket off him, and carried him outside with the chain clanking behind. They laid him down by the stone pillar, then stepped back.

A few at a time, a crowd gathered, standing well back but forming a rough circle with Kov and the pillar in its center. As he considered them and their pinned-together tabardlike garments, it occurred to Kov that they dressed as they did in order to slip out of their clothes and dive into the water as fast as possible. They lived in fear, these people—*like most misers,* he thought. All that gold, heaped up and stored where no one could even see it! Yet, of course, it would be his job to correct that situation, his for the rest of his life, hundreds of years that would warp his very soul. *I will not end up like Otho,* Kov told himself, *not all bitter and greedy, I won't, I can't let myself!*

One of the burly fellows who'd carried him out stepped forward, grabbed him, and hauled him up to prop him against the pillar. Kov considered sliding back down, but the crowd in front of him was parting, murmuring, to let someone through. Dressed in her glittering scales of gold, Lady blazed like a tiny sun in the fresh dawn light.

"Welcome to our river," she said, and she smiled. "Soon you will be one of us, bound to the water as we are."

"Never," Kov said. "I cannot escape you, but I'm a man of earth, and earth will dam up a river when it's stubborn enough."

Everyone in the crowd gasped aloud, and Lady's smile disappeared.

"Think of the gold, Kov," she said. "The gold will be yours as well as ours, you know, for those who belong to a river own the fish in it." She stroked the front of her dress. "We have so much gold, and you shall have a share of it."

The dazzle from the golden scales got into his eyes, and through them, he felt, into his brain. He wanted to touch it, to stroke the dress itself, not the woman underneath, to feel those golden scales under his fingertips. With a shake of his head, he shut his eyes. He heard her chuckle to herself.

"They say that the lust for the sun's blood runs strong in the blood of the Mountain Folk," she said, "and I think they speak the truth."

Kov crossed his arms over his chest and kept his eyes shut. He could hear the dress jingle as she walked up to him, then felt her fingers touch his hair. She separated out a lock; then he felt the sawing of a small knife. The lock of hair came away in her hand, and she stepped back again.

She spoke first in her own language, then in Deverrian. "Look at me, Kov, because what I am about to do with this hair concerns you greatly."

The urgency in her voice opened his eyes. A man in a green tabard was handing her a small glass vial filled with some sort of liquid. When she held it up to the sun, he could see that it was oil. Solemnly she stuffed the lock of his hair into the vial, then stoppered it. The man in green took it from her with a bow.

"Should you try to escape from our river," Lady said solemnly. "I shall burn this hair, and your soul shall burn within you. Better you should stay among us!"

A man in a yellowish tabard stepped forward, bowed, and knelt down. With a small key he unlocked the shackle from Kov's ankle.

"Let the dance begin!" Lady called out.

The villagers answered her call in their own language. Someone out of sight began to pound on a drum; a flute player joined in. All those in the circle began a solemn dance, moving a few steps in one direction, bobbing their heads, then moving back in the other, yet they always moved more steps deosil than widdershins, so that the circle did make progress around the pillar. As they danced, Lady chanted in her own language, swaying back and forth, first calling out, then murmuring softly, moving her hands in the air as if she were weaving some sort of ensorcelment.

It should have been impressive, but Kov was remembering Dallandra, with her beautiful face and cold-steel eyes, picking up his staff and talking about the dweomer upon it as casually as she would have told him that coltsfoot herb would ease dropsy. With as little fuss she could call forth rain out of a clear sky. She would have no need of stamping feet and silly chants to bind a man to her. *There's no true dweomer here!* he thought, *not that I'd better let them know I know it.* At last the music ended, the dancers stopped, and Lady stood smiling at him, her face flushed, her eyes wide under their fan-shaped brows.

"You may have the freedom of our river," she said.

"My humble thanks, my lady," Kov said. "I shall serve you always."

Her grin widened into triumph. Apparently she couldn't tell a lie when she heard one, either. Kov silently worked a small spell of his own, not that real dweomer lay behind it. *Earth is stubborn, earth is slow,* he told himself, *rocks will stop the river's flow.* He now knew, deep in his heart, that the threat to his soul would come not from her and her people, but from the gold itself, all that gold, piled up, glittering, waiting for him like a pouty lover.

"Since I belong to the river now," Kov said, lying solemnly, "I crave a boon. I wish to learn to swim."

"You don't know?" Her smile vanished into a wonder almost comical. "Well, then, by all means, you shall learn! The very best of our young men shall teach you."

"Well and good, then." Kov bowed as low and as humbly as he could. "My heartfelt thanks!"

Learning to swim would take him away from the underground chamber for at least some part of the day. Kov intended to be a slow learner, positively clumsy, in fact, to have access to the sky and air for as long as possible while he schemed out a way to escape, far from the golden treasure's spell.

Laz, of course, had no need of the Dwrgi Folk's bridge. In his hunt for Faharn and his men, he flew over the Dwrvawr a good many miles to the north of the village, where the river ran through a high plateau of tumbled boulders in dry gullies, expanses of patchy brush and dry grass, bordered by hills so sharply ridged that it seemed they'd been cut with knives. An incessant wind blew down from the north, bringing a chill with it at night.

The wind caused him a great deal of trouble. After some days of flying, Laz had gained control of his blunted wings under normal circumstances. As long as he flew with steady strokes straight ahead, or glided on a rising thermal, he could control his motion as well as he always had. Landing, however, or making tight turns presented difficulties. Those maneuvers required a perfect camber that, with damaged wing tips, he couldn't always achieve. He would just manage to get the right angle to land or turn when a gust of wind would tumble him, squawking, from the sky. When he attempted to land, a wind gust would fling him backward. At times he even dropped his sack of belongings, which generally came untied during its fall. He would have to land as best he could, transform back to man-shape, and laboriously pick everything up and repack it with his damaged hands.

After some days of this aggravation he decided to risk the tunnel working. Half spell, half ritual, Laz had pieced it together on his own from hints that he'd found in the ill-fated Hazdrubal's teachings and the *Pseudo-Iamblichos Scroll.* At first he'd had no particular goal in mind, other than his usual curiosity about what would happen if he tried such-and-such a bit of dweomer. In human form, he'd gotten no results worth speaking of. In raven form, when he existed on the etheric as much as on the physical plane, he'd opened a long tunnel to and through the astral to—somewhere. At first he'd not recognized the strange roads he'd opened, misty tracks that led him through landscapes that seemed real but that changed at whim. In the library of the temple of Bel in Trev Hael he'd found a copy of the *Secret Book of Cadwallon the Druid* and at last understood the treasure he'd unearthed by accident.

The mother roads, the fabled mother roads that could take a man or a raven anywhere he wanted to go—they were a prize worth running risks for, Laz had decided. He'd used them to travel to the ruins of Rinbaladelan, then back to the temple of Bel up north of Cengarn. The summer just past, the working had nearly killed him. He'd opened a tunnel above the temple and used it to rejoin his men in the forest. Just as he'd come free, the tunnel had closed behind him with a snap like the jaws of some great beast.

Thinking about his narrow escape still made him shudder. He had no idea why the tunnel had closed so suddenly, very nearly leaving him on the astral. Had he not escaped, he would have died. Worse yet, he might have been trapped on the astral with no hope of rebirth. As he perched on a dead tree, out in the Northlands barrens, remembering the risk gave him pause. He knew now how deadly a dweomer working could turn, when the sorcerer understood only some of its properties.

Yet, in the end Laz decided that the rewards of the mother roads outweighed the risk. They had a peculiar property that made them useful for more than one reason. Since they were driven by thought, they responded to thought. On a sunny morning, once the Dwrvawr and its water veil lay well behind him, Laz opened a tunnel through the higher worlds. He knew that he had only a few moments to travel before his physical body began to dissolve into a stringy mass of etheric forces, so he flapped hard, flew fast, faster, panting for breath, his wings aching, until he saw at last a pale brown meadow, where a dead river flowed in a sluggish stretch of thick silver water. Nearby stood a tree, half of which burned with perpetual fire whilst the other half bloomed green in full leaf. Beyond that tree lay forest, dark, tangled, and forbidding, where he'd never dared venture.

Laz landed on the riverbank to rest and to examine the sack he carried in his talons. It appeared to be whole and unharmed, though he decided to wait to open it to see what had happened to the objects inside until he was safely back on the physical plane. Sometimes they survived these trips; sometimes he found only a strange mass of fibers and a greasy sort of ectoplasmic slime, which tended to evaporate fast in actual physical air, leaving a stink of decay behind it.

As soon as he recovered his strength, Laz pictured Faharn in his mind, brought back every memory of him that he could, and combined them into an image of Faharn, still based on memory. He visualized Faharn's neatly braided mane of black hair, glittering with silver charms in the sunlight, his cornflower-blue eyes that marked him as the member of a clan with slaves among its ancestors.

All at once the image changed and lived: Faharn was standing beside his bay horse, unfastening an empty nose bag from the horse's halter. Laz focused on the image and kept his mind upon it as he hopped up onto his sack. With a caw that echoed, strangely hollow, across the dead meadow, he leaped into the air and flew. The image hovered in the air in front of him, always seemingly just a few yards away, never coming closer, till at last it disappeared into a shimmering silver lozenge of pure force: the gate out.

Laz swooped through the gate and found himself flying over a herd of horses, tethered out in a sparse patch of grass. He circled around and saw below him a scatter of crude tents, a campfire burning, and men, pointing up at the sky, yelling and waving. Voices floated up to him, "The raven, the raven!" With a squawk of greeting Laz circled lower until finally he found Faharn. He dropped his sack at Faharn's feet, then tried to land in front of him. His damaged wing tips betrayed him yet again. He skidded to a halt on his tail feathers, then leaped up with a shake and a croak of rage.

"You're back!" Faharn sounded on the edge of tears. "Feathers and all!" Tears or no, he grinned as if his face would split from it. "Thank the gods! Thank all the gods!"

Laz formed an image of his physical body, transferred his consciousness over to it, and banished the raven. He heard a click, saw a flash of blue light, felt every nerve in his body vibrate, and regained his human form. For a moment he stood dazed, blinking at the sunlight around him. The men—those he could recognize—started hurrying over to greet him. The strangers stayed some distance away, staring, murmuring among themselves. More than once Laz heard someone say "mazrak" in a hushed voice.

"Back, indeed," Laz said. "With many a strange tale to tell you, too. Here, let me get dressed." He knelt down and opened the sack. His clothing had stayed intact and free of the obnoxious ectoplasm. The black crystal, too, lay safely wrapped in rags.

Laz pulled his shirt over his head, then put on his brigga and laced them, a slow process with his maimed hands. When he finished, he paused to look around him. The camp sat in the middle of open land, mostly grass, though trees grew along the streams that wound through it. Stretching off to the horizon were grass-covered mounds of varying sizes, ranging from a mere ten feet or so across to massive artificial hills. They were all too circular in shape for natural features. Some, in fact, looked as if giants had leveled their tops with huge knives, while others peaked like roofs.

"Where are we?" Laz said, pointing. "What are those?"

"First question: about three hundred miles east of Braemel, as close as we can reckon," Faharn said. "Second question: the Horsekin around here, and there aren't a lot of them, call this the Ghostlands. Those barrows are the graves of our ancestors, I suppose. I don't know who else would be buried in them."

"A very good point." Laz flashed him a grin. "And I'd guess that no one's going to look for you out here. Barrows always harbor evil spirits, right? No one's going to come poking around them, therefore."

"That was my thinking, yes. Though I can see how the superstitions got started. There have been times when we've heard things in a barrow, a funny scraping sound, and something else." Faharn paused, then shrugged. "Almost like someone talking. The wind, probably, or the earth shifting inside."

"Probably. Spirits or no, you look well."

"We've done well enough, though the winter was hard. We had some deserters desert." Faharn smiled with a twist of his mouth. "We've lost men since you left us, but then I picked up a few, too."

"So I see. What happened between you and Pir?"

"We split the band between us." Faharn's voice turned flat. "That woman of yours chose to surrender to the Ancients, and he went with her. So did a lot of our men."

"That I know. I scried for them."

"Oh? How much did you see? He's taken your place with her."

"I'm not in the least surprised." Laz fished his belt out of the sack and wrapped it over his shirt. "Pir has always had a way with the fillies."

Faharn hesitated on the edge of speaking. Laz finally got the buckle fastened and looked up to find Faharn staring at him with a peculiar expression.

"You're not angry?" Faharn said.

"It's her right to take a second man, isn't it?" Laz said.

"According to the laws, yes, but—" Faharn hesitated, and he looked oddly disappointed by something. "But it's none of my affair, of course."

"Of course. I'll be her first man still." Laz knelt down again and pulled his boots out of the sack. "What about these new men? I see that some of them are carrying falcatas."

"Deserters, all of them. Can I help you with your boots? I'm guessing those crystals are what injured your hands."

"You've guessed right. No, I can get them on eventually. It's a bit of a struggle, is all. Here, deserters from what?"

"Regiments. They're Gel da'Thae horse warriors. They're more than a little fed up with the direction this Alshandra cult has taken. The rakzanir get more control over the priestesses every day, or so they tell me."

"Oh, do they? Now that's extremely interesting."

Laz got the first boot on, tucked in the brigga leg, then glanced up. Faharn was watching him, his head cocked to one side, his eyes narrow.

"What's wrong?" Laz said.

"Nothing, nothing," Faharn said. "I suppose I thought you'd be angry about Pir and your woman."

"Her name is Sidro, by the by." Laz pulled his second boot on. He tucked his brigga leg into it, then stood up. "And I don't own her any longer."

"Of course not. Sorry." Yet still Faharn hesitated with that peculiar expression on his face.

What is this? Laz wondered. *Did he want her himself?* If so, he'd had an odd way of showing it, back in the forest camp. Laz decided that the problem lacked both importance and interest. He felt perfectly confident that Sidro would always choose him over any other man around.

"Now," Laz said, "what I want to do is head south and find them all, Vek as well as Pir and Sidro, and the others. What will the rest of you do?"

"I'll come with you," Faharn said. "And I'll wager that everyone else will, as well. Ye gods, there's nothing out here! There's no reason to stay."

Some of the men—those from his old band—cheered. The new men nodded and agreed more quietly. Most of them were still wearing their gray regimental shirts, Laz noted, stained with varying amounts of dirt.

Laz spent the rest of that day talking with his band of outlaws, particularly the new men. They'd grown suspicious, they told him, of the convenient visions of a handful of priestesses, the ones that their leaders favored. One of the new men in particular, Drav, was more than willing to explain at some length. He was a hulking, beefy sort, a full-blooded Gel da'Thae with a swagger and a face full of tattoos that marked him as a member of a highly placed mach-fala. He'd been an officer in Braemel's top regiment.

"So," Drav said by way of introduction, "you're a mazrak, are you?"

"I can hardly deny it," Laz said, grinning. "Does that make you want to dispose of me in Alshandra's holy name?"

Drav spat into the dirt. "Better a mazrak than a hypocrite."

"Indeed. Tell me more."

"Look, I never much believed in all this Alshandra talk at first. It was just a way to keep the Horsekin in line and obedient. But then I started thinking, well, maybe there's something to it. The men under my command believed, and it gave them fire and courage. Good enough, think I." He paused, then began to underline his points by stabbing one thick finger into the callused palm of his other hand. "But then the priests got to the rakzanir. First they chased Exalted Mother Grallezar out of town. Didn't like that. Then they started talking about killing slave women to make the Lijik Ganda shit their brigga. Really didn't like that. Then they started running good men onto the long spear just for grumbling about their orders. Couldn't put up with that."

"I see," Laz said. "If you stayed, could you have been raised up on the haft yourself?"

"Pretty damn likely." Drav grinned, exposing pointed teeth. "And all those damned Horsekin, parading around, the stinking bastards. They don't understand discipline. Never will. Resent it if you give them direct orders. Cursed if I'm going to bow and scrape and beg the pardon of a lot of stinking Horsekin."

"I couldn't agree more," Laz said. "How do you feel about the Ancients?"

Drav shrugged. "Never known any," he said, "I'm willing to wait and see if I like them or not. The rest of the men here most likely feel the same."

Since Faharn had managed to steal some extra horses as he'd led the men east, Laz had a mount when they broke camp and headed south. Every morning, however, he assumed the raven form and flew ahead of the band, simply because no one was exactly sure of where they were. Judging direction by the sun's position allowed them to head roughly south and little more. When Laz flew high he could see the lay of the land for miles and choose landmarks that they could sight upon to keep traveling in a reasonably straight line.

The barrows provided many a good mark, but by the second day he saw fewer and fewer of them. By the third day, he realized that they were coming close to the last of the graves. He flew up high, then leveled off, looking to the south. A handful of mounds stood, widely scattered, on the grassland. Off to the east he could see woodland, hazed with blue in the hot sun. To the west, the ground swelled and rose into downs, natural hillocks unlike the barrows. Straight ahead to the south, the grassland began to narrow, caught between the downs to the west and patches of forest cover toward the east. At the far horizon he could just make out a sharp line of intermittent hills, the beginning of the broken tableland and its thick forests and canyons that marked the border between the Northlands and the plains of the Ancients.

Laz flew back to his men, circled low so that they could see him, considered landing, then stayed in raven form. He didn't like the look of the forest just ahead. A stand of old growth, dark and tangled, stretched for some miles. At the edges it bled out into a straggling collection of second-growth saplings and brush among old pines, many of them stunted and twisted by the constant winds blowing off the Ghostlands. All his dweomer faculties seemed to have gone on alert, whispering of danger. He turned toward the east and flew lower, swooping over the trees.

Just at the forest verge he saw a caravan, a merchant caravan, judging by the long line of mules and the heap of pack panniers. Men wandered among the trees, picking up deadfall for firewood. No danger there—Laz flew higher and decided to follow the broad dirt road that wound eastward through the old forest. A few miles on he saw another camp, and the sight turned him cold even as he flew above it in the summer sun.

In the middle of a clearing stood a red banner, tattered, stained with smoke, but bearing the gold hunting bow and arrows of Alshandra. Around it, rolling up bedrolls, saddling horses, and inspecting their weapons, were roughly thirty men. Some wore the brown shirts of a Gel da'Thae regiment; others wore leather tunics, painted with geometric designs—Horsekin warriors. Some wore bandages as well or had an arm in a sling, others seemed unharmed. They all looked sullen, snarling back and forth at each other like men will do when they're hungry and exhausted. Their auras, which the raven could see with his etheric-tinged eyes, clung to them, shrunken and gray with despair.

The horses, some of whom bore wounds, stood head down, already tired out here in the morning, stock that had done the hard work of carrying cavalrymen without a taste of grain. Laz saw no sign of a baggage train, nor could he pick out an officer as he circled high above. They were raiders, no doubt, who'd lost a good stiff fight and were trying to get home.

And what lay just ahead of them on the road? Those merchants, all unknowing, traveling with fat mules and panniers of food and hay, guarded only by men with quarterstaves and one red-haired swordsman. *Well, it's none of my affair,* he thought. Yet something he'd noticed about the caravan made him turn back west to take another look at it. As he flew over it for the second time, he noticed a dark-haired lass, vaguely familiar, among the men. *That couldn't be Wynni,* he thought, *way out here.* Yet the resemblance brought Marnmara's warning back to mind, a warning about atoning for evil done in lives long past. *Which way will you go on the road, Laz.* He estimated that some twenty souls rode with that caravan, and all of them would likely be dead by sunset.

The raven croaked out an oath in his native Gel da'Thae, then turned north and flew as fast he could back to his men. He circled in front of them to make them halt, then managed to land reasonably smoothly near Faharn, who dismounted to come speak with him. Laz transformed back into human shape with a flash of blue light, then hunkered down for modesty's sake. Faharn knelt on one knee to listen.

"Something of interest," Laz said, "a few miles ahead of us I spotted a band of Alshandra's raiders. They are doubtless about to attack a rich-looking merchant caravan that's ahead of them on the road."

"Huh, I'd rather we took that caravan for ourselves," Faharn said.

"Just so." Laz, as usual, had a lie and some half-truths ready. "We can either let the damned raiders exhaust themselves taking the caravan, and then fall upon them, or we can present ourselves as rescuers, in which case the merchants will doubtless share what they have willingly. Your new men are all trained horse warriors, and they're fresh. The raiders I saw look like they've already been beaten once."

"The decision's yours, of course." Faharn considered briefly. "But I'd prefer to save the merchants' arses for them."

"Good lad! I agree."

Faharn smiled and glanced away as if he'd been given a splendid compliment.

"I'm going to fly off and warn them," Laz went on. "Then I'll be back to transform and join you. We've got to hurry, but don't tire out your mounts too badly."

"Right."

In a flash of blue and a quiver of nerves, Laz changed himself back into the raven form. As he flew off, he could see his men following at a walk-trot cavalry pace.

Aethel's caravan had camped that night at the western edge of the forest. Out in the grassy meadows the mules had good grazing, evening and morning. The broad, flat road ahead looked like easy traveling, and, or so Aethel assured Berwynna, there were no more strange villagers ahead. Some hours before noon, the muleteers loaded up the pack animals, those that rode mounted their mules, and they set off westward. Far ahead lay a scatter of trees and a wink of silver that meant sunlight reflecting from water. At the horizon rose a gentle swell of hills, marking the beginning of the downs, Aethel told Berwynna.

"We be still a good hundred fifty mile from home," Aethel said, "but soon, some miles down the road, we'll come to a hill that does mark the halfway point of our journey. It always does gladden my heart to see it, though some say evil spirits do live upon it."

"Evil spirits? Truly?"

"So some say." Aethel winked at her. "I have my doubts."

They'd gone another mile, perhaps, when Berwynna noticed the raven. It came flying fast out of the north, a black mark on the clear warm sky at first.

"Dougie," Berwynna said. "I think that bird's heading straight for us."

"So it is." Dougie shaded his eyes with his hand. "And it's a fair big bird for a raven, too."

About the size of a pony, Berwynna suddenly realized, when the raven swooped down low. The caravan halted in sheer surprise at this impossible sight and turned into a milling confusion on the road as the enormous raven circled overhead. It was cawing in a loud shriek, over and over. Berwynna suddenly realized that it was trying to speak.

"Bandits, bandits! Danger, danger!" she called out. "Be that what you're telling us?"

"Bandits, danger!" the raven called back. "True, true!"

With a last flap of wings it flew away, heading back north. Aethel raised his quarterstaff high and took charge.

"Bring the stock round in a circle! Hobble the mules! Get your staves ready, men! Berwynna, ride into the middle of the circle of mules and stay there!"

The mules picked up the mood of the men. They began braying and kicking as the muleteers pulled the leather hobbles out of pack-saddles and various sacks. One muleteer had to grab a mule's halter and steady it while another fought to get the hobbles on its forefeet. Berwynna's own mount laid back its ears and tried to buck. Dougie grabbed its halter with both hands and pulled it down.

"Listen, lass!" Dougie said. "I can't stay with you if we get attacked. If this blasted animal tries to buck again, you make a fist like this—" He held up a clenched fist. "And hit it hard between the ears."

"I will."

Aethel suddenly yelled, a wordless screech of alarm. Berwynna twisted round in the saddle and looked back at the forest verge just as mounted men trotted out of the trees. They yelled in return and kicked their mounts to a gallop.

"Horsekin!" Richt yelled. "Ah, shit!"

The muleteers left the stock to its panic and rushed to grab quarterstaves. Dougie drew his long sword and ran toward the forming battle line. Berwynna tried to urge her mule in among the others, but it ignored her yanks on the halter rope and swung around toward the danger as if it wanted to see what might happen. All around them the other mules brayed and jostled one another.

The galloping mob of Horsekin slowed to a trot and split in two. Each half swerved off the road, then trotted around, readying themselves to attack the band of mules and men from the sides like two halves of a pair of iron tongs. *We're doomed!* she thought. *They're high up on horseback. Our men are on the ground.* Even Aethel and Richt had dismounted to fight. The bandits paused, letting their horses blow and recover their breath, just long enough for her to get a good look at them—tall men, all of them, carrying curved swords, with huge manes of curly black hair and pale faces covered in bright-colored tattoos. At a yell from their leader they inched their horses forward and began to surround the circled muleteers.

Berwynna's mule brayed, tried to rear, then kicked out. All around her, the other mules began to bray as well, to rear and buck as if they were trying to free themselves from their packsaddles and panniers. The hobbled mules swayed back and forth. One of them tried to kick out with its hind legs only to fall when it lost its balance. The fall, and its anguished brays as it struggled to get back to its feet, broke the last of the herd's morale.

The mules panicked and ran. A few raced down the road, others across the meadow, a few back toward the forest. Most of them, however, charged straight into the gang of bandits on the left. Perhaps in their mulish minds they thought safety lay among the horses. Be that as it may, they disrupted the barely-begun charge from that side of the road.

Yelling curses, the bandits to the right charged. Berwynna's mule kicked out, then joined the panic and galloped straight for the bandit pack. She heard screams and yells rising from the battle in the road as she yanked on the mule's rope with one hand and its mane with the other. She kicked it hard and repeatedly on its right side and finally got it to swerve away to her left just before it reached the bandits, who had finally gotten their own horses under control and were moving forward. Alternately yanking and kicking, she forced the mule back toward the battle in the middle of the road.

What she saw sickened her. Men bleeding, screaming, striking out with staves while the bandits and their swords cut and swung relentlessly—as she watched, Aethel staggered back, his throat pouring blood, and fell under the hooves of a horse. Dougie—where was Dougie? She saw a blade flash up, and his red hair. A bandit screamed and fell from the saddle as the horse buckled to its knees.

More hoofbeats, this from behind her—she turned to see another pack of men, too many, too fast for her to count, racing across the grassland. At the head, someone familiar—Laz! Of all men to be there, Laz! He was yelling orders in some language she couldn't understand as part of the Horsekin mob swung around to face this new threat. Swords flashed up, blood on the blades. A horse screamed with an ugly half-human sound, then fell dying into the road.

At the sight, Berwynna's mule panicked again. When it reared, she hit it between the ears as hard as she could and brought it down. With a bray it broke into a dead run and raced across the meadowlands. She yanked, screamed, could do nothing to stop it. All at once it reared, came down with a jolt, and bucked before she could set herself. She tumbled over its head and fell hard into the tall grass. It leaped over her and raced off.

Berwynna clambered to her feet. Her back ached like fire, but she could see three Horsekin riding straight for her, and from somewhere she found the strength to run. Tripping and stumbling she sprinted through the grass. *Trees,* she was thinking, *if I could only get to the trees.* But the forest verge stood far away, and the three riders gained steadily. Long before she reached it, they caught her.

She heard one yell a single word as they pulled up their foaming horses and surrounded her. One of them, more human looking than the others, dismounted and made a grab at her. She dodged, ran straight into the flanks of a horse, and twisted away, but he grabbed her by the arm with one huge hand. She kicked him in the shins and screamed, kept kicking and screaming as he struggled to grab her with both hands.

The other men began yelling at him, perhaps to hurry, perhaps to just let the lass go, because she could hear other horses galloping toward them. Her captor held on grimly with one hand, yanked her hard and slammed her up against his body. He slapped his other hand over her mouth—his mistake, because she got a good hunk of flesh between her teeth and bit down as hard as she could. Blood filled her mouth and made her gag. He yelped and pulled his hand free. His grip loosened just enough for her to squirm away. She stumbled backward, but as she fell, she kicked up and got him sharply between the legs with the toe of her riding boot. He yelped again and doubled over.

His two companions began yelling at him as the hoofbeats pounded closer. Berwynna just managed to get to her feet before horses surrounded her. One horse rammed into her, but she managed to keep her feet by throwing her arms around its neck and clinging as its head swung down toward her. She could hear men yelling in a mix of languages and see the flash of metal above her. All she could allow herself to think of was getting free of that melee before it killed her by accident. She let go the horse, ducked, dodged, saw a brief opening as a bleeding horse fell to its knees. She raced through it just before another horse closed the gap. She reached open ground and began running toward the road.

"Wynni!" Dougie's voice, a blessed, blessed sound, reached her over the screams and shouting.

Berwynna saw him racing toward her through the grass, his sword in one hand. Behind him a rider was galloping, a Horsekin rider, swinging down with his deadly saber.

"Dougie, 'ware!" Berwynna yelled at the top of her lungs.

Dougie twisted around a moment too late—the saber swung down and caught him full in the back. He pitched forward, and the rider turned his horse and galloped off, heading toward the forest. Yet he never reached it. As he passed one of the few muleteers who was still standing, the man swung his quarterstaff with the full weight of his body behind it and cracked the horse across a foreleg.

The horse went down, tumbling his rider into the road. The muleteer swung again and struck him on the side of the head.

Sobbing under her breath, Berwynna ran to Dougie and flung herself down beside him. He was already dead, his back split open, the spine broken, blood and flesh, so much blood, and a glimpse of shattered bone—Berwynna staggered to her feet to see Laz running toward her, holding a quarterstaff at a clumsy angle in both maimed hands. Out on the road, the battle was over. Men lay scattered across it, dead or dying, both Cerr Cawnen men and Horsekin. Wounded horses sprawled in the dirt or tried to get to their feet. A few hobbled mules huddled together.

Berwynna barely saw any of it. The sight of Dougie's shattered body filled her mind and her eyes. She would see it forever, she knew, no matter how long she might live, at the merest thought or mention of him. It seemed horribly unjust, that all her memories of loving him would be stained forever by that sight. Laz glanced in the general direction of the body.

"Wynni!" Laz said. "For the sake of every god, come away!"

She nodded, let him grab her arm and lead her back toward the road. The survivors from the caravan and the rescuers, Laz's men, she assumed, since he'd brought them, were trying to gather themselves and their wounded. Richt knelt in the dirt by Aethel's body and wept. Two of the muleteers had tied the man who killed Dougie hand and foot; they dragged him along, then threw him down like a sack of offal.

Mic came running toward her, Kov's staff in hand. "Thank the gods," he kept saying, "thank the gods you're safe."

"But Dougie's dead," she said.

"I know. I saw. I thought you'd died with him."

"I wish I had."

"Don't say that," Mic's voice shook badly. "Please don't say that."

"I won't, then."

Laz was giving crisp orders in the strange language that, she abruptly realized, had to be Horsekin. Only then, still stunned as she was by grief and fear, did it occur to her to wonder where Laz had come from. *He just dropped out of the blue sky,* she thought. And remembered the raven. She caught Laz's arm as he walked by.

"That was you," she stammered. "The raven, I mean. That was you."

"You are clever, aren't you?" Laz gave her a lopsided grin. "No time to talk now, alas. We've got to get ourselves out of here. If those bastard swine return—"

He let the sentence hang there.

"True enough," Mic said. "Let me see if I can get Richt back on his feet."

"We can't leave Dougie here," Berwynna said. "We've got to bury him properly."

"We will." Laz turned and looked out toward the meadow. "Faharn took a couple of the men out to fetch him. We'll bury our own dead and leave the others here for my compatriots."

She stared, puzzled.

"The ravens," Laz said. "You're in shock, Wynni. You'll be able to think again in a bit. Mic, do you know who these men were? Gel da'Thae cavalry, that's who. Those tattoos are their regimental numbers and notice: they're wearing identical shirts, all cavalry issue. Not that it matters to our dead, I suppose, but bandits they weren't. This bodes more than a little ill."

"True spoken," Mic said. "Bandits would keep running. Cavalrymen won't."

Laz hurried off. Numbly Berwynna turned toward the meadow and saw a pair of men approaching, carrying someone wrapped in a blanket. A third man was leading a Gel da'Thae horse, unharmed except for a scratch along its neck. While she watched, they slung Dougie's body over the saddle. Something shiny slithered out of the blanket and fell upon the ground. Berwynna ran over and picked up his long-bladed hunting knife.

"We bury sword with lad," one of the men said, "when we can."

"He'd want that," Berwynna said. "My thanks."

His face smeared with blood and tears, Richt had gotten to his feet and stood talking with Mic beside Aethel's body. Six of the muleteers had survived mostly unharmed as far as she could see, and two more sat on the ground, badly wounded and sobbing. One of the men Laz had brought with him was helping two of the unharmed men take the weapons from the dead and dying Horsekin in the road while others were leading captured horses toward the mules. The lone Horsekin prisoner had hauled himself up to a sitting position and watched all this with expressionless eyes. Berwynna pointed him out to Laz.

"That be the man who killed Dougie," Berwynna said. "Bain't?"

"It is."

"I do want a word with him."

"Be careful, now. I know he's tied up, but these swine are dangerous."

"Dougie's knife be here with me."

Before he could say more, Berwynna strode away, the long knife clutched in one hand. *Dougie's never going to hold this again,* she thought. *Or hold me.* Her grief turned into a spear of ice, shoved into the place that once had been her heart.

The prisoner sat on the ground. The muleteers had tied the man's hands together, forced his arms down over his bent knees, then slid a quarterstaff twixt arms and knees to keep him from escaping or causing more trouble. Indeed, the only part of him that he could move was his head. He tipped it back to look Berwynna over with narrow eyes, pale gray eyes that marked him as a human being, she realized, not Horsekin. His hair, crusted with blood from the quarterstaff blow, was a pale brown. A tattoo of a boar, not some Horsekin marking, decorated his left cheek.

"So you be the one who killed him," she said. "My betrothed, that was."

He refocused his gaze on the empty air beyond her.

"You did stab him in the back, you coward!"

Still no response.

"Go ahead, ignore me now, but I'll be having vengeance on your clan for this."

"Oh, will you?" He deigned to look at her. "A lass like you? I suppose you think you can swing a sword."

"There be no need for me to. I'll be begging my father to wipe you and yours off the face of the earth."

"And I suppose your father's some great lord." Contempt dripped from every word. "As if there were any up here."

"He's not, but the silver dragon himself."

He considered her again, his eyes flicking this way and that. "You look human enough to me," he said at last, and he laughed.

Berwynna stepped forward and entwined her fingers in his hair. She heard someone shout, heard men running toward her, but she wrenched his head back and held the knife blade against his throat. He stopped laughing. His pale eyes stared up at her, wide and suddenly wet.

"You bastard scum," she whispered.

With one smooth stroke she slit his throat. Blood sprayed and dappled her shirt sleeve. She let the dead thing go and stepped back with a jerk of his hair to make his head slump over his knees. She wiped the knife blade clean on the back of his shirt, then looked up to realize that she was standing in the midst of horrified onlookers.

"Well?" Berwynna said. "It be no different than cutting up venison, except I always do feel pity for the deer."

Some of the men pressed hands over their mouths as if to choke back curses. Mic, however, merely looked at her, his eyes as calm as if he were contemplating some distant truth.

"He did kill my Dougie," Berwynna said.

The men all nodded, as if agreeing with her unspoken right of vengeance. Mic sighed with a shake of his head.

"You're Rhodry's daughter, sure enough," Mic said. "He's going to be very proud of you when we find him."

"If we do live that long," Berwynna said.

Mic winced but made no answer.

As animals go, mules are the geniuses of the four-legged world, but terror can blunt the finest intelligence. Berwynna's mule, with its halter rope flapping and the saddlebags banging against its withers, ran east until it could run no more. It pulled up, foaming and snorting, in open meadowland only to realize that it was facing yet another terror: being alone with no herd in sight, not so much as a single other mule or horse to join. It stood shivering, head down, until at last it caught its breath and felt its strength return.

It raised its head, sniffed the wind, looked around, and saw a dirt road. It could smell the droppings of other mules, recently passed that way. In its six years of life, it had learned that roads meant men who gave you nose bags of grain, stables in winter, and piles of hay. With a snort it set off walking down the road, though unfortunately, it continued on east rather than turning back toward its former herd.

Between them Laz and Richt got the remnants of the caravan organized. They had six captured horses as well as the nine mules who'd been hobbled in time, those carrying the caravan's food. As they worked, four more mules returned; with their panic over, they had found their way back to their herd. One of the men who'd deserted with Drav had been killed, leaving them his mount and falcata as well. Two of Laz's original outlaws were dead as well, and another had a mangled arm.

Horses or not, with badly wounded men the caravan could travel neither far nor fast. Some miles down the road stood one of the southernmost barrows in the middle of a stretch of open land. Fortunately, it stood some twenty feet high and perhaps a hundred yards across. Boulders and stones poked out from the thin soil on its sides and lay scattered all round, as if perhaps its walls had once been higher. At the top grew a pair of straggly trees, bent and twisted Cerrgonney pines.

"That's someone's grave," Laz said. "A lot of someones, mayhap."

"It be so," Richt said. "We do call it the Ghost House."

"It's also the only high ground for miles. We'll never reach the downs by tonight."

"True enough. Say you we camp on the barrow?"

"I do. Gather up your dead so we can bury them there."

"No need of that. Our folk, when the soul does leave the body, we value not the body at all. The wild things shall have their share of the flesh. Leave them lie with the other dead, out in the open air."

Laz stared. He couldn't decide if he admired the custom or found it revolting, but at the moment it hardly mattered.

"We'll take Dougie, though," Laz said. "For Berwynna's sake."

"Good." Richt shook his head. "Never have I seen a lass such as her. I do think mayhap it be true, that the dragon be her da."

"Oh, it's true. I'll swear it to you, and this is no time for me to be making jests, is it now?"

Richt shook his head again, then hurried off to give orders to his remaining men. They stripped the bodies of Aethel and their other dead comrades, then laid them out in the meadow. Dougie, however, they buried in the side of the barrow when they reached it. Mic helped the muleteers dig a deep trench. They put Dougie's claymore in his hands, wrapped him in his plaid, and laid him in, then began to shovel the dirt on top. Berwynna watched them without speaking or weeping.

"He'll lie with other brave men," Laz told her. "Only the best would have been honored with one of these barrows."

"Just so." Berwynna's voice sounded thick with tears, but none fell. "Tonight I'll be finding me two sticks or suchlike that I may tie together for a cross. He did believe in Lord Yaysoo, and he shall have a cross for his grave." She turned away, and at last she wept, her shoulders shaking as she doubled over. She clapped her hands over her face as if she were trying to shove the tears back inside. "My apologies," she sobbed out.

"What?" Laz said. "Ye gods, tears are the best thing for grief. Weep all you want. They'll heal you."

"Naught will do that."

"Mayhap not, naught but time."

Berwynna sat down on the ground by Dougie's grave. Laz walked away to give her the only gift he could, privacy.

By the time that the men got their improvised camp into some sort of order, the sun was setting, throwing long shadows over the western downs, turning the clouds at the horizon into streaks of blood. Mic, Richt, and Laz walked to the edge of the barrow to discuss their situation.

"Thanks to you," Mic said, "we've beaten them off this time. I wonder if they'll come back to try again."

"I have the horrid feeling that they'll do just that," Laz said. "We have things they need—mules, horses, and food."

"They be able to see us up here plain enough," Richt said. "And when we do leave, there be but one road through this wretched country. They'll be a-following us."

"Roads are where you make them," Laz said. "We'd better find a different one."

"And risk a mutiny?" Richt lowered his voice. "The only thing my men do think of is making a run for Cerr Cawnen."

"How far is it?" Laz said.

"Many a long mile yet. Ten nights away, or twelve, most like, if we want not to kill the wounded men by traveling too long a-day."

Mic sobbed once, then buried his face in his hands.

Laz turned away to allow him to compose himself. *If the muleteers won't follow the raven,* he thought, *they can go on and be slaughtered without us.* On the other hand, it occurred to him, dividing their force might be the worst possible move. In the morning he'd scout, he decided, and see how many of those raiders were left, and if they looked like they had the stomach for another fight. With a shrug Richt left them, striding fast back to camp.

"Well, I have a few more tricks to play," Laz said to Mic. "By now you must have realized that I have dweomer."

"I assumed so. If you can turn yourself into a bird and fly, it's rather obvious."

"So much for my pitiful attempts at deception!" Laz grinned at him. "Let me think about this."

Mic managed a watery smile in return. *I can't do one cursed thing to stave off the ugly fate awaiting us,* Laz thought, *but they don't need to know that now.* As they walked into camp, an odd idea occurred to him: he might be able to ask for help. He'd been an outlaw and outcast for so long, with nothing to fall back on but his wits, that he'd forgotten the simple idea of asking for help.

He had the black crystal. It seemed to be linked to dweomermasters among the Westfolk, and even though they were most likely too far away to reach the caravan, for all he knew someone might be nearby, someone, anyone, better disposed toward them than a pack of Horsekin raiders. That night he took the crystal and sat between the pair of trees. For a long time, while the moon rose and slowly crawled toward zenith, he bent his mind to the crystal and sent out a message of desperation.

He wasn't in the least surprised when no one answered.

All that night Berwynna dreamt about Dougie, that they were back on Haen Marn, sitting among the apple trees and laughing at some jest, or lying in each other's arms up in his chamber. She woke at dawn to a sour reality and a worse fear. Like the men, she was assuming that the Horsekin would return and, this time, win. What would happen to her if they didn't kill her along with everyone else? She decided that rather than find out, she'd fight as best she could to ensure they did kill her. *Maybe Father Colm was right about Heaven,* she thought, *maybe I'll see Dougie again there.* The thought was less than comforting.

Around her the camp was waking in an eerie silence. The muleteers rose and tended the animals without speaking more than a few necessary words. Everyone grabbed their share of the breakfast rations and ate alone, as if looking at their fellows would somehow remind them how doomed they all were. Even the mules and horses ate fast, pausing often to raise their heads and sniff the air, testing the wind for enemy scent. Berwynna took a bare portion of bread and sat down on a rocky outcrop next to Mic to eat.

"Where's Laz?" she said.

"Off somewhere," Mic said. "I wish I'd never let you come with us."

"I came on my own. You didn't let me, so it's not your fault."

Mic tried to smile and failed.

Berwynna left him to his silence and wished she were back home on her island, where they'd always been safe. An island. The thought struck her suddenly, that while she'd not seen a single loch or pond in days, there was more than one kind of island in the world. She stood up and considered their situation from the top of their artificial hill. In the east the forest hid their attackers, but the forest was now a good ten miles away.

"At least we'll be able to see them coming," Berwynna said.

"I suppose so," Mic said, "for all the comfort that is."

"Oh, come now, Uncle Mic! We're not dead yet, and I've been thinking."

He gave her a look of such condescending pity that she decided to keep her thoughts to herself.

Not long after Laz appeared, pulling on a shirt as he climbed up the side of the barrow. When Richt and Mic got up to go speak with him, Berwynna trailed after to hear the news, predictably bad.

"I spotted them, all right," Laz said. "The slime and their swine have regrouped right at the forest verge, but they also seem to be laying low and licking their wounds. I suspect that they're waiting for us to take to the road again. I suggest we don't."

"Easier said than done," Richt said. "If we do turn south, I know not the way. We be lost then, for certain."

"If we keep going west, we'll be dead." Laz sounded curiously indifferent to the prospect. "I counted twenty-four of them, two of whom are wounded. There are seventeen of us, with five wounded. They have sabers, and they all know how to swing them. Your men have never touched a saber or a sword in their lives. Do you like those odds?"

"Of course not," Mic said. "Very well, I'll present the idea of turning south to the rest of the men."

"You be not in town council!" Richt stepped forward. "Present it? I be master now, and I'll tell them."

"But will they listen to orders?"

"Oh, and I do suppose you know my craft better than I do?"

"Stop it!" Berwynna snapped. "You both be a-feared, but bickering will get us nowhere. There be somewhat else we can do. There be many a rock all round here. What if we do build a wall around our camp? The Horsekin, they would have to climb the barrow, then climb over the wall. While they try, it will be lots easier to kill some."

"Splendid idea!" Laz said. "They seemed to be in no hurry to leave their camp. When I left, they were roasting one of your mules, the bastards, or large chunks of it to be precise, over various fires. I suppose half-cooked mule is better than naught for breakfast."

"We do have higher ground than them, anyway, bain't?" Berwynna finished up. "Dougie did always say that it makes a difference in a fight, who be higher."

Richt and Mic stared at her for a long moment.

"Well?" Berwynna said.

"You are, of course, precisely right," Laz said. "We can also cut branches, sharpen them into stakes, and set them around on the level ground at the edge of the barrow, which means my disgusting compatriots will have to dismount and pull them up if they want to ride up."

"We can throw rocks at them if they do try," Berwynna said. "If we do hit a couple of them in the head, they mayhap will have to stop. And two of the muleteers do have hunting bows."

"So do some of my men." Laz gave her a lazy grin. "This might be almost entertaining."

"Huh!" Mic snorted profoundly. "Richt, my apologies."

"And mine to you," Richt said. "Very well. Let's go tell the others."

Giving demoralized men hope has something of the dweomer about it. The muleteers and the men in Faharn's band worked so hard and so fast that soon their improvised dun wall rose to four feet high. In the morning, Berwynna filled every available container with water from the nearby stream and piled them up in the center of the circle. In the afternoon she fetched small rocks that could be used for weapons. By firelight the men sharpened branches into stakes. As Berwynna tore up a blanket to make bandages, she found herself thinking of Dougie. Her eyes would fill with tears, but she would wipe them away and go on working.

With the first light of dawn some of the men pounded the stakes at the perimeter of the wall in a random pattern while others led the stock out to water and graze. Laz once again disappeared, then returned with the news that the raiders were just breaking their own night's camp.

"We've got a little while more," he said. "Enough to put another round of stones on our wall."

"I wonder if they'll send out a scout first?" Mic said.

"If so, our position should give him somewhat to think about." Laz paused, sniffing the wind like a horse. "Well, all we can do now is wait."

Berwynna glanced at the sky. The sun had climbed halfway to zenith.

Some days previously, Rori had flown to the edge of Horsekin territory, a wide stripe of grazing land that bordered on the tundra and ice of the far north. He'd seen horse herds guarded by small encampments, a pitiful few signs of life dotting an empty expanse. Since he'd always heard the Horsekin described in terms of large numbers—the Hordes, indeed—he found the emptiness puzzling.

When he flew south again, taking a different route, he discovered the reason. A long column of some two thousand riders, wagons, and extra horses was trudging along, heading to the south and west. He flew low enough to take a good look at them. While he saw mounted warriors riding guard, the majority of the travelers seemed to be women, children, and slaves. Blankets and animal skins covered the crude wagons, which, judging from the lumps under the lashings, looked full of household goods and supplies.

A migration, then, they were continuing the gradual move south of the Horsekin that had led to the overthrow of Braemel and Taenbalapan. But where did this group intend to settle? Rori's understanding was that the land around those two Gel da'Thae cities had already received all the immigrants it could support.

That night, when they made camp, Rori amused himself by swooping down and scattering the horses, which they'd foolishly neglected to hobble, then took a turn over the camp, high enough to be out of range of their bows and throwing spears but low enough to determine that the warriors were indeed northern Horsekin. Their officers, however, looked like well-armed and disciplined Gel da'Thae. These tribes, then, were certainly heading south at the request of the rakzanir who ruled the mountain cities. It was possible that they meant to found a new city, perhaps even around that fortress he'd seen a-building earlier in the summer.

Potentially this movement of peoples represented a threat, but there were far too many of them for one dragon to rout. Rori caught and killed one horse for his supper, then headed south to find a place to eat in peace and lair for the night. Over the years he'd become used to raw meat, but that night, chewing on cold horseflesh, stiff with rigor, made him remember feasts he'd attended in the past, where roast meats graced every table and the smell of fresh-baked bread perfumed the air. Sweeter than the food was the company of fighting men like himself, or as he'd been back then, drinking and laughing, enjoying every moment of the lives they were wagering in a long gamble against the Lady Death. Bard songs and warm fires in winter—they haunted his dreams that night.

In the morning, when he woke, Rori put those thoughts out of his mind. With a roar, he sprang into the air and flew onward toward his rendezvous with Prince Dar.

Toward noon he left the northern foothills behind and flew over the barrow fields. Far ahead, where the tablelands began, lay a natural stone spire that was directly north of Twenty Streams Rock. He was planning on heading south once he reached that landmark, but something nagged at him. *Turn east,* the nag seemed to say. *For the love of every god, turn east.*

The sun had reached zenith by the time Rori surrendered to the nag and turned east. He passed over patchy forests and shallow streams, winking silver in the sun. In but a few miles on, he saw the tiny figures of mounted men at the forest verge. They were lining up in a rough marching order around a tattered red banner bearing Alshandra's holy bow and arrows. He dropped lower, smelled Horsekin, and roared to the attack.

Down he plunged, wings folded, until at the last moment he swooped upward, flapping hard, twisting this way and that to avoid spears or arrows that never came. When he leveled off and looked down, he saw riders on the ground and horses galloping off in all directions. A rider clung to the back of one panicked warhorse heading east down the road. Rori stooped like a falcon and struck, sinking the claws of one paw into the screaming rider. He rose high, shook the paw, and watched the Horsekin plunge howling to his death. The rest of the men below ran, rushing for the cover of the trees.

That will give them somewhat to brood over, he thought, *them and their cursed Alshandra!* He swung wide to turn toward the south and Cengarn, but as he did, he spotted what appeared to be more horses farther off to the west. With a smooth heft of one wing, he swooped back. Below him he saw a large, flat barrow, further fortified with a ramshackle stone wall and guarded by a ragtag group of human beings and a pair of dwarves. He was willing to wager that he'd found the Horsekin's prey.

He adjusted his wings to glide down lower and circled around the hill, far enough away to avoid panicking the horses and mules tethered in the midst of the defenders. He was planning on calling out a greeting, but one of the dwarves got in before him. At Rori's distance the voice sounded thin and faint, but he recognized it.

"Rhodry! It's Mic! It's Mic! Help us!"

"Mic!" Rori called out. "Ye gods! Here, I'll land!"

The entire mob inside the wall answered him with a roar of cheers. Rori glided past, turned to the west, and settled on the road downwind of the improvised fort. Mic, who'd grown stout over the years, came puffing down, staff in hand, to join him. The other dwarf followed, dressed in baggy shirt and brigga. She, Rori was startled to realize, was not a man of the Mountain Folk at all, but a young human woman with a long knife clutched in one fist. Her hair was dark, and her eyes cornflower blue—*Eldidd coloring,* he thought, *but all the way up here?*

"Mic it is, indeed!" Rori sang out. "And here I was a-feared you and Otho had been slain by Horsekin. Long years ago now, it was."

"Naught of the sort," Mic said, grinning, "but Otho's gone to his rest, slain by old age and naught more. I cannot tell you how much it gladdens my heart to see you."

"No doubt. Did you know there were Horsekin raiders on the road behind you?"

"Know? They attacked us once already, and it's a marvel that any of us are still alive."

"Then it's a good thing I scattered them." Rori allowed himself a long rumble of laughter. "They won't be following you any longer, I'll wager."

Mic's eyes filled with tears, but he grinned, then turned to call out the good news to the others still in the improvised dun. Rori took a good look at the lass. The calm way she looked back and the wide set of her eyes, her short but sturdy build, reminded him of someone—of Angmar, he realized suddenly.

"Here," Rori said in as gentle a voice as he could manage. "Do you come from Haen Marn?"

"I do," she said. "You be my father, or so I were told. I be

Angmar's daughter, one of them, for we be twins, Marnmara and me. My mam be well, though truly she were fair taken aback by the news that you be a dragon now."

"No doubt." Rori found himself unable to say more.

"Ah, indeed, this is Berwynna," Mic said, "and truly, she's your spawn, no doubt about that! Ye gods, we've got so much to tell you. And you to tell us, no doubt."

"Such as how I came by these wings?" Rori recovered his voice with a gulp and a snap of fangs. "Here, I don't dare go any closer to your mules and horses. As long as I'm with you, the Horsekin aren't going to attack, so you can leave them inside that wall and camp outside of it."

"Well and good, then," Mic said. "I'll go tell the others."

The dwarf hurried back up the hill, leaving Rori alone with this strange lass, his bloodkin. She was a pretty little thing, he decided, but nothing about her struck him as delicate. She stood with one hand on her hip, the other holding the dangerous-looking knife at an easy angle.

"Da," she said, "you be hurt! That thing on your side—"

"—is an old wound. I have hopes that it will heal soon."

"Be there somewhat I can do for it?"

Rori was about to dismiss the offer, then remembered that she had hands. "There is," he said. "When we find willow trees, you can brew me up a medicine from the bark, if you'd be willing."

"Of course I be willing." She smiled at him. "I be your daughter, after all."

Her smile reminded him of Angmar's. The resemblance acted like a spark in the dry kindling that had become his heart over the years. He remembered how it had felt to love a woman, one like himself as he'd been then. The blood of two races ran in their veins, dwarven and human for her, elven and human for him. They had each lost other loves. They had understood each other's sorrow when they'd met and found a way to assuage it for a little while. Now here was their child, considering him gravely, as small in relation to a dragon as a hound would be to a human.

"It gladdens my heart to meet you." Rori made his voice as quiet as he could. "But what, by all the gods, are you doing out here in the middle of this blasted wilderness?"

"Looking for you." Suddenly she turned away, and tears choked her voice. "My betrothed, he were with me, Da, but the Horsekin, they killed him."

"Oh, did they now? Don't trouble your little heart, Wynni. We'll have our revenge."

She turned back, and through her tears she smiled. "My thanks," she said. "That eases my heart somewhat."

"Good. Now, here, I'll take you and Mic back to the island. You'll be safe there."

"And desert the caravan? I can't do that."

Her soft words struck him like a blow. Had he really been thinking of leaving all those other men to the mercy of the Horsekin? *Dalla was right,* he thought. *I stand in danger of losing my human soul.*

"No more can I," Rori said briskly. "Just a passing thought. We'll get everyone safely to—where were you all going?"

"A place called Cerr Cawnen," Berwynna said. "I know not where that be."

"A good long ways ahead of us, that's where, at least a hundred miles away, maybe two."

Berwynna said nothing, but her mouth slackened, and her eyes filled with tears. With a little frown she wiped her eyes on her sleeve.

"Then we'd best start soon, hadn't we?" she said.

"I like your spirit, lass, but I've got a better idea. Let me talk with Mic and your caravan leader. If we head straight south, we'll reach safety far sooner. Have you ever heard of the Westfolk?"

"I have." She started to say more, then choked it back. A look he could only call terror flitted across her face.

"What's wrong?" Rori said.

"Naught." Her bright smile came back, but he noticed the knife trembling in her grasp. "I just be so weary, Da, and so sad, too, thinking of my Dougie dead and gone."

"No doubt! Well, the prince of the Westfolk sent me off to scout for Horsekin. I'm to meet him at a place called Twenty Streams Rock, which is—" He paused to work out how long the journey would be for a caravan rather than a dragon. "Well, five or six days away rather than thrice that number. I'll escort you there, and then we'll decide what to do next."

"My thanks." She walked over to him and with her free hand stroked him on the jaw. "I always did think I'd run to my da's arms one fine day."

"At the moment I don't have any, alas. But here, don't look so distressed. Someday mayhap I'll become a man again. There are powerful sorcerers among the Westfolk, and they tell me that they might be able to discover how to reverse the spell."

Berwynna flinched, looked away, looked back, then suddenly turned and ran back to camp. As she climbed the hill, she passed Mic and a Cerr Cawnen man, who came on down to greet him. Mic introduced the fellow as Richt, the new caravan master.

"My master in the craft, Aethel," Richt said, "he be dead, alas."

"That saddens my heart to hear," Rori said. "Now, I owe you my thanks for saving my daughter's life."

Richt made an odd noise, half a laugh, half a yelp of terror. "Ye gods!" His voice shook. "It be true, then. Our Berwynna, she be a dragon's spawn."

"Not precisely," Mic said. "I'll tell you the tale later. For now, I'm more interested in what we're going to do next."

In her grief over Dougie and her terror of Horsekin raiders, Berwynna had quite simply forgotten about the dweomer book. While Richt and Mic conferred with Rori, she ran back to camp. She noticed Laz's men standing in a tight knot between the two trees with Laz in the center of the group. They were arguing about something, but she couldn't understand a word of their language. They ignored her, as did the muleteers from the caravan, even when she began searching through the pack panniers, hoping desperately that her saddlebags had turned up on one of the returning mules. She never found them.

When she asked the muleteers, none of them had seen a pair of tan leather saddlebags with dwarven runes upon them. She went through every pannier and sack again—still nothing.

The mule she'd been riding had galloped off into the wilderness and never returned. She forced herself to admit that the magical book, which may well have been her father's only hope of returning to human form, had disappeared. *And I'm to blame,* she thought. She knelt in the dirt among scattered packsaddles and panniers and cursed herself. Why had she taken it? Why? It could have been safe on Haen Marn instead of wandering through the wilderness on the back of a panicked animal.

Wolves would doubtless find the mule and pull it down to eat it. The book would be lost forever. In sheer frustration she began to weep. When she heard someone walk up behind her, she twisted around and saw her uncle, looking at her sadly.

"Ai, weeping again?" Mic said in Dwarvish. "Mourning your Dougie, no doubt! Ai, my poor little lass!"

"Worse." Berwynna scrambled to her feet. "Uncle Mic, I've got to go hunt for my mule, the one I was riding, I mean. I had my saddlebags on the saddle, the ones Grandfather Vron gave me, and in them—"

"No!" Mic shook his head vigorously. "You are not going out there, whether it's alone or with a guard. Wynni, we've got to get out of here."

"But Da's here to protect us—"

"He can only do so much. For all we know, there's a whole army of Horsekin around here somewhere. We've got to get off this road and start south today."

"But I had—"

"Hold your tongue!" Mic laid a heavy hand on her shoulder. "I won't hear it. You could be killed out there. Ye gods, you nearly were! Those men who tried to grab you—do you want to end up raped and a Horsekin slave?"

"No, no, of course not."

Now was the moment, Berwynna realized, that she should confess, tell her uncle that she'd taken the book and lost it again. *But no one else knows,* she thought. *Maybe I'll never have to tell Da or anyone else.* Yet such would be a coward's trick, she realized, one unworthy of her Dougie's gift.

"Wynni, are you listening to me?" Mic said.

"What? I'm sorry, Uncle Mic. What did you say?"

"I said, here come the men to load the mules. Come along, let's not get in their way."

Mic grabbed her hand; she pulled free.

"You don't understand," Berwynna began. "Do let me explain."

"Here, what's all this?" Laz walked up to them, with his men close behind him. They walked warily and kept their hands on the hilts of their weapons. When they formed a half circle behind him, some of the men turned around to keep watch, as if they expected another attack at any moment. The man called Faharn stood next to Laz and glowered like a winter storm.

"Wynni," Laz said, "I know your heart aches for your Dougie, but—"

"It be not only Dougie!" Berwynna drew herself up to her full height, not that it amounted to much over five feet. She spoke in the Mountain dialect so Laz could understand her. "It be the book, that book with the dragon on it, the one Dougie did bring to Haen Marn. I did carry it in those saddlebags, and now it be gone."

Laz did the last thing she would have expected: he laughed. "So you did steal it," he said, "and here I thought Mara had just mislaid it."

"I did, and I know not why. It were sitting on a bench among the apple trees, and somehow I did feel there were a need on me to have it. It did will me to pick it up."

"Wynni!" Mic said with a groan. "Be honest, now! Books don't will people to do things."

"Oh, I wouldn't say that." Laz's mood changed to the utterly serious. "I've had that experience myself, with things that had dweomer upon them."

Berwynna felt a thin sliver of hope that she'd not disgraced herself. "Be that true?" she said.

"Very true." Laz held up his hands with their stumps of fingers. "This is the result of listening to a pair of wretched dweomer crystals. The book might well have influenced you. I know that the wretched thing could move itself."

"It what?" Mic's voice turned feeble. "That's impossible."

"But, Laz," Berwynna said. "There be no dweomer in my soul."

"Very true. That's what makes you so vulnerable to it. Mic, that book is crawling with guardian spirits. I've no doubt they could move the thing and bend Wynni to their will. The only question is why they wanted to." Laz frowned, thinking. "Well, here, let me scry for it."

Laz turned a little away. Berwynna could see the change in his face: a slackness, a loss of focus about the eyes. After a moment he shrugged. "I suspect it's still in the saddlebags. All I see is a vague impression of darkness. How were you carrying it? Did you have those oiled wrappings around it?"

"That, and one of my dresses." Berwynna felt like weeping in frustration. "I did wish no harm to befall it."

"Alas, unless someone finds it and opens the bundle, I'm blind to it."

"What about the mule? Could it be that you can scry for it?"

"I never saw your mule, so I cannot. But don't be too harsh on yourself, Wynni. For one thing, we don't truly know what was in the wretched book. For another, its spirits were in charge, not you."

"My thanks. Yet my heart does ache with shame—"

"Tell your heart to hold its tongue." Laz flashed his knife-edge grin, but she saw no humor in his eyes. "Mic's right about one thing. You've got to get this pitiful excuse for a caravan moving again." He hesitated, then shrugged. "As for me and my fellow outcasts, we'll be leaving you."

"What?" Mic said. "Why? Are you daft? Those Horsekin outnumber you."

"It's the dragon," Laz said. "He hates me, you see. I don't know why, but he does, and he'll kill me. My one chance is to try to slip away. I've told my men that if he comes after me, they're to run like the hells are opening up under them. There's no reason for them to perish miserably with me."

Berwynna spun around and looked for her father. A good distance away, Rori was sitting on his haunches like a giant cat, his tail curled around his forelegs. He was looking off to the east, most likely watching for their enemies.

"But the Horsekin!" Mic repeated.

"We'll have to take our chances with them," Laz said. "I don't suppose any of us will be much of a loss should they catch us, after all, since we—"

"You saved our lives," Berwynna interrupted. "Let me go talk with him."

Berwynna took off at a trot before Mic or Laz could stop her. She ran to the edge of the barrow, scrambled down the side, and hurried over to the dragon. He lay down with his front legs stretched out in front of him and lowered his head to speak with her.

"Is somewhat wrong?" Rori said. "You look troubled."

"I be so," Berwynna said. "Da, you do know that we did nearly die, all of us, when the Horsekin did attack the caravan."

"I do, truly. And?"

"Know you why I didn't die?"

"I don't, though I was wondering about that."

"Some Horsekin, they nearly did capture me. I did fight and nearly get free, but in the end, they would have taken me. There were three of them, and I were cut off from our men. But just then, rescuers did ride up, men we'd not seen before, men who be outlaws among the Gel da'Thae because they worship not the demon Alshandra. They did ride and fight and save us, but two of them, they were slain, Da. They did give their lives to save mine and Uncle Mic's and the rest of the men, just like my Dougie did die fighting to save us."

The dragon opened his massive jaws in surprise. "By every god," he said at last, "then those men are heroes to me, outlaws or not. I wish I had some splendid boon or gift to give them, but alas! All those old tales about dragons having treasure? They're not true."

"That does ache my heart, Da. But truly, there be a boon you could grant them."

"Indeed? And what might that be?"

"I do fear to ask for it, lest you say me nay. There be danger in the asking, you see."

The dragon rumbled with laughter. "Wynni," he said, "I'm as sure as I can be that you're my daughter. You're as crafty as a dragon hatchling, aren't you? You want me to promise this boon before I hear what it is."

"Well, that be true, Da." Berwynna heaved what she hoped was a pitiful sigh. "The boon, it would cost you so little."

"Oh, very well." Rori paused to rumble again. "I hereby most solemnly grant your boon."

"Da, you be so wonderful!" Berwynna would have thrown her arms around his neck, but they would have reached a bare quarter of the way. "I always did dream that my father would be so grand."

"Enough flattery, hatchling! What's this boon?"

"There be a Gel da'Thae man with us named Laz Moj. He does tell me that you hate him, and he fears you would slay him on the spot. Please, Da, he did save my life and Uncle Mic's. Please don't harm him."

"Laz Moj?" The dragon's silvery brow furrowed. "I don't recognize the name."

"He be a mazrak, a raven mazrak, from here in the Northlands."

The dragon growled, a huge sound like a hundred dogs. Berwynna stood her ground and laid a gentle hand on his jaw. When she stroked him, he stopped growling.

"Of all the wretched dweomermen in the blasted Northlands," Rori said, "it would be him. It's a good thing you wheedled that boon out of me."

"But, Da, you'll not kill him, though, will you?"

"He's safe from me. I gave my word, and I promised you a boon, and you shall have it. Huh! You remind me of another sister of yours, one you've not met. Alas, you won't meet her, either, because she's gone to the Otherlands. Rhodda, her name was, and she could charm anything out of me when she was a little lass." He growled again, but it was a wistful sort of sound. "It's just as well you can't join forces against your poor old father."

"Poor old father? And you a dragon?"

"I wasn't a dragon back when Rhodda was young, and it's a pity, too. She might have been more tractable."

Berwynna felt a cold touch of regret, that she'd never be able to meet this sister. She'd just found out that Rhodda existed only to hear that she was dead. *Just like Dougie,* she thought, and to her horror the memory picture of his broken body rose again in her mind.

"Here!" Rori said. "What's so wrong?"

"I did just remember how the man I did love so much died." Berwynna gasped for breath and managed to choke back her tears. She refused to let her father see her weep. "I'll be going back to camp and telling Laz that he be safe from you."

When Berwynna climbed the barrow wall, she saw Laz and his men saddling their horses. She ran over to them and caught Laz by the arm.

"It be safe," she said. "He did promise me that he'd not slay you, Laz, because you did save my life and Uncle Mic's. So don't leave."

Laz stared at her.

"When I did ask," Berwynna went on, "he did grant me a boon, that he'd not harm you."

Laz laughed, one good whoop of laughter, and shook his head in amazement. Faharn stepped forward and spoke urgently in their language. Laz shot him a disgusted glance and answered in the same.

"He's telling me I shouldn't trust you," Laz said to her. "By the black hairy arse of the Lord of Hell, I owe Haen Marn too great a debt to go around accusing its daughter of lying to me. Very well, Wynni. Let's go talk your father. He needs to know that the book's gotten lost, and since he's promised not to harm me, I'd best be the one to tell him. Don't say one word about it until I do."

"Laz!" Faharn snapped in the Mountain dialect. "Be not a fool!"

"That advice comes too late," Laz said. "Let's see, I was born some thirty years ago now, and so it's thirty years too late." He laughed again, and his eyes gleamed with excitement. "Let's go, Wynni. I want to see if your father keeps his promises."

Faharn began talking fast in their language, but Laz slipped his arm through Berwynna's and marched her off across the barrow with Faharn trailing miserably after them. The dragon lay where Berwynna left him, waiting for them. When they climbed down from the barrow, Rori raised his head and growled, but only faintly.

"So," the dragon said. "You're the mazrak, are you? Laz Moj, is it?"

"That's my name, truly," Laz said. "May I ask why you've always hated me? I honestly cannot remember ever doing you harm."

The dragon considered him for a long cold moment. "Mayhap you don't," he said at last. "But I do. Listen to me, Laz Moj. I made my daughter a promise, and I'll keep it as long as you treat me and mine as well and faithfully as you'd treat your kin and clan. But if you ever do me or mine the least bit of harm, then the promise ends. I'll crush you without a moment's thought." He lifted one clawed paw from the ground. "Do you understand me?"

"I do, most decidedly." Laz took a step back. "I promise you I have no intention of doing them any harm." He held up his maimed hands. "Do you see these? Berwynna's twin healed them. Your woman Angmar gave me the shelter of her hall. I owe them and, through them, you a great deal of gratitude. Doing them harm is the farthest thing from my mind."

Rori slapped the ground with his tail, then switched it back and forth like an angry cat. "Good, but you don't know who else I consider mine. Prince Dar and his royal alar, indeed, the Westfolk, all of them—not one small bit of harm, Laz Moj, not by dweomer, not by the sword, not at all, naught, nothing." Rori thrust his huge head forward. "Do you understand that?" His upper lip curled to show fang.

"Ye gods, I've never even met these people! Why would I harm them?"

Their gazes met and locked. The dragon's tail slapped the ground again as if it had a life of its own. Berwynna felt afraid to so much as breathe as they stared at one another. He was terrifying, her father, when he wanted to be. Somehow she'd not expected this when she'd longed to find him, that in an instant he could turn so frightening, so wild. With a toss of his head and a half-turn of his body, Laz looked away at last.

"Good," Rori said softly. "I think me you do understand."

"I do," Laz said. "I understand in the marrow of my soul, albeit that marrow's more than a little frozen at the moment. In terror, that is."

Rori laughed, his deep good-humored rumble. Laz took a deep breath and managed to smile, then turned to Berwynna.

"Wynni," Laz said, "you have my undying thanks for this."

"You owe her your life," Rori said, "just as she owed you hers. The debt's been repaid. Remember that."

"Oh, fear not! I shall."

"Good." The dragon lurched to his feet. "Now that we understand each other, Laz, you'd best get your men and what's left of that caravan on the road. Richt knows where we're heading. We can talk more later. I'm going to go look for those Horsekin now, so both of you, get back on the barrow. These wings can knock a man over when I take flight."

Berwynna opened her mouth to ask about the book, but Laz caught her eye.

"Come along," Laz said. "We'll talk more tonight, just like your father wants. I agree that we need to get on the road. We're giving you a horse to ride, Wynni. It wears a thing called a bridle, and you should be able to control it."

"I be glad to hear that," Berwynna said. "Not that I know how to ride."

"You'll learn," Rori put in. "You have to. Now go, both of you!"

Rori waited until Laz and Berwynna had gone a safe distance away before he took to the air. He soared high over the barrow and the camp, then turned and headed back east. He saw no sign of the Horsekin raiders on the road except for tracks leading into the forest. When he flew over the trees, he used the road as a guide, still saw nothing, then began to swing back and forth at angles to the road. In the thickest part of the forest, hiding among the old-growth trees, he could just make out a few large shapes that might have been horses.

He dove and flew so close to the treetops that they shook and dropped leaves. When he roared, he heard the panicked neighing of horses and the braying of mules answer him. Men shouted to one another. Although he heard animals moving in a rustle of underbrush and a crack of breaking branches, nothing broke free and tried to run. The Horsekin must have tied and hobbled their stock.

He took another turn over, looking for a spot where perhaps he could break through the canopy or even knock down a few of the smaller trees, but the raiders had chosen their hiding place well. Old-growth timber stood like a dun wall around and over them. And what if he reopened that wound in an attempt at breaking through? He roared a second time. Again he heard panic, but again, their discipline and their ropes both held, keeping them and their animals beyond his reach.

The third time he roared it was out of sheer frustration. He flew up high, turning to wing away from the forest. He would go back to the barrow and wait there for a while, he decided, then swoop back to see if they'd foolishly left their improvised lair. He badly wanted to kill something, to release all the rage he felt at the very thought of Laz Moj, kept as safe by his promise to Berwynna as the Horsekin were by the forest.

As soon as he'd seen the man, Laz's image had wavered and blurred into three images, shifting from the sharp-faced man in front of him to Lord Tren to Alastyr, the vilest of them all in his fused memories. It had taken his entire will to refrain from raising one huge paw and killing him on the spot.

And all because of his newfound daughter and her begging that boon—although, as he thought about it, Dallandra as well had spoken to him of forgiveness and mercy, back in the summer past. Mercy. Once he'd understood that word. Now—had he forgotten it? Did it mean nothing? Long ago, his ancestor Prince Mael had written that mercy toward a noble lord's inferiors was a good thing, one of the qualities that marked a man as noble. *I'm not a man any longer,* he thought, *noble or common! And I'm glad of it!*

But was he truly? He thought of Berwynna, the daughter he'd never known he had. On Haen Marn she had a twin sister—and a mother. Angmar had returned. He could see her again, if he could face letting her see him in dragon form. Once he got their daughter to safety, he could fly off and find Haen Marn. If he dared.

For a fourth time he roared, a huge trembling of sound that echoed across the barrens. With the roar he sent his thoughts away, troublesome, painful thoughts that vexed him more than spears or arrows ever could. What counted now, he reminded himself, was getting what remained of the caravan to safety and delivering his report to Prince Dar. He refused to let himself think beyond that.

Rori settled down on the barrow to brood and wait, but although he stayed until the sun was low in the sky, the Horsekin never left their refuge in the forest.

Berwynna knelt by Dougie's grave. Since the wooden cross she'd made would never last beyond the summer, she'd gathered small rocks, which she laid into the dirt to form a cross shape that would endure. She patted the earth down around it with both hands.

"Farewell, beloved," she whispered in the language of Alban.

"May you ride in Lord Jesu's warband forever, just like you wanted."

"Wynni!" Mic was calling to her in Dwarvish. "Come mount up!"

Berwynna got up and blew the grave one last kiss, then turned and walked off to join her uncle and the caravan without looking back.

With such a late start, the caravan could travel only a few miles south that day. Still, Richt kept everyone moving as long as possible through the unfamiliar country, until they'd left the road far behind them. If anyone wanted to follow them, Berwynna supposed, they could track them by the trail that the mules and horses trampled into the grass. She doubted if anyone would, thanks to the silver dragon. She kept a watch on the sky, hoping to see him, but it was late afternoon before he rejoined them.

At times he circled high above them; at others, he flew a crisscross pattern over their line of march; always he stayed within their sight and the sight as well of any possible enemies. When near sunset Richt finally called a halt, the dragon landed nearby, just far enough away to keep from frightening the stock.

"Very well, Wynni," Laz said to her, "it's time we told your father the truth about that book. Someone else will tend your horse for you."

Had Laz not gone with her, Berwynna might well have lacked the courage to tell the silver dragon about the lost book. As it was, she found herself lagging behind as he led the way through the tall grass. When he saw them coming, Rori lowered himself to lie with his legs tucked under him. The sunset light dappled his silvery hide with a pale orange and gleamed on his scales.

"What do you want?" Rori said to Laz.

"I've somewhat to tell you," Laz said, "because it may concern you." He glanced at Berwynna. "We had a book of dweomer spells, I think it was, written in the language of the Ancients, but thanks to bandits and recalcitrant mules, we've lost it."

For that "we" Berwynna could have thrown herself at his feet in thanks. Instead she merely nodded.

"Not the dragon book?" Rori said. "White leather-bound, and a black dragon on the cover?"

"The very one, alas."

"Do you know if it was written by a creature named Evandar?"

"I don't, but Evandar had somewhat to do with it. Wynni's betrothed brought it to her, and he told us that Evandar had shown him where to find it."

Not quite true, that Dougie had gifted her with the book, but Berwynna decided that she would let it lie rather than admit to a theft—if indeed, theft it was.

The dragon rippled his wings as if he were about to lift them free of his body, then settled back into the grass. "Then it did concern me, greatly even, or so a Westfolk dweomerwoman told me. How did you lose it?"

If Laz could face an angry dragon who hated him, Berwynna decided, she could face one who was her bloodkin.

"I were the one, Da." Berwynna stepped forward. "It were in my saddlebags, and when those raiders, they did attack us, my mule did panic and throw me. Then it did gallop off, and never did it return."

"Ah, I see." The dragon considered this briefly. "Then you didn't lose it. It was taken from you by those murdering scum when they attacked. You're hardly to blame."

Berwynna wanted to feel relieved. She wanted with her very soul to have the burden of guilt she felt lifted. Yet still it nagged at her. *We should tell him the whole truth,* she thought. She tried to muster the courage to do so, but Laz was speaking again.

"I've been thinking about getting it back," Laz said. "In the morning, when it's light, I could change into the raven while you guard the caravan. If I see this wretched mule, which can't have gone that far in two days, then I could fly back and tell you, and you could go off and fetch it. No doubt it would do for your breakfast."

Rori glared at him. "Trying to curry favor, are you?"

"Trying to show you that I'm not whoever it is you think I am."

The dragon rumbled with laughter. "I'll give you this, Laz Moj. You don't lack guts in this life."

Laz stared at him gape-mouthed, then suddenly grinned. "I think me I begin to understand somewhat." Laz glanced Berwynna's way and stopped smiling. "But this is no time to discuss it."

"True spoken."

Berwynna could tell that she was being left out of some secret, but considering her role in losing the book, she decided against demanding to be let in.

"About that idea of mine—" Laz said.

"It's too dangerous." Rori shook his massive head. "I've been flying over the Northlands for some days now. The Horsekin are up to something, all right. I've seen more than one band of them prowling around. Some of them have archers. Could an arrow bring the raven down?"

Laz sucked in his breath with a little hiss.

"I take it that means it could," Rori went on. "Besides, I don't want to leave the caravan. My daughter's life means more to me than the book. Once you've all reached safety, I can fly back north and hunt for the saddlebags myself. Wolves aren't going to eat a book, even if they should kill the mule."

Laz nodded in agreement.

"But, Da," Berwynna joined in. "Be it that you want not the book? What you say does make me wonder if you do or not."

Rori made a sound that fell halfway between a growl and his rumbling laugh. "I don't know," he said at last. "I truly don't know if I want it or not." He lowered his head in order to look at her face-to-face. "And that's the only answer I can give you today."

"Well and good, then, but I—"

Berwynna broke off speaking when Rori stood up, clumsy on his short, bowed legs. His tail slashed through the grass behind him. "I'm going to hunt," he announced. "Leave me!"

Berwynna found herself glad to do just that. She followed Laz as he ran back to the caravan with no pretense of courage. Already the men had lit campfires against the gathering night. When she reached the edge of the warm glow she stopped, out of breath, and turned to look back. The dragon was just launching himself into the air in a blur and thunder of wings. She watched as he circled, gaining height, then flew westward to disappear into the last glow of the sunset sky.

Berwynna's mule had nearly reached the river when it smelled a herd close by. It stopped walking and threw up its head to sniff the wind—a herd, most assuredly. When it brayed, it heard a distant answer. As it trotted toward the sound, it kept testing the wind. The scent of two-legged things came with the scent of other mules and of horses, a different scent than the two-legged things it was accustomed to. When at last it saw the herd, turned out to pasture for the night, it saw the two-legged things as well. These had manes of black hair—very different than the other ones, who had short light manes, but the mules and horses looked and smelled like its old herd.

It was a huge herd, too, covering a long stretch of grass. No wolves could threaten any herd this large. Cautiously, with one eye out for a stallion, the mule took a position out on the edge. Another mule nickered in friendly greeting. No one challenged it. With a sense of overwhelming relief, it lowered its head and began to graze.

"Dalla?" Sidro said. "Laz, he be coming this way."

"What?" Dalla said. "You're sure?"

"Truly. I did dream of him last night, and when I woke, I did know the dream were true. There be somewhat wrong with his hands. They be scarred, and some of his fingers, they be gone."

"Are you surprised? From the way you described what happened when he touched those crystals together, it's amazing that he's not dead or at least blind."

Sidro sat down in the grass near Dallandra, who was perched on a fallen log, nursing little Dari. Every now and then Dari let go of the nipple to whine and squirm in her mother's arms.

"Her bottom be sore," Sidro said.

"I know. I put some oil on it. It's those beastly rags we were using at the Red Wolf dun. Out here I've been filling her carry sack with grass. The rash already looks better."

"That be a splendid idea, the grass. Then when it be soiled, you just pour it out and pull more. I do wish I'd known that, back when I had my own little one."

A good many miles west of Cengarn, they were sitting at the edge of the royal alar's camp, watching the men strike camp. Sidro could see Pir walking among his share of the horses, talking to one here, stroking another's neck there. The geldings and mares clustered around him or followed when he moved on, though the golden stallion kept his distance. Whenever one of the mares rubbed up against Pir, the stallion would lay his ears back, but he never attempted to bite the herd master.

"Have you told Pir about Laz?" Dallandra said.

"I haven't." Sidro felt the familiar anxiety rise, trembling her hands. "I know not what to do, Dalla."

"Well, I'm not you, but if I were, I'd tell Pir and see what he says."

"You be braver than I."

Sidro stood up and shaded her eyes with one hand as she searched for Pir, who had momentarily disappeared from view. He reappeared by standing up; most likely he'd been checking the hooves of one of his horses.

"Sooner or later he'll have to know," Dallandra said.

"True spoken. I'll tell him this very night, after we do make camp."

Yet Sidro found one excuse after another to put off telling him that night, and the next as well, until she dreamt of Laz again. She woke to gray light and the sound of rain on the tent roof. Beside her in their blankets Pir lay asleep, one arm thrown over his face. Cautiously she sat up without waking him. She took her tunic from the ground and pulled it on. Over the winter she'd sewn them both Westfolk clothing with the help of the other women in the alar. Although her embroidery still looked clumsy to her, compared to the beautiful craft of the others, she'd grown used to the comfort of the loose linen as opposed to her old heavy leather dress.

We're happy here, she thought, *Pir and I.* Another thought sounded in her mind like the clang of a brass bell, loud and threatening—Laz, riding closer every day. She realized that she was thinking of Laz as a storm cloud, sweeping into view on a sunny day.

"What's wrong?" Pir yawned and sat up. "You look frightened."

"Do I?"

He cocked his head to one side and considered her. "I can smell fear on you," he said.

Sidro took a deep breath, then decided to just blurt the truth. "It's because Laz is on his way here."

"Are you certain?"

"Yes. The bond between us, the magic we shared—of course I'm certain."

"Ah."

She waited, but he said nothing more, his face abruptly masked, distant from her. The distance wrung her heart.

"I don't know what to do," Sidro said.

"Don't you want him back?" Pir said.

"I don't know."

"Well, that's something, more than I thought I'd ever get."

"Don't say that! You deserve more. You've been so good to me, I—I don't know what to say, I don't know what to do. Will you go off with Laz and the rest of the men if he doesn't want to stay here?"

"No. You asked me once if I was happy here. Well, I've made up my mind about it. I have my horses, and for the first time in my life, I have friends. I won't be leaving."

"Well, I don't want to lose you, and now I'm studying with Val, too, but you know that Laz won't want to stay with the Westfolk. He's not going to ride at the prince's orders just so he can be my First Man."

"Laz will never ride at anyone's orders. He'll want you to go away with him."

"Oh, yes."

"And most likely you'll go."

"I don't know that." *But when he touches me,* she thought, *can I really say him nay?*

Pir smiled, a brief flicker of a smile, then reached over and caught her hand. "Well, then, we'll see when he gets here. That's all we can do, wait and see what happens then."

He was right, she supposed. Bitterly, bitterly right—she felt as cold as if a sorcerous snowfall had fallen from the clear summer sky. What was Laz going to say when he found her with the horse mage instead of staying faithful to him like a patient slave? *It's my right to have a Second Man,* she told herself. She knew, as well, that she wasn't afraid of Laz, that it was herself, her own weakness for him, that frightened her. Every time he touched her, she felt her sense of self melting away.

But thinking of the ancient laws of the Gel da'Thae reminded her of something important. *I still have one weapon,* she realized. Laz was as Gel da'Thae as she was. Some things they would share forever, no matter how far from home they were. One weapon, if she could bring herself to use it—and she'd not have to say a word.

With a dragon for an escort, what was left of Aethel's caravan met no more trouble as it made its way south. Every morning Rori would fly ahead, then return to tell Richt and Laz the best route to take while he circled above, on guard against enemies. They picked their way through tangled primeval forest, dismounted to lead the horses and remaining mules along the narrow paths beside streams, luxuriated in the few patches of meadow they came upon, and finally rode down one last canyon to see the open grasslands stretching out before them in the golden light of late afternoon.

As she looked out across the seemingly endless green, bowing and rising in the wind like the waves in Haen Marn's loch, Berwynna had never felt so alone, so desolate, despite the men around her, human and Gel da'Thae both, including her beloved uncle, riding next to her. *What would Dougie have said if he could have seen this?* she wondered. Once again she saw the image of his shattered flesh and cursed her memory for refusing to scrub it away.

"Are you all right?" Mic said in Dwarvish.

"No. Just thinking about Dougie."

"I wondered. I miss the lad, too." Mic rose in the stirrups and looked out across the grass. "Empty out here. Rori told me we'd be safe, though, once we reached the plains."

When Berwynna glanced at the sky, she saw her father, so distant that he looked as small as a white bird. *I lost the book.* That thought returned to her whenever she looked at her father, despite his apparent indifference to the book's fate. Thinking about the book was so much less painful than her memories of the man she'd loved that she was willing to dwell on it, as if it were some foul-tasting medicine brewed by her sister to chase away a worse ill. During their ride south, Laz had scried often for the dragon book. He'd never seen anything but the darkness inside its wrappings.

The silver wyrm circled lower, then landed a safe distance from their horses. When Laz and Richt dismounted, Berwynna joined them. Riding a heavy cavalry horse, far too large for her slight frame, had made her legs ache so badly that she dismounted at every pause. She decided that she was beginning to hate horses, all in all, and mules even more. The three of them walked over to the dragon, who was sitting with his front legs stretched out in front of him like a hound at a hearthside. In the sun his scales glittered around the pink stripe of the old wound on his side.

"The Westfolk camp is about two miles ahead," Rori said. "They've seen me, and so I expect someone will come to meet us, probably Dallandra, the Wise One of the royal alar."

"Does that mean a dweomerwoman?" Laz said.

"Just that. I wouldn't advise lying to her. Sidro's mentioned in the past that you have a penchant for that."

Laz winced and considered the grass growing between the dragon's paws.

Sure enough, when Berwynna looked to the south, she saw a group of some dozen riders coming, most of them mounted on horses whose coats shone a beautiful golden color, except for one woman's silvery mare. Behind them trailed a man on a roan.

"There's Dalla," Rori said. "And the man in front is Calonderiel, the warleader. Behind them—some of the archers, I suppose. Cal never goes anywhere without an escort. Ah, wait! There's Ebañy! Wynni, you have another uncle, and here he comes, my brother, that is, there on the roan horse."

"Evan the gerthddyn?" Laz said.

"He goes by that name, too."

"Then I have somewhat to give back to him. My apologies, I'll return straightaway."

Laz turned and strode off, heading back to his men and the remnants of the caravan, waiting in the tall grass. *The Ancients,*

Berwynna thought, *the fabled Ancients!* The riders dismounted only a few yards away, because their horses showed no fear of the dragon, much to Berwynna's surprise. Some of the men stayed with the horses while the rest, led by a woman with ash-blonde hair and gray eyes, walked over to the dragon. The man Rori had called Ebañy stayed a little off to one side and smiled, but Berwynna could see him assessing everyone with a cool gaze. Although her newly-found uncle looked like an ordinary human being, the other West-folk shocked her. She'd heard about their strange ears, but no one had told her about their cat-slit eyes, their slender height, and the sheer beauty of their alien faces.

Rori spoke to the woman in a language that Berwynna had never heard before, and she answered in the same. He seemed to be telling her who everyone was, judging from the way she looked at each person in turn. Occasionally Berwynna heard names, and eventually her own. The woman smiled at her and spoke in Deverrian. "Welcome, then, Wynni. I'm Dallandra. Your father tells me that you have the heart of a dragon, though fortunately not one's scales."

"My thanks." Berwynna curtsied, as best she could in her old brigga, simply because she had no idea of what else to do. "I be honored to meet you."

Dallandra smiled again, then returned to her discussion with the dragon. Eventually the two of them told the others what they'd decided, that everyone who was willing would come to the Ancients' camp, while those who preferred to camp elsewhere could find another spot, though one close enough for safety's sake. By then Laz had returned, carrying a bundle wrapped in embroidered cloth.

"I'll discuss it with my men," Laz said.

"The Ancients tell me that there were Horsekin raiding on the Arcodd border," Rori said in Deverrian. "Take no chances." Rori swung his head Dallandra's way, but he continued to speak in Deverrian. "Dalla, I smell wyrd in all of this. The man who led the caravan—he died defending it—was Jahdo's grandson."

Dallandra tossed up her head like a startled horse, and her mouth framed an O. "Wyrd, indeed," she said at last. "And an ugly wyrd, at that. My heart aches for Jahdo and Niffa, too." She shook her head and paused before speaking again. "Laz, we have friends of yours in our camp."

"I know." Laz gave her a lazy grin. "I scried for them."

"Of course." She considered him for a long moment. "You look as if you've met with some painful ill luck."

"You could say that, truly." Laz held out his maimed hands and the cloth-wrapped bundle. "Evan the gerthddyn! I believe this belongs to you."

Berwynna's newfound uncle strolled over and took the bundle. He unwrapped the rags to reveal something shiny and black, then laughed.

"I never thought to see this crystal again," Evan said.

"There it is," Laz said, "and I wish I'd never stolen the accursed thing. We have a fair bit to discuss, you and I."

"And so we will, tonight, I hope. What about the white one?"

"Lost. It's at the bottom of Haen Marn's lake. I'll explain that, too. I wish I'd never found it, either."

"Where was it?" Dallandra stepped forward. "I've wondered about that for months."

"In Rinbaladelan, fair lady." Laz made her a bow. "And therein lies another long tale."

"Which I very much want to hear, but not out in the middle of nowhere. Ask your men where they'll camp, Laz. I want to get back to the alar."

After much discussion, Laz's men, even Faharn, decided to make a separate camp. They unloaded their pack animals about a quarter of a mile away from the sprawl of Westfolk tents. The remaining Cerr Cawnen men, however, chose to take refuge among the Ancients. Laz watched them leading their stock through the grass till they disappeared among the gaudy tents.

"What about you?" Faharn said.

"I'll camp here with you all," Laz said, "but I'm going to go fetch Sidro first."

As Laz set off through the tall grass, he was considering what he would say to Sidro. He'd been raised in a world where women had the final say over who would be their lovers. If she wanted to keep Pir as her Second Man, he had no real objection, provided they both came with him when he led his men back to the Northlands. As her First Man, however, he was planning on asserting his rights by bringing her back to spend the night in his tent.

Laz had almost reached the camp when he saw Sidro, walking out to meet him. She wore Westfolk clothing, an embroidered shirt and leather leggings. Her raven-dark hair, long enough to trail along her shoulders, gleamed in the sunlight. He stopped walking and let her come up to him, but he could feel his sexual scent spreading out toward her in greeting, his beautiful Sisi, his again at last.

Yet when she drew closer, he noticed that she was carrying a bundle wrapped in a blanket. He turned cold—she couldn't mean it, she really could not mean what that bundle signified to a Gel da'Thae man. She looked frightened, he realized, but when she stopped some three feet from him, she forced out a smile.

"Here." She shoved the bundle against his chest with shaking hands. "Here are the things we shared in the cabin."

"No!" Laz snapped. "You can't do this to me, Sisi. You just can't!"

"I can, Laz. Here!" She thrust the bundle at him again, and this time her hands were steady. "Here's the knife, the red pottery plate, the two books, and this is one blanket from our bed. I've kept the length of linen, because you gave that to me as a gift."

Laz tried to step to one side; Sidro dodged with him and thrust the bundle forward again. Laz began to wonder if he were having a nightmare. She could not mean it, she just couldn't! He could smell his scent changing, shrinking back into his body, turning into something acrid with the taste of defeat. If only he could get close to her—he thought of a ploy, something temporary that would give him a chance to win.

"I could be your Second Man," he said. "If you and Pir come with me, I—"

"That would be worse, wouldn't it? Faharn would gloat, and the other men would sneer. Better to just end things between us cleanly."

Once again she held out the bundle. Once again he tried to dodge around it—if only he could get her in his grasp, then she'd yield to him as she always had before. He was sure of it, but once again she swung around to face him and shoved that accursed heap of things in between them. Laz decided to change tactics. He raised his hands to display his maimed fingers.

"Sisi, I need you." He allowed a quaver into his voice. "Please, can't you see how much I need you?"

She wavered—he could see it in her eyes—then shook her head. "No, Laz," she said. "You've got others who'll help you."

"I don't understand! Why have you changed like this?"

"Don't you remember when you told me that I didn't know how to be free? Well, I've learned."

"I didn't mean free of me!"

She considered him for a moment, then laughed. Laz cursed himself for the slip.

"Oh? So the truth comes out, does it?" She continued to hold out the blanket-wrapped bundle. "Pir and I are happy here. We're going to stay."

Laz realized that he could think of not one word more to say, not a truth, not a lie. He stared at her and tried to capture her gaze, but she focused her own on the bridge of his nose. She remembered that little safeguard against ensorcellment, too, and he cursed himself again for ever teaching it to her.

"You've got to take it, Laz," Sidro said. "It's the law of our kind."

"I'm an outlaw, remember?"

When she pushed the bundle into his chest, he stepped back sharply. She considered him for a moment, then loosened the knot in the cloth. Laz had a moment of hope that she was about to take it back, but when he stepped forward, she shoved the wretched thing into his chest again. He raised his arms and let it fall between them. When it hit the ground, the unknotted blanket opened and spilled its contents. His two books, his translation of the *Pseudo-Iamblichos Scroll,* wrapped in its dragon cover, and the chronicles of the war at Highstone Tor, slid out to lie in damp grass. He stooped and grabbed them before they could soak up the moisture, then realized what he'd done. By taking even the smallest part of those offered goods, he'd agreed to the break between them.

She knew it, damn her! he thought. *She knew I couldn't let the books lie.* Rage coursed through his body, hotter than blood. Although he stood up fast, Sidro had turned and was already hurrying away.

"Sisi!" he called out, but all he could hear in his own voice was the rage. "I still love you."

She paused and glanced back, looking over her shoulder.

"As much as you can love anyone," Sidro called back. "You'll forget me soon enough." She turned on her heel and strode away, hurrying back to the Ancients' camp.

Laz stood staring after her. The sun was setting, the night wind was picking up, but still he stood, watching cooking fires bloom among the Westfolk tents. *Pir didn't even have the decency to come greet me,* he thought. *But then, why should he?*

"He won, the sneaking sly little bastard!"

A woman was leaving the tents and hurrying toward him. For a moment hope flared; then Laz recognized Dallandra.

"Laz!" she called out. "I'd like to hear that tale about the white crystal."

"It will have to wait until the morrow." Laz considered face-saving excuses, then damned them all and told the truth. "I've just been bruised in my very soul, and I need to go lick my wounds like a whipped hound."

With the books held tight against his chest, Laz strode away. He refused to pick up the rest of the things that Sidro had given back to him. *I'll get her back,* he promised himself. *Somehow or other, I'll get her back!*

Pir was sitting cross-legged in front of their tent, merely sitting and staring out at the sunset sky, yet Sidro considered him the most beautiful sight she'd seen in many a long year. When she sat down next to him, he turned his head and smiled at her.

"You didn't think I could go through with it, did you?" she said.

He reached over and took her hand to squeeze it. "I thought you wouldn't want to go through with it," he said. "Glad to see I was wrong."

"So am I." She leaned her head against his shoulder. "So am I."

He slipped his arm around her waist and pulled her close. They sat together until the sun set and darkness sent them inside their tent.

After consulting with Prince Daralanteriel and Calonderiel, Rori left the royal alar under the guard of Arzosah and Medea and flew off north. He intended to take another look at that forward encampment he'd seen building, to say nothing of the migrating Horsekin. Grallezar had often described the Alshandrite leaders' favorite tactic, to move the fanatical believers of the far north down to the cities in order to ensure a majority of their supporters in the formerly free towns. She'd lost her own position because of just such a migration. Her city, Braemel, had been the last Gel da'Thae stronghold free of Horsekin influence. Dar had pointed out that this new group might have been going to try to move farther south and rebuild another of the ancient cities that their ancestors had destroyed, a potentially more dangerous move than building near the new fortress. Once the Horsekin reclaimed and fortified one of the old cities, it would take far more men than they had available to pry them out again.

As he flew, Rori kept an eye out for Berwynna's mule as well as for bands of raiders. When he reached the barrow lands, twice he saw stray mules, which he caught, killed, and ate. Neither of them carried a riding saddle nor, therefore, saddlebags. To search he flew a wider course, angling back and forth from east to west over a likely stretch of territory while still making progress toward the north. He saw no more stray mules and no bands of Horsekin raiders, either. The unit that had attacked Aethel's caravan had most likely managed to reach the new fort in the north.

Perhaps they had Berwynna's mule, perhaps not. He found himself curiously indifferent to the fate of that book. He simply could not decide whether he wanted to leave the dragon form and return to his former body. *I'll be old,* he thought, *old, half dead, unable to fight, unable to fly.* In return, what would he gain? Hands, of course, the company of other men, and Angmar, back and within in his reach. Only the last gain seemed worth the losses.

If he found the book, and if the book contained the dweomer

workings that Dallandra suspected it did, then in a strange way the decision might be made for him. He remembered his silver dagger, lost in Bardek, and how it had made its way back to him just as Jill had turned up to take him away from Aberwyn. The silver dagger had been a messenger of Wyrd. The book might well be another. If so, it would turn up, and then perhaps he would be able to make a decision. Perhaps.

As he flew onward, he put the matter out of his mind. It was more important, to his way of thinking, to discover what the cursed Horsekin were up to. Yet somewhere, deep in his soul, he heard a voice taunting him for a coward.

Every day at noon Angmar climbed the stairs of Avain's tower to bring her firstborn daughter a meal. Despite her bulk, Avain ate but little: porridge in the morning, a plate of meat and bread in the middle of the day, a bowl of soup in the evening, a few apples when they were in season, or at times nothing at all before she went to her bed, a heap of straw upon the floor. Angmar had tried to get her to sleep in a proper bed in years past, when Avain was smaller, but she'd always refused. Now no bed in Haen Marn's manse would have fit her.

Avain was sitting at her table by the window, watching the water dance in her silver basin, when Angmar came in with a plate, covered with a bit of linen to keep off the flies.

"Your meal, my love," Angmar said.

Avain looked up with her strange round green eyes, lashless and unblinking. "Dougie's dead," she said. "Poor Dougie."

"What?" Angmar set the plate down with shaking hands. "Ah, ye gods, the poor lad, indeed!"

"Wynni, she be with her da. Dragons!" Avain smiled and got up from her stool. "Dragons, Mama! Silver dragon, black dragon, green dragons, lovely dragons."

"But what about Dougie?"

"He be dead, Mama." She spoke in a calm, ordinary voice. "Wynni be safe with her da."

"With Rori, you mean?"

"With her da, truly."

"If her da flies this way, will you tell me?"

"Of course, Mama." Avain held her arms out from her shoulders. "Lovely dragons! Avain want to fly, Mama."

She tossed back her head and roared, then ran around and around the room with her arms outspread. As she watched, Angmar was thinking of her first husband, Enj and Avain's father, who had loved tales of dragons. He had blamed himself, Marn, son of Marnmara, for his strange daughter's affliction, sure that somehow he'd attracted a dragon's soul into her body as it grew in the womb. Everyone had called him daft. *But he was right,* Angmar thought, *may the gods forgive us, he was right!*

GLOSSARY

Alar (Elvish) A group of elves, who may or may not be bloodkin, who choose to travel together for some indefinite period of time.

Alardan (Elv.) The meeting of several alarli, usually the occasion for a drunken party.

Astral The plane of existence directly "above" or "within" the etheric (q.v.). In other systems of magic, often referred to as the Akashic Record or the Treasure-House of Images.

Banadar (Elv.) A warleader, equivalent to the Deverrian cadvridoc.

Blue Light Another name for the etheric plane (q.v.).

Body of Light An artificial thought-form constructed by a dweomer-master to allow him or her to travel through the inner planes.

Cadvridoc (Dev.) A warleader. Not a general in the modern sense, the cadvridoc is supposed to take the advice and counsel of the noble-born lords under him, but his is the right of final decision.

Captain (Dev. *pendaely.*) The second-in-command, after the lord himself, of a noble's warband. An interesting point is that the word *taely* (the root or unmutated form of *-daely,*) can mean either a warband or a family depending on context.

Deosil The direction in which the sun moves through the sky, clockwise. Most dweomer operations that involve a circular movement move deosil. The opposite, widdershins, is considered a sign of the dark dweomer and of the debased varieties of witchcraft.

Dweomer (trans. of Dev. *dwunddaevad.*) In its strict sense, a system of magic aimed at personal enlightenment through harmony with the natural universe in all its planes and manifestations; in the popular sense, magic, sorcery.

Ensorcell To produce an effect similar to hypnosis by direct manipulation of a person's aura. (True hypnosis manipulates the victim's consciousness only and thus is more easily resisted.)

Etheric The plane of existence directly "above" the physical. With its magnetic substance and currents, it holds physical matter in an invisible matrix and is the true source of what we call "life."

Etheric Double The true being of a person, the electromagnetic structure that holds the body together and that is the actual seat of consciousness.

Falcata (Latin) A curved and weighted saber derived from the earlier falx—an ancient weapon, carried in our world by Hispanic tribes of the second and third centuries BC, rediscovered by Gel da'Thae swordsmiths.

Gerthddyn (Dev.) Literally, a "music man," a wandering minstrel and entertainer of much lower status than a true bard.

Gwerbret (Dev.) The name derives from the Gaulish *vergobretes.*) The highest rank of nobility below the royal family itself. Gwerbrets (Dev. *gwerbretion*) function as the chief magistrates of their regions, and even kings hesitate to override their decisions because of their many ancient prerogatives.

Lwdd (Dev.) A blood-price; differs from wergild in that the amount of lwdd is negotiable in some circumstances, rather than being irrevocably set by law.

Malover (Dev.) A full, formal court of law with both a priest of Bel and either a gwerbret or a tieryn in attendance.

Mach-fala (Horsekin) A mother-clan, the basic extended family of Gel da'Thae culture.

Mazrak (Horsekin) A shapechanger.

Rakzan (Horsekin) The highest ranking military officer among the Gel da'Thae regiments, a position that bestows high honor on the mach-fala of the man holding it.

Remembrance, Day of (Elv.) A festival at the spring equinox where bards perform special poems commemorating the ancient cities of the Far West. See "alardan."

Rhan (Dev.) A political unit of land; thus, gwerbretrhyn, tierynrhyn, the area under the control of a given gwerbret or tieryn. The size of the various rhans (Dev. *rhannau*) varies widely, depending on the vagaries of inheritance and the fortunes of war rather than some legal definition.

Scrying The art of seeing distant people and places by magic.

Sigil An abstract magical figure, usually representing either a particular spirit or a particular kind of energy or power. These figures, which look a lot like geometrical scribbles, are derived by various rules from secret magical diagrams.

Tieryn (Dev.) An intermediate rank of the noble-born, below a gwerbret but above an ordinary lord (Dev. *arcloedd.*)

Wyrd (trans. of Dev. *tingedd.*) Fate, destiny; the inescapable problems carried over from a sentient being's last incarnation.

TABLE OF INCARNATIONS

643	696	718	773	835-843	918	980	1060s	Early 1100s	1150s
Brangwen	Lyssa		Gweniver	Branoic		Morwen	Jill		Branna
Madoc		Addryc	Glyn	Caradoc			Blaen of Cwm Pecyl	Drwmyc	Voran
Blaen	Gweran		Ricyn	Maddyn	Maer	Meddry	Rhodry	Rhodry	Rori
Gerraent	Tanyc	Cinvan	Dannyn	Owaen	Danry	Gwairyc	Cullyn		Gerran
Rodda	Cabrylla		Dolyan				Lovyan		
Ysolla	Cadda		Macla	Clwna	Braedda		Seryan		Solla
Galrion	Nevyn	Nevyn	Nevyn	Nevyn	Nevyn	Nevyn	Nevyn		Neb
Rhegor					Caer				
			Dagwyn	Aethan	Leomyr		Gwin		Warryc
			Saddar	Oggyn			Ogwern		Oth
				Anasyn				Kiel	
Ylaena				Bellyra	Glaenara			Carramaena	Carramaena

TABLE OF INCARNATIONS

643	696	718	773	835-843	918	980	1060s	Early 1100s	1150s
				Lillorigga		Lanni		Niffa	Niffa
				Bevyan				Dera	Galla
				Merodda		Mella	Mallona	Raena	Sidro
Adoryc				Burcan			Sarcyn	Verrarc	Aethel
			Mael		Pertyc Maelwaedd		Rhodda	Lady Rhodda	
				Olaen				Jahdo	Jahdo
				Maryn				Yraen	Clae
				Elyssa			Alaena	Marka	
							Rhys		Ridvar
							Sligyn	Erddyr	Cadryc
				Brour		Tirro	Alastyr	Tren	Laz Moj
							Perryn		Pir
				Trevyr					Nicedd